COURTING DARKNESS

By Robin LaFevers

HOUGHTON MIFFLIN HARCOURT
Boston   New York

hmhco.com

The text was set in Adobe Jenson Pro.

Book design by Whitney Leader-Picone
Map by Cara Llewellyn

Library of Congress Cataloging-in-Publication Data
Names: LaFevers, Robin, author.
Title: Courting darkness / by Robin LaFevers.
Description: Boston : Houghton Mifflin Harcourt, [2019] | Summary: When
Sybella discovers there is another trained assassin from St. Mortain's
convent deep undercover in the French court, she must use every skill in
her arsenal to navigate the deadly royal politics and find her sister in
arms before her time — and that of the newly crowned queen — runs out.
Identifiers: LCCN 2018021262 | ISBN 9780544991194 (hardback)
Subjects: | CYAC: Assassins — Fiction. | Courts and courtiers — Fiction. |
Kings, queens, rulers, etc. — Fiction. | Brittany (France) — History —
1341–1532 — Fiction. | France — History — Charles VIII,
1483–1498 — Fiction.
Classification: LCC PZ7.L14142 Co 2019 | DDC [Fic] — dc23
LC record available at https://lccn.loc.gov/2018021262

Printed in the United States of America
DOC 10 9 8 7 6 5 4 3 2 1
4500739480

To fierce, determined girls everywhere.

Especially those still discovering *how* to be fierce.

You are the true heroes.

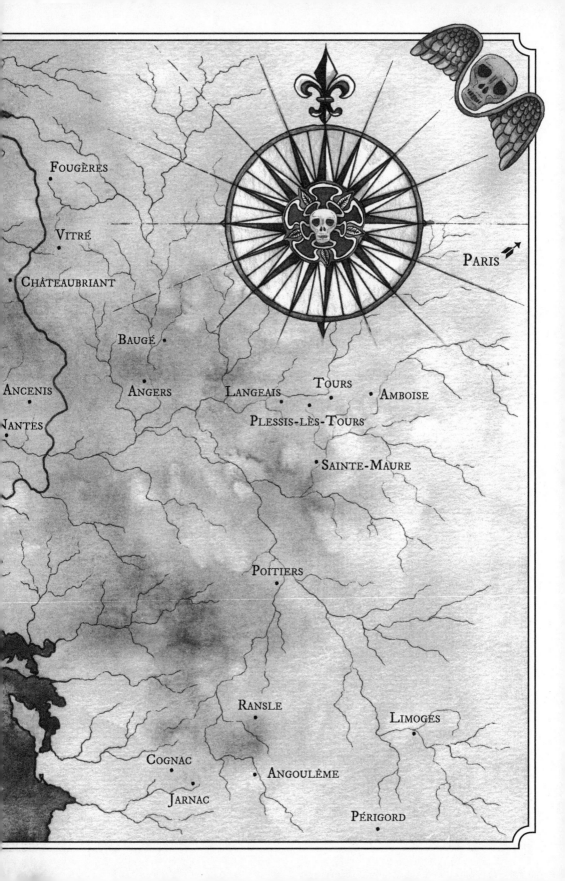

Dramatis Personae

From the Convent of Saint Mortain, patron saint of death

SYBELLA D'ALBRET, Death's daughter, lady in waiting to the duchess of Brittany

ISMAE RIENNE, Death's daughter, lady in waiting to the duchess of Brittany

ANNITH, handmaiden to Death

LADY MARGOT, Death's daughter, lady in waiting to Louise de Savoy, countess of Angoulême

LADY GENEVIEVE, Death's daughter, lady in waiting to Louise de Savoy, countess of Angoulême

The Breton Court

ANNE, duchess of Brittany, countess of Nantes, Montfort, and Richmont

GAVRIEL DUVAL, a Breton noble, half brother to the duchess

ISABEAU, Anne's sister (deceased)

DUKE FRANCIS II, Anne's father (deceased)

The Privy Council

BENEBIC DE WAROCH, "Beast," knight of the realm, captain of the queen's guard

JEAN DE CHÂLONS, prince of Orange

CAPTAIN DUNOIS, captain of the Breton army

PHILLIPE MONTAUBAN, chancellor of Brittany

JEAN RIEUX, former marshal of Brittany

BISHOP OF RENNES

FATHER EFFRAM

The d'Albret Family

ALAIN D'ALBRET, lord of Albret, viscount of Tartas, second count of Graves (deceased)

SYBELLA D'ALBRET, Death's daughter, lady in waiting to the duchess of Brittany

PIERRE D'ALBRET, second son of Alain d'Albret, viscount of Périgord and Limoges

JULIAN D'ALBRET, third son of Alain d'Albret (deceased)

CHARLOTTE, daughter of Alain d'Albret

LOUISE, youngest daughter of Alain d'Albret

TEPHANIE BLAINE, lady in waiting to Sybella

Breton Nobility

VISCOUNT MAURICE CRUNARD, former chancellor of Brittany

ANTON CRUNARD, last surviving son of the former chancellor

JEAN DE ROHAN, viscount of Rohan, lord of Léon and count of Porhoët, uncle to the duchess

Followers of Saint Arduinna

AEVA, Arduinnite, lady in waiting to the duchess of Brittany

TOLA, Arduinnite, lady in waiting to the duchess of Brittany

Breton Men-at-Arms

SIR LANNION, second in command of the queen's guard

YANNIC, squire to Benebic de Waroch

LAZARE, charbonnerie, member of the queen's guard

GRAELON, charbonnerie

The French Court and Nobility

CHARLES VIII, king of France

ANNE DE BEAUJEU, sister to the king, regent of France

PHILIP DE BEAUJEU, Duke of Burgundy, husband to Anne

MAXIMILIAN OF AUSTRIA, the Holy Roman emperor

Princess Marguerite, former dauphine of France, daughter of Maximilian of Austria

Louis, Duke of Orléans

Simon de Fremin, a lawyer

Seguin de Cassel, general in the king's army

The Cognac Court

Count Charles Angoulême

Louise de Savoy, countess of Angoulême

Jeanne de Polignac, mistress to Count Angoulême, lady in waiting to Louise

In France

Jasper, a mercenary

Valine, a mercenary

Andry, a mercenary

Tassin, a mercenary

Richard of Shrewsbury, claimant to the throne of England

The Nine

Mortain, god of death

Dea Matrona, mother goddess

Arduinna, goddess of love's sharp bite, daughter of Matrona, twin sister of Amourna

Amourna, goddess of love's first blush, daughter of Matrona, twin sister of Arduinna

Brigantia, goddess of knowledge and wisdom

Camulos, god of battle and war

Mer, goddess of the sea

Salonius, god of mistakes

Cissonius, god of travel and crossroads

PROLOGUE

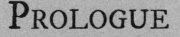

Sybella

Rennes, Brittany
November 1489

s I stand on the battlements of the besieged city, looking out at the disarray before me, it is clear the god of Death has taken to the field. While this could be said of any battle — death and war are old friends, after all — today He rides a black horse, a pale-haired rider hunkered down in front of Him.

Annith. The most skilled of all of Death's handmaidens and the sister of my heart.

She has done her part to avert this war — taken her shot using the last of the arrows forged by the gods, which flew as straight and true as if guided by their own hand. But now the French have seen her. Understand that it was she who shot at their king. And even though he is unharmed — harming him was never the intent — they are on her like jackals on a rotting carcass.

"Reload!" calls out Aeva, one of the dozen followers of Saint Arduinna who stand beside me along the ramparts.

Death and Annith ride hard for the gate, Mortain covering her with His body — a body from which four arrows protrude — protecting her life with His own. No, not His own, for He is the god of Death, I remind myself. But Father Effram's warning has taken root in my heart.

"My lord, you do know what will happen if you choose to involve yourself in mortal affairs, do you not?"

The French archers release a second volley of arrows. As one, the Arduin-nites and I return fire. But our arrows are too late. Mortain is hit yet again, taking two more to His side. Annith twists in the saddle, trying to hold onto Him.

It does not work, and they plummet to the ground. Annith begins crawling toward Mortain under yet another shower of French arrows. By Fate or chance, one of them buries itself in Death's chest, and I feel the pain of it as if it comes from my own. Ice-cold fingers of dread trail down my back before wrapping themselves around my heart.

As a lone hound brays in the distance, I shove away from the battlements and race down the stairway to the gate. More hounds join the first, raising their voices in an unholy lamentation. For a moment, the world hangs suspended, like a drop of sap oozing from a tree, and in that moment I know. The god of Death—my father — is gone. He has passed from this world.

By the time I reach the gate, the French have fallen back, as if even they sense the magnitude of this moment. Nuns from the convent of Saint Brigantia swarm toward the fallen Mortain as Annith throws herself on his body, weeping. As much as I am hurting, she will be even more so.

Before I can reach them, a laugh rings out — an incongruous, joyful sound in the solemn stillness.

Puzzled, Death reaches for his chest, his hand coming away red with blood. Although I am half a bowshot away, I hear him say, "I am alive."

It feels as if the earth I am standing on gives a dizzying spin.

He is alive. But even as far away as I am, I can see that he is no longer Death.

A great chasm opens inside me, a dark yawning maw that threatens to swallow me whole. If Death no longer walks amongst us, then what purpose am I to serve? What use will there be for my dark talents and skills?

I fear the answer was writ long ago, when I was born into the family that raised me. The family that nearly killed me and drove my mother into Death's arms.

And that answer terrifies me far more than death ever has.

CHAPTER 1

Genevieve

Cognac, France

 was born in the upstairs room of an ancient roadside tavern, a group of common whores acting as midwives. My mother, too, was a whore, although perhaps not so very common. Would an ordinary woman invite Death to her bed on a dare?

I emerged covered in slime and blood, my face—indeed, my entire body—as blue as a wild hyacinth. Hushed whispers and murmurs of sympathy followed the horrified silence my arrival caused, until Solange, the oldest among them, grabbed me from my mother's slippery hands and swatted my backside.

Nothing. I did not cry or whimper or even draw breath. But old whores are as wise as old cats, and Solange did not give up. She bent down to place her wrinkled lips on mine, and blew.

According to my mother, my chin quivered, a fist curled.

Solange blew again, her determined breath somehow shoving away the cold hands of my father as He reached for me.

I drew a deep breath of my own after that, followed by a lusty cry. The women thought me a miracle, moved that one had been visited upon them just as if they were the Magdalena herself.

All except my mother, who knew precisely who she'd invited into her bed nine months earlier. It wasn't until I was four years old and clutched at her hand as she headed up the stairs with her night's customer that my parentage was confirmed. "His heart," I whispered into her lowered ear as I rubbed my small chest. "It's beating strangely."

Less than an hour later, he was dead.

It is that same panicked beating that has brought me to the lowest levels of the castle today — a heartbeat as close and intimate as if it is beating against my own ribs.

I follow the deep *ba-bump* through the narrow, twisting corridors of the dungeons, stopping when a gaping black hole appears at my feet. The darkness that oozes up through the metal grate is as thick and solid as a coiled snake.

At first, I think it a hatch to the river that runs nearby. *Or perhaps* — wrinkling my nose — *the sewer*. Until the next heartbeat reverberates through me, one long, deep *ba-bump*. I never feel the heartbeats of others unless they are close to dying. That is when I finally understand the nature of this pit.

It is an oubliette.

A dungeon designed specifically for those who do not even warrant the mercy of a clean death.

Nameless dread that cannot be explained by the presence of death thrums through me. My hand clenches. I should turn and walk away. Return to the sumptuous, brightly lit rooms of the castle proper.

I am getting ready to do just that when the heartbeat stops. The pressure in my chest grows, stretching against my ribs, seeping into the very marrow of my bones. Trepidation and despair sweep through me, as if the world itself has just been torn in two.

And then the pressure stops. Is simply gone, like the passing of the wind.

"Who's there?"

The croaked question shatters the absolute silence, causing me to leap back. The dead do not speak.

Oubliette. To forget.

If it were called by any other name, I could turn and walk away. If it were empty, it most assuredly would hold no interest for me. But someone is down there, someone else the world has forgotten. That he is dying — well, there is no way I can ignore it now. While I was sired by the god of Death and sent to His convent to train in His arts, I have had precious little opportunity to explore them since I have left.

"Who are you?" The voice is low and hoarse, but it is the commanding tone of it that startles an answer from me.

"No one. A shadow." My words float down into the darkness on the barest exhalation of breath. Hopefully he will think them naught but a fevered dream as he lies at Death's door.

There is movement below, as if someone is shifting position, straining to look up. A moment later, I hear him rising to his feet. I scramble back from the hole, my footsteps quick and silent.

When I am well away from the oubliette, I allow myself to run, returning through the labyrinth of underground corridors to the main floor of the castle.

Who are you?

His question follows me like a ghost, as if the forgotten, dying man has looked into my very soul and seen the doubt and uncertainty that has plagued me for the last year.

Who, by the Nine, *am I?*

When I finally reach the main section of the palace, I pause to brush off my skirts and smooth my hair. I arrange my face into the bland, subservient mask I have worn for the past five years, then step into the warmth of the light.

Oddly, it is far colder against my skin than the living blackness of the dungeon.

CHAPTER 2

Sybella

Rennes, Brittany
One Week Later

he loss of my father, still sharp and raw, drives me to the city gates, as if I'm hoping that he will return. But of course, he does not. Even so, like one of the restless souls that still hover where their bodies fell, I hover in the shadows of the gate and stare out at the empty field beyond.

No. Not empty. A small holly bush appeared three days after Mortain fell, springing wholly formed from the earth soaked with his blood. Its leaves are dark green and glisten with bright red berries. Holly has always been sacred to Mortain.

Beneath the miraculous bush, humble offerings have sprung up like toadstools after a rain—a silver coin, loaves of coarse brown bread, a comb of honey, a bundle of willow twigs, a black ribbon. The branches are rumored to bring love to the forlorn, health to the sick, and peace to the dying. It is the last that I find most believable. He was the god of Death, after all.

I have often wondered why my god bid me live when I sank to the bottom of that river nearly six months ago. He did not just whisper encouragement in my ear, but put his cold hand upon mine and pulled me to the surface, into the waiting arms of one who loved me.

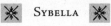

Was it simply a gift for all I had suffered? Or was there some purpose I had yet to serve? Or mayhap it was naught but a parent's instinct to assure his child's survival.

He saved me once before. When I was fourteen years old and in pain beyond bearing, I tried to take my own life. On that day, I was told by my old nurse that I was sired by Death and not Count d'Albret, my mother's husband and the man who raised me. I was taken to the convent of Saint Mortain then, where I spent the next three years learning Death's arts.

Even that was not my first brush with death. I very nearly did not survive my own birth, arriving with the birth cord wrapped twice around my neck, my mother's body unable to let go of me, already regretting her decision to bring me into this world.

If not for the promise my true father had made to her, I would have gone with her into death. But promise he did, and the god of Death is not one to break such promises. Instead, I lived.

And he, he . . . did not.

Anger as bright and red as one of the holly berries flares in my belly. Anger that one so newly come into my life has left it far too soon. Why did my father save me, only to abandon me once more? Why did he bid me live if he would not be here to guide my hand? It was only through Mortain's existence and grace that I found a place in this world. A purpose.

I reach out and grab a piece of holly, ripping it from the bush. Whether it is to hurt the bush or because I need some reminder of who I am, I cannot say. But the leaves are sharp with thorns, and I cut myself. A drop of blood wells up, as dark and red as one of the holly berries.

Is this blood still mingled with that of the gods or will I, too, become fully human?

Behind me, someone coughs. Shoving the holly into my pocket, I pull a dagger from my belt and whirl around. But it is only a wizened priest, sparse white hair fluttering slightly in the breeze, who stands there.

"Father Effram," I hope he cannot hear the disappointment in my voice.

"How am I able to feel everyone's heart beating but yours?" In the days since Mortain fell, that is the one gift of his that I know still remains — my ability to sense the heartbeats of the living.

Father Effram's eyes dance with a mischievous light as he spreads his hands wide and lifts his shoulders. "It *is* a very old heart, Lady Sybella." The twinkle in his eye reminds me of Annith's claim that the ancient priest does not merely follow the patron saint of mistakes, but once walked the earth as Saint Salonius himself.

"What brings you outside the city gates, Father?"

"There is a . . . problem that requires your attention."

"What sort of problem?" Anticipation stirs in my chest. I have been prowling the city since the battle, searching among the jubilant townspeople, relieved merchants, and dispersing mercenaries to see what other gifts might still remain. The right sort of problem could reveal those answers.

"I'm afraid one of the prisoners has overpowered his guard and taken a hostage."

I turn and begin walking back to the city. "Which prisoner?"

"The former chancellor Crunard."

I look sharply at Father Effram.

"What does he want?"

"Annith."

"Does he not know that she has returned to the convent of Saint Mortain?"

"Apparently not."

"And the hostage? Who is he?"

When the priest does not answer, I grow uneasy. "Father?" I prompt.

He sighs deeply, reaching up to tug at his ear. "The bishop."

I stop walking. "Surely you jest."

"No jest, my lady."

While the bishop is a member of the duchess's Privy Council and one of her spiritual advisors, he and I have only one thing in common — our mutual dislike. Of all the members of the duchess's inner circle, he is the one who insists on clinging to his prejudice and judgment of me.

Every deed I have done out of love, he ascribes to self-interest. Every action born of my loyalty, he has suspected of treachery. Even my devotion to Mortain is tainted in his eyes, due to my own dark past, my depraved family, and the nature of my god.

It is like looking into a mirror that reflects back all the worst fears I ever had about myself.

For seventeen years, my self-loathing had been honed to a razor-sharp edge. It was only Mortain's grace that was able to dull it and cleanse me of despair. That I should be asked to save the bishop's hide now, when those old wounds have opened, seeping even older doubts and fears, seems a cruel fate.

"Let him pray to his God. If he is worthy of being saved, then surely He will send someone."

Father Effram's gaze meets mine squarely. "He has."

"Someone other than *me*."

He scratches his nose. "God makes use of what tools He can find."

I stare at him a long moment before huffing out a resigned breath. While this is not the answer I seek, I will not turn down a chance to pit my skills against a known traitor. Even if I cannot kill him, I am spoiling for a fight. Any fight will do.

Besides, it will pain the bishop greatly to be saved by the likes of me. That is reward enough.

CHAPTER 3

hen we reach the north wing where Crunard is being held, three guards stand in front of the closed door, weapons drawn. Good. Crunard will not be escaping with his hostage. When they see us, to my astonishment, they abandon the door and rush toward us, weapons drawn.

Fortunately, it is a long hallway.

I flip my knives so that I hold them by the tip. I wait one heartbeat, and a second, hoping beyond reason that Mortain can still marque those meant for death. The precepts of my faith have always insisted that to kill without his marque to guide our hand is to step outside his grace and risk becoming naught but a murderer.

But no marques appear, and the men are almost upon us. Fortunately, the precepts of Mortain also grant us the ability to kill in self-defense.

"Down!" I shout to Father Effram. I let one dagger fly, then the next.

The closest guard reels back, clutching his eye. Behind him, the second man checks his stride, dropping his sword as his hand claws at the knife embedded in his throat. The third guard steps around the others, sword raised.

He is a big man, thickset and heavy. Either it has not registered that I have just mortally wounded his two friends or he is stupid, so certain he has a killing blow that he moves slowly, like an executioner at a beheading.

In the time it takes for his sword to arc toward me, I retrieve the stiletto from my left sleeve. Ducking in low, I launch my entire body at him, aiming for his gullet.

The move brings me up against his chest, my blade sinking deeply into the hollow of his throat. For one crystalline moment, we are pressed together in an embrace, his sword flailing uselessly behind me. I twist the stiletto, shoving it in deeper.

Just as I leap back to avoid the blood, a great, dark, flapping thing rises from his body and tries to wrap itself around me. I do not know who is more shocked, the soul as it hovers in disbelief near his lifeless husk, or myself as I realize that the ability to experience the souls of the dying is a gift of Mortain's that is still left to me.

But there is no time to savor that. As I hurry to collect my knives, Father Effram pushes to his feet. His cheeks are pink, his eyes bright with . . . fear? Excitement? Admiration? I cannot tell.

As I approach Crunard's chamber, I feel more alive than I have in days, my skin tingling with anticipation, my heart leaping at the challenge before me. There are three — no, four — pulses beating in the room. I tighten the grip on my long knife, no longer caring that it is the be-damned bishop I am saving.

On my signal, Father Effram raps smartly on the door. "Monsieur Crunard? I have the woman you asked for."

As the key turns in the lock, I utter a silent prayer for Mortain's guidance. If some of his gifts are left to me, then perhaps a tenuous connection still exists between us as well. A connection that could allow me to know his will.

As soon as the door begins to open, I kick against it with all my might, forcing it back against the wall with a crash.

Crunard stands behind the door, his sword pointed at me, my long knife holding it at bay. A fallen guard lies on the floor behind him. Another stands with a sword pointed at the bishop, who cowers in the corner.

Crunard glares at Father Effram. "This is not Annith!"

"Annith is not coming."

There is the briefest flicker of surprise and disappointment before Crunard gains control of his features. "She has already left?"

I cannot help it — I laugh. "Did you truly think your daughter would bid you a fond farewell? Not only are you a traitor to our country, but you have treated her and her mother abysmally."

My barb finds a home. "I did not even know she existed until mere months ago."

"That does not excuse any of it."

Crunard's jaw tightens. "I think you forget that I am the one holding the hostage."

"I think you forget that the bishop and I do not care for each other in the least. I am more interested in your motives than his safety."

"I want out of this prison."

"To what end? So you can betray the duchess a second time? And why today?" As I speak, I move carefully, so slowly that to the untrained eye it will look as if I am holding still.

"So I can find my son."

The son he claims is being held hostage by the French regent. "The duchess already promised she will inquire after his whereabouts when she arrives in France." I am closer now to the armed guard standing over the bishop — almost within striking range.

Crunard's free hand clenches into a fist. "I do not trust that the duchess will do it. I wish to search for him myself." His eyes are as clear and guileless as a babe's, but his gaze shifts ever so slightly. He is lying. Of that I am certain.

I raise my knife. Properly applied, the tip would do very little damage, but might yield up the truth behind his lies. The thought unnerves me. Mortain has only been gone a handful of days, and already my mind turns back to the dark instincts of my past.

I smile, but I do not think it is reassuring. "You can trust the duchess. She is not doing it for you, but for Annith, who would like to meet this brother she so recently learned of." I tilt my head. "How will she feel about this newest trick of yours? Killing innocent guards, threatening the bishop, further dragging her family name through the mud."

His face grows white with fury. He takes a step toward me, the tip of his

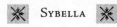

sword lowering ever so slightly. It is the smallest of openings, but I take it. "Father! The door!"

When the guard glances toward the door, I lunge at him. Before he has time to react, I grab him by the hair, jerk his head back, and slit his throat.

Blood spurts out in a crimson rain, staining the floor as well as the cowering bishop. I do not stop long enough to comfort him, but launch myself at Crunard, bracing for the impact of his sword against my dagger — hoping my blade will be long enough.

Instead of resistance, I find Crunard standing with his sword stuck in the closed door, Father Effram sprawled at his feet. I check my momentum as Crunard pulls his gaze from the dead guard to my oncoming rush, then shift my weight to my back leg and swing my front leg up to kick the hand still holding the sword.

There is a loud snap as the contact breaks his wrist. He bellows, and his grip goes slack. Before he can do more than that, I step in close and point the long knife at his throat.

His face is pale, beads of sweat gathering on his brow. His pulse beats rapidly against the blade's edge.

I glance at Father Effram on the floor. "Are you all right?"

"Fine. I am fine." He tries to leap up, but finds himself yanked back down. "If somewhat stuck." He tugs helplessly at the hem of his robe caught in the door. "If you could be so kind, my lady?"

My lips twitch as I reach out with one hand to open the door long enough for him to retrieve his robe. The priest springs to his feet. "I *do* serve the patron saint of mistakes," he mutters, dusting off his robe.

The sword embedded in the door is at the exact height of Father Effram's heart. "It is just as well that you do. That mistake saved your life."

Father Effram glances over his shoulder, the blood draining from his face. To give him something to think about besides how close he came to death, I tell him to go see what the bishop is whining about.

As he hurries off to that corner of the room, I step away from Crunard to peer around the desk to the man on the floor. His heartbeat is weak and irregular.

"Who is he?"

"The sentry on duty when my friends arrived. His injury was an accident."

The man's shirt is stained red with blood. "Since when is a chest wound an accident?"

"I had a sword pointed at him, but he wasn't supposed to throw himself on it. He was outnumbered, after all."

"He was supposed to ignore his duties and see to his own safety?" I snort. "Not everyone is as cowardly as you and takes the easy way out."

"Please," he says, "tell me. What was easy about my sons dying one by one as they fought for their country? Or having my last surviving son taken captive in a futile battle for Brittany's independence?"

Cupping his useless hand, he takes a step closer. "Tell me, what was easy about learning that son was held hostage by the regent of France? And that the only way I could save him was to turn my back on everything I had fought for my entire life? I have been forced to sit here for a year, unable to do anything to find him. Please, do tell me how easy that was."

Merde. That *cannot* have been easy. "Maybe that was not the right word," I concede. But then, nothing about our country's fight to remain independent of France has been easy. Before he can say anything else, I point my knife at him. "Do not go anywhere."

"I won't." Even though his eyes stay firmly on mine, the muscles in his body tense, gathering strength to make a break for the door.

I sigh in exasperation. "I tried to give you a chance," I remind him, then kick his left knee. It is a gentle tap — meant to deter, not destroy — but he is old and not expecting it. He shouts as he crashes to the floor. Assured he will not go anywhere, I finally hurry over to the injured man and kneel beside him.

His eyelids flutter, and a groan of pain escapes his lips. "Must warn the duchess . . . Crunard —"

I place my hand on his shoulder. "Shhh. He did not escape, monsieur. Your brave deed gave us the time we needed."

His breathing becomes easier. "And the bishop?"

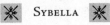

I glance over at the bishop, whom Father Effram is helping to his feet. "He will live." I try to keep the annoyance out of my voice.

The man gives a faint nod, before his eyes drift shut. The bishop and Father Effram approach us. "Will he make it?" Father Effram asks.

I shake my head. Father Effram kneels beside the dying man. "What is your name?"

"William."

"Tell us what we can do for you, William."

"So thirsty."

Eager to do something to ease his agony, I rise to my feet and snag an ewer that sits on the desk, then return to William's side.

He is too weak to lift his head, so I rip off a corner of my underskirt, dip it into the water, and dribble it into his mouth. He is dying. I *know* it. But there is no marque on his forehead; no deathly shadows lurk upon his mortal wound.

A wave of despair washes over me at the finality of this moment, for both William and me. There truly are no more marques of Mortain to guide the living into death. To guide *me*. How am I to navigate such a world? What will keep me from straying too far into the shadows?

But I am not the only one of Mortain's daughters serving here at court. "Where is Ismae?" I ask Father Effram.

He considers me a moment. "I believe she is with the duchess."

"Go and fetch her, if you please. She is death's mercy," I murmur. "She will know what is to be done."

His face softens. "But you too know what is to be done, Lady Sybella. And you are already here."

"Just get her," I snap.

He rises to his feet and heads for the door. "Best send for Duval as well," I call after him. The duchess's half brother and master strategist will need to know of Crunard's newest betrayal. "And take the bishop with you. He is no doubt anxious to get out of his bloody robes."

As the bishop passes me on the way to the door, he pauses to utter a short prayer for William. He does not so much as glance at me or utter a single word of thanks. I nearly laugh. Even now, after I have saved his sorry life, he cannot bear the sight of me. Whether it is because I am Mortain's daughter or because of the more human aspects of my past, I do not know.

Dismissing him from my mind, I turn my attention back to the guard. Since there is nothing else I can do, I take his hand in mine.

Father Effram is wrong. I am useless in this situation. I am — *was* — death's justice, never his mercy. It was Ismae who bestowed the mercy that death could deliver. Not I. I was only ever to serve as his vengeance.

William groans again, a heartbreaking whimper of pain. I grip his hand tighter, as if by doing so I can will him into death.

It is close now. I can feel his soul frantically beating against his body, wanting to be free. I do not know whether to be grateful that I can still feel such things or enraged that I must feel them with no way of knowing what I am supposed to do.

His heartbeat falters and stumbles, then struggles to keep going — like a valiant horse that is pulling too heavy a load. It would be so easy to free him of that.

I reach up and run my hand gently along his brow, then down his cheek. "Be at peace, dear William." I place my palm over his struggling heart. I close my eyes and breathe deep, growing still inside. How can I ease this man's plight?

Slowly, an answer comes, filling both my heart and mind with a presence that is far wiser than I. And that . . . presence . . . knows the absolute rightness of what to do.

I press my palm more firmly against his chest, using no more pressure than I would to caress my sister's cheek. *Rest now.*

With a faint sigh of relief, his heart stops. In the silence that follows, William's soul rises from his body, like some wary cat unfurling from a hiding place, then rubs against me. In thanks, I realize.

I allow myself to savor the peace the soul feels. The peace that it in turn brings me.

The soul does not linger or try to force itself upon me as most do, but simply

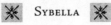

floats up to the ceiling, where, like all souls, it will wait three days before finally departing.

When I look away, I find Crunard watching me. I blink twice, trying to reorient myself.

"He is dead," I say.

"Is he, now?" Crunard's eyes are sharp and bright.

"Which means in addition to your crime of treason, you are a murderer." I utter the words harshly, hoping they will hide my sorrow. "This was no casualty of war or battle, but your own selfishness and greed."

His face contains multitudes — anger, disappointment, frustration — but no regret, no sorrow, no remorse. Indeed, it feels as if there is almost a belligerent ferocity lying just beneath the surface. "I do not think it was *I* who killed that man," he says softly.

The wily fox, they used to call him. And no wonder. "You are mistaken. I simply placed my hand on his heart and prayed that his death be easy."

"And Mortain chose to honor your wishes?" His scorn is palpable.

"Yes," I say, trying to keep the wonder from my voice.

CHAPTER 4

he sound of others approaching from the far end of the hallway is a welcome distraction.

"Have you sent for Beast?" Ismae's voice is as familiar as my own. It was the first voice that reached through my grief and despair when I arrived at the convent. If not for her gentle coaxing, I would have run away rather than allow myself to be trained by the nuns who served Mortain.

"No," Duval answers. "He is not scheduled to return until tomorrow." The heels of his boots are clipped and hard upon the floor.

"Duval." Ismae's voice is filled with both compassion and warning.

His footsteps slow. "What?"

"Whatever Crunard was planning, it failed. Do not . . . do not act rashly."

"Says the woman whom I spent nearly a year trying to restrain from killing half the nobles at court." His words do not hide the pride or love he holds for her, although he would be appalled to know that.

"It's been a long time since I tried to kill anyone," Ismae grumbles.

Duval ignores her protest. "Why do you think I would do anything rash? Crunard has only betrayed our country and my sister, poisoned me, tried to kill you, and has now repaid the leniency we showed him by littering the hallway with bodies."

Father Effram clears his throat. "I believe that was Lady Sybella, my lord."

Gavriel Duval appears in the doorway, his gray eyes filled with a barely contained fury. I do not even pretend that I was not eavesdropping. "What took you so long?"

"Stepping over the trail of bodies you left in the hallway." Duval's voice is dry as bone, but the harshness in his face is softened by gratitude. "Once again, we owe you a debt of thanks."

Before I have time to rebuff his sincerity, Ismae pushes past him, shaking her head in exasperation. But silent questions — and envy — lurk deep within her probing gaze. "If you wanted to get out of your stitching duties, I'm sure there was an easier way."

I shrug carelessly. "It's important I keep my skills honed, especially in light of my upcoming trip to the French court."

As she draws closer, she scrutinizes my face, my gown, my very soul, to assure herself that I am okay.

"Your concern is almost insulting."

"Hush." She reaches up to wipe something from my cheek. "You're covered in blood."

Without taking his eyes from Crunard, Duval clears his throat. "Would you mind telling us what happened here?"

Ismae grimaces at his stuffy formality, but I know it is the mask he wears when his emotions run high. "Of course, my lord. Your prisoner Crunard was ungrateful over his improved conditions and decided to take advantage of the duchess's mercy. He bribed or coerced three of the duchess's men to his cause and used them to take the bishop hostage, killing a fourth guard in the process."

Duval turns on his heel and strides over to where Crunard sits on the floor. "Why? What was worth these four men's lives?"

"My son."

A vein in Duval's temple begins to pulse. "Do you really think Anton would want you to slay his countrymen in his name? If so, he was right about you all these years — you do not know him at all." The disgust on Duval's face is palpable. "I should have had you killed months ago," he mutters.

"But you didn't." Crunard smirks. "And now you cannot, because it would be in cold blood and your honor" — he nearly spits the words out — "would never allow that."

"You have no idea what my honor will allow, old fox."

"I beg to differ. It will keep you from ever truly winning."

The words sting, as Duval has done everything in his power to keep Brittany independent of France. That they will now be joined by a marriage contract rather than outright conquest is thin comfort. Duval looks away a moment, as if arguing with himself. Without warning, he turns back around and gives Crunard a healthy clip to the jaw.

The older man's eyes widen in surprise as his head snaps back, then close as he slumps into unconsciousness.

I shoot Duval a look of annoyance. "If I'd known we were allowed to do that, I would have clouted him myself."

Duval flexes his hand as he takes in Crunard's injured wrist and twisted knee. "It looks like you got a good shot at him. But you are truly all right?"

"If either one of you asks me that again, I will prove how fine I am by stabbing you with my knife."

That elicits a begrudging smile out of him as Ismae announces, "Clearly, she is fine."

When more guards arrive to remove the bodies and return Crunard to the dungeon, Ismae accompanies me to my room so I may change. "Knock first," I warn her. "I don't want Charlotte and Louise to see me covered in blood and trailing the scent of death." Such easy violence is precisely why I am determined to keep my sisters from our family.

Ismae raps on the door. When there is no answer, she opens it and waves me inside, then pulls me over near the banked fire and begins unlacing my gown.

"Well?"

She and I have been prowling the palace and surrounding parts of the city like vultures, waiting for someone — *anyone* — to die so we could see how death worked in this new, upended world.

I take a deep breath before answering. "There are no marques any longer."

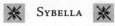

Saying the words out loud feels as if someone has carved my heart out of my chest, leaving it empty and hollow.

Her hands on my laces still. "Truly?" she whispers.

"Truly. Not on the guards rushing me, not on the man holding the bishop hostage, and not on the soldier who lay dying in my arms. Even as he passed into death, no marque appeared."

Ismae's silent disappointment fills the room as her fingers resume their work. "So, that is it. His gifts have left us."

I give a quick shake of my head. "Not all. I am still able to feel heartbeats and sense souls as they leave their bodies."

She lets out a breath. "Well, that's a good sign."

"Are you still able to sense the presence of life?" For all that we are half sisters, her abilities have differed somewhat from mine — all of Mortain's daughters have variations in their gifts and skills.

"Yes," she answers slowly. "But I was never certain if that was Mortain's gift or the convent's training."

I glance at her over my shoulder. "Do you dare try poison?"

Blushing, she pretends to struggle with a knot. "It still does not appear to harm me in the slightest. But again, I wasn't sure whether that was one of his gifts or some strange aspect of my own body."

To hide how happy I am for her, I smirk. "And they say I am impulsive."

She lifts her shoulder in a half shrug as she unfastens my belt. Before she can remove it from my waist, I quickly hide the holly twig in my palm. I start to tell her of my prayer for the dying man, and the surety with which the answer came, but find I cannot. It is still too new, too nebulous. I am afraid that speaking of it will cause the connection to shatter, and I am too selfish to risk that.

CHAPTER 5

Genevieve

t is a few days before I can break free from the others and return to the dungeon.

Margot's confinement began this week, so there were many trips to the chapel for the ritual blessings, final feasts, and celebrations with the household. My absence would have been noted — and commented upon — something I am desperate to avoid. But at last Margot has been sequestered to her room in anticipation of the babe's birth.

Descending the staircase, I let the bustle and chatter of the castle fall away like an unbearably stiff cloak. Fortunately, the sense of impending dread has left me, but the sense that the world has shifted in some unnamable way remains.

As I step into the corridor that leads to the dungeon, the darkness folds itself around me like a welcoming blanket. I pause for a moment, listening for potential guards or the sound of the prisoner's heart beating. But there is nothing. I place my hand upon my chest to be certain, but there is only the steady rhythm of my own heart.

A fleeting sense of sorrow shafts through me for the passing of a life, unknown and alone. However, it is the passing of that life that has drawn me here — giving me a chance to explore death more closely.

There are so many lessons Margot and I had not yet received from the nuns at the convent of Saint Mortain before we were sent away.

We know only a handful of ways to kill a man, and have even less understanding of how our arts work.

That is what I am hoping to learn from the dead prisoner. Provided the guards have not lugged the body away, it will be a perfect map for me to study.

It is not until I am standing almost upon the grate itself that I hear the sound of . . . panting? No, huffing. Followed by a grunt.

The sounds of a living human. Disappointment slams into me like a fist, and I nearly crush the apple I have brought for my lunch. He had to have been close to death for me to have heard his heart. Yet now he is down here breathing and grunting. How can I explore the mysteries of death if the man is still alive?

"Ives? Have you returned?" The deep rumble of the prisoner's voice is more proof he is not as dead as he should be.

"You have been alone so long your enfeebled mind is conjuring ghosts for company."

There is a faint whisper of movement, and though I cannot see through the murk, his regard is palpable as it reaches through the dark to take my measure. "While my enfeebled mind has conjured many ghosts these last long months, you are the first to smell of apples."

I loosen my grip on the fruit in my hand, the full impact of his situation finally registering. He has been locked down here for months. Was near death but a few days ago.

"I do have an apple. Would you like it?"

"Yes." The force of his hunger causes his voice to crack.

It is a simple thing, to bring such reverence to a man's voice. The apple is too large to fit through the grate, so I reach for the small knife at my belt and slice it in half. "I will drop it down, one half at a time."

There is a rustle as he comes to stand beneath the opening. I peer down, but see nothing in all that sooty darkness. "It's coming through the center," I tell him, hoping he can catch it rather than have it land in the filth I can smell all the way from here. I drop one half, then the other, holding my breath until I hear the quiet slap of them landing in his palm.

A long silence is followed by a juicy crunch and a grunt of pleasure. As he gulps down the fruit, I am filled with satisfaction. I have helped someone. Even if it is only to keep them from starving one more day. It is the same feeling I had as a child when I found a stray cat behind the tavern and would sneak it a saucer of milk. Although the satisfaction tonight is tenfold.

"Who is Ives?" I whisper, wondering if I should be worried about the guards.

A long pause. "One of the ghosts."

Something in his voice feels unspeakably sad, and I find myself wanting to change the subject. "And what of you? Why are you not a ghost? You seemed near death but days ago."

"I was. Until it rained and filled the seep so I was able to quench my thirst."

So, I did not imagine it. "Does no one bring you food or water?"

"They did. Once." There is a note of wistfulness in his voice.

"I will bring more if I can."

I regret the whispered promise before I reach the first corridor leading out of the dungeons, where reality begins to chase away the last dregs of satisfaction. I cannot come back. I have no convincing pretense for being down here. Count Angoulême would ask questions, poke and prod and watch me more closely.

My role in this household is one of a biddable, humble attendant, not someone who possesses such morbid interests or would dare to explore death if she stumbled upon it. Too many years have been spent cultivating that bland demeanor. It is beyond foolish to risk it for some unknown prisoner.

And yet my soul is hungry for such risks. A taste for them was fed to me with my mother's milk, then nurtured and honed by the convent. To not take them feels like leaving fruit to wither and die on a vine.

CHAPTER 6

hen I reach my chamber, the countess of Angoulême sits in a chair by the fire, waiting for me. I hide my surprise with a warm greeting. "My lady." I sink into a deep curtsy.

She motions me to my feet. "Where have you been, Genevieve?" I cannot tell by her expression how long she has been waiting.

"Roaming the halls. You know how restless I get when cooped up for too long."

She wrinkles her nose. "I do not understand your need to gallop about. I have always thought it was odd, ever since we were children."

I nearly laugh. She and I never knew each other as children, but first met when we were twelve years old. She, too, was a ward of the regent, one of the "girls" Madame Regent raised as her own. There were others as well, including the young dauphine, Marguerite, once destined to be queen of France.

"I only gallop when I am outside, my lady. Indoors, I keep to a trot."

She studies me with thoughtful eyes. Once she would have laughed at my jest, but with her new elevated station, she inspects each word for any sign of disrespect or overfamiliarity.

She moves her hands to her belly. While it is softly rounded with child, she is not as far along as Margot. Does it bother her that her husband's mistress — her own lady in waiting — will be bearing his child before she does? Deciding to ignore — or forgive — my jest, she says, "My lord husband wishes to see you."

Caution wars with curiosity. The count has not summoned me in over a month. "Ah, then. Best not keep him waiting."

Louise's heavy brow creases faintly as she searches yet again for the sign of disrespect she fears.

I reach down to take her arm and pull her to her feet. "After all," I say cheerfully, "he is an important man with much to do."

"Do you know why he wishes to see you?" Her dark brown eyes meet my own, hesitant questions lurking in their depths.

"No." I allow a faint hint of surliness to color the word. It is a trait of mine she knows well. "I have probably offended or transgressed in some way." Louise has always been too timid and biddable to do anything improper, but secretly enjoys when others take such risks. Her mouth quirks up in a faint smile, the questions fading from her eyes.

The thick oak door to Count Angoulême's room stands open. He sprawls in a chair at his desk with his back to the fire, a decanter at his elbow, a half-full glass in his hand. The room is cloying with the thick, too-warm scent of vetiver, cloves, and wine. I do not go in, but remain in the doorway. "My lord? The countess said you sent for me?"

He waves me forward. "Come in, come in. Don't hover. And close the door."

The first several times he asked me to close the door, I hoped it meant he had news from the convent regarding my duties. It did not.

Biting back a sigh of resignation, I do as he commands.

When I reach the chair in front of his desk, he pours a glass of wine, places it in front of me, and motions for me to sit.

I remain standing.

"Where have you been?" My heart pounds for one long, painful moment — does he know about the oubliette? "You've been scarce of late."

"I have been keeping my own company, my lord."

"That is too bad. I miss your earlier visits. It was refreshing, being interrogated by a young demoiselle less than half my age."

My cheeks flush at this reminder of my behavior when Margot and I first came to Count Angoulême's household, nearly a year ago. I had had the misfortune of attracting the king's eye. Being his older sister as well as the regent, Madame wanted me far away from the French court — and her younger brother. Fortunately for her, Louise was traveling to her new home in Cognac and needed attendants of her own. Margot and I were assigned to accompany her.

I could not accept that our lives could be so easily uprooted on such a whim and was convinced it was all part of the convent's master plan for us. Especially since Angoulême was their ally and the one who first agreed to sponsor us at the French court for the convent.

When I say nothing, he takes a sip of wine, his heavy-lidded gaze meeting my own. "No demands today that I put you in touch with the abbess of your convent immediately?"

I stare past him into the fireplace. "That gained me nothing, my lord. Once it became clear it was like beating a dead horse, there was no choice but to change my strategy."

He rises to his feet — slowly. I cannot tell if he wants to intimidate me or show himself to his best advantage. Whichever his intent, it fails. "Did you just call me a dead horse?"

"Never, my lord."

He comes out from behind the desk and sits upon the edge, crowding me. The chair presses against my legs, but I will not sit and give him the advantage of height. His knee pokes forward to rest ever so faintly against my thigh. "And what is this new strategy of yours, dear Genevieve?" His eyes are still slightly swollen from last night's revelries. His nose is so long and sharp it could scythe wheat, and strikes a discordant note above lips that are as full and ripe as a woman's.

It is hard to keep the contempt from my voice. "Wait as ordered until the convent sends further instructions."

"They have forgotten about you," he says, not without sympathy.

My fists clench. "I doubt that, my lord. Have you yourself not spent the last few months claiming how unforgettable I am?" He has not been subtle in pursuing me.

The sympathy shifts to something else, and I immediately regret my own stupidity. My anger made me careless.

He reaches up with his finger. Moving it across my skin, he draws a line from my temple down to my jaw. "You are unforgettable." I know a modest maiden would recoil, in coy surprise if not outright shock. But I cannot — will not — give ground in this game he insists on playing.

"Such a stubborn chin. And those cheekbones! They could cut as surely as any blade."

"Then you had best be wary and not play with sharp things."

Slowly, to be certain I know he is ignoring my implied threat, he runs his finger back up to rest at the corner of my mouth. "But your lips tell a different story."

In the haze of anger that descends upon me, I see only two choices. I can bite his repugnant finger clean off or take it in my mouth and wrap my tongue around it — simply to shock him.

Fortunately, my wits return. "My lips tell the story of a man who tried to pet a wolf he thought was tame. In the end, he lost his finger." I shift my body, crowding myself back against the chair behind me. It causes his knee to slip and he nearly tumbles forward. He catches himself, but not before wine has slopped out of the goblet and onto his sleeve.

"I grow tired of this," he growls.

I allow my own displeasure to shine through. "No more than I. Surely this is not what the convent of Saint Mortain had in mind when they asked you to sponsor me at court." Indeed, in the past year it is as if his arrangement with them has faded into naught but a threadbare memory.

His lips flatten, but he does not argue. Instead he rises from the desk and returns to the chair behind it. "I have something for you. A gift."

My breath hitches in my throat. That's how it started between him and Margot — with a gift.

"Sire, I do not wish anything from you. It is enough that you give me food and shelter until the convent calls upon me."

"Take it," he insists, holding a small pouch out to me.

Reluctantly, I reach for it, my fingers closing around the thick silk. "This will not change anything between us."

He stares at me over the rim of his goblet. "I would be disappointed if it did. Open it."

I pull my gaze from his and fumble with the silk ribbons. When I turn the pouch upside down, a luminous white pearl on a thin chain of gold tumbles into my palm. It is lovely, but I do not tell him that.

"Do you know the meaning of a pearl, my dear?"

Most maids would not know the sexual implications a pearl implies, but I do.

"It celebrates the beauty of irritation," he continues.

I jerk my head up at his unexpected answer. He smiles into his goblet. "I look forward to seeing you wear it."

I close my fist around the gift, glad it is not breakable. "That will not happen, my lord."

"Oddly, I find your never-ending irritation to be somewhat beguiling. It is puzzling to be sure, but you are young and I am patient. You are dismissed." He lifts his goblet in salute, then turns away from me.

Nearly dizzy with his shifting humors, I head for the door. It is only when I am in the hallway and have taken a dozen steps away from his chamber that I allow some of the tension to leave my body. I lean against the wall a moment to collect myself. Unbidden, the memory of Margot receiving her first gift from Angoulême washes over me.

"Why did he give it to you?" I ask.

She is looking in the small, occluded mirror in our room, a chain of gold with three red garnets glittering in the candlelight as she turns this way and that to admire it. Her hair is almost the exact color of the jewels. "Because he likes me, silly."

"Nothing good will come of it," I warn.

She turns around to face me and grimaces. "You sound just like old Sister Claude fussing at her birds."

When we came to the French court together, Margot and I, it was to be a great adventure. Two of Mortain's own daughters, planted right under the long nose of the French regent, who was causing our country so much grief.

And at first, it was. We would spy on the courtiers, mimic their mannerisms and comportment. But the longer we were at court, the more Margot was pulled into the courtiers' games and flirtations, and the more scornful of me she became.

"What were you doing in there?"

My head jerks up to see Margot herself standing in the hallway, glaring at me. I blink at the contrast between the Margot of my memory and how she looks now. Her red hair is as lush as ever, cascading around her shoulders like rich autumn leaves, but almost everything else about her has changed. She is rounder now, ripe to bursting with the babe she carries in her belly. Her eyes no longer sparkle with mischief or boundless energy, but are puffy and haunted-looking. I have heard the other women say she is not sleeping well. "What are you doing here? You're supposed to be confined to your rooms."

"I snuck out to find you. So?" Her mouth twists with jealousy. "What were you doing in Angoulême's office?"

I close my hand tightly around the pearl necklace. "Nothing."

She takes a step closer. "I don't believe you."

I sigh and tilt my head so she will see I am bored by this conversation. "If you must know, I was asking if he had any word from the convent."

Some of the sharpness leaves her face as she barks out a laugh. "You are three times a fool, Gen."

I shrug aside her scorn, happy enough that jealousy no longer clouds her thoughts. "Time will tell," I mumble as I turn to walk away.

"Wait!" she calls out, lumbering after me.

As much as being near her is like pouring salt into a fresh wound, I do not have the heart to force her to shuffle after me, clumsy and awkward. I slow my pace. "According to you, we have nothing to say to each other."

"I have something I must tell you. *Ask* you," she corrects.

I slowly turn to face her, but she is peering down past her belly at her feet. She has not talked to me — or asked me anything — for more than four months. I cannot imagine what has changed her mind. Something unfamiliar flutters deep in my belly, and I cannot tell if it is annoyance or hope. That I can still feel hope where she is concerned angers me. "So ask." I resume walking, but more slowly.

She grabs my arm. "Would you stand still for a minute?"

I am so startled by the faint note of desperation in her voice that I stop. "What?" Concern creeps in past the armor I have erected between us. "What is wrong? Is it the babe?"

"No. Yes. Maybe. I don't know."

Her voice sounds so lost, so close to despair and maybe even fear, that I find myself caring in spite of my vow to never again give a fig for anything she says or does. "Should I call a doctor? The count?"

"No!" she says, her face stricken. "It is nothing like that." Her eyes slip from mine to study the tapestry on the wall behind me. "It is just . . . I have a favor to ask."

This time it is I who bark out a laugh. Of course she wants something. "I cannot imagine what it is that I could do for you. You have made it abundantly clear that I have nothing to offer you anymore."

"There is one thing that *only* you can do for me."

Her words snag me like a hook. But I cannot make this easy for her. Not after all the pain she has caused me, so I simply wait in silence.

Her cheeks grow pink, and she fidgets with her hands. That is when I notice she is holding a red silken cord. I recognize it immediately — it is one she cut off of her finest dress when we first came to court, thinking it would make an excellent garrote. It has sat unused for five years.

Her hands grip the cord tightly, as if drawing on it for strength, then she thrusts it at me.

Keeping the pearl necklace carefully concealed in my left hand, I take the cord with my right. "Is there someone I am to strangle for you?" I do not even try to keep the disbelief from my voice.

"Saints no, Gen! Stop searching for the convent in every single thing!" Her voice is low, but it feels as if she is shouting.

I glare at her mulishly. "If you're asking a favor, mocking me seems an unwise approach."

"Would you just listen?" The note of desperation is back, so I relent.

She glances left then right to be certain we are alone, and lowers her voice to a whisper. "This has nothing to do with the convent, but everything to do with the Nine. There is no one else I can ask. You and I are the only ones who still worship the old saints here."

Even though the Church insists we call them saints, they are gods to me. And the convent. She has my full attention now.

"I need you to make an offering to Dea Matrona." She nods at the red cord I now hold in my hand.

"And how am I to do that?"

"Under the light of a waxing moon, you must untie the knots and bury the cord with an offering at the base of a silver birch. If you do, it is said that Dea Matrona will widen my passage so that the babe can pass through easier, allowing for a less painful birth. I would do it myself, but in my current condition" — she flaps her hands at her overripe body — "I cannot sneak anywhere, let alone be certain I can lower myself to the ground or get back up again. Please. Will you do this for me?"

The faint note of panic is unmistakable now. She is afraid. Afraid of what is coming and her powerlessness to stop it.

"But we are not friends anymore. Surely only friends do these sorts of things for each other."

"But we *are* sisters." Margot's eyes burn into mine. "Surely you would do this for a sister."

"You have treated me more like a maidservant than a sister for nearly two years."

She has the grace to be embarrassed. "Everything is a trade with you — a negotiation. If you will do *this*, then I will do *that*."

I do not understand her frustration. "That is how the world works."

Exasperated, she nearly stamps her foot. "Will you do it?"

I stare down at the red cord, wanting to shout at her that if she had only listened to me, none of this would have happened. She would not need to invoke Matrona's help or fear the pain of childbirth. Instead I say, "Tell me exactly what I must do."

CHAPTER 7

ell past midnight, when all the others are either asleep or engaged in bedplay, I slip from my room carrying the red silken cord and a small sack filled with all the things Margot said I would need.

No one sees me, and even if they did, they would simply assume I was on my way to meet a lover, for that is the way of things here at Cognac.

At the French court, our lives were constructed to make us pious, disciplined, and obedient. But the court at Cognac is designed around sensual pleasures, self-indulgence, and a great passion for the arts. After my upbringing at the convent and the austerity of Madame Regent, it felt as if I had been plucked from a barren winter tree and set down amidst a vibrant and dissolute summer garden.

I hated it. I still do.

Although, it amuses me greatly to think how Madame Regent would feel if she learned she had installed us in a den of libertines.

Outside, the gray clouds scuttle across the moonless sky. There is barely enough light to see my way through the castle's courtyard down past the farrier. I cut a wide berth around the kennels for fear of setting all the count's hounds to baying.

When I reach the castle wall, I let myself out through the small north gate that opens onto the field beyond. The entire countryside looks as if it has been dipped in charcoal dust, naught but shades of gray as far as my eye can see. Luckily, the silver birch is the lightest of them all, making it easy to spot.

The wind picks up, moving through the yellow dying birch leaves so that they sound like ghostly whispers. I ignore the shiver that trickles along my shoulders and kneel on the ground. Using my knife, I begin to dig, stabbing the blade into the earth at the base of the tree, the dirt rasping against the metal.

Of all the ways I had hoped to use my knife when I left the convent, preparing the ground for an offering to Dea Matrona on Margot's behalf was not one of them.

I stop to push the hair out of my face. Everything about this is wrong. It is so wrong it makes my teeth ache, and my bones want to dance out of my skin. This is not what the convent wanted for us.

And yet, what *did* the convent want? For they have never, in all the five years, contacted us.

I begin digging again.

Margot comes from nobility, so the transition to the French court was easy for her. She, like the other highborn girls in Madame's household, were confident enough in their own noble blood that they allowed themselves to disdain the rules occasionally, especially when Madame was away.

I never allowed myself such luxury, afraid my humble beginnings would show through if I relaxed my guard.

The hole finally big enough, I wipe the blade on my skirts, shove it back into its sheath, and reach for Margot's sack.

It wasn't until we arrived at the French court that Margot's contempt for my roots began to show. Something about being among royalty brought all Margot's snobbery to the surface. Although she still talked to me, she began to act as if I wasn't good enough to share her table, let alone her bed. As if we were not both daughters of the same god and I was truly naught but a whore's get and she a grand lady.

And yet here I am kneeling in the dirt, praying to Dea Matrona on her behalf to guarantee the safe birth of *her* bastard child.

I rip open the sack, remove a loaf of bread, and place it in the hole. Next comes the egg, which I set carefully atop the bread so it will not break. I take the red silk cord, untie each of the knots, then arrange it on top of the egg and bread, making certain no lines cross or overlap, which might cause the birth cord to tangle or wrap around a limb or neck. Once that is done, I use both my hands to shove the loose dirt back into the hole, packing it firmly into place. I uncork the wineskin and sprinkle a smattering of wine onto the tamped-down earth before leaning back to admire my handiwork.

Something is missing. A prayer, mayhap. But surely it is Margot who should be praying?

The wind rustles in the leaves overhead, a dozen dry, raspy voices reminding me that she is not here — only me. And whatever ways she has wronged me — and there are many — I do not know that she must pay for them with a difficult birth.

I bow my head and pray, asking Dea Matrona to bless Margot as she enters motherhood, to bless her babe, so that it will be hale and healthy, and to bless the birth so that both will survive.

By the time I return to the castle, a sense of melancholy has descended over me. I am unwilling to return to the chamber I once shared with Margot and mope over her betrayal. Instead, my feet carry me to the small altar I have built in the rooms near the dungeon.

This entire floor is only ever lit with one torch set in an alcove, even though many alcoves line the wall. I decided to turn one of them into a place to worship the Nine away from the prying eyes of those who have fully embraced the dogma of the new Church.

Before arriving in France, I had not had many dealings with the Nine. They had always seemed as distant and remote as royalty. For the first half of my life, I knew them only as stories told by my mother. Of the wild, untamed Saint Mer, who ruled over wave and sea. Of Brigantia, whose wisdom was recognized by the Church, her skill and knowledge of healing taught not only in Brittany, but in France as well.

My mother spoke often of Dea Matrona, mother to us all, and her twin daughters, one each for the two sides of love. My mother had little fondness for the fierce huntress Arduinna, patron saint of virgins and love's sharp bite. Saint

Amourna, however, as patron saint of the beguiling nature of love, was a favorite of hers — of all who worked in my mother's profession. According to my aunt Yolanthe, back in the mists of time, women like my mother and aunts were consecrated to her and their work considered holy.

Of the other gods, my mother had less to say, although they sometimes appeared in her stories. The terrible Camulos, god of war, and the far older and wiser Saint Cissonius, patron saint of travelers and crossroads. She also told tales of Saint Salonius, the patron saint of mistakes, whose tricks played on the other gods were the stuff of myth and legend.

And of course she told me of Saint Mortain and the convent that served Him.

At the convent my relationship with Mortain was straightforward enough. I would believe in Him and serve Him, and He would give me a path to a better life. Some of the girls thought of Him as their father, but for me, the word *father* conjured up sturdy Sanson, the tavern keeper, with his heavy beard, stained leather apron, and thickly muscled arms.

However, since being in France, I have found great comfort in the Nine. Visiting this altar is one of the few ways I am able to remember my own self, my true flesh and blood and purpose.

Nine short candle stubs sit in one of the alcoves. There is enough food left in the sack to make another offering here. But as my fingers close around a loaf of bread, I realize there is something else I can do with the food. Something that would bring me even more satisfaction than a second prayer for Margot.

Besides, it is a risk, and I am as hungry for those — for *action* — as the prisoner is for food. I rise to my feet, take the lone torch, and use it to light my path back to the oubliette.

"Hello?" I whisper as I set the torch into a bracket in the wall. "Is anybody home?"

A rustling from below. "You have caught me just in time," the deep voice rumbles. "I was about to go out visiting."

"That *is* lucky," I agree. "I suppose you have already eaten your dinner, as well, and are not hungry?" The thick silence that meets my question reminds me he is not simply hungry, but starving, and I curse at my careless jest.

"I have recently dined on mildewed straw and a bony rat." His humor mostly manages to hide the strain in his voice. "I cannot imagine you have anything that can tempt me after such a fine meal as that."

"I am not one to be deterred by such a daunting challenge." I follow his tone, but am careful not to overstep again.

"Well, do your best. I will not stop you."

I cannot help but smile as I set the bundle down. "How far from the grate to the floor?"

"Two men's lengths."

I do not know if he is tied up or chained, but with that great a distance, he cannot leap up and grab me, or overpower me in any way.

Unless he is lying.

Just to be certain, I glance around the antechamber until I spy a small piece of stone — a pebble from some past guard's boot or a crumbling corner of the castle wall. I toss it down through the grate. The length of time it takes for the pebble to hit the bottom reassures me that it is as deep as he says.

"Smart girl," he whispers. He does not know the half of it. Once I had told him I would return, I began carrying the needle case from my sewing basket with me. I select the sturdiest needle and use it to pick the padlock on the metal grate.

It is old and rusty with the damp air, but within seconds I hear the satisfying snick of a lock giving way. The bolt screeches in protest as I pull it back. I wait, ready should the sound have drawn anyone's attention. A guard perhaps. Or a jailor. When no one calls out or approaches, I lift the heavy iron grate, wincing as the hinges creak.

"Here." I toss down a wineskin filled with water. When I hear the slap of it hit his hand, I lie flat on my belly and lower the sack down as far as I can. "And the rest. Ready?"

"Yes."

I let go.

I do not know what I expect — a ravenous growling as he rips into the food, a gluttonous snarling as he snuffles through it like a pig through slops. Instead there is silence, as if some miracle has been laid before him.

Mayhap it is a miracle, to him at least.

At last I hear rustling as he unties the sack and begins pulling out supplies: bread, cheese, and another apple. When he finally speaks, it is a strained rasp. "Thank you."

Part of me wishes to sit and listen to him eat — hear every bite he takes, every moan of pleasure the food will bring him. But I also know what it is to be hungry — the relief of having food again. I know that desire to shove it into your mouth so fast you can't even swallow, so that before you know it, you are retching it back up. "How long has it been since you've truly eaten?"

"The apple you brought with you was the last food I've had."

"Then do not eat too quickly," I caution him. "Else it will turn your stomach." I do not linger to see if he takes my advice, but push to my feet and begin walking the perimeter of the outer chamber, giving him time to be alone with the first food he has eaten in days.

Truly, it is a wonder he is still alive. After a dozen laps around the chamber, I allow myself to return to the oubliette. There are no sounds of eating — or retching. "Are you all right?"

"I think I have died and passed into the Otherworld."

"If that were the case, I do not think I would be able to hear your voice." I do not know if that is precisely true. I have been around death so rarely that I have no knowledge of what shape my gifts from Mortain might take. Perhaps I could hear his voice, alive or dead.

"Then clearly I have been visited by an angel."

A surprised snort escapes from me. "I can assure you, I'm no angel."

"You have come bearing food, water, and hope. If that is not the act of an angel, I do not know what is."

"You are ridiculous," I say, even though his words warm the deep part of me that is hungry to do something important, something that matters. And feeding a starving man feels important. Unless he has committed some horrible crime. "Why are you in the dungeon?" The question feels like yet another risk — akin to poking a coiled snake with a stick.

"I am not sure that I know." His words are careful, measured, and I cannot help but wonder if that is what all guilty men would say, given the chance.

"Surely you did something to end up in an oubliette?"

"Are you so very confident of justice in this world?" he asks softly.

His words give me pause, for no, I am not at all certain of justice in this world. Have indeed seen very little of it. "Fair enough. What do others think you did to deserve such a fate?"

"As best I can tell, I was in the wrong place at the wrong time. Saw something I should not have. And you?" he asks. "Why are you here? Are you some bored lady in waiting? A servant exploring the dungeons for your own gain? Some spy sent to rescue me?"

His questions feel like darts that have hit home. I am all of those things. "Are you deserving of rescuing?"

"Oh, yes. Would the Nine have sent me hope, then water, and now food if they did not believe my cause to be just?"

Hearing him speak so casually of the old saints makes the fine hairs along my arms stand up. "You are Breton?" I have never heard of anyone in France who still worshiped the Nine.

After a considering pause, he says, "Yes. And you?"

"I, too, am from Brittany. And to answer your earlier questions, I am neither a bored lady, a spy, nor a servant. I am far closer to your own circumstances than you might think — a prisoner, of sorts. One who has been gone too long already and must return before my absence is noted."

"Will you come again?" The question hangs in the air like a feather.

"I do not know," I tell him. "I shouldn't have come at all."

"I'm glad you did."

When I return to my room, it feels less empty than it has in weeks. That is when I know that I will be returning to the oubliette.

CHAPTER 8

Sybella

rom the height of the eastern tower, I can see that the holly bush is slightly larger than yesterday, as is the crop of offerings beneath its branches. It is hard to keep my fingers from drifting to the twig hidden in my belt, even as I mock myself for doing so. And yet I cannot bring myself to throw it away.

Harder still is not picking at the scabs that have begun to form over old wounds. Especially now that the essence of what made me more than simply the sum of those wounds has been taken from me.

But not all of it has been taken. I am still able to experience the souls of the dying. Indeed, it is the soul of the guard who died with my hand on his chest that brings me to this tower today.

It has been a full week since the battle. While souls normally linger for only three days before moving to the Otherworld, those that suffer a violent death often take longer, if they ever move on at all. And today, with no people nearby to distract me with their heartbeats, I am able to sense a few that remain. They bump and flutter, restless and unsettled.

For my entire life, this ability to sense souls has felt more like a curse than a gift. When I was a child, their cold, chill presence brushed against me with icy wings of terror. In the end, they were nothing to be afraid of, although it took me a long time to learn that.

It is the souls of the newly dead — like those I killed yesterday — that are the most disturbing. The forced, unwanted intimacy, the eager, hungry way they flock to my warmth, the shocking and unwelcome invasion of their final thoughts shoving their way into my mind. I have learned to protect myself from them, with practice. But there is always that initial violation before I can resist. However, in this new upended world, like a beggar with scraps, I will grasp this remaining gift with both hands and call it a feast.

As the wisps of faded souls flutter against me, I close my eyes, trying to think how best to invite them to me. As it turns out, I do not have to. Merely having the thought causes them to flock to me like moths to flame, the dark gray ripple of their invisible wings barely detectable.

It is the weight of their souls and memories that nearly causes me to stagger. The neigh of a war horse. A flash of steel. An aching regret for a pair of lips that will never be kissed again. A surge of honor here. A wave of shame at being bested there. It is like running my hand through the small stones in a riverbed, each one cold, vividly colored, and uniquely formed.

Except for one — one of them is shockingly vibrant, so much so that I wonder if one of the wounded on the battlefield was overlooked and that he passed into death but recently.

Before I can fully explore this, I am distracted by a living heartbeat mounting the stairs behind me. My eyes snap open, and I quickly lower my arms. The heart beats in a rhythm so slow and deep and steady that I recognize it immediately.

Beast.

His physical presence has all the subtlety of a small mountain, and as he draws closer, the tattered remains of the lingering souls retreat. He slips his arm around my waist and pulls me close — the only man in the kingdom who could survive taking such a liberty with his throat intact.

He leans in and places his lips against my ear. "You are brooding." The warmth of his breath causes me to shiver. "I was on my way from the training yard to change for the council meeting and could feel it all the way down in the courtyard," he murmurs.

I am both vexed and pleased by this connection between us that allows him to know my thoughts so very well. "You've straw for brains if you think that."

"So you are always telling me." He presses a kiss into the top of my hair, and I allow my head to drop back against his shoulder. It is like leaning against a boulder, implacable and solid. And warm. This particular boulder gives off a ferocious heat.

They have always called him Beast, for truly he looks the part, with his nearly mythical strength and grotesque appearance. Many fear him. But many more — mostly young children and those who have fought with him — are able to see past the ugliness to the kindness and humor that shine in his eyes.

Unless those eyes happen to be lit with battle lust — then one must say a hasty prayer to the Nine and get out of his way. But for me, being with him is like basking in the warmth of the sun after a long winter, chasing away the dark shadows that lie as heavily upon me as a chill.

If I do not say something — and soon — I fear I will begin to purr. "I never brood. I am taking some fresh air, that is all. You have no idea what it is like to be stuck in a roomful of ladies sewing and talking, talking and sewing, from dawn until midnight, their tongues as fast and sharp as their needles. It is enough to drive me mad."

"I thought you liked sharp, pointy things."

"I prefer them to be deadlier than a simple sewing needle."

"I have no doubt that even a simple sewing needle would be deadly in your hands." He places another kiss upon the shell of my ear, his lips soft and fleeting. Between the crowded palace and our respective duties, our time alone is rare.

And forbidden. The behavior of a lady in waiting to the duchess must always be maidenly, modest, and above reproach. Many would condemn us for our stolen moments. Others would try to use it as a weapon against us. Fortunately, the duchess is a romantic at heart and turns a blind eye.

"So what *were* you brooding on? It can't be Charlotte or Louise, for I passed them just now, happily playing in the garden with Tephanie."

"Did you take a blow to your head in the training yard that has robbed you of your wits? I am not brooding."

He purses his mouth, drawing his face into a most comical arrangement of scars and lumps. "Is it because the duchess has ordered Ismae to remain here in Brittany with Duval?"

I snort. "There is your problem. It is Ismae who is brooding, not me. Mayhap it is she you heard."

He shakes his great head. "Only your brooding seems to get past my thick skull." He reaches up and scratches his ear. "It must be Annith, then. You are worried about her returning to the convent with Balthazaar."

Balthazaar. The name of the former leader of the hellequin is still unfamiliar on my tongue. "As if Annith and Balthazaar aren't match enough for anything the convent should think to put in their way." In truth, this oaf has named every one of my worries so far.

"I heard about your encounter with Crunard, but you can't be brooding over that. Knowing you, it was the high point of your day."

"If you ever think something so foolish, I will gut you and dance while you bleed."

That surprises a laugh out of him. "You will be the death of me, Sybella."

"Ah! That is why you court me. You are only curious to learn what it is like to die at the hands of one of Mortain's own."

"I have been found out." He lowers his head, his lips brushing against mine. The harshness of his ugly face, his sheer physical strength, should feel menacing, but it doesn't. Instead being with him fills me with both light and hope, something I have had far too little experience with. I lean in to him. Heat curls up from deep within my body, the sensation still new and unfamiliar. This feeling of desire — of *want* — is something I'd thought lost to me forever.

His mouth on mine is slow and deliberate; the rough, callused tips of his fingers slide down my shoulders, feather light along my arms, down to my hands. When they reach the heavy ring on my finger, he stops kissing me and pulls my hand up closer to study it. I resist the urge to yank it away. After a moment of silence, he rubs his thumb over the black obsidian that hides a sharp barb tainted with poison. "I thought you'd given this to the duchess." His voice is carefully devoid of emotion.

"I did," I say lightly. "But it was only meant as a way out in her darkest hour, and she was eager to be free of it."

"Would that she had thrown it in the midden heap," he grumbles.

I remove my hand from his and place my palms against his cheeks. "It is a weapon now, Beast. Nothing more. I swear it." Before we can resume where we left off, I feel another presence on the stairs behind us. A much smaller, younger presence. "We have company."

Beast steps crisply away, looking neither rushed nor guilty, and is standing by the ramparts when the page reaches us.

"Sir Waroch," he says breathlessly. "Lord Duval asked to see you right away. I'm to tell you that riders from the house of Rohan have been spotted."

Beast and I exchange a look. "Rohan?" he asks.

"Yes, my lord."

"Very well. Go on. I'll be right behind you."

The lad bobs a bow before turning to clatter back down the stairs.

"Rohan!" I repeat when the boy is out of earshot. This cannot bode well. As one of the most powerful nobles in Brittany, he sided with the French crown instead of the duchess. "He has been safely tucked up in his lands in France for the last year. What does he want now?"

Beast shrugs his massive shoulders as he heads down the stairs. "I'm sure Duval has been plotting all the possibilities out on a chessboard. Maybe he will tell us at the council meeting."

As Beast disappears out of sight, something niggles at the back of my mind. What if Crunard knew that Rohan was en route? The families have been allies for many years. How easy would it have been for Crunard to slip among Rohan's men and leave when they departed?

I had asked, *Why today?* Crunard did not have an answer for me, but what if I have found it anyway?

As I turn to follow Beast, a shock of cold brushes along the back of my neck. Like a spoiled, persistent cat, the vibrant soul tries one last time to gain my attention, but I brush it aside, too concerned with thoughts of the living to pay it any mind.

CHAPTER 9

ver the last harrowing months, the duchess and her council have plotted and argued and planned for a crushing defeat even as we made a desperate bid for victory. Thanks to Annith, aided by Saint Arduinna and Mortain, now Brittany and France are to be united by marriage. While Brittany will not maintain full independence from France, it is the duchess's heirs who will rule over both.

It has not been a smooth or easy process, for there are many different opinions among the council. And while I respect most of them, I rebelled at their decision to hold today's meeting without the duchess.

It is possible they did it for precisely the reason they said — to allow her to pursue happy, girlish joys and prepare for her upcoming marriage. Or it could be something else entirely. Something they are not even aware of. Now that she is officially betrothed to the king of France, they no longer see her with the same . . . not respect, for I know each of these men holds her in high esteem and would die defending her. But something more insidious than that — as if now that she is to marry, they no longer judge her to be the mistress of her own fate.

If that is so, they have sorely underestimated her.

And me. I smile, thinking of the surprise I have in store for them. That coupled with the news I have to share with the council makes this the first meeting I have ever truly looked forward to.

With nearly an hour before the meeting starts, I turn toward the garden where Beast saw my sisters playing. It is a rare opportunity to

spend a few quiet moments in their company. While they are more precious to me than life itself, my duties to the convent and the duchess have left me little time for them. It does not help matters that my temperament is not well suited to tending to young girls.

The garden is nearly empty this time of year, the heavy clouds keeping most of the courtiers inside close to the roaring fires. Tephanie sits on a stone bench, poking dutifully at the linen in her embroidery hoop. She keeps one eye on the girls, who are searching the bushes for the last remaining flowers before the next storm comes. When my foot crunches on the gravel path, Tephanie's head snaps up, face alert. Good. She has put aside some of her timidity. As one of the few who has lived in my family's household, one of the few who has seen firsthand the cruelties they are capable of, she knows the dangers that await those who let down their guard.

"My lady!" She hops to her feet and bobs a curtsy, holding her hoop close to her chest. Her furtive gesture has me longing to peer over and see what she is working on, but I refrain. She is loyal beyond measure, stood by me when others did not, and has followed me into my new life with no questions asked. The least she deserves is her privacy. "How are the girls this morning?"

"They are well. With so many new guests and the bustle of preparations for the upcoming trip, they seem to prefer the gardens." She smiles shyly. "I cannot say that I blame them."

"Nor I. You may sit back down," I tell her. "I only came to visit with the girls for a short time before I must meet with the council."

"They will be happy to see you."

Even though there is no censure in her words, they poke at me like her needle does at her linen. When I spend more than an hour with them, I grow as restless as a caged animal.

"Since you are here, do you mind if I fetch some fresh embroidering silk? I have used up all my red."

"Of course. Take your time. I do not need to be anywhere for nearly an hour. And you might want to get a fresh needle," I add. "I think the one you're using has grown dull."

She blushes, as if I have scolded her.

"Tephanie." I reach out and briefly touch her arm. "It was not an order, merely a suggestion. It looked as if you were having to force it through, which was causing your thread to snarl."

She takes a deep breath. "Of course, my lady." She bobs a curtsy, sets her hoop face-down on the bench, then hurries inside.

My glance lingers briefly on the hidden embroidery before I turn and make my way along the stone path to my sisters. Louise watches a lone thrush, perched on a bare branch, warbling his sad winter song. Charlotte is crouched over a bush, her face creased in concentration. Intrigued, I head first in her direction. She glances up as I draw closer. Realizing it is only me, she returns her gaze to the bush without saying a word. Her lack of greeting pinches my heart, but I do my best to ignore it. She is always thus — feeling no need to make idle conversation or greeting. "What have you there?"

"A spider."

A huge spider's web spreads across half the bush. While its corners are securely fastened, the stiff breeze causes the threads to flutter delicately, like fine lace. "Webs are beautiful, are they not?" I ask.

"Yes." The word comes out almost breathlessly. That is when I see she is not staring at the web, but at the spider itself. It is big and fat and nearly as large as her thumb.

"Louise!" she calls out. "Come see this!"

"It is only a spider," I tell her, knowing Louise will not enjoy it nearly as much.

"Yes," she says impatiently. "But look what it's *doing*."

I peer closer at the web. The creature scuttles across the fine silk to a large fly trapped in one of the sticky strands and begins spooling out web, using it to bind the fly. I look again at the intent expression on Charlotte's face, and a trickle of apprehension runs down my spine.

Louise arrives just then. "What is it?"

"A spider," Charlotte tells her. "Hunting a fly. Watch."

Impatiently pushing a strand of her hair away from her face, Louise peers closer, then leaps back abruptly and grabs my hand. "It's killing it! Make it stop!"

I squeeze her hand. "I can't, sweeting. That is how they eat and feed their young."

"I don't like it." Her voice becomes shaky, and she turns her face into my skirts.

"Don't be such a baby," Charlotte scolds as she scoots even closer to watch.

She has always been a curious child, I try to tell myself. Has always been inquisitive, snooping and sneaking, collecting details about the world around her like a miser collects coin. And who can blame her? In our household, the more one knew, the better one could avoid deviously set traps. She has also lived among our family for ten years now, long enough to be touched by their darker impulses.

Which is why she must never return to them. That and her own personal safety, although she is, thankfully, too young to realize that.

"Uh, my lady?"

Tephanie's voice is a welcome distraction. Not only is she better at comforting Louise, but I can ask if she has noticed this type of behavior with Charlotte. When I turn to greet her, my world tilts, like a crystal goblet that teeters on the edge of a table before shattering.

A heavily muscled man holds her close, a long hunting knife pressed firmly against her throat. His face is one I know well, from both my nightmares and my childhood. Indeed, his looks favor his father's so much that it is like twisting a dull, rusty blade in an old wound.

Bitter acid of fear and anticipation floods my body, drawing my skin tight over my bones, my muscles tensing with readiness.

Mortain has been gone from my life for less than a week, and already the family that raised me has found a way back in.

CHAPTER 10

he sight of my brother Pierre sends me reeling down a deep hole full of ugly memories and heartbreak and death. So much death. My mother, Pierre's mother, Charlotte's and Louise's mothers. Our brother Julian. Even my own death, narrowly escaped.

The man who raised me and committed those atrocities, gutted with a knife.

Pierre is one of that man's children who eagerly embraces his legacy of cruelty.

Mayhap this is the reason Mortain bid me live — to protect my sisters from the horrors visited upon me.

Two men stand on either side of Pierre. Like him, they are dressed in red and yellow tabards. The man on the right is tall and wide-shouldered. A beard covers most of his face, and his eyes are as hard as flint. His height and long limbs mean he will be fast, with a long reach.

The other man is shorter, but thicker through the shoulders and chest. He holds himself with a careless strength that bespeaks a sea-soned soldier. However, it is his eyes that disturb me most, for they are flat, as if no soul or heart or anything decent lives within.

I shift my focus to the scar on my brother's left eyebrow, the one I gave to him when I was ten years old and he tried to kiss me a second time. I am older now, and far more deadly. "Pierre."

At our brother's name, Charlotte looks up from the bush and slowly stands before taking one careful step away from me. Whether to give herself room to run or to disassociate from me, I do not know.

"This is convenient. I come looking for one sister and find all three. I knew your pet would prove useful." His casual grip on the knife at Tephanie's throat sends a shard of ice through my gut. He doesn't care if he kills her or not. He grins, a cruel twist of his lips that has haunted my dreams for as long as I can remember. "You didn't think I'd forgotten you?"

I force my own lips to curve in a mocking smile. "Of course not." I had, however, hoped he would not remember until we were safely in France. "But I *did* think you had returned to Périgord for the winter." I fill my voice with arch amusement. The scent of fear would only embolden him further.

"What I want could not be found in Périgord. If you and the girls come easily, I will not have to hurt this sow you seem to have grown so fond of."

Terror tries to chase all the breath from my lungs, but I rein it back in. "Is this some newfound brotherly responsibility you are feeling toward our sisters?" As I talk, I pull Louise nearer so she is tucked close against me, shielded by my skirts. "You are not a nursemaid, and the girls mean nothing to you."

"They belong to me now and are the bargaining chips I will use to form new alliances and rebuild our family's influence. Now bring them here, or I will be forced to do something you will regret."

Even though I can feel Tephanie's eyes on me like a frightened calf, I do not dare look at her. "Kill her or not, I don't care."

Louise gasps. I squeeze her hand, trying to reassure her it is naught but a lie. "And you may take the girls as well. I have grown weary of them."

Pierre smiles, pleased at his easy victory. Overconfidence has always been his great weakness. "Ah, but I will not leave you behind. You are still of marriageable age and hold some value. Besides, you have much to answer for." His eyes glint darkly, hinting at the malevolent punishments he has in mind.

Ignoring the cold fear that trickles along my skin, I keep my voice light. "Dear Pierre. I forget you were never the clever one in our family. Let us talk this through. Surely I will serve you better by waiting upon the duchess. My presence here could do much to repair the damage our family has done to her."

"Not clever, eh? How do you suppose I got in here undetected?"

"By wearing Viscount Rohan's colors, which is practically cheating."

The vein in his forehead throbs as he takes a step forward, dragging the forgotten Tephanie with him. "Cheating? This is not some game of cards we are playing." He stops and cocks his head like a curious vulture. "Or is it? I'd forgotten how you could make anything into a game." His eyes gleam with a spark of admiration, and I fear I will be sick. If there is anything about me he admires, I must cut it out like rotting fruit. "Tell me, was it a game when our brother Julian died? Did you enjoy luring him to his death?"

"No!"

"You may as well have swung the sword yourself. And our father's death was by your hand."

Charlotte jerks her gaze from Pierre to stare at me, and Louise shoves her face into my skirt.

"He is not dead," I say coolly.

Pierre's eyes bore into mine, alight with cold fury. "You left him lying in a pool of his own viscera. Even when the surgeons stitched him back together, he did not regain consciousness. He is as good as dead. Do not fool yourself, Sybella. You are no more suited to the duchess's court than a wolf is to a lapdog. You are a d'Albret. You lie like one. You kill like one." He takes a step closer. "Heartlessness and cruelty are your weapons of choice. Your d'Albret blood is thicker than your desire to be a lady in waiting to some mewling queen."

The need to scream at him that I am not of his blood is so strong, I fear it will burst from my throat. But I can feel Louise trembling beside me. See Charlotte watching Pierre and me carefully. With all the death and upheaval they have gone through, I cannot tell them we do not share the same blood.

Besides, to admit that is to hand Pierre a weapon. A weapon he will be quick to use as we struggle over custody, and I will not give them up. Not to him. Not to the d'Albret family.

"I think you underestimate the toll these last months have taken on me. I want nothing more than to lead a simple life, with simple pleasures. To serve my queen and to guide my sisters to womanhood so that they may make suitable marriages." I will take the one on the left first. He looks faster than Pierre or the other man.

Pierre snorts. "And how will you do that? You can offer them nothing. You have no lands, no husband, nothing you can call your own. You cannot sign a

betrothal contract to ensure your own future, let alone theirs. You will live in a room at the beck and call of a fickle young girl. That is no kind of security to offer anyone."

Compared to what the d'Albret family has to offer, it is paradise on earth.

"Perhaps that is so," I say, as if flirting with some admirer. "But I cannot just pick up and leave the duchess's side with no explanation. I must obtain her permission." As we talk, I continue to pull on Louise's arm until she is all but hidden behind me. To Pierre, it will merely look as if I am shielding the younger girl from him, which I am.

But I am also freeing up my throwing hand.

Thankfully, he does not see me as much of a threat. "She is our sovereign and, as you yourself noted, soon to be queen of France. To slight her could set the family honor and fortunes even farther back. Besides, you cannot provide better marriages for our sisters than the duchess can arrange once she is queen."

He laughs. "She will put the crown's interest first, while I will see to my own interests. Very different things."

I shake my head in disbelief. "You don't truly expect the three of us to simply prance out of the palace, with no one trying to stop us, do you?" The man on the left is slapping his knife against his thigh, waiting impatiently. The one on the right has a crossbow, but it is strapped to his back, leaving both hands free to snag the girls. Fools. I curl my fingers up until they make contact with the tiny catch at the base of my wrist sheaths.

"They would not dare to try to stop me. You all belong to me. Even if someone were stupid enough to try, with our blades at your throats, they would not risk interfering."

Neither Pierre nor his men bear Mortain's marque. I cannot help but feel as if I stand on the edge of a precipice. They intend to take us alive, and I don't know if killing them is considered self-defense.

But it *will* allow me to save my sisters. I press against the catch on the sheath, and the hilt of my knife slips down into my palm, then I shrug, as if bored by the conversation. "As I said, you are welcome to the girls. And the maid." Behind me, Louise's small body grows rigid with betrayal and shock. "There, now. Go to him." I release her hand and lean down to nudge her forward, whispering, "Drop to the ground when I say 'spider.' Blink twice if you understand."

Her solemn eyes blink once, twice. As those worried, frightened eyes stare up at me, I realize I cannot kill Pierre in front of her.

Charlotte glances over at me, her face clear and unafraid. I cannot tell if she heard my instructions to Louise or not. "Go on, sweeting. Go to Pierre." I speak loud enough for my brother to hear. "He will take care of you."

Charlotte lifts her skirts and begins picking a slow, careful path forward. "I wondered when you'd arrive." Her young voice is clear, high, and utterly steady. "To be honest, I thought you'd be here weeks ago."

She manages to inject a faint element of disdain into her words. Clever girl. That will further enrage him, which will make him even more careless.

"Enough!" he snaps. "Be silent and do as you are told." As he scolds her, I inch my fingers along the knife until I have the tip grasped firmly in my fingers. To disable and not kill is a far more difficult throw. I will have only one chance. It must be quick, and it must be true.

As Louise slowly walks toward our brother, she starts to cry. Pierre scowls, his face flushing in anger. "Make her be quiet! Someone will hear."

"Spider!" I shout.

As I launch my dagger, both of my sisters drop to the ground. My blade hurls through the air, a darting flash of silver, before slicing across the back of Pierre's hand.

He bellows in pain as he drops his knife. There is a second yelp of pain as Tephanie stabs him with something, and he loosens his grip on her long enough that she can break free.

A moment of stunned silence follows as what has just happened registers with Pierre's men. *Slow*, I think to myself. *Just like him.*

They reach for their weapons, but too late. I have already pulled Ismae's crossbow from the folds of my overskirt and am slapping a bolt into place. I let it fly, aiming for the man drawing his sword. I do not wait to see where the bolt lands, but reload while turning toward the second man. The bolt pierces his wrist, hopefully shattering it. At the very least, he will be unable to use his own bow anytime soon.

Reloading again, I glance back at the first man, swearing when I see my aim was off and I caught him in the throat. He holds a hand up to his neck, trying to stop the flow of blood. He is not dead now, but will be shortly.

Cradling his injured hand, Pierre glares at me. The malevolent loathing in his eyes has the weight of a physical blow.

"Leave," I tell him. When he hesitates, I say it again, louder. "Leave! I have two more bolts and six knives. You are finished here. Besides, your friend is gravely wounded. Best you get him somewhere he can die in peace."

I can feel Louise's and Charlotte's eyes on me, wondering who this creature is who has taken over their sister's body.

Pierre grits his teeth, lips white with pain. "I will have what is rightfully mine by birth. And I will crush you in the process. The law is on my side."

"Mayhap, but the duchess is on mine."

The taller henchman is propping up the one bleeding from his throat. "Sir?" the man says gruffly. Pierre turns on him so savagely that I fear he will strike the injured man. Instead he swears, and strides for the garden gate, leaving his two wounded companions to struggle after him.

When they reach the gate, Charlotte rises to her knees, her cool gaze moving from Pierre to me, then back to Pierre again. For one heart-stopping moment, I do not know if she will follow him or remain with me. In the end, she stays where she is.

When Pierre and his men finally disappear from view, I drop the crossbow and race forward. I reach Louise first, grab her up into my arms, and hold her close, petting her head. "I was lying, sweeting. It was all lies to keep you safe. Do you hear me? None of it was true."

Finally, she looks up at me, her face red and swollen, her tear-filled eyes wide with fear. She nods and throws her arms around my neck. Relief, as sweet and gold as honey, flows through my limbs. "Let's see to your sister."

Charlotte is already standing and brushing the grass off her skirts. I pull her into a one-armed hug, which she allows for a second before stepping away. I grab her hand and hurry toward Tephanie.

"Are you all right?" I ask softly.

"I am fine," she says, even though her hand still trembles.

"You know I didn't mean any of what I said —"

"I know, my lady! Here." She reaches for my sisters' hands. "I'll take the girls. Now go and do whatever it is you must!"

I want to hug her for her understanding. Instead I pick up my skirts and tear out of the garden, hurrying down the path that leads to the courtyard. They cannot have gotten far — all three were wounded, and one was surely dying. When I turn the corner into the courtyard, however, I am assailed by a wall of heartbeats, and my steps falter.

The palace yard is filled with at least fifty of Viscount Rohan's men, with more pouring in through the gate. Some are mounted, others are on foot, but all are wearing the exact same tabard and cloak as Pierre and his men. I pause, trying to pick out the three familiar figures, but they have been swallowed by the crowd.

For a moment, I am pinned by indecision. I can call for the palace guard, but what to tell them? That my brother was here and demanded custody of our sisters? Something he has every right to do? That it was done at knifepoint will matter little, I fear.

No. What is between Pierre and me is best handled privately, at least for now. And without knowing why Rohan is here, it cannot be wise to alert him to this breach in our security.

And then, as if the gods have answered a prayer I have not yet had time to utter, I see Beast, striding on the other side of the crowd, half a head taller than most. He has not changed for the council meeting and still bears his weapons from the training yard. "Beast!"

His head snaps up, his gaze finding mine at once, knowing immediately that something is wrong.

"Pierre!" I call out over the heads of the milling crowd. I hold up three fingers and point them toward the gate.

Beast's face shifts at once, becoming hard and lethal. With an abrupt explanation, he grabs the nearest horse, leaps onto it, and puts his heels to its flanks.
Hapless soldiers scramble out of his path as he gallops toward the gate in pursuit.

A horse entering the courtyard just then prances out of his way, the woman
rider swerving as she tries to calm her mount. A second prayer answered.
"Ismae!" I call out.

She takes one look at my face, then quickly steers her horse to a mounting
block. I reach her in time to hold the reins while she dismounts. She is scowling
by the time her feet touch the ground. "What's wrong?"

"Pierre was here."

Her face blanches, and her hands reach for the knives at her wrists. "Where?"
Her voice is steady, deadly.

"Gone. Beast has just ridden after him." I quickly fill her in.

"Where are your sisters now?"

"In the garden with Tephanie. I must get back to them."

Ismae nods. "Go. I will find reinforcements and meet you in your room."

I turn and race back to the garden. If I were planning such an abduction,
I would have a second team of men ready to snag the girls if my first attempt
failed. Fortunately, Pierre is not that clever.

Chapter 11

Genevieve

y plan to let Margot know that the offering was safely made is thwarted when Louise is struck by a fierce bout of morning sickness that lasts three entire days. Finally, the sickness passes and Louise does not need all of us to attend her every minute. As I make my way to Margot's chamber, a messenger arrives for Count Angoulême.

Margot will have to wait.

I give the messenger some time to deliver his message, then contrive to be strolling by Angoulême's office door within minutes of his departure. Angoulême looks up from his desk as I pass and calls out to me.

"Genevieve!"

"Yes, my lord?"

"You saw the messenger arrive." It is not a question.

"Yes, my lord." The curtains are drawn against the chill, and a fire crackles in the hearth. There is a brace of candles on his desk as well as blank sheets of parchment, a pot of ink, and a stack of fresh quills. Out of habit, I glance down to see if I can recognize any of the wax seals.

"He brought news of the duchess and the situation in Brittany." He reaches out and straightens one of the letters on his desk.

"And?" Will the man make me pluck each word from his tongue?

"The king and the duchess of Brittany are to be married."

The words are so unexpected, so unwelcome, that I draw back as if he has struck me. "You cannot be serious."

He shifts in his chair, scowling in irritation. "Of course I am serious. Why would I lie about such a thing?"

"But it makes no sense!" I insist. "Last we heard, the king was marching on Rennes to besiege it."

The count reaches for the decanter on his desk. "It seems that the principals involved decided it would be better for everyone if they married instead."

I shake my head. "That cannot be. The late duke was opposed to such a union. The countries have been enemies for as long as I can remember."

"I am aware." The count's voice is dry as dust, for he fought alongside the duke in many of those skirmishes.

"Why would the duchess betray all that he fought for? All that *she* has fought for?"

"Oh, come now." He fills a crystal goblet with wine. He does not offer me any. "Marriages are naught but contracts between powerful families. France has been occupying Brittany for months and threatening her borders for years."

"But agreeing to marry is the ultimate surrender. Why would she trade away all her bargaining power like that?"

He slowly leans back in his chair, studying me. "Is that what you think of marriage?" My hands itch to punch the condescending look off his face. "What else was the duchess to do? She had run out of options."

"Resist. Wait for her husband, Maximilian, to arrive with help."

"It was only a proxy marriage," he points out. "And she waited for months and months. No meaningful help came. He was too consumed by his own wars. She pawned every crown jewel she possessed to procure mercenary troops. Begged and appealed to every ally, each of whom sent just enough help to ease their conscience, but not enough to do her any good. She was truly out of options." He takes a sip of wine. "It was the best choice she could make under the circumstances."

The explanation makes sense, yet every bone in my body resists what he is telling me, and I feel sick inside. "What of Princess Marguerite? Will they just set her aside? She will not be happy with that. Nor will her father."

Angoulême snorts derisively. "No one imagines either of them is happy. Maximilian may take some action against France or Brittany, but that action will be tempered by the fact that France now holds his daughter hostage."

I feel sick for Marguerite as well. She was much beloved by the king, as well as Madame. Since she was three years old, she has been pampered and indulged and raised with all the royal magnificence due a future queen of France. Now that has been taken from her.

It changes not only the dauphine's position, but mine as well. If Brittany and France are now allies, if they are one country unified under one ruler, where does that leave me? Or the convent? Do they still answer to the duchess and serve her interests above all else? "Will Brittany remain independent, or shall it become part of France?"

Angoulême looks down into his goblet. "I am certain it is part of France now." He swirls the contents. "Why else would the king go to all the trouble to marry such a thorn in his side as your duchess has been to him?"

His words set my teeth further on edge. That is when I finally understand my own distress. The marriage makes Brittany's independence simply a point to be negotiated on a contract. I thought what the convent was fighting for was more important than that. And now it seems that I was wrong. "I still am not sure I believe it. Is it possible she was forced into it?" If that is true, then surely there is still some role for me to play.

"Now you are just being absurd."

"Even so, shouldn't you at least send a message to confirm the truth?"

"Foolish girl! Do you not think the regent has me watched for just such a misstep?"

I stare at him in bemusement.

He laughs outright. "Do you think I can write to the duchess's Privy Council or your precious convent whenever I please? Do you think my comings and goings and, yes, even my correspondence, are not scrutinized by the regent? Come now, Genevieve. Surely the convent trained you better than that."

"Of course they did, my lord," I snap back. "But I also assume that you have means of working around those obstacles, else what use would you be to the convent?"

His nostrils flare in agitation. "You forget yourself. Perhaps time will bring some clarity. Now leave. I have work I must do."

"With pleasure." I lift my skirts and storm from his chambers.

My head is a swirl of questions both heady and sobering. Was the duchess coerced? If so, and if she is on her way to the French court, why have I not been called to take action? Surely I am the most well placed initiate of the convent. Indeed, my connections with the French court could prove most helpful, even if she has not been forced into this marriage.

Hope, bright and shining, surges through me. In my darkest moments, I have come close to believing what both Angoulême and Margot claim — that the convent had forgotten about us. But now there is a chance their need for me could not be greater.

CHAPTER 12

Sybella

ephanie and the girls stand in the doorway that leads back into the palace, closer to people than the abandoned garden, yet not so far that I will not know where they have gone. Tephanie has managed to calm Louise, while Charlotte is carefully smoothing her gown over and over.

At my approach, Louise looks up. The hesitation on her face cuts me to the quick. "Come," I say, as if their entire world had not just been turned upside down. "Let's return to our chambers." I take each of their hands in my own. Charlotte tries to tug away, but I refuse to let go.

If I had a choice, I would keep some truths from both of them all their lives. Even though they have lived in the d'Albret household and have seen much, they do not fully understand all that they saw. But today they have witnessed more violence, cruelty, and hate than most girls are exposed to in a lifetime. I cannot simply ignore it. Between Pierre's accusations and my own actions, I must tell them something.

When we finally reach our chamber, I pull the girls inside while Tephanie closes the door behind us. I kneel in front of them, not letting go of their hands. Louise's enormous brown eyes look like crushed autumn leaves. Was I ever that young? That innocent? I must have been, but I can no longer remember it.

And Charlotte. The look on Charlotte's face guts me even more, for it is filled with both familiarity and knowing. She has seen some version of this before, and she believes that whatever I am about to

tell her will likely be a lie, or at the very least, an attempt to put too fine a polish on what is naught but a lump of lead.

"First, you need to know that I did not mean any of what I said to Pierre. I *do* care about you — about Tephanie — but wanted Pierre to believe otherwise."

"Why?" Louise's voice is whisper quiet.

"I hoped if he thought I did not love you, he would not bother to hurt you. It is like you pretending your favorite doll is not your favorite so Charlotte will not tease you with it."

Her face clears in understanding even as Charlotte scowls at me.

My voice grows softer, for these next words are hard to get past the sorrow that fills my throat, the wound still fresh. "You must also know that I did not kill our brother Julian." Although I now know we shared no blood, I will always think of him as my brother. "He was killed trying to protect me, and while I love him all the more for it, you can be certain that will weigh on my conscience for all eternity."

"Who was trying to hurt you?" Louise's voice is small.

How do I tell her it was her father? I reach out and cup her tender cheek in my hand. "Someone who enjoyed cruelty for its own sake and had no care for those he hurt."

"Oh." That seems to be enough for her. She has not been around him much. He did not bother himself with his children until they could be of use to him. When I turn to Charlotte, however, I can see that she knows precisely who it was that tried to hurt me. She regards me for a long moment before nodding, as if she has deigned to believe me.

Unable to resist, I quickly hug her for her faith in me, then I plant a quick kiss on her forehead before doing the same to Louise.

Behind me, the door opens, followed by a murmur of voices. Ismae has arrived and has brought reinforcements. Lazare — a slender man whose face is as sharp as any blade and his eyes as cutting — is with her. He is one of the mysterious and maligned charcoal-burners who serve the Dark Mother, the one to pray to when the Nine have forsaken you. Maybe that is who I should look to for guidance now. Especially since she favors the scarred and wounded, those without hope.

Lazare is one of the first to leave the depths of the forest to serve the duchess. He is swift and deadly. We have fought together many times. I trust him implicitly. Next to him is a small gnome of a man grinning widely and nodding his head in enthusiastic greeting. Yannic, Beast's loyal companion, is short and crooked, his movements clumsy and awkward, but his heart is bigger than a mountain, as is his courage. Even better, the girls know both of them, since they traveled with us when we made our escape from Nantes.

Smiling, Yannic reaches for Louise's ear and pulls a small rock from it. She blinks. "How did you do that?" she demands. He winks at me, and I know that all will be well between them.

As Yannic and Lazare distract the girls, Ismae takes my arm and pulls me toward the door.

"What?" I ask, frowning. "Did Beast find Pierre?"

"He has not returned yet. But you and he are due in the council meeting."

The council meeting! *Merde*, that seems like a lifetime ago. "Have I not missed it already?"

"No. Dunois and Duval were just heading down as I was coming to your room."

"Did you tell them I was not coming?"

Ismae stares at me blankly. "Why would I?"

I pull my arm from her grip. "Surely my sisters need me more than the council does."

Ismae gives a sharp shake of her head. "You yourself said that Pierre and his men were wounded. And Beast is close on their trail. If your brother had other reinforcements, they would have already made their move. They are gone. At least for now."

I say nothing. My instincts scream at me to grab my sisters and go to ground, like a hunted fox, burrowing in the safety of the earth until the danger has passed.

Ismae grabs my arm again. "Look at them."

Louise and Charlotte sit on the floor with Tephanie and Yannic, playing some sort of game with small stones. Lazare leans against the wall behind them, not smiling exactly, but not scowling either.

"They are fine," she whispers. "And that council meeting is part of keeping them safe." She gives my arm a shake. "You and Beast cannot both be absent. Besides, you are the one who invited the duchess to this meeting — one the council specifically wanted to have without her. You owe it to her to be there."

I scowl. "How did you know I invited her?"

Her mouth quirks up. "Because when I went to tell her of it, she explained you already had."

Ismae takes full advantage of my hesitation and grabs my shoulders, spins me around, and shoves me toward the door. "The continued safety of your sisters depends on the duchess. She is your best protection against Pierre and his plotting. The stronger she is, the more she will be able to protect you. And with Beast in pursuit, he will not come back. Besides," she says more gently. "I am also your sister. Do you not trust me to keep them safe?"

I make a face at her. For all that I do not like it, she is right. My best hope for their welfare is to continue my plan to accompany the duchess to France and get my sisters safely under the French crown's protection. Pierre would not dare challenge the queen of France.

Which means I must attend the council meeting.

By the time I reach the large double door, I have put myself back together. If I am not precisely the same person I was when I got up this morning, it is a close enough approximation that no one should be able to tell.

The guard nods in recognition and opens the door to admit me. When I enter the room, it feels as if I have stepped from a black winter storm into a soft spring day. The room is buoyant — with relief and jubilation.

Grave Chancellor Montauban looks five years younger than he did a mere week ago, his face no longer haggard with worry. Jean de Châlons, the duchess's own cousin, is actually smiling — transforming his predatory face into one that is charmingly handsome. He is precisely the sort of man I would have trifled with. Once.

The stalwart Captain Dunois, who has served the duchess all her life, still looks like an enormous bear, but at least he is no longer a grumpy one. While he is not smiling, exactly, there is an absence of tension in his face that is nearly a smile.

They are — of course — still savoring their victory. And why not? They are not the ones whose past enemy has just breached their walls and held a knife to their throat. My limbs threaten to renew their trembling, but I grip my skirt and squeeze ruthlessly until the weakness passes. Even though it feels as if some hound has just dug up all the dead, rotting remains of my family's past, I will not let the privy councilors see that.

Fortunately, not everyone is seated, which makes my entrance less noticeable. Chancellor Montauban stands near the door, talking with Duval. "I thought the regent was going to sew the king's mouth shut if he did not stop agreeing to your concessions."

Duval grins boyishly, and I realize how rare a sight that truly is.

The bishop is dressed in a fresh red robe and already seated at the table. His skin hangs a little looser than before, as if his close call with death has shrunk him somewhat. "It is a shame the regent was born a woman, else she would have made a fine ruler."

Duval casts an annoyed glance his way. "The king's sister has been a formidable enemy, whatever her sex, and I am glad she had no further advantage to add to her arsenal."

The bishop does not so much as acknowledge me as I pass behind him to reach my chair, and it is all I can do to keep from knocking his be-damned miter off his foolish head.

"Besides," Duval continues as he moves to take a seat at one end of the table, "in all our dealings with the regent, she has been harder than a rock and just as implacable as her father was before her. If not for the king's sudden affection for the duchess, we would be in a much weaker position."

"Fortunately, now all that is left for us to do is to get this marriage behind us." Chancellor Montauban attempts to smooth over the ripples in the water. "Then most of our problems will be over."

"Except we will have to find Duval a new hobby," Châlons adds with a grin.

Everyone laughs — more giddy relief than true humor. Duval shrugs good-naturedly. "It will take a while to grow accustomed to things being at ease between our two countries."

I finally reach the far end of the table and take a seat next to Father Effram, putting as much distance between me and the bishop as I can. The old priest gives me a smile of welcome, but I busy myself adjusting my skirts, hoping Father Effram's shrewd eyes will not see more than I wish him to.

"Shall we start?" the chancellor asks.

Duval looks around the table. "Beast was supposed to be here."

I concentrate on not meeting Duval's eyes. I've no intention of explaining that Beast is chasing after my vile brother to the entire council.

Dunois shrugs. "He was, but clearly he got waylaid. We can start and fill him in later."

Duval begins. "The wedding is to take place in two weeks' time at Langeais castle. King Charles has been most generous, filling our treasury with funds. We now have the ability to outfit the duchess and her escort in the full honor they deserve."

Chancellor Montauban, who has spent the last few months trying to rattle coins from our empty treasury, leans forward and steeples his hands together. "That was very generous of them."

"Generous?" Duval's lips twitch in wry humor. "Or self-serving?"

The chancellor spreads his hands in a calming motion. "Come, Duval. There is no need to malign this noble gesture."

Captain Dunois shoots the chancellor a penetrating look. "Surely you realize it was a way to ensure that the mercenaries and our troops were paid off and dispersed."

"And thank God for that," Duval mutters.

The mercenaries we had contracted to fight against France became more of a threat than an ally when our coffers ran dry. They came close to holding the entire city hostage for their pay. "And do not forget this noble gesture did not include allowing the duchess to rule over her own duchy," Duval points out. "The king needed a great deal of convincing on that. He was determined to oversee it in her name."

A spark of anger thaws some of the ice in my belly. Even a duchess — a soon-to-be queen — must beg for scraps at her own table.

"It required three extra pages in the betrothal contract," the Prince of Orange adds. That same betrothal contract removes him from the line of succession. If he is bitter about that, it does not show.

Duval turns to him. "Any word from Maximilian?"

"His scouts have likely not reached him yet, but he will hear soon enough. He will be most displeased." The prince's words are strained, for the emperor is his liege, and his conflicting loyalties place him squarely in the jaws of a vise. "Nor can we blame him. His wife has just entered a betrothal agreement with his enemy. He will feel woefully betrayed."

"It was a proxy marriage," Duval is quick to remind him. "And the bishops have assured us it was not binding."

Captain Dunois leans back in his chair and folds his arms across his chest. "If Maximilian wanted the marriage so badly, he could have sent the needed troops. The entire motive for the marriage was to gain his aid and protection in our fight against France, which he was unable to provide." The captain's disgruntlement matches my own, so I am happy to hear him give voice to it.

Châlons scowls and continues speaking. "He has not only lost his bride and her dowry, but his own daughter was to be queen of France. He has had two ripe plums snatched from his hand."

His words cause something already brittle and fragile inside me to snap.

"Does your cousin know you think of her as some plum to be plucked, my lord?" My voice is cold as the winter sea.

He turns to me, as if unable to believe a woman has just challenged him. But then he sees who is speaking, and if there is one thing a predator like the prince recognizes, it is another predator. His annoyance turns to circumspection, and he spreads his hands wide in a gesture of surrender. "I mean no disrespect to my cousin."

I hold his gaze a moment longer, wishing to draw out his discomfort. It is a petty victory, but it also soothes the hot, bitter place deep inside me. Before I can release his gaze, however, the loud scrape of the door latch draws our attention.

Beast is back is my first thought, and I am filled with dismay that he will have to explain his absence before all assembled. Especially if he has dragged Pierre back with him.

But it is not Beast. It is the duchess herself who stands in the doorway. Flustered, the council leaps to their feet. The duchess is young and short of stature, but her innate nobility and regal air make her seem both taller and older than she is. That and her barely contained anger. I feel Father Effram watching me, but pretend I have eyes only for the duchess and her surprising arrival.

Her frigid gaze surveys the room, looking at every man as she goes around the table. "Why has this meeting been called without my knowledge?"

Chancellor Montauban steps forward and holds a chair out for her. "Your Grace, we are but seeing to the planning of your upcoming trip to Langeais and didn't think you needed to be bothered with such details. Especially as you have so many other pressing matters you're involved in."

The duchess seats herself before turning to her brother. "Is this true?"

He gives an imperceptible shrug. "For the most part, Your Grace. We have also just received reports from our various allies, and until we knew whether they contained good news or bad, we saw no reason to burden you with them."

"Do our allies' reactions no longer affect me?"

Duval winces. "Of course they do." He takes a half step toward her, and much of his formality falls away. "Please, we thought only to leave you to the pleasantries of planning a wedding rather than scheming and tactics and politics. You have been so happy this last week. We thought only to allow you to enjoy it a bit longer."

The duchess's face softens. In an uncharacteristically public show of sisterly affection, she places her small hand on his cheek. "I know, Gavriel, and I am thankful for all you have done and continue to do to protect me. But there is a good chance I will not be privy to council meetings in France, and I would welcome any information and knowledge we possess before embarking on my journey. Now, please be seated, all of you."

As the others seat themselves, Duval steps into the uncomfortable silence caused by her arrival and turns back to the prince. "We understand Maximilian's disappointment with the turn of events," he says. "What will his countermove be, do you think?"

"None that I have heard; however, the news went out only a handful of days ago. I am sure he will weigh all his options."

"Given how reluctant he has been to fight France outright, we will have to hope that his views on that will continue." Before the prince can respond, Duval turns to Captain Dunois. "What have you heard from our other allies?"

The older man shrugs. "Spain is not happy, and is making noise about a possible abduction."

Duval's interest turns razor sharp. "They are planning an abduction? When do they think to move?"

"No, not planning one. They speculate that the duchess has been coerced. Britain is even less happy with us, demanding immediate payment for their loan of troops, as well as implying the king has exerted some undue influence over the duchess and she is being forced into this marriage against her will."

A sigh of annoyance escapes the duchess.

"Not so much against her will," Duval murmurs, "but because she was out of options. However, this appears to be a recurring theme among our allies. We will have to watch carefully and quash those rumors if necessary."

As they discuss the ways to counteract such rumors and ensure the duchess's safety on her upcoming journey to France, it is all I can do to keep myself firmly in my chair. Where is Beast? Why is he not back yet? And then I remember it has not even been an hour. And that Pierre likely had horses waiting outside the city. I fight back an urge to pound my fist on the table and warn them that our enemy has breached our walls.

Except he is not their enemy, but mine.

And there is no guarantee any of these men will protect my sisters from him.

The realization chases my anger from me faster than water douses flames.

What would it be like to have so many willing to fight for your safety? To simply assume your world would be safe and you were worthy of such efforts?

What would it take for these men to feel that way about my sisters?

I nearly laugh. They likely do not even remember that I have two sisters.

Something dark and ugly rises up in my throat. While I am perfectly able to take care of myself, my sisters are not. They have only myself and Beast to see to their well-being. How would these wise and noble men react to the news of Pierre's abduction attempt?

Duval would give us his full support. Dunois as well, perhaps. The chancellor would *want* to support my family, as long as it did not jeopardize his main responsibility, the duchess. Former marshal Rieux and the Prince of Orange? No. They are not the sorts to lift a finger to help someone else — especially if there is not something to be gained from it. They are like all the men throughout the years that could never be bothered to concern themselves as d'Albret went through wives faster than most men go through horses. They did not even question the rumors or gossip, merely dismissed them as such.

The chancellor might fuss and cluck, but would not endanger his other charges. Clearly there is only so much protection to go around. Especially when the law is on Pierre's side.

There will be no help from this quarter. The duchess has more courage and integrity than two-thirds of her council. She is the one who has offered my sisters protection, although I wonder how many in this room even know that?

Anger, hot and acrid, fills my belly. Surely my sisters are owed such protection.

But Pierre has shown just how ruthless he is. How much of that will spill onto the duchess? Is this roomful of protectors enough to deter my brother? By accepting her protection for my sisters, am I putting her in harm's way?

My path ahead seemed so clear — in exchange for my continued service, the duchess offered to foster my sisters. But that very oath of loyalty I swore to her now puts her at risk. How in the name of the Nine do I thread that needle?

The king, I remind myself. He is the missing piece in all of this. Pierre would not dare move against the king. In truth, the king's protection could likely be the only thing that will deter my brother. And it is the duchess who has access to that.

The war is over. France and Brittany are now allies. Even better, the regent is widely known to keep a veritable stable of young noblewomen, girls sent to her at a tender age so she could train and shape them into womanhood. Surely two more young girls can easily hide among their numbers.

Indeed, I *know* that two girls can.

Remembering the news I bring for the council eases some of the coiled tension from my body. That same news also reminds me that I do not embark on this adventure empty-handed. I have additional protection to offer the duchess. And my sisters.

I shift my attention back to the conversation. The duchess is speaking. "Is there any word on what Rohan wants?" the duchess asks.

"Not yet," Duval admits, "but he claims he is here on the king's business, and I cannot imagine it will be to our advantage."

Chancellor Montauban shakes his head. "Could the French simply have sent him to offer his support and congratulations?"

Duval, Dunois, and Châlons all exchange knowing glances, but say nothing.

The chancellor looks at them in exasperation. "You are a suspicious lot."

"We have been enemies for a long time now, and are more accustomed to

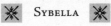

suspicion than trust," the duchess says. "Old history will not be forgotten so quickly."

I lean forward. "Speaking of matters of suspicion and trust, Your Grace, we may have some additional assistance in that area."

The chancellor frowns at me, clearly not wishing to encourage that line of thought. "The convent of Saint Mortain has hidden two of their initiates deep within the French court. Their orders were to burrow like little moles until they were under the nose of the regent and the king himself. They have been in position for years, waiting to be called into service. They could prove excellent guides as we try to navigate this complex, unfamiliar terrain of being allies with the French."

Duval visibly brightens. "This is most welcome news, Lady Sybella."

They will also be two more able-bodied and skilled assassins I may call upon to protect my sisters against any future moves Pierre might make.

CHAPTER 13

Genevieve

ne of Margot's waiting women opens the door, motions me inside, then quickly shuts it behind me so a draft does not follow me in.

My eyes take a moment to adjust to the darkness. The curtains block out any hint of daylight for fear it will harm the mother's or babe's eyes. Cloth has been draped from the ceiling in great poufs and swathes, softening the room and making it feel far smaller than it is. The only light comes from the roaring fire and two candles. As is intended, the room is as warm and close as a womb.

When I was five, my aunt Bertine found herself with child. She was already round and ripe of figure, so it was easy enough for her to hide it from her clients. But there were other men, more than a few, who enjoyed lying with a woman heavy with child, her lush fullness causing their own virility to stir. She worked up until the eighth month. Noblewomen, however, are confined to their rooms several weeks before the babe is due. It is nearly suffocating, and I do not know how Margot can stand it.

"Gen? Is that you?" Margot's voice comes from behind the bed's rich curtains.

"It is." As I approach, the waiting woman draws back.

"Leave us," Margot commands.

"But, my lady! You should not be alone —"

"I am not alone. Genevieve is here. Now go."

Tsking in disapproval, the woman leaves the room and closes the door quietly behind her.

"Well? Did you do it?" she asks.

"I said I would, and I did. Here." I reach out and give her a piece of the silver birch bark from the ground beneath the tree, knowing she will not rest until she has proof.

Once, my word would have been proof enough.

She grabs the bark, closes her eyes, then brings it to her lips. "Thank you." Like quicksilver, the expression on her face changes from relief to suspicion. "Why did you not come sooner? It is past noon."

Instead of shaking her for her ingratitude, I pull up the waiting woman's stool and sit down. "There has been news of the duchess."

Margot flops back onto her mound of pillows. "Oh."

I lean forward. "The duchess and the king of France are betrothed. There will not be a war, but a wedding, instead."

She blinks sleepily. "Well, that's good. I suspect everyone is tired of war."

"But, Margot, think of what this means for us. It is possible the duchess was forced into the marriage against her will. Even if she wasn't, the political action has moved from Brittany to France, where we are conveniently placed just as the convent planned. They will need us, Margot. I am certain the convent will be contacting us any day with instructions. Perhaps we will be needed to forestall the marriage. At the very least, we can tell the duchess all that we have learned of the regent's moves against her so that she will know just how little the woman is to be trusted."

Margot's head lolls to the side as she considers me. "*We*, Gen? What do you think I will do with this news? Leap up from my birthing bed, grab a horse, and ride with you to the French court, waving our daggers to fend off all who would naysay the queen?" She laughs, three high, brittle notes. "There is no *we* in this game of yours. There is only you."

"This is no game, Margot. The duchess will be at the French court in less than a fortnight."

Margot leans forward. "But that is no guarantee the convent will call you. You are like some poor dog that does not know when to quit begging for scraps."

"Very well." My voice is stiff, guarded. "What would you like me to tell them when they do contact us?"

"Tell them?"

"About you. What shall I tell them about *you*, Margot? How would you like the story to go? Shall I say that you seduced the count? Or that he seduced you? Shall I say you got caught in a web of your own design? Or were in turn caught in a snare fashioned by Angoulême?"

"Do not act as if you have not had lovers before!"

"Of course I've had lovers. We both have." In truth, she was my first lover and I hers, practicing our skills until we were ready to use them with those we knew less well. "But this is about turning your back on the convent and abandoning our sworn duty to them."

She looks as if I have slapped her. Before I have a chance to feel guilty for that, she leans forward, her face contorted with spite. "Don't you dare blame this on me. It was because of you that we were sent to molder in this rustic court."

"That wasn't my doing, but the regent's!"

"If you had not thrown yourself at the king and caught his fancy, we would still be there, ready to aid the duchess upon her arrival."

She is jealous, I realize. Jealous that I was the one who caught his eye, not her. "I did not throw myself at him," I say between gritted teeth.

"No. You're right. You did not have to throw yourself at the king. It was no doubt all those tricks you learned at your mother's knee."

Her words chase the air from my lungs. That she would throw the origins of my birth at me goes against all the convent's precepts. Her face changes again, shifting to sly and knowing. "You worry the convent will be upset to learn of my fate? What makes you think they aren't the ones who ordered me to do this?"

Her words are a swift, brutal kick to my gut and cause my entire body to flush with heat, then cold. I grip my knees with my hands. "*Did* they?"

The smug satisfaction on her face nearly causes me to retch. "Yes, they did."

The enormity of the betrayal sends me reeling. That the convent had chosen her for such an assignment and not me is bad enough. But that she never mentioned they had contacted her is even more painful. "When did they tell you?"

She shrugs. "A few weeks before the count gave me the garnet necklace. That was no simple act of chance, Gen." She says this as if I am some slow-witted child.

"How? How did they contact you?"

She looks down to arrange a strand of her hair. "In a letter. It was sent to the count, and he gave it to me."

"Where is this letter?"

She snorts. "You think I kept it? I could not risk Louise finding it, so I burned it."

"Were you ever going to tell me you'd heard from them? Or just keep it to yourself?" What I truly want to ask is *Was there any word of me? Any action they wanted me to take? Any task they'd assigned to me?* But I will bite my tongue clean off before letting her see how badly I hunger for that information.

"You didn't need to know." She avoids my eyes and adjusts the neckline of her bed gown.

I cannot help it — I reach out and grab her arm, forcing her to look at me. "That was never how things were between us. Why did you keep it from me?"

She pulls out of my grasp. "Because you turned into a sour old woman who refused to take any pleasure in what is all around us, and I was sick of it. Sick of your fake piety and your lofty airs. You act as if your eagerness to do the convent's work makes you better than I am, but we both know just how false that is."

"I do not give myself airs. I have been trying to stay strong. For you, for me, for the convent. For Mortain. I have been trying to do what was asked of us."

"Doing the convent's bidding was always more important to you than it was to me, Gen. You always cared more, while I hardly cared at all."

Another brutal blow. "Why? Why would you not care?"

Her face twists with some ugly emotion I cannot name. "I think the more important question to ask yourself is why do you care so very much?"

Before I can answer, she leans back against her pillows, folds her hands, and rests them on her stomach. "It is because you had no place else to go, Gen. No other life to lead. But I did. I had many choices before me, while you had none."

I can hardly catch my breath as she rips all remaining vestiges of our old friendship to shreds.

"Now I think you should leave. All this talk cannot be healthy for the baby."

Slowly, stiffly, I rise to my feet. I want — desperately — to give her a chance to take it back, to say she is sorry. Anything but to leave it like this. But she says nothing.

"You are wrong," I finally say, my face hot, eyes burning. "I had as many choices as you did. It is just that I have never seen shame in whoring nor understood the need to lie to oneself by dressing it up with silk and jewels."

And with that, I take my leave.

CHAPTER 14

anton, whore, tart, strumpet, harlot, *abricot*, camp follower, *poule de luxe*. Of all the names people gave my
mother and aunts, whore was they one they chose to
call themselves. It was honest, Yolanthe explained. Far
better than being called a luxury hen.

All of them had choices. Not many — no woman does. Laundress,
tanner's wife, brewess, spinner, weaver, gong farmer. Was it truly better
to shovel other people's shit or spend your days up to your elbows in
others' piss than to be paid for a tumble?

It was the Church, Yolanthe insisted, that perverted their trade to
serve their own derision of women. It was the Church, she claimed,
who erased Saint Amourna's true past.

When I arrived at the convent, the nuns did not shame me for my
mother's profession. To them, all of us who arrived on their doorstep
had our own unique set of tools that could be used in serving Mortain.
Besides, if Mortain had seen fit to lie with our mothers, who were they
to shame us — or Him — for His choice?

Margot is wrong, I think as my feet carry me down the hallway. *I
have just as many choices in my life as she did.* I could marry. A tanner,
a guildsman, a blacksmith, any number of men in the trades would
be glad of me as a wife. In truth noblewomen, for all their privilege,
have fewer options than I do — they may marry or go into a convent.
But their alternatives provide them with food and shelter and clothing,
while not all mine guarantee me even that.

Indeed, that is why so many of us found our way to the convent
— it gave us some measure of freedom. While we swore an oath to
serve Mortain, within that oath was a variety of ways in which to
serve.

That is why I still keep my contract with the convent. Once I walk away from that, my opportunities are greatly reduced.

Although, I must admit, the choices and autonomy promised by the convent have not materialized like I'd hoped.

Margot is right about one thing. I *have* always cared more than she did. But not for the reason she thinks. It was never because I had no place else to go or no other options. It was because I wanted to prove to the world that I *did* have a choice. That was what allowed — allows me still — to keep believing they will call me into service. If not, I will have wasted ten years and been sent away from those I loved for nothing.

I am not willing to accept that.

When I reach my room, I let myself in and bolt the door behind me. It is a small chamber, given to Margot and me. It is too hot in summer and too cold in winter, but it was ours and ours alone. It was here that Margot and I would test each other on our convent lessons. Where we would practice the moves Sister Thomine had drilled into us, praying no one would hear the thumping that ensued as one of us inevitably hit the floor.

It was here that I waited in vain as Margot joined me less and less until she finally stopped coming at all.

I stride over to the two trunks shoved up against the far wall. I have never looked through Margot's trunk. Not once. Not in Amboise when she first began to avoid my company, nor in Cognac when she finally cut me out of her life.

But today I must know if the convent ordered her to have an affair with Count Angoulême. Margot saves every small scrap of her life. If she received a letter from the convent, she would not have burned it. It would be in this trunk.

But it is locked. I reach for the small sewing kit in my pocket and unfold the leather flaps to pull out a large sturdy needle. Beneath my careful coaxing, the lock quickly gives way.

The trunk is nearly bursting with scraps of fabric, coils of ribbon, velvet pouches, and old gloves. There are dried flowers, small silver charms, a gold bracelet, and a jeweled stiletto I stole for her off a young, arrogant Italian ambassador. I paw through it all, looking for letters or parchment. My knuckles graze something hard — a rough wooden practice dagger. The sight of it nearly guts me. I made it for her when we first arrived at court and we were desperate for something with which to practice our skills. Was that a lie too?

I push the dagger aside and resume rifling. I find one of the silver powder boxes given to each of us by the convent. Instead of powder, it contains night whispers, a poison that kills when inhaled into the lungs. My hand closes around it, and I set it aside. I can still use it, even if Margot no longer has reason to.

Next to the box is a hairnet of gold thread and white pearls. Only they are not pearls at all, but cunningly designed wax beads that hold poison. The wax has shriveled somewhat, but the poison might still be usable.

It is not until I reach the bottom of the trunk that my hand meets parchment and my heart skips a beat. But there is no black wax seal, and when I glance at the words, I see it is a love note from her first lover in Amboise. There are two more letters from admirers but no other correspondence.

I slam the lid of the trunk shut. Would she truly have burned instructions from the convent? She who kept every note and small gift sent by her admirers? Any one of those would have gotten her in serious trouble with the regent. Far more so than correspondence from the convent would have endangered her with the count.

Unless it was instructing her to seduce him for the convent's own ends. He might not take kindly to such orders.

I shove to my feet, stride over to the hearth, and grab the poker. Even though she hasn't been up here in months, I sift through the ashes, hoping some scrap of the burned letter might still be there. After I have stirred every trace of ash at least twice, I toss the poker aside.

There is nothing. Nothing to indicate whether Margot lied or was telling the truth.

Nothing to subdue the trembling in my hands her spitefulness has caused.

Nothing to punch or kick or fight with. Nothing to pummel or beat or drive away.

I take two steps toward the door. I want to march back to Margot's room and demand she tell me the truth. But that has never worked with her. The more

I wanted something — her cooperation, her approval, her affection — the more she withheld it.

But she will never have that kind of power over me again.

Anger and frustration crackle through my limbs, and the walls themselves feel as if they are closing in, crowding me until I can scarcely breathe.

I retrieve my wooden practice dagger from my own trunk, then shove it into my belt. I cannot stay here a moment longer.

⁓

The deepest floor of the castle is as dark and empty as always. I grab the lone lit torch and make my way to the chamber I have used since we first arrived at Cognac. Margot came with me exactly twice, quickly giving up our practice sparring sessions for the other entertainment Cognac had to offer.

But for me, these sessions have been as necessary as air — connecting me to the convent and who I truly am, what I am meant to be. They were my best — and only — defense against despair.

With the chamber lit only by my single torch, I take up the position Sister Thomine drilled into us. Within moments I am moving in old familiar rhythms: lift, strike, kick, again. It is as calming as the lullaby my mother sang over my cradle.

I continue until my muscles burn with fatigue and my skin no longer itches. I continue until sweat trickles down my neck and along my ribs and the question about Margot's letter no longer burns like a branding iron.

Only then do I allow myself to lean against the wall to catch my breath. I dread returning to the castle. Perhaps I will sleep here tonight and skip dinner altogether. My stomach protests by gurgling loudly. Grimacing, I rub my hand across my hollow belly. I am too hungry to miss supper.

That's when I remember the prisoner.

The half-starved, forgotten prisoner rotting in his cell is the best company this wretched place has to offer. I will dine with him tonight.

CHAPTER 15

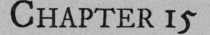

 y lady?" Captain Dunois's voice greets me in the hallway as I emerge from the council room. He has been
waiting for me.

"Yes, my lord?"

"I wanted to convey my appreciation for your handling of the
Crunard situation. Your timely actions kept the matter firmly contained. Thank you."

His praise is a welcome balm to my tattered spirit. "Thank you,
my lord. I am always pleased to use my skills to help the duchess."

"As you have demonstrated time and again."

The ugly memory of Pierre in the garden shoves his compliment
aside. I wonder what Dunois would say about my handling of that
situation — or asking Beast to go after him.

Or my decision to say nothing about it at the council meeting.

"Do you by any chance know where Beast was this afternoon?"

It is the question I've been dreading. Do I tell him the truth?
The part of me that has steeped for years in the shame and despair
of the d'Albret family is reluctant to share my past with him. Let
alone tell him of Pierre's visit and threats. I feel as if I am somehow
responsible for it all. And am I not? Was it not my own actions that
brought him here?

It seems better — easier — to wait until Beast returns and we can lay the entire episode at Dunois's feet, tied up as neatly as a bale of wool.

Although how the matter will be neatly resolved escapes me. What will Beast do if he is able to find Pierre? Kill him? Assuredly that would be the easiest and most satisfying solution. But it would not resolve the custody of me or my sisters — the next male d'Albret in line for the title would inherit that duty along with the family estates.

"My lady?"

"The last time I saw him, he was riding out the main gate into the city. He was ... in quite a hurry. I assumed he was on some business for you or Duval."

"No, but he has plenty of his own duties that could draw him off in such a fashion." Captain Dunois pulls on his chin for a moment, considering.

This lie sits queasily in my stomach. "Was that all, my lord?"

"No." He glances at the hallway around us, which is deserted now. "I wished to speak with you about some concerns regarding our upcoming trip to the French court." He picks his words carefully. "The French court is not accustomed to women of your skills. Since France no longer worships the Nine, they have no convent or saint that encourages such behavior. They will likely not know what to make of it and could easily consider it a stain on your character."

A chill settles along my skin, and it is all I can do not to rub my arms. "So I must keep my sisters and the queen safe without letting anyone see how I do it, lest my protecting of them suggest that I am unworthy of the queen's regard?"

"My lady, you know how much I admire you and your skills, but the French king will not appreciate the nuances of how Brittany chooses to worship the Nine. He will see it as irregular at best, and as heresy at worst. It is one of the reasons Duval was so insistent on the duchess maintaining rule over the duchy — so the king would continue unaware of the nature of Bretons' faith. And of all the Nine, it is Mortain that most threatens the Church, for he competes with God Himself in matters of life and death."

"Once, perhaps, but no more," I remind him.

He throws his hands out to his sides. "But how to explain that to them when I cannot even do so to myself?"

I have no answer, since I am no more able to than he. How does one describe what happened on the battlefield that day? How does one explain the transformation of Death?

"Whatever the case, I think it important you not reveal that you worship Mortain or serve him."

That he is right does not make his words any more welcome. While I knew my faith would be uncommon in France, I did not know it would make me anathema to the king. "Very well, my lord. While this will be inconvenient, I thank you for the warning." It is hard not to feel as if all my paths to safety are narrowing.

But the duchess has promised her protection. And the king dotes on her and will grant her every wish. He has already demonstrated that. All I must do is remain unobtrusive and discreet.

As if sensing my despondency, Captain Dunois continues. "Beast, too, will have to tread carefully. His exploits and battle lust are well known to both the French army and the court. Many there will have faced him on the battlefield. They will not bear him any love. Indeed, they may protest his presence in their midst."

"This will not come as a surprise to him."

The older man reaches up to scratch the back of his neck. "There is more you should know about the French court." He squints down at the toe of his boot. "While it is as decadent and indulgent as any court in Europe, unwed maids are held to a much higher standard."

"It is the same here," I point out.

He nods, still fascinated by his boot. "True. But the duchess has a romantic heart and is generous with those who have served her well. While she may be happy to turn a blind eye to your, ah, alliance, the regent will not. She keeps a firm hand on that sort of thing. It is just one of the reasons so many noble families send their daughters to be her wards — they can be certain of the stringent moral standards she will hold them to." It is hard to tell who is more uncomfortable with this conversation, the captain or myself. "She has even gone so far as to interfere with the king's paramours, although one imagines somewhat less so now that he has reached his majority.

"She will no doubt hold the new queen and her attendants to those same high standards. You will need to use the utmost discretion in your dealings with Beast, lest the connection draw your reputation into question."

"Thank you for the warning, Captain Dunois, although I expected as much. Well, perhaps not the revelation about the king." I smile wryly so he will not see my embarrassment.

As I watch Captain Dunois disappear down the hall, I feel like a brittle autumn leaf that has been caught up in a windstorm. I have been praised, warned, and admired, all within a quarter of an hour. All by the same man.

I wonder which of those he will feel when he learns what transpired this afternoon.

CHAPTER 16

y noxious brew of emotions propels me down the hall, the lies I have just told sitting like a lump of lead in my gut. I cannot even enjoy Captain Dunois's hard-won respect without the actions I was forced to take against Pierre tainting it. I should have killed the bastard when I had the chance.

But that is far easier to say without Charlotte and Louise standing here with their wide, frightened eyes. Nor do I think that would have warranted Captain Dunois's respect any more than what I did. But by not killing Pierre, I feel as if I have allowed a poisonous serpent to roam free, endangering not only my sisters, but Beast.

Would killing Pierre have been the right thing to do if not for my sisters' presence? How thin is the line between self-defense and willful murder? I fear it will be too thin for me to recognize as I cross it.

I cannot even turn to my sisters for comfort right now, afraid they will see my anger and be frightened by it.

It frightens me.

Anger, along with violence, is the favored currency of my family. The family I want no part of, and yet is always there — in my memories, in the world, in my actions.

When I step outside the palace, the gathering storm clouds have grown so dark that the late afternoon sky looks as if night has already fallen. The wind that howls through the courtyard mirrors the storm in my own heart.

I draw my cloak more tightly around me. *Go ahead and try*, I mutter. I would welcome the chance to fight something — even the wind.

Because I still can, I slip one of my knives into my hand, conceal-

ing it among the folds of my cloak — but only barely. I am not required to hide
who I am just yet.

The courtyard is still full of Rohan's men, but the chaos is giving way to
order as the castle's steward and stable master see that all the men and horses
are cared for.

I plunge through the crowd, not caring whose arm I jostle or elbow I bump.
A heavily bearded soldier looks up with a growl of warning. I meet his gaze,
praying he will start something. Instead, he mutters an apology and steps aside.
Coward, I want to shout at him, but he has given way and that will have to be
victory enough.

Deciding to put my anger and restlessness to good use, I head for the perimeter wall that separates the palace from the rest of the city. I want to know how
Pierre got in.

Rohan's troops had only just arrived as I chased him out of the garden. If
Pierre had come through the gates prior to the troops, the sentries would have
questioned him. He would not have risked that.

Unless he was there with Rohan's knowledge. I turn sharply and begin walking the perimeter. No, that cannot be. The houses of Rohan and d'Albret have
never been close allies. Indeed, they have often competed for the same crumb of
power or land. They would not collaborate on this.

Which means Pierre likely breached the palace wall. A ladder, grappling
hooks, a rope. Any of those could create a way in. In addition to the main gate
tower, there are two smaller gates. They are also guarded, but by fewer men. If
Pierre gained entrance there, one of the sentries will know.

As I scan the thick stone walls of the palace's outer bailey for any signs of
forced entry, yapping hounds of guilt nip at my heels. Could I have prevented this?

It is not possible to keep my sisters locked inside the palace every moment
of every day, nor personally guard them every second. If so, how would I serve
the duchess?

When I reach the southern gate, a frisson of unease slithers through me. The guard who should be on duty is not at his post. I tighten the grip on my knife and pull a second one from its sheath. At the door, I pause. There is nothing. No sound. No beating hearts. Frowning, I slip around the corner, then cautiously peer inside.

A man is sprawled on the floor.

Swearing under my breath, I hurry to his side. The sentry lies face-down in a pool of dark blood, a knife protruding from his back. It is a common weapon, the kind many soldiers favor. Because it is so unexceptional, it is precisely the sort I would choose for such a task.

I slip my own blade back in its sheath, then gently pull the dagger from the dead man. "I am sorry," I whisper as I reach out to turn him over.

The moment my fingers touch his shoulder, his soul unfurls from his body and rushes at me. Even as I reel in shock, I recognize it at once. It is the vibrant one I encountered just a few short hours ago while up on the battlements, where I was cradled in Beast's arms. Laughing and complaining of my small problems. Ignoring this very soul and accusing him of acting like an indulged cat.

My stomach curdles at my own stupidity. *This* is how I could have prevented Pierre's attack. By listening to this soul's warning.

Sickened and ashamed, I open myself to the dead guard.

A sense of outrage crashes into me like a wave, nearly causing me to sway. Outrage at treachery inside the walls of the palace. Outrage that some coward would strike him in the back. Outrage that he had become the weak link in the duchess's defenses.

As the first wave of emotion recedes, bewilderment takes its place, resulting in a dizzying swirl of images: Pierre's face, the tabard of red and yellow, the bitter taste of betrayal, a lingering sense of loss. The man is young, not yet married, and just setting out to make a name for himself.

When he has finally quieted, he pauses, radiating a faint sense of indignation as he studies me.

"I'm sorry I failed you," I whisper. "I should have heeded your warning.

Please forgive me." The soul withdraws in on itself, feeling as if it is not in any position to grant or receive forgiveness.

But the soul is wrong. It was my error, not his, that allowed Pierre to get as far as he did. My arrogance and complacency did this. While I did not kill the guard, everything that came afterward is my fault.

I close my eyes and let the caustic shame and bitterness burn through me, turning that arrogance and complacency to ash. When I have grown accustomed to the pain of it, I open my eyes and stare down at the fallen guard.

How can I grant this loyal man the peace he deserves? I do not have a misericorde, the most rare of Mortain's weapons that will instantly send a soul on its journey, relieving it of the need to linger for three days. Only Ismae has that.

But . . . the misericorde is made of Mortain's own bones, or so they said. I am no longer certain if I believe that to be true, if I ever did, but within that legend is the seed of an idea.

I take the point of my knife and prick the thick pad of my littlest finger. Dark red blood oozes up. I stare at it for a moment. Blood and bone, the very stuff we humans are made of. The very stuff the gods themselves were once made of. Held sacred by all the Nine, and the new Church as well. Flesh of my flesh, bone of my bone.

"You have served your duchess and country well," I whisper. "May the Nine grant you peace." I reach out and smear the drop of blood onto the man's forehead, the precise spot where the marque of Mortain most often appeared when he still guided my hand.

The results are as shocking as they are sudden. The soul grows buoyant, lighter, as if unraveling from the tether of earthly guilt and fear. After a brief flash of delighted awe, it circles me once, twice, and a third time, then rushes upward and dissolves, becoming a part of the very air itself.

I gape openmouthed as I look back down at the body, then at the space above it. The soul is truly gone. Was that gift always available to me? Or is it something new caused by the shift in the Nine?

I look down at my own finger, a small drop of blood brilliant against my white skin. A sense of lightness fills me. Like that soul, I almost feel as if I could rise up into the air.

Even with the passing of Mortain, I might still contain mysteries I have not yet discovered.

CHAPTER 17

y the time I get back to the palace, dusk has fallen. Torches are lit along the wall, their flames stretched thin, sparks fluttering in the strong wind.

The courtyard holds easily twice as many of Rohan's men as when I left earlier. Disappointed that Beast is not there waiting for me, I snag a page hurrying from one of the outbuildings and tell him to fetch Beast from the garrison. The boy tries not to let his annoyance show — I have probably just delayed his dinner — but bows smartly and does as instructed.

Surely Beast is back by now, and I am anxious to hear what happened. I must also let him know what has transpired here this afternoon. We will need to assign double watches on the lesser used gates as well as arrange for a proper burial for the fallen sentry. This has been an important reminder that not all our enemies became allies when we signed the betrothal agreement with France.

While I linger in the shadows waiting for Beast, I listen for any whispers of why Rohan and his men are in Rennes. There is talk of horses, complaints about the crowded quarters, and assurances that Rohan will put all this to rights soon enough. My ears perk up at that, and I take a step closer, only to have the page call out to me.

My pleasure at how quickly he has returned turns to dismay when I see he has brought not Beast, but Captain Lannion. "My lady." Captain Lannion bows. "How can I be of help?"

"Beast is not back yet?" He has been gone more than four hours. It should not be taking this long.

"No, my lady. Is there something I can do for you?" His voice holds a faint note of concern.

Captain Lannion and I have traveled together, camped and fought together, but I am not ready to share my concerns with him. "Thank you, but no." After one last polite bow, he returns to the garrison.

My mind is as unsettled as a harried fox. Pierre did not have that great a head start. And two of his men were mortally injured. Beast should have been back by the time the council meeting was over, though clearly there were scores more of Rohan's men just outside the gates that he had to search among and wade through.

Or Pierre himself could have had more men waiting outside. Of course he did — he never travels with less than half a dozen retainers, and often ten times that. True fear runs along my skin, drawing it taut. *Have I sent Beast straight into a trap?*

No. I clench my hands into fists, then open them again. No.

Pierre would not travel with that many men, not on this sort of mission. And Beast is not called Beast for nothing. When he was but fifteen years old, he rode into a d'Albret stronghold to ascertain the safety of his sister, Louise's mother. He did not see her, but was met by twelve of d'Albret's men-at-arms. He walked away — leaving eight dead and four to limp back to explain their defeat to their enraged liege. The battle lust Saint Camulos gifted him with served him well that day, and it will serve him again. Pierre's men are no match for it.

Besides, I remember how insulted I was by Ismae and Duval's fussing and clucking over me. I'll not insult Beast by doing the same to him.

But Sweet Jesu, this loving someone is hard. Might as well rip a piece of one's heart from one's chest and feed it to wild pigs.

～⁊⁊～

By the time I reach Captain Dunois's office, my shoulders are so stiff that my entire back aches. It is bad enough that Beast is not back yet, but now I must admit that I lied to Captain Dunois. And tell him of Pierre's visit, flaunting my family's sordid history.

I remind myself that Captain Dunois already knows my family's history. He knows of the treacheries and deceits they have perpetuated in the past. He did not hold me responsible then, and he will not hold me responsible now.

But who is to say he should not?

Pierre's visit today was an ugly personal matter. One that should never have come so close to the duchess or cost her any of her men. It should not truly have even concerned Beast, except that he stuck his big lumpen nose into my affairs months ago and has refused to budge from my side.

As I raise my hand to knock on the captain's door, the knowledge that I am the one responsible for bringing this mess to the duchess's door writhes in my gut like small white grubs in newly turned earth. I try to use my anger at Pierre to erect a shield between me and these unwelcome truths, but the anger is no match for the carefully honed edge of my self-loathing.

"Come in," the captain calls out.

When I enter, he looks up from the letter he is penning, his face creasing in concern. "My lady, are you all right?"

"Yes, my lord."

His frown deepens. "Do you have news of Beast?"

"Yes. And no."

"Go on." Although he hides it well, there is a faint note of unease in his voice.

For a moment, the enormity of what I must tell him overwhelms me.

The truth. As simply as possible. With no nooks or crannies for me to hide in. "The story has two parts."

Dunois sets his quill on the desk and gives me his full attention. Because I wish to rush and get it over with, I force myself to utter the words calmly. "There has been an incident."

Captain Dunois waits as patiently as a mountain, and I think of all the soldiers who must have confessed to him over the years. My hands clench the back of the chair in front of me. "My brother Pierre paid a visit today. He came upon me and my sisters in the garden."

Dunois rises so quickly that the force of it shoves his chair back. "Your brother was here? How in God's name did he get past the guards?"

"He and two of his men dressed in Viscount Rohan's colors."

"And so had free access to the palace grounds." His eyes narrow. "But you are all unharmed?"

"Yes."

He studies me carefully. "Are you certain?"

"I am fine."

"Perhaps," he concedes. "But you are also shaking."

I let go of the chair and wrap my arms around my middle. "It was cold outside, and my search for Pierre's means of entry took a while. That is the second part of the story. One of the guards had been murdered."

Dunois runs his hands over his close cropped hair. "Where?"

"At the south gate. We should send someone for his body as well as arrange a double watch on both the south and east towers."

Captain Dunois reaches for his sword. "Agreed. We should also double the guard on you and your sisters."

Of all the responses I was anticipating, concern for my family's safety was not one of them. "That brings us to the third part of the story."

Something in my voice causes him to pause. "Beast?" he asks quietly.

"Beast. He was in the courtyard as I was pursuing my brother and his men. I . . . I asked him to follow them so I could return to my sisters. I was uncomfortable leaving them alone any longer than I had to."

"In case your brother had additional men still on the premises."

"Yes. Exactly so."

He busies himself strapping his sword belt around his hips. "Which is why I think we should place an extra guard on your family."

"Ismae, Lazare, and Yannic are with them now."

Dunois nods. "They're good, but Lazare needs to keep training every moment he can in order to be equal to the others of the queen's guard. But that is a most excellent use of Yannic." He pauses, "I wonder who else . . ."

I try to direct him back to the matter at hand. "But Beast has still not returned."

"I am not overly concerned about Beast, my lady. Not yet anyway. I am more interested in ensuring this does not happen again."

"I appreciate your concern for my family, but my sisters are . . . They do not trust strange men easily. I fear your effort to help them will only cause greater distress."

His gruff face softens, and in that moment, I see his full awareness of all that I have suffered, of all that I want to protect my sisters from. "What if they were not men?"

My heart shifts, expanding as Dunois's astute kindness works its way in. "Who are these non-men you have in mind?"

"The followers of Arduinna. They have little enough to do while waiting to leave for France. But more important, it is the very nature of their service to their goddess — to protect the innocent."

I cannot believe I did not think of this sooner. Although to be fair, he is not aware of the longstanding animosity between the followers of Saint Arduinna and Saint Mortain.

For the first time in more hours than I can count, the knot inside me loosens. "That is an excellent idea, my lord. I will speak with them in the morning."

He reaches for his gloves. "Now I'd best see to doubling the watch and sending someone for that poor soldier."

"Thank you. Should I tell the duchess what has transpired, or would you prefer to do so?" It is not a conversation I relish, but neither will I shirk it.

He comes around his desk and busies himself pulling his gloves onto his blunt fingers. "That is not necessary."

"Surely she should know."

"She does know. She knew full well when she offered your sisters protection what Pierre was capable of. That's why she offered them safekeeping. Besides, I am going to double the guard around the palace, and you are going to double the guard around your sisters. We have taken care of the problem. I do not inform her of every tactical decision I make, and this is no different."

He folds his arms and leans against the edge of the desk, considering me as he weighs some inner struggle. "You are not the only one to have an ugly family history, you know," he says at last.

I am so astounded by his words that I can only blink in response.

He picks up a heavy silver inkpot and begins studying it. "Beast's family, too, has its skeletons." While Beast himself has told me of them, I am stunned that Captain Dunois would speak of it. "I do not know how much he has told you —"

"All of it, my lord."

He nods. "I had hoped so. But there is one thing that Beast does not know yet. I wish to tell you as well, for he will not be happy when he learns of it. Like you" — he glances up from the inkwell long enough to send me a piercing look — "he may try to blame himself or use it to pull away from those he cares about."

Merde. The clarity with which Captain Dunois sees me is most unsettling.

"It is about Beast's father."

"His father?" The word invokes a lifetime of Beast's pain and fury and anger. A lifetime of his mother's hatred for being born to her through the rape of a French soldier. "He claimed to have no father."

"Lord Waroch is dead," Captain Dunois says quietly. "But the man who sired Beast is not."

I reach out to steady myself once more against the chair. "Are you certain?" I think of Beast, and the years of ill treatment by his mother, a young boy's understanding of the unfathomable sins of his father.

Captain Dunois stares at the inkwell morosely. "I knew — *know* — him, I'm afraid. When he returned from the war, he was not shy about boasting of his exploits, nor of how he treated the lady of the keep he had commandeered — Beast's mother."

"My lord, why are you telling me this?"

"I tell you because his father is high up in King Charles's army and known to frequent the French court. There is a chance Beast will run into him during your time in France. I did not wish him to do so unprepared."

"Would it not be better for Beast to remain unaware of this?"

Dunois grimaces and sets the inkwell down. "There is a strong family resemblance. I fear that if they meet, it will be obvious to both of them. I don't want Beast taken by surprise."

"But why tell me?"

"Because it is the part of himself that Beast hates the most, my lady. The part that kept him from even allowing a woman into his life. If he erects a wall between you when he learns of this, I want you to breach it."

Our eyes meet in a moment of perfect understanding. "I will not let him cast me away so easily."

He gives a ghost of a smile, then stands and heads for the door. When he reaches it, he pauses. "The gods set all this in motion years ago, my lady. None of this is your fault," he says softly. "Not Pierre, not the guard. You must also know this: There is no place Beast would rather be than pursuing those that mean you harm. Relieve yourself of that burden, at least."

Then he is gone, and I am left struggling to accept both his unexpected trust and the absolution he has so generously given.

When I return to my chambers, I thank Ismae, Lazare, and Yannic, then dismiss them until morning.

Ismae lingers. "Any word on Beast?"

"No, though Captain Dunois does not think it is time to worry yet."

"He is likely right." She bids me good night and follows Lazare out of the room. Yannic pauses in the doorway, his gnarled hand outstretched to give me something.

It is small and round. A black pebble, I think. "Is this one of your lucky ones?" He has them blessed by saints or priests or whomever he can find before using them in his deadly slingshot. "Thank you. It is lovely. Who was this one blessed by?"

He makes a cutting motion at his throat, lolling his head to the side, eyes closed.

"Mortain?"

He shakes his head.

Frowning, I try again. "Balthazaar? Before he left?"

Yannic waggles his hand back and forth. Not wanting to press him further, I close my palm around the pebble. "Thank you."

When he is gone, I close the chamber door and cross over to my small trunklet. I lift the lid and place the stone in the box, then retrieve the sprig of holly from my belt and lay it next to the pebble before closing it again.

When I turn toward the far corner of the room, I see Tephanie sitting beside the bed, her face pale, her hands tightly clasped together.

Even though the bed curtains are tightly drawn, I keep my voice low. "Tephanie."

Her head snaps up, her face brightening. "My lady!"

I motion her away from the bed to the fireplace. "Thank you again, for seeing to my sisters."

"Of course, my lady. I am honored to be of service."

"That may well be, but this sort of service is far more than you bargained for." She starts to protest, but I hold up my hand. "Tephanie." My voice is as gentle as I know how to make it. "You are pale, and your hands still shake. You were not meant to be a guardsman, but a beloved and devoted companion. While I would be sad to see you go, I cannot help but feel you would be happier in some other role. One that does not put you in harm's way."

Her hand flies to her cheek. "Oh no! I wish to serve you and the girls. Please don't send me away."

I reach out and tuck a strand of her mousy brown hair behind her ear. "Dearest goose, it would not be dismissing you, but seeing that you are safe." For the briefest of moments, she allows her cheek to rest against the tips of my fingers, then quickly pulls away. "You understand, I cannot guarantee that something like this will not happen again?" I say softly.

She plucks nervously at her skirt. "I know, my lady. But few who are suited to the task of caring for young girls would be prepared for such things. I know your family and what to expect. I will be more alert from now on. I grew careless."

"This is in no way a reproach of you or how you reacted! None of us expected Pierre to be so bold. You were courageous and kept your head, and for that you have my eternal gratitude." Tephanie is one of the few who have found a place in my heart, and I would not hurt her for any reason. And as I gaze into her large brown eyes, eyes that are practically pleading with me, I realize that sending her away would hurt her. "If you truly wish to stay, I would be honored to have you."

As moved as I am by Tephanie's devotion, she is also one more person I will have to protect. All while hiding every weapon, skill, and talent I possess. It is beyond galling and I want to rail at the stupidity of a world that requires such rules. But I cannot do that without fear of drawing the judgment I wish to avoid. *Merde.*

But Tephanie will be under no such scrutiny. "Tephanie, do you still have that knife I gave you in Nantes?"

She looks at me blankly for a moment before her face clears. "Yes, my lady!"

I shove aside the rug in front of the fire. "Fetch it, then. Tonight we will begin your first lesson."

CHAPTER 18

Genevieve

 return to the dungeons bearing a large sack of food. When asked, I told the kitchen servants I was taking it to Margot. They were surprised, as they had sent up a separate tray less than an hour before. I smiled and told them that with the babe, Margot had the appetite of three men.

Reassured by this good sign, they piled my tray high with all manner of food — plenty for both me and the prisoner.

I quickly transfer it to a sack, fill the empty wineskin with water, and return to the dungeon. As I draw near the oubliette, I can hear the prisoner moving. I slow my steps so I may listen better. He is breathing heavily, panting almost. A faint whooshing sound comes in a steady rhythm, pauses, then starts up again. I am so busy concentrating that I do not mind my feet and stumble on an uneven cobble and nearly land on my face.

"Ah, my ghost has returned."

"Just how many ghosts do you have visiting you?"

"Too many." His voice is bleak. "But you are my favorite."

"You only say that because I come bearing food."

My words are met by silence. "You do?" He is not quite able to hide the faint tremble of hope in his voice.

"I do." When I reach the thick iron grate, I set the torch nearer to it than I have in the past, as I will need some light in order to get all this food down to him.

Mostly to give him something to do besides salivate while he waits for me to open the grate, I ask, "What were you doing just now?"

"What do you mean?"

"When I got here, you were doing something. Moving. Panting."

There is a long moment of silence interrupted only by the screech of the bolt as I slide it free. "Exercising." The word is filled with both faint defiance and sheepishness. "I cannot have my body become as enfeebled as my mind."

I almost laugh at how closely his actions match my own of just a few moments ago. I wrest the hatch open, lie flat on my belly, and lower the sack down as far as I can. "Here."

There is a faint *whoomp* as he catches it, then rustling as he unties the knot and retrieves his dinner: bread, cheese, two meat pies, a small game hen wrapped in laurel leaves, an apple and cheese tart. "This is a feast." His voice holds a note of wonder.

I smile in pleasure. "It should satisfy you for at least an hour or two."

As he begins to eat, I scoot closer to the grate. "How long have you been here?"

"Not sure," he says around a mouthful of food. "I can remember the hot sun on my back and the smell of ripening wheat. But whether that was a year ago or two, I cannot say. And you?" His question startles me. "How long have you been here?"

I open my mouth, a lie at the ready, then stop. I am so tired of lying. Every breath I take, every word that crosses my lips has been a lie, and I am sick of it. Besides, he is alone in a dungeon, by all signs completely forgotten by everyone. Surely anything I tell him is no different than telling a dead man. "Just over a year."

"And in all that time you have never wandered down here before. What brought you that first day?"

His deep rumble of a voice is gentle. It is a safe voice, a voice that is naught but darkness and breath. No face. No body. No past. No future in which to tell any of the secrets I might share. Only this moment when I do not have to wear a mask or dance to a tune I loathe. "Curiosity." I do not tell him of the beating heart, or the promise of death that held for me, or the sense of dread that day.

"It is curiosity that brings you today?"

"No. Today it is anger," I say without thinking. But it is not the whole of it. It is yet another lie.

In the darkness, all the words I have been unable to speak for months, nay, for years, press down upon me, heavier than the stone walls that surround us. "No, what truly brings me is pain."

There is a faint whisper of movement. I cannot be certain through the murk, but I think he tilts his head, studying me. His regard is as tangible as a touch. "What hurts?"

"My heart." I do not think I say it out loud, but somehow in the absolute quiet of the dungeons, he hears it.

"Ah." His voice is full of sympathy. "Heart wounds are the hardest to heal."

"Do they *ever* heal?" The question sounds small, like one a child might ask, and yet it feels like more of a risk than any I have yet taken.

"In a manner of speaking. But they leave a scar. How much of one depends on how well you tend the wound."

I scoff in disdain. "How does one tend a heart wound? Poultices will not reach it. There is no salve that can be placed upon it, nor splint nor bandage."

"Time," he says softly. "Time is the best salve for heart wounds. Reminding oneself of the small joys and comforts that can still be found in the world. A voice in the dark, a friend, the smell of fresh apples. All of those, over time, can help."

He is speaking of me. *I* am the voice in the dark, and it is *I* who smell faintly of apples. "You don't know what you're talking about," I tell him, but the words lack heat. It is a far cry from the large, important things I envisioned doing when I first ventured forth from the convent. But it is better than nothing.

"Let us talk of anger, then, for anger can warm as well as any fire." I can practically hear him rubbing his hands together, as if over a flame. "Who has earned your anger?"

"Everyone," I whisper. "Every rutting one of them." As soon as the words are out, I feel lighter, as if I have thrown off some heavy, suffocating cloak. "But mostly Margot."

"And who is this Margot who has earned your wrath?"

She *has* earned it. "She is my . . . sister."

"Ah, is there any relationship as complicated as that of a sibling? I think not." There is a rustle of sound. I grow very still, ready to flee if he is making some attempt to see through the grate, but the sound quickly stops."

"Do you have brothers or sisters?" I ask.

"Three brothers. All dead." His voice is short, clipped. I remember the ghosts he spoke of and wonder if I have just seen a part of his own heart wound.

It is oddly comfortable, sitting in the dark sharing secrets. It is what my mother and aunts used to do after a long night's work, when their customers had gone. They would climb into their beds and tell an amusing story, whisper some juicy bit of gossip, or some odd tidbit about one of their customers. It is as welcome and familiar as a small fire on a cold winter's day.

For a moment, I am filled with homesickness, something I have not felt since I was seven years old and spent my first few weeks at the convent. But this homesickness is different. I do not miss the tavern with its creaky beds and bug-ridden straw. What I miss is that part of me that used to feel safe, that used to thrill in the exchange of secrets, that used to care enough to feed a starving cat.

Who are you? That question has haunted me since the prisoner first asked it. Tonight, I feel closer to the answer than I have in a long time.

❧❦❧

Even though it is late when I return to the main floor, there is a surprising amount of activity. The kitchen is still bright with light and voices, and I pass three different servants rushing by me. When I recognize Marie, I reach out and stop her. "What is going on?"

She spares me a harried glance. "It's Lady Margot, my lady. The babe is coming!" And with that, she bobs a curtsy and hurries on her way, arms full of clean linens.

And even though Margot has turned our friendship to ash and salted the earth beneath our feet, I murmur a quick, silent prayer to both Mortain and Dea Matrona for a safe, easy birth.

But maybe not *too* easy.

CHAPTER 19

Sybella

dress carefully in a black brocade gown for the audience with Viscount Rohan. Ismae has a similar gown that she wears so the two of us may stand at the duchess's shoulder, a lethal reminder not to underestimate the future queen.

But first, I must see to my sisters' safety. And to do that, I must face the followers of Arduinna.

Not only are those who follow the patron saint of love's sharp bite noted for their ferocity and martial skills, but they have a longstanding animosity toward Saint Mortain and those who follow him. I can only hope their friendship with Annith and the role she and Mortain played in bringing peace to our land have gone a long way toward healing that.

I find the Arduinnites in a small chamber just off of the duchess's solar. They, too, will be posing as ladies in waiting to the duchess so she will not be defenseless at the French court. Aeva is standing with her hands stuck out awkwardly at her sides, like some ungainly heron. Large swathes of beige and black silk are draped around her body, her legs braced as if she has just dismounted from her horse. When she sees me, her eyes narrow. "If you so much as smile, I will gut you with my knife."

I bite the inside of my cheeks to keep from doing precisely that. "I would not dream of it." The greeting is somewhat harsh, even for

a follower of Saint Arduinna, but Aeva is one of the prickliest of them all. The younger Arduinnite, Tola, does not look fully at home in her new gown, but neither does she look like she is within a hair's breadth of yanking it off.

"Why are you here?" The challenge in Aeva's voice is unmistakable. Whether it is because I serve Mortain or because it is simply more comfortable to challenge me than to be embarrassed over the gown, I do not know.

"Don't scowl so!" I chide her. "I am here attending the duchess this morning. Besides, you look even more ridiculous in your fancy gown when you screw up your face like that. Here." I step forward, dodging the beleaguered seamstress pinning up the hem. "Pull the sleeves down toward your wrist. It will free up more room at your shoulders. See?"

Glaring at me, she pinches the wrist of her left sleeve and gives it a tug. As she rotates her shoulder, the scowl lessens somewhat. She does not so much as grace me with a thank-you. "What other tricks are there to surviving such finery?" she grumbles.

"For one, you must move more slowly to give your skirt time to get out of your way."

She opens her mouth to protest, but I talk over her. "Except when you must run. Then lift it up, like so."

"How am I supposed to fight when I must hold up my skirts?" she protests.

"It is most vexing," I concede. "My fighting tends to be less out in the open than yours, and for this assignment that will hold true for you as well." I turn to the chair where she has set all her weapons, my hand hovering over one of the knives. "May I?"

"Why?" she asks warily.

"So I may see if it is possible to fit it under your sleeves like I do."

"Very well," she says, as if allowing me to pluck one of her teeth from her jaw.

"If you'd rather I didn't . . ."

She scowls even deeper, and this time I cannot help but laugh. "You are easier to bait than a mad bear. I am only trying to help, but will leave you alone if you'd rather."

"Stay. I will no doubt need all the help I can find in this monstrosity."

The seamstress gasps in distress. Aeva looks down at her. "I mean no disrespect. The gown is much lovelier when others wear it. It is not meant for such as me."

This appeases the other woman somewhat. Before Aeva can offend her further, the duchess enters the room followed by Ismae. We all curtsy.

After she greets us all by name, she turns to me. "Have you been fitted for your gown?"

"Yes, Your Grace."

"Good," the duchess continues. "Once you have finished with Aeva, I need you and Ismae to attend me. The councilors are gathering in the great hall."

For a moment, guilt raises its insistent head, but I hold Captain Dunois's reassurances close. I glance down at the harried seamstress. "How close are you to having all that you need?"

"Close enough," she mumbles around the pins in her mouth. "What I don't have, I'll guess."

Aeva brightens considerably. "That is a good plan."

"You may work on Tola's gown," I tell the seamstress. "I will help Aeva out of hers."

The seamstress rewards me with a relieved "Thank you, my lady," before hopping to her feet and hurrying toward the younger Arduinnite.

Aeva smirks. "Are you my handmaiden now?"

"Hardly. Step down from the pedestal, you belligerent goose, so I can get at your lacings."

I can see by the set of her mouth that she wants to shove me away and claim she can do it on her own, but she cannot. To assuage her wounded pride, I tell her, "It is merely an excuse. I have something I must ask of you."

A spark of interest causes her suspicion to recede, and she steps to the floor without further argument. "What?"

"Turn around so I may tend to your gown." I give a silent prayer of thanks when she complies. It is hard enough to ask this vexing woman a favor, especially

one that is so important to me. I would rather she did not see my face when I do it.

She pulls her long braid out of my way, exposing the marque of Arduinna at the nape of her neck. My fingers long to touch it and see if it is raised like a brand or merely stained upon the skin. Instead, I begin untying the lacings at her waist. "I request the protection of Arduinna."

She starts to turn around to look at me, but I tug on the laces to keep her facing forward. "For yourself?"

I cannot decide whether I am insulted or flattered by the incredulity in her voice. "No. For my two young sisters. Ismae and I are to accompany the duchess this morning, and I have run out of people I can trust to watch them."

"Watch them against whom?"

"Our brother. He wants custody of them but does not have their best interests at heart." I can only hope the words I don't say speak as loudly as the ones I do.

She turns to face me, her prickliness and animosity gone. "We will gladly help protect them." Her words are as solemn and binding as an oath.

My throat tightens in response. "Thank you. Once you are back in your own clothes, I will take you to their chambers."

Dressed in their short fur robes and leather leggings, bows slung over their shoulders and knives at their hips, Aeva and Tola accompany me to my sisters' chamber. Lazare and Graelon wait just inside the door.

Graelon nods a pleasant greeting, but Lazare studies the others with equal parts suspicion and defiance. In the final confrontation between the duchess and France, before the king decided marriage would be the better option than war, many followers of the Nine banded together to aid their country, the Arduinnites and the charbonnerie included. But these two are as prickly as hedgehogs. Having them in the same room together will be like carrying dry grass and tinder in the same bucket and hoping it doesn't catch fire. "I do not believe you have met before. Aeva and Tola are followers of Arduinna and have agreed to help watch the girls. Aeva and Tola, may I introduce you to Lazare and Graelon, two of the charbonnerie who have not only loyally served the duchess, but are my friends as well."

As they study each other with wary eyes, Tola comes to the rescue.

"That was quite a trick with the cannon fire when the army was at our gates," she says with true admiration. "I would give much to learn how to do that."

Lazare turns to the younger Arduinnite. His lip gives half a curl upward, which for him passes as a smile. "Pretty words won't pry that secret from me."

Tola's eyebrows raise slightly. "Is that a challenge, charbonnerie?"

Lazare leans against the doorjamb and folds his arms. "If you care to take it as such."

Baring her teeth in what some might call a grin, Aeva leans toward him. "We are up to whatever challenge you care to issue."

Lazare blinks lazily, but it does not hide his spark of interest. He is hungry for a challenge, and the Arduinnites are happy to provide it.

"Excellent." I nudge Aeva and Tola into the room. "You can compete over who is better at overseeing the safety of my sisters." By the time I close the door, Lazare is smiling to himself.

Tephanie hurries forward to greet us, her eyes wide and her mouth open in surprise. "M-my lady. I did not expect you to return so soon." Although she is speaking to me, her gaze is fixed with fascination upon the other two women's unusual attire and the bows slung across their shoulders.

"Louise? Charlotte?" I call out. "I have people I'd like you to meet."

Louise jumps to her feet and comes running, while Charlotte follows at a slower pace. Louise stops short when she is close, apparently somewhat taken aback by the appearance of the Arduinnites. Giving the girls a moment to adjust, I perform the introductions.

When I have finished, Charlotte says, "Are they here to guard us?"

I glance at her sharply. "If I meant that, I would have said so." I do not know

if she is trying to worry her sister, or poke at my tender places, or if she simply has a natural talent for doing both at the same time.

Tola squats down in front of Charlotte so that they are nose to nose. "Who do you need guarding from?" There is no mockery or dismissiveness in her manner, which is what wins Charlotte over in the end.

"Our brother." Charlotte studies the two women. "Which of you is more skilled with the bow?"

"Oh ho! You go straight to the heart of the matter, don't you? Well," Tola says in a conspiratorial tone, "Aeva would claim that she is, but she would be wrong." She leans closer to Charlotte and whispers, "I am better."

Aeva rolls her eyes and offers her hand to Louise. "Come, let me tell you a story about who is truly better with a bow . . ."

Shyly, Louise takes her hand and allows herself to be led from my side. As they all make themselves comfortable in front of the fire to better hear Aeva's story, the constricting tightness around my heart eases a bit. Two of those I love are safe and protected. Now there is only one that I must worry about.

CHAPTER 20

y concern over Beast is like a nagging suitor who will not take no for an answer. It is ardent. Insistent. And wholly invasive.

I reassure myself that if Pierre had cut Beast down, he would have returned his broken body to me on a platter, but it is thin comfort.

As I stand behind the duchess while she receives Viscount Rohan in the great hall, I distract myself by turning my worry and anger on the viscount, glowering at him while I run my finger along the edge of my hidden blade. It is easy — so easy — to step back into this fuming anger at the world around me — like finding a favorite gown I had somehow misplaced. And if it allows me to get under Rohan's skin, so much the better.

I am certain there has been some mistake." The duchess's voice does not waver.

Rohan is of middle years with the look of a lazy, self-indulgent predator who is inclined to let others do the hard work of rounding up his quarry. "I'm afraid not, Your Grace. The king has invested the governorship of Brittany in my hands. Effective immediately."

He pretends he does not notice my unrelenting scowl, but I can feel his heart begin to beat faster. Good. He is unnerved by my attention. He gestures to his second in command, who steps forward and holds out a scroll. Duval takes it from him and begins to read.

The duchess's face is impassive. "I have placed the duchy under the guidance of Chancellor Montauban. The king did not object nor put forth any other names when we last spoke of it. Not even yours."

Rohan tries to shrug as if he is indulging a child, but the movement is too calculated to be truly careless.

"Where do you plan to reside?" the duchess asks coolly. "You cannot spend nearly so much time at your French holdings as you have this last year."

I smile at the veiled rebuke of his collusion with the French. Rohan's glance flickers in my direction before bowing in acknowledgment of the reprimand, his arrogance wilting somewhat along the edges. "I shall take up residence at my main holding in Josselin."

Duval finishes reading, his mouth curving disgust. "The letter does seem to claim Rohan is to be governor of Brittany. It is signed by the king and bears his seal."

Duval's confirmation further inflames my temper. The king promised the duchess one thing, yet within days he has already changed his mind. I cannot help but wonder what other promises will be broken, what other wishes will not be honored. My sisters and I may have the duchess's protection, but will the king allow her to honor that?

It feels as if my staunch bastion against Pierre has sustained a crack in its foundation.

"We shall see," the duchess says brusquely. "Once I am in France and can discuss this with the king, you can be certain this misunderstanding will be put to rights."

Her words are sure and confident, and for a moment Rohan looks nonplussed. Pressing her advantage, the duchess leans forward in her chair. "Remember this. My people have been through much while you were safely retired to your lands in France. You will treat them with a gentle hand and allow them to rebuild their lives, or I myself will ride back at the head of an army to oust you from this office. Do you understand?"

Rohan forces his features back into their casual arrogance. "But of course, Your Grace." He must raise his voice to be heard over a rustle of movement toward the back of the room. "My only wish is to serve the interests of you and the king to the best of my ability."

Courtiers begin ducking and stepping aside as a small black shape flaps toward the front of the chamber. Still unaware of the disturbance behind him, Rohan gives a shallow bow. "You have nothing to fear from me."

That is when the bird attacks him.

With a rushing of wings and a rather desperate caw, a wild-eyed crow with a viciously sharp beak descends upon Rohan. *Perfect.* The viscount ducks in surprise, the men around him drawing their swords.

"Stop!" My voice rings out, cutting through the disarray as I step off the dais.

Rohan tries to maintain his dignity while dodging the wings and beak of the unsettled bird attempting to land on his shoulder. For that *is* what's happening, I realize. The crow is exhausted and looking for a place to land. "The creature is attacking me!" Rohan waves his arms to fend it off.

I step closer, ignoring the drawn swords. "Hold very still, monsieur." My voice is low and urgent. "This is no ordinary crow, but one sent by the convent of Saint Mortain."

Rohan pales and grows motionless. Even though he has spent the last year in France, he is Breton enough to tremble at that name.

With Rohan no longer waving at him, the crow alights on the man's shoulder, clinging precariously to the silver fox collar of his doublet.

Rohan flinches as I take a step closer. "Let's hope the bird is not an ill omen of this new venture of yours, a warning to turn back." Suspicion and alarm battle for control of the viscount's features. "Or worse. He could be a harbinger of your own death." I whisper the words as lovingly I would as an endearment.

Rohan is mine now. "Get him off of me!" He means for it to come out as an order, but it sounds more like a plea.

I am so close now that it looks like Rohan and I are partnering in a dance. His widened eyes follow my hand as I place the back of it on his shoulder.

The crow eyes me with disdain, as if doubting my wits to think he will fall for such a trick. However, it is not his wits I am counting on, but his hunger. For the last three days I have carried a bit of dried venison in my pocket, waiting for a messenger from Annith. That he happened to arrive during Rohan's audience with the duchess is the saints' own luck.

The crow catches the scent of the treat. When he lunges for it, I clasp his feathered body between my hands, his heart beating frantically as I remove him from Rohan's shoulder. When I step away, I twist my fingers to give him his treat. He jabs, capturing it in his beak with a triumphant look in his black eyes.

"You'd best be careful for the next few days," I warn the viscount. "One never knows what such a messenger can portend."

As I leave the room with the crow safely cradled in my hands, I can only hope Rohan was as discomfited by my performance as I was by the news he brought.

CHAPTER 21

hile Ismae escorts the fuming duchess to the solar, I hurry to the chamber that used to serve as office to the abbess when she was in residence. It will be the best place to retrieve the message and read it away from prying eyes.

I have not set foot inside the room since the former abbess of Saint Mortain was banished. Was it truly only two weeks ago? While it is empty, some faint echo of her presence still remains. Or perhaps it is simply my own animosity toward her and her callous disregard for me or my well-being.

Nervous and impatient, the crow squawks. I tuck him safely in one of the three empty cages behind the abbess's desk and trade him another treat from the nearby jar for my message. I march over to the chair and plop myself into it, then stretch my feet up and rest them on the desk. If any remnant of the abbess remains, let us see how she likes that.

The door opens, and Ismae pokes her head in. Her eyes widen as she takes in the location of my boots, but she says nothing. Wise girl.

"The duchess said I may come see what Annith had to say."

I wave her over, unroll the message, and begin reading.

> *Dearest Sybella (and Ismae, who I imagine is reading over your shoulder),*

I cannot help it, I laugh. Ismae nudges me with her elbow. "As if you wouldn't be reading over my shoulder if it were addressed to me."

> *We arrived at the convent three days ago. As you can imagine, Balthazaar's appearance has thrown every-*

thing into chaos. Truly, it is as if a cat has landed among a flock of pigeons. Sister Beatriz fainted when he was introduced! The older sisters, while less flamboyant, were equally dramatic. Both Sister Vereda and Sister Claude cried openly when they came face-to-face with him.

The younger girls (and nuns) seem to take his presence more in stride. Aveline and Sarra appear bored by the whole development. Yet when they think no one is watching, I find them staring at him with hungry, resentful eyes. I do not know what it means for their relationship with him, but we will have our hands full while this is all sorted out.

However, you are leaving for France soon, and I wanted to get this information to you as quickly as I could. The two novitiates I told you about left the convent almost a year before either of you arrived. They were near my age, although I'm afraid I wasn't close with them — I was too focused on my training at the time.

I have spent hours poring through the convent registry, and there is only the smallest reference made to the girls' departure. I include it below:

September 1484. Margot and Genevieve left for France today. They are to pose as nieces to one of Duke Francis's allies, and as such will be tutored at the French court. They will be in position to feed us critical information in a timely manner, and will be available to us should we need to move against the crown. Although we shall do nothing for at least a year or two until they are well and truly established and beyond suspicion.

There is no mention made of who the ally was or where he lived. Further, I have found no evidence of any communications of theirs ever being received by the convent, nor any correspondence *from us, either directing them to act or giving them instructions.*

There was so little written about them I broke down and asked Sisters Claude and Vereda how the girls were to be contacted, should their services be needed. The answer was most unsatisfactory. When hidden initiates of Mortain are to be called into duty, they are given a crow feather, either by a messenger from the convent or by letter.

How we are to do that, when we do not know where they are, is unclear to me. I asked Sister Vereda if she has Seen either one of them, but she gave me such a garbled answer that I am certain Balthazaar's arrival has temporarily deprived her of her wits. The entire strategy is so weak and flawed that we may as well have set the girls adrift on a raft in the open ocean. I fear that they have burrowed deep into the court awaiting instructions that never came. Yet one more thing to lay on the reverend mother's long list of crimes.

I do not know how helpful my memories of them will be. Margot had red hair, brown eyes, and freckles. She promised to grow into a woman of great beauty. What I remember most about her was that her gifts from Mortain had not yet appeared—even at twelve. Since it was the same with me, I took great comfort in that. However, that is not helpful to you.

Genevieve stands out even less vividly in my mind. Her hair was too light to be brown, but too dark to be blond. She was of average height and well muscled, for she threw herself into her training here. Her face was thin and somewhat fox-shaped, her eyes brown. But that was five years ago. Appearances change so much in those five years between twelve and adulthood! They could now be fat or thin, their hair darker, their faces rounder. There is a good chance they may even have grown taller, since many girls have not reached their full height by that age.

Dearest Sybella, I am sorry I have so little to give you. In truth, I feel as if I am sending you into a haystack to hunt for a needle. But if anyone can ferret out fellow daughters of Mortain, it is you.

Please give dear Ismae a hug for me and know that all is (mostly) well here. I will pray for you and the duchess each and every day.

Annith

And just like that, my small nugget of hope for the future and my promises to the council vanish like ashes in the wind.

CHAPTER 22

Genevieve

I always knew the crow feather that would call me into service would not appear in the first year, or even the second, but I was certain it would come. I spent hours wondering whether the messenger would be a man or a woman and what guise they would wear. I had nothing to go by or signs to look for. I knew only that someday, someone would arrive bearing a crow feather, the signal that the convent was calling me into service.

Today, the first day of Margot's labor, I wish more than ever that messenger would arrive. There are a thousand other places I would rather be than here in this castle as Margot crosses the threshold into her new life, a threshold she can never uncross.

The men are lucky. By custom, they are not allowed anywhere near the birthing room. Indeed, the farther away they are, the better. So they have embarked on an extended debauch of hunting and drinking and eating, then hunting some more.

I, too, make myself scarce. In part because of Margot's own command for me to stay away, but also to avoid the silent questions in the other attendants' eyes. I have no wish to explain to them why I am not at my best friend's side as she begins her grueling ordeal.

On the second day of Margot's labor, I disappear to the castle dungeon bearing two sacks. When I reach the oubliette, I lower one of the sacks down into the prisoner's waiting arms. Instead of lingering, I turn to leave.

"You are not staying?"

I clench the sack in my hand and keep my voice steady. "I have something else I must do today."

"Very well. Thank you for the food." And that is the end of it. He does not poke or prod or pepper me with more questions.

I retrace my steps back toward the main landing until I stand in front of my altar. Today, as Margot labors to bring her child into the world, it seems a good time to remind the gods that we are here.

I open the remaining sack and retrieve a flint to light the candles. Next I remove a piece of the silver birch bark, two small willow twigs fashioned into a cross with a leather tie, one of Margot's forgotten ribbons, an owl's feather I found outside, and a broken-off corner of a small loaf of bread. It is hard to know what Saint Camulos requires, but I have decided on an arrowhead I found outside the farrier's hut. For Saint Salonius I have brought a knucklebone, and for Saint Cissonius, a pinch of salt. Last, I lay the pearl necklace Angoulême gave me in front of Dea Matrona's candle. It is the most valuable thing I own.

I sit back on my heels. "Please," I whisper. "Watch over Margot and her babe."

For a brief moment, it feels as if the very fabric of the air around me thins, allowing some indefinable essence of the Nine to reach through and assure me. It is like another forgotten piece of myself falling into place.

I slip from my knees onto the floor to continue my prayers. As I watch the bright flames of the candles, a deep sense of peace comes over me.

❧

I awake with a start. Unsure where I am, I know only that my heart is racing. I push myself up from the floor and see the altar, then put my hand to my chest in an attempt to calm myself.

But my heart beats slow and steady, which means it is not *my* heart that is racing.

I leap to my feet, pick up my skirts, and run as fast as I can back through the wending hallways, the furious pounding of the heart drawing me to it like a lodestone. I take the stairs two at a time.

When Bertine's babe came, she huffed and puffed and strained like an ox trying to pull too great a load. Only instead of pulling, she was pushing. The other women sat around her, holding her up, one of them sitting with her back to Bertine's, giving her something to push against. In truth, it seemed as if it took all eight of them to bring that babe into the world. When it came, it came in a rush of blood and shouts of pain.

I can hear the screams before I am halfway up the stairs to the birthing room. That's when my own heart starts to pound. If Margot had wanted me by her side, she would have sent someone. But she did not. Even so, I must know what is happening.

By the time I have reached the fourth floor, my breath is coming in ragged rasps, my hands and feet icy cold. The door to the room is ajar, so it is easy enough to stand and observe unnoticed.

Five women surround the bed, all of them working frantically. Margot herself lies sprawled in the middle, her belly twisted and misshapen, her legs spread open. Blood is everywhere.

My heart — or is it Margot's? — beats louder, more painfully.

I want to step farther into the room, but my feet have grown roots, binding me to the floor. The midwife stands near Margot's shoulder murmuring soft words before placing a thumb on her forehead.

She is administering last rites.

No, I want to shout. *She is not dying! She is not even one of yours! She is Mortain's.* But I cannot find the words. Even if I could, I am not certain I am allowed to say them.

Margot's pale, exhausted face turns to me just then, her eyes flying open so that we are staring at each other. She opens her mouth — to shout? to call my name? — but it twists in a grimace as another birthing pain racks her body. It squeezes and squeezes, her back arching as she rides it out. When it recedes, her face relaxes once more, and I wait for her to turn this way again.

Except she does not.

A moment later, I am met with a silent raw scream that is so full of anguish, I must grab on to the doorjamb for fear it will knock me over. There is no piece of Margot to reach or hold on to, only pain and fury that comes in a long, hot wave, pouring over me, filling up all the space around me, nearly drowning me in outrage and despair so complete that there is no room for anything else.

In that same moment her heart simply stops. It is so sudden and unexpected that the room grows dim and distant, and I nearly lose my grip on the door. The beating of my own heart feels naked and alone against my ribs.

A giant fist wraps itself around every organ in my body and squeezes so tightly that I must double over to draw breath. With Margot's scream still ringing in my ears, I turn and stumble down the hall like a drunken lord.

By the time I reach the end of the hallway, my feet are working again and I begin to run. It is the first time I have ever run from anything, but I do not know what else to do and know only that I must be away from here.

I race down three flights of stairs to the main floor. When I reach the door, I fling it open, but outside it is pouring sheets of rain. The porter grabs my arm, pulling me back inside. "You can't go out there, my lady!"

I stare at him blankly, not comprehending. When he slams the door shut against the winds, I realize I am trapped. Trapped inside with Margot and her death and all the things I do not want to face.

I turn back to the stairs, ignoring the porter's questions. I go down instead of up, down one flight, then another, until I reach the floor of utter darkness. Of stillness and quiet. Of emptiness. If I can just stand in this emptiness for a moment, I am sure that the maelstrom inside me will cease.

Breathe, I tell myself. But my arms and legs will not stop shaking, and I cannot draw a full breath.

I bend over, grabbing my knees, trying to force some air into my lungs. When they do finally work again, instead of drawing in a great gulp of air, a ragged sob escapes, the sound so harsh and raw that I clamp my hand over my mouth so I will not have to hear it again.

Did I botch the offering to Dea Matrona somehow? Lay the cord in the wrong position? Not sprinkle enough wine on the earth?

Were my thoughts and prayers not sincere enough?

But they *were* sincere. As angry as I was, I never once wished for her to die. Surely Dea Matrona knows that.

But not too easy.

Those simple words, flippantly said, circle back to me.

No. I shake my head. There is a world of difference between *not too easy* and wishing death. A lifetime of difference. Those words cannot be responsible for Margot's fate, and if they are, it is simply that Matrona was looking for an excuse.

My bones itch and tremble, eager to be moving again, to escape these thoughts, these feelings.

I begin pacing the antechamber lit by the lone torch. I walk until I am exhausted, my limbs weak. Only then do I allow myself to stop and rest against the wall.

But as soon as I close my eyes, the image of Margot lying in a pool of her own blood rises up, seared into my vision.

The horror of it shoves me from the wall, forcing me to keep moving.

After a while, I have no idea how long, I find myself standing by the grate, staring down into the oubliette. I want to forget. More than anything right now, I wish to forget.

Exhaustion sets in, and my legs slowly fold under me. I lean forward, pressing my body against the cold stone floor.

"Hello?" the prisoner calls softly. "Is it you?" His voice is laced with concern, but I cannot bring myself to answer, afraid of what will come out of my mouth if I dare open it.

"Are you well?" he whispers now, his voice coming from directly beneath the grate. I lift my hand and place it on the grate so he will see that it is me.

"Another heart wound?" he asks softly.

"Yes." The word bursts from me, more gasp than answer. *Say it,* I tell myself. You cannot hide from it forever. "She is dead." My throat closes up, and my mouth gapes open in a silent wail I can no more stop than I could the storm. I stuff my fist into my mouth, determined that no sound will escape.

I thought I knew death. Understood it. Studied it so that it was familiar to me. But nothing at the convent has prepared me for this — this pain and desolation and sense of having someone ripped from my heart.

Especially someone I no longer even liked. Who had earned my animosity and was happy to toss it back in my face. "How can I feel this way about someone I have grown to hate?"

The prisoner shifts on his straw. When it comes, his deep voice feels like the most solid thing in a world gone mad. "Sometimes," he says softly, "the death of those we hate is harder to bear than that of those we love." A sense of some old hidden pain floats up from the oubliette, mingling with mine. "I think once they are dead, all the things that might have been, all the truces that might have been called, all the broken pieces that might have been mended, are now sealed for all time. It is final, this hate."

Oh, how he is right. That hate, which should have protected me, does not. The world has been altered in some irrevocable way that I cannot mend or put back together.

"Breathe." The prisoner's voice comes again out of the dark. "A slow, deep breath in, then out."

"I'm trying," I snap, but my words catch on a sob.

"Just keep trying." His voice is as patient as the standing stones at the convent. "Your body will remember, even if you cannot. Deep breath in . . . out." In the silence that follows, I hear him take in a deep breath of his own, then slowly let it out. When he takes the next breath, my own lungs respond, following his lead, filling themselves with air. And slowly, in the darkness, with his words as my guide, I relearn how to breathe in this new, broken world.

CHAPTER 23

Sybella

ephanie grasps her knife awkwardly, glancing up at me with a hopeful look in her eye. "Like this, my lady?" Her voice is pitched low so as not to wake the girls.

"No." I reach out and adjust her grip. Her fingers are stiff, but I manage to coax them into the right position. "Like that." When I look up, she is blushing. I step back and pretend I haven't noticed. "Do you remember the strike I showed you the first night?"

"Yes, my lady." Her movements are stilted and leaden, as if she has never used those muscles before and her mind must struggle to direct the movement.

"There you are! You're getting the feel of it now."

A quick knock interrupts us, and the door opens to reveal a young page standing breathless in the doorway. "Beast has returned, my lady. He just rode into the stables."

The relief that floods my body is so complete that for a moment I am as boneless as a piece of old rope. "Thank you." As he takes his leave, I turn back to Tephanie. "It is getting late, and your arms are trembling with fatigue. It is probably a good time for us to stop."

"Of course, my lady. *That* is our reason for stopping. Not because Sir Waroch has returned." Her eyes gleam with rare mischief that is like watching the sun peek out from behind a cloud. I cannot help but

smile. I snag a small linen towel from the back of one of the chairs and toss it at her. "Hush, you." She smirks happily as she blots her face with the towel.

Beast is back.

I return my knife to its sheath, lift my cloak from its hook, and pull it around my shoulders. "You will likely be asleep when I return, so I will see you in the morning."

Outside the room, Aeva considers me with an air of suspicion. "Where are you off to at this late hour?"

My eyebrows shoot up. "Not that it is any of your business, but Sir Waroch has returned, and I wish to know what he learned of my brother." Then I soften. Since they are guarding my sisters, they deserve the whole truth. "It is not widely known, but Louise is the daughter of Sir Waroch's beloved late sister. He cares for her welfare as much as I do."

Aeva's calculating look is replaced with one of understanding.

"Now go inside, sit by the fire, and make yourselves comfortable. I'm sure Tephanie will enjoy the company."

After they let themselves into the chamber, it is all I can do not to take the stairs two at a time. Joy and relief beat against my ribs. He is alive! And likely unharmed if he was able to ride.

The stable yard is dark and nearly deserted except for a handful of posted sentries. A lone lantern draws my eye. Beast is stripped to the waist, washing himself in icy water that spurts from the pump. Yannic works the lever with one hand while holding a bundle of clean, dry clothes in the other.

Beast cups another handful of water, causing his bulging muscles and sinew to flex. The lantern light reflects off the faint rivulets of water that trail down the myriad scars covering his thickly muscled arms and back. Every time I see those scars, I wonder anew that he has been able to survive so much damage and live. Beast has claimed it is a gift from Saint Camulos himself, that the saint's followers heal quickly. Perhaps that is so, but I suspect his own iron will and pigheadedness have something to do with it as well.

Beast stops washing and lifts his head, his gaze going unerringly to mine from clear across the yard. He reaches out to Yannic, who lets go of the pump and hands him a towel. After scrubbing himself dry, he trades the towel for a shirt, tugs it over his head, and begins making his way across the yard.

I want to launch myself at him, to feel with my skin and bones that he is whole and safe. I want to fuss and cluck at him like a mother hen, which would only embarrass us both, so I clasp my hands firmly behind me. "You're back."

"Don't sound so disappointed." Drops of water still cling to his thick, spiky lashes, making his eyes stand out in the torchlight.

Unable to help myself, I reach out and put my finger on his cheek to wipe away an errant drop of water. "Well, you *are* large and ugly and take up a lot of room."

He steps closer. "Fortunately, you have more than enough beauty for both of us." He shakes his head. "I deserve you as much as an ox deserves to drink from a crystal goblet."

I snort. "Where you see a crystal goblet, the rest of the world sees chipped, cracked earthenware. Trust me, my beauty is only skin deep. My soul has more lumps and scars than you ever will."

"Mayhap that is why I love it so." There is no more space between us, just the immovable solidity of his chest, the planes of his stomach. "Do you wish to know what hap —"

I place my fingers upon his lips. "Later. Now it is enough that you are back."

"You were worried?" He sounds both pleased and disbelieving.

Worried is far too small a word to contain the all-consuming fear and dread I felt in the days he was gone. "No, you lummox. I would never worry about someone as hardheaded and stubborn as you."

"You are adorable when you lie." His voice is naught but a deep rumble.

"I am never adorable." I place my hands around his neck. "And if you do not kiss me," I whisper against the side of his jaw, "I will be forced to stab you instead, and that would get blood all over the cobblestones."

His warm breath grazes my cheek. "The sweetness of your courtship is impossible to resist."

"It is one of my gifts." I slowly pull his head lower until his lips are close enough for me to reach. When our lips touch, all the fear and worry and shame and anger I have held close for the last three days vanishes.

Like some great alchemist trick, Beast pulls all of that from me, taking all of it in so that I am left only with joy at his safe return. And wanting. So much wanting. The want curls deep in my belly with velvet hooks. I take fistfuls of his shirt, heat radiating from his skin and the warm, solid muscle beneath it. His hands on me are both heavy with strength and as light as those of a lute player. I want to feel those hands all over my body. To know that he is safe with every inch of my skin. To have there be no more distance between us.

"Sybella," he whispers against my mouth.

"Here." I pull my lips from his and slide along the wall to a door. My hand fumbles a moment, then opens it.

Beast blinks at the room behind us, his brows raised.

"It is no accident that I waited for you here against the wall of the tack room." I take his hand, pull him inside, and close the door behind us.

Later, as we rest upon a pile of saddle blankets, I run my fingers along his chest, tracing every scar, every muscle, every rib, as if they hold the key to this man and his generous heart. "So tell me. What happened? Why were you gone so long?"

He settles his head more comfortably on the saddle he is using as a pillow. "There was a swarm of Rohan's men just outside the city. It was impossible to find Pierre, at first. It wasn't until he left his dead retainer where he fell that I was able to see where he'd been. But he had a fair head start. By the number of hoof marks in the ground, he had nearly a dozen men waiting for him."

I prop my head up on my elbow. "And you went after them — alone?"

"Of course not. I had help."

"Who?"

He grins. "The charbonnerie camp was not too far from there, so I collected six of Graelon's men, and we settled in to follow."

"Why not just return once they were free of the city?"

"I wanted to track them long enough to be sure they would not simply lie in wait, ready to attack us again when we leave for France."

I tap him lightly on the chest. "Smart man. Where did they go?"

"South, beyond Nantes. They demanded hospitality from the local lords on the first and second nights. When they got past Nantes, I thought we'd finally be able to move against them, but they reached their own holding and were joined by a battalion of men before picking up the road to Gascony the next morning. That is when I decided they would not be doubling back." He captures my hand in his, holding it still. "I am sorry he got away."

"Do not apologize. Even you cannot take on an entire battalion of men."

He lifts my hand and kisses it. "For you I would take on the entire world."

And he would. I can see it so clearly in my mind—with a battalion full upon him, wading his way through them like a farmer scything wheat. I shiver.

"But," he continues, "I am not that foolish." He sighs. "It was easier. Before I met you. Before I knew Louise. It is harder now to find my courage."

"That is called wisdom, and well that you should acquire some." I am silent a moment as the weight of the confrontation with Pierre presses down on me once more. "I should have killed him."

Beast studies me for a long moment. "Did he bear a marque?"

"No. But neither did the guards involved in Crunard's escape attempt. It appears that marques are no more."

Hearing the despair in my voice, he leans down to kiss the crown of my head.

An old familiar wave of shame washes over me. Unable to meet his eyes, I look down and pluck at one of his chest hairs. "I wanted to kill him," I whisper. "I wanted to with all my heart, marque or no. The only thing stopping me was Charlotte and Louise." I look up at him. "It was one thing to have those impulses

when Mortain was guiding my hand, but that is no longer the case. Surely being so quick to kill makes me just like Pierre."

He tightens both arms around me, as if trying to squeeze such thoughts from my head. "No." The word is quick and certain. "You were sired by Mortain, not d'Albret."

"I have done horrible things and caused untold damage long before I came to serve Mortain. I hold darkness inside me like an acorn holds a seed."

"You are wrong," he whispers against my hair.

I am quiet for a moment, unable to accept the comfort he offers. "At the convent, we used to soak apricots in poisoned honey, for the sweetness disguised the poison. And while the fruit itself is not toxic, a lifetime spent soaking in the poison made it so." I pull away from him so I may see his face. "What if I am that apricot? No matter that I was born of Mortain, if I have spent my whole life steeped in the d'Albret poison, how can it *not* have tainted me?"

Beast brings his hands up to cradle my face, his eyes fierce with certainty. "You are not an apricot. You are a blade that has been brutally forged, painfully hammered, and wickedly honed. You are steel, not poison. You are deadly, not depraved. They are very different things, Sybella."

His words soothe something in my heart. I want so desperately to believe him. At the very least, no matter how far I fear I have gone, how beyond salvation I have ventured, he will always accompany me on that road.

CHAPTER 24

n the morning of our departure for France, Ismae and I wait for the duchess near her chamber door, the silence between us thick with all the last-minute things we wish to say, the farewell we have no choice but to make. Instead, Ismae shoots a disgruntled glare at Tola and Aeva, who wait farther away from the door, just beyond hearing. "I do not see why the Arduinnites get to go when I must stay here."

Her grousing nearly causes me to smile. "It is their magic that brought this miracle into being. When their leader offered their services, the duchess thought it impolitic to refuse. Besides, with Rohan's arrival, I am guessing you will have more intrigue and scheming than you had planned for."

Her face brightens, but before she can respond, the duchess appears at our side, resplendent in a black satin traveling gown complete with a fur-lined cloak.

"Your Grace." We both sink into deep curtsies.

Her face is pale, her head held high. "If you will come with me," she murmurs, "I have one stop I must make before we depart."

"Of course, Your Grace."

It is but a short walk to the cathedral. At the wide ornate doors, the duchess pauses. "I must say goodbye to Isabeau." Her voice falters only slightly.

Duval emerges from inside the vestibule where he has been waiting. She turns gratefully to him. "Thank you for meeting me."

He takes her hand in his and gives it a bracing squeeze.

"Wait here, if you please," she tells us. Duval looks once at Ismae, his gray eyes the exact same color as the walls of the mausoleum. It is easy to forget that Isabeau was his sister as well. Indeed, it is easy to forget that they were all a close-knit family rather than a political dynasty. Duval has served his sister since she was born, making it his duty to see to her safety and well-being. And now they will be parted. Duval can likely count on two hands the number of times he will see her again. If that.

I do not mean to listen, but the cathedral is as quiet as a grave, and its high open ceilings allow sound to echo freely. "You will see that candles are lit for her daily?" the duchess asks.

"I will."

"I knew when I married — whoever it would be — I would have to leave Isabeau behind." Her voice breaks. "But I did not want it to be like this."

Duval reaches out and pulls her into his arms. "There is naught you could have done. She was always plagued with ill health."

"While that is true, I always wonder how much the constant worry of war and a lifetime of intrigues hastened her death."

"You protected her from it as much as you could."

"As you protected me. I cannot thank you enough for everything you have done, Gavriel. I would have given up a hundred times if not for you and your determination —"

"Hush. It will not change now. I will simply do it from afar."

Her composure crumbles, and she allows herself to lean against his chest. "I do not know if I can live in the midst of those who have been our enemy for so long."

His arms tighten around her. "Ah, but I know that you can. If not for you, we would be a conquered people with a new overlord. You found a way to win the king's heart. You wrested victory from defeat. It is your child who will inherit the French crown. The woman who did that will easily meet whatever the French court may throw her way."

She pulls away, wiping at her eyes. "If I was strong, it was because you were the iron at my back. So have a care for yourself. Do not plot too hard. Do not let Rohan unsettle you too much. I will speak to the king immediately and see that he is removed and returns to his lands in France."

The smile Duval gives her is bright, but even through the dim light of the cathedral I can see the faint melancholy that tugs at its corners. "All will be well," he assures her.

The sound of a distant trumpet drifts in through the cathedral's door. "Now," he says more briskly, "the traveling party is assembled, the baggage train is loaded. All they are waiting for is you."

She nods, straightening her shoulders. In that gesture the young girl who will sorely miss her older brother disappears and the young queen-to-be takes her place. When Duval escorts her back to us, Ismae stares at him a brief moment, realizing for the first time, I think, just how much this goodbye is costing him and why the duchess wished her to stay.

Our departure requires speed as well as some discretion. Not only is the marriage arrangement most irregular, but the bishops involved have not, in fact, effected a miracle and produced the required dispensation by the pope.

Even so, our traveling party has all the subtlety of a mummer's parade. Part of it is inevitable. It is impossible to hide fourscore knights, three litters, and a baggage train the size of a small village. Add to that a collection of travelers who are adorned in their grandest finery — surcoats in gay colors, ornate hats that flutter in the breeze. They remind me of a flock of self-important pheasants, plumage bobbing as they chatter excitedly.

At the duchess's appearance, a small cheer goes up from the crowd. She receives their jubilant adoration with a gracious smile as Duval escorts her to Chancellor Montauban, with whom she is to ride pillion.

Ismae walks beside me as I make my way to my own horse. I do not relish saying goodbye. The farewell we just witnessed has nearly ripped off the chains that keep my own feelings tightly contained, and I fear they will spill out into the courtyard in a jumbled mess.

Ismae sighs. "For all that you are sharp-tongued and ill-mannered, I shall miss you. And if I thought you would not slap me, I would hug you goodbye."

"Since I am the bossy one, it is I who should hug you," I point out, then wrap

my arms around her and pull her close, savoring the feel of her, her strength, her stubbornness, and her unwavering loyalty. "I shall miss you, dearest sister," I say, planting a quick kiss on her cheek. Before she can so much as squeak in surprise, I let go, grab the pommel of my saddle, and mount my horse, not caring how unladylike it might look.

The horse prances a bit, eager to be on its way, and Ismae twitches my skirts into place. "Have you decided how you will look for the convent's other initiates?" she asks.

I busy myself testing the length of my stirrups. "Not yet. The red-haired one will be easiest to locate. I will search for her first."

"If all else fails, you can simply hand every woman at court a crow feather and see how she reacts," she suggests.

"It may well come to that," I mutter. The trumpet blares again, crisp and loud in the chill air. We are out of time.

A hush falls over the crowd as a priest of Saint Cissonius comes forward. He grasps a large wooden staff with both hands, bows his head, and prays. When he is finished, he reaches into the pouch at his waist and casts a handful of salt upon the ground.

It is not until the salt touches the earth that it hits me — I am truly leaving. A sense of loss and mayhap even panic ripples through me. Brittany has been the seat of all my darkest memories and vilest hours, and to leave that behind is no loss.

But, I realize, looking up at the rooftops of the townhouses and the church tower, I was safe here in Rennes — at least for a time. I was also welcome in this city. Indeed, it was one of the most welcoming places I have ever lived, second only to the convent. I was respected here, admired even. Everything good about myself — my friendships, my faith, my belief that I was someone with something to offer — is tied up in this place. And now I am leaving.

It has been hard enough to cling to faith here in Brittany, one of the last places the gods once walked the earth. One of the last places where lives have been touched by those gods — although I must remember more than ever to call them saints. How much harder will it be to keep faith alive in a land that has been stripped bare of their wonder and mercy and gifts? How will my faith not crumble like week-old bread?

At the head of the party, Beast raises his gloved hand, then motions us forward. We are on our way.

I do not look back.

CHAPTER 25

Genevieve

move numbly through the days, ignoring the sad, drawn faces and the quiet tears of the other women. My own grief is like a moat between us, only instead of being filled with water, it is filled with thorns and nettles and spikes.

It is unbreachable.

I also avoid the entire fourth floor of the palace, having no wish to encounter Margot's enraged soul as it lingers.

Count Angoulême sends for me twice, but I ignore the summonses, keeping mostly to my rooms, sneaking out only to exercise my body in the dark of the dungeons.

I do not visit the prisoner. He has seen me in my darkest hour, my guts spilled out onto the dungeon floor, more fully exposed than if I had paraded naked before a host of leering men. That he was deeply kind makes it all worse somehow. I did not ask him for such kindness and do not wish to be beholden to him because of it.

❧

It is hunger that finally drives me from my room. When I am certain that dinner is over and most of the kitchen staff have retired for the night, I go in search of food.

That is where Angoulême's steward finds me, pilfering cheese and bread from the larder. "My lady?"

I whirl around, stuffing the food into my pockets. "Master Gelais. You startled me."

"I am sorry, my lady. That was not my intent. Count Angoulême requests your presence in his office."

"I am not up to seeing him just now. Please send my sincere regrets."

The steward shifts on his feet, looking uncomfortable. "I am afraid refusing is not an option, demoiselle." His eyes are full of resolve, and for one ridiculous moment, I wonder if he will throw me over his shoulder and drag me to the count. I welcome the rush of anger that thought brings. But he is only the messenger. I will save my wrath for Angoulême.

When we reach the count's chamber, the steward opens the door, ushers me in, then closes it behind me.

Angoulême's study is in disarray. A travel pouch is open and filled with dispatches. Large maps lie on his desk, held in place with weights at each of the corners.

I curtsy. "My lord." My voice is colder than the winter sky. Surely he knows I hold him responsible for Margot's death. He cannot think to seek comfort with me, or worse, try to offer me such comfort. My grief is still raw and fresh and deeply colored by my anger at him. I square my shoulders. Let the count try to comfort me. I welcome the chance to cross swords with him and point out just how much this death falls on his shoulders.

He pushes the map aside and gives me his full attention. "Why have you refused my summonses?"

I stare at the floor in front of me. "Because I was mourning my sister, my lord."

"You're not the only one who grieves."

My head snaps up, angry words gathering on my tongue.

"She asked for you, you know," he continues. My heart — my heart does not know whether to leap for joy or dissolve in a fresh wave of sorrow. Why had no one told me? Fetched me to her side? "And yet you did not come."

I force my voice to steadiness. "What did you wish to speak to me about that had your steward threatening to drag me here?"

His lips flatten into a thin white line, and for a brief moment, I do not know what he will do. "I have been summoned to Langeais to attend the wedding of King Charles and Anne of Brittany. I must leave tomorrow and will be gone through Christmas."

My mind can scarce make sense of his words. How can the world continue as if nothing has happened?

"I should have left two days ago," he continues. "But I could not. Not with all that has happened."

I am filled with outrage that he thinks to dance at the king's wedding while his young mistress lies cold in a grave merely days old. "The abbess of Saint Mortain should be there. She often attends affairs of state. Will you tell her how Margot died?"

He looks away, reaching for the dispatches. "There has been a message from her."

"When? What does she say?"

He pulls a letter from his travel pouch, and my heart skitters nervously in my chest. Though I have waited for this very thing for five years, I am suddenly unsure I want to see it. "Under orders of the king and the Church . . ." Although he reads softly, his voice feels thunderous in the thickly charged air. "The convent of Saint Mortain has been ordered to disband."

The words crash into me, knocking me off my feet and shoving me into deep water where I cannot regain my footing. "I do not believe you." My voice sounds breathless. Desperate. "What reason would the duchess have to do such a thing?"

"I do not believe it was the duchess who was behind this decision. My guess is that the king's bishops used the opportunity to cluck in his ear about the old-world beliefs still practiced in Brittany and he acceded to their wishes in the matter."

My chest feels so tight I can scarce get the next words out. "What of the other Nine? Are their convents and abbeys to be disbanded as well?"

"I do not know, as I am not involved in those. And the king does not know

I am involved in this one either," he adds pointedly. "The letter from the abbess explains it all."

The impact of the news works its way into my limbs, and I begin to tremble. "But how am I to serve the convent?"

He looks down at his desk, but not before I see the pity in his eyes. "You aren't. The abbess has instructed me to be your permanent legal guardian."

Bile rises in my throat, hot and bitter.

This is not happening. *Cannot* be happening. My head begins to shake from side to side, an emphatic *no*. "They will not have so easily dismissed all my years of service. The abbess would call me back to the convent to give me this news herself."

He slams his hands on the desk, the sound of it cracking like a whip. "You foolish girl. She is protecting you! If she sent you a message, it would lead the Church fathers right to your door, and you would be subject to the same punishments that they will suffer." His voice softens. "They are trying to spare you that." He tosses the letter onto the desk between us. "See for yourself."

I stare at him a long moment before allowing my eyes to glance down to the parchment. I immediately recognize the black wax seal of the convent. That at least is real. For the first time, I consider that what he says might be true. If he has proof, then there is nothing left of my life. There is no place for me to go. I carefully unfold the sheet. The handwriting is elegant and graceful, and the missive is signed by the abbess. I force myself to read the words on the page.

They say exactly what the count has claimed.

"It is what will happen to all the initiates," Angoulême says in the face of my continued silence. "Suitable husbands will be found for most. Some might find their way to other convents, although more conventional ones under the Church's purview."

"What of the abbess? The nuns? Many are past marriageable age." In truth, most were flatly against marriage to any man.

He shrugs. "They are not my concern. You are."

I feel as if I will be sick. "What does that mean, exactly?"

"It means I am to arrange a suitable marriage for you."

His words are all the more upsetting for their sincerity. He truly believes he is doing what is best for me, and being gracious in the process. "But I have no wish to marry."

"Are you sure? There are any number of men among my court that would make a good husband, and your charms have not gone unnoticed, Genevieve. I will even let you pick."

His generosity is a surprise. I would have expected him to use this to his advantage. More than before, I am at his mercy. I must get out of here and find someplace to think through the full implications of this. "Thank you, but marriage was never something I aspired to."

He leans back in his chair and folds his arms. "Other arrangements can be made." The look in his eyes makes his meaning perfectly clear.

"No, my lord." My voice is not angry or bitter or defiant. "I will not follow in Margot's footsteps." I will not step into that snare.

Something in his manner shifts. "Am I so very repulsive? Have I not shown you kindness and a life of ease and luxury?"

That I do not want this life, that I do not want *him*, has wounded his pride.

"My lord, you already have many women who seek nothing more than to cater to your every desire. I cannot offer you anything they do not. And you yourself have said I am stubborn and contrary."

He smiles, a slow, unsettling gesture. "Perhaps that is why I desire you? I have never been with anyone as . . . contrary and stubborn as you, that is certain. You know I am fond of you." He leans forward, planting his elbows on the table, growing serious again. "I can grant you many things — safety, shelter, a home, a rich and luxurious life with no hardship."

He is utterly sincere, thinking he offers me my every wish on an engraved silver platter. "Thank you for your most gracious offer, my lord, but I shall pass."

There is a long moment of silence in which he studies me with an assessing quality that only increases my unease. "Genevieve, you should think long and hard about refusing my offer." He picks up his wine and takes a sip, drawing the moment out. "It is not like you have anywhere else to go."

His words so closely mirror Margot's that it is all I can do not to flinch. "I will find something, my lord." For all the tumult inside, my voice comes out firm and steady.

He sets the wine down abruptly. "Tell me, how do you think the regent would react to learning that your mother was a common tavern whore?"

His words are like an ax that cleaves the earth from my feet. Margot betrayed me.

At the convent, we were taught that our birth stories are among our most precious possessions. Each of our stories carried the history of how we came to be marqued for His service. They were sacred. And Margot told Angoulême. She betrayed my secrets. Bile fills my throat again, and this time I fear I will retch all over the count's fine carpet.

"So are you a whore, my dear?"

The word in his mouth is hard and ugly, and I want to snatch it from his tongue. He uses it to shame me, to shame my mother and my aunts, but they are not deserving of his — or anyone's — disdain.

It is the very reason I hold my family origins so close. Not because I am ashamed, but because I cannot bear the way the world sees them. Some long-forgotten part of me rises up and takes control of my body. I place one hand on the chair in front of me and wave the other in the air. "La, my lord! You know how fond Margot was of telling stories." The words skip nimbly off my tongue, as if that long-forgotten part of me knows precisely what to do.

He studies me for a moment, then stares down at the wine in his cup. "I wonder if this is one of her stories. It has the ring of truth in it to me."

I force all the fury I possess to burn away my fear till it is naught but a faint metallic tang in my belly. "Truly, my lord?" I fold my hands in front of me and tilt my head. "Is that why I have worked so hard to avoid your advances? Why I pray so fervently in the chapel twice a day? Is that what is behind my utter devotion to the countess? Not to mention the convent?"

He shrugs again, but there is a faint crease of doubt between his eyes.

"Margot was a great liar. We all know that."

He scowls. "She did not appear so to me."

"Is that because she told you she loved you?" I ask sweetly. "Ah, I see by your face that she did. Well, she did not. It was a lie. She grew to love this soft life rather than the convent and its purpose and became your mistress to advance her financial security and position."

He shoves his chair back, as if needing to put distance between himself and my words.

"Did she claim you were a fine lover as well? Another lie. She told me of your huffing and puffing, your soft belly and graying hairs." I lean forward confidentially. "Did she also tell you that you were her first lover? Yet another lie. He was a knight at Amboise. Young and firmly muscled, with shoulders so broad they nearly blocked out the sun. And his sword was as long and as skilled as they come." Each word I speak is like a blow, so that when I am finished, he will feel as if he has been pummeled into the wall behind him. "Besides, are not all women whores to you, my lord? And what of you? You sleep with every woman between fourteen and forty who crosses your path! What would you call that?"

He smiles thinly and without humor. "I am not paid to sleep with them."

"No? Did Louise not bring a pretty dowry to this marriage? Was that not required in order for you to consummate it? How is that different from what a whore charges?"

He slams both his palms on his desk and rises to his feet. "You forget yourself!"

I step forward and lean into his space, nearly pressing my nose against his. "No. *You* forget yourself. No matter who my mother was or was not, I was sired by the god of Death, and you will be wise to remember that." Without giving him a chance to respond — or mayhap I'm afraid I will reach across the desk and strangle him — I turn and stride toward the door.

"Stop!"

Out of habit, I obey, my hand poised above the latch as I look over my shoulder. He leans forward in his chair, his eyes hard. "You do know that the punishment for masquerading as nobility is death?"

I grit my teeth and turn to face him. "And who aided me in that masquerade, my lord? I wonder what the punishment for that would be?"

"I would tell them that you lied and deceived me as well."

"And I would produce this" — I wave the message from the convent — "to prove that I did not."

His nostrils are pinched white and his muscles bunched. For a moment I fear he will leap up from his chair and wrest it from my hands. But instead he shrugs. "It will not come to that. You have had a shock, especially on top of your recent loss." The pity in his voice makes me want to claw at his face. "I will not press you, but when I return after Christmas, I expect you to have come to terms with this new arrangement."

In answer, I yank open the door, step through it, and then slam it behind me so hard that the latch rattles in its case.

CHAPTER 26

y rage is a living beast, driving me down the corridor, my steps so heavy it is a wonder the stone does not crack beneath my feet.

Margot has betrayed me.

The *convent* has betrayed me.

In truth, even Mortain has betrayed me, or how else can all the roads I've taken, all the lessons I've learned, all the skills I've acquired, put me right back on a path that leads to my mother's life? One for which she sacrificed much so I would not have to share it.

It is the most twisted, cruel, ironic fate I can imagine, and I cannot decide who is most to blame.

Margot betrayed years of friendship and sisterhood in exchange for . . . what? A garnet necklace? A position as the count's favorite? A softer life? I do not believe her claim that the convent ordered her to do it. I cannot allow myself to believe it.

The memory of what the convent itself has just done surges up again, nearly choking me. This is not something I ever expected to feel again—the pain of having those I cared most for trade me away.

When I finally reach the safety of my room, I bolt the door firmly behind me before storming over to the one small window and shoving aside the curtains.

I hold the letter up to the weak sunlight and inspect it more closely. It is the official black wax, the correct seal. The handwriting looks right, although in truth, I have never seen the abbess's handwriting, so I would not recognize it. But it is her name, and the formal language used is much the way she would talk. There are no flaws or signs of forgery.

Besides, what would Angoulême gain by forging this? Eventually the convent would learn of it, and it would take a braver, bolder man than he to risk crossing those who worship Death.

Which means that this is what the convent truly wishes.

Rutting figs. They cannot do this to me. I will not let them. No one, not even Mortain Himself, gets to keep me on a leash for the rest of my life. Besides, if they have disbanded, how will they even enforce such an order?

This realization gives me room to breathe. And in that small space comes a second realization. Many fates hang in the balance. How many other girls — many younger than I — will find themselves in hastily arranged marriages that they have not chosen? And how many of them came to the convent precisely because they or their mothers wanted to avoid those marriages?

What will happen to Sister Beatriz, with her silly, pigeon-headed ideas of how to seduce a man? Not to mention ancient Claude and her aching joints, or Sister Vereda, the even older blind seeress. Where are they to go? No man would have them. Nor even one of the Christian convents.

For all that this letter enrages me about my own fate, it also spells disaster for the entire convent. All the emotions that have been threatening to boil over for the last three days distill down into a black, hardened mass. If they think to strike a bargain over my future without my consent or agreement, they have sorely misjudged me.

A knock at the door startles me out of my reverie. "Demoiselle Genevieve?" It is the steward. "The count has requested your presence at dinner, my lady. It is his last night here before he leaves."

My hands clench. I will not sit in the great hall pretending to be merry and joyful. I glance around me, looking for some excuse to send him away. But there is nothing.

He knocks on the door again. "Demoiselle? I know you are in there."

"I am sorry," I call out as my gaze lands on the washbasin. "I am ill."

There is a long pause. "I don't think the count will accept that. He is most insistent that you join him."

I grab the basin and move to stand near the door. "It is impossible." I stare at my fingers, take a deep breath, then jam one of them down my throat — a trick Sister Serafina taught me when I accidentally drank one of her potions instead of the tonic she had prepared for my cough.

I gag, but that is all. I shove again, this time farther down, and am relieved when my entire guts begin to turn themselves inside out. It is not a quiet thing.

"Oh." I can almost feel the steward back away from the door. "I will tell the count you are truly ill. Would you like something sent up? A broth, perhaps?"

"No thank you. I do not think I could keep anything down right now."

I heave and retch once more just to convince him, shuddering as I place the basin in a far corner of the room. If the count himself appears at my door, I will simply hand it to him and send him on his way.

Angoulême's peremptory summons crystallizes what I will do. Must do. *I am leaving*, I want to shout triumphantly at the steward's retreating footsteps.

The decision is as sure as an arrow finding its mark.

I do not know where I will go or how I will get there or what I will do when I arrive. Only that I will search out new choices for myself. Ones that do not involve the count or marriage or a room above a tavern.

I will be alone — out in the world without the protection of the convent or the patina of the French court. Or even a friend by my side.

No. I do not need friends. They are a heartbreak waiting to happen. That I would even wish for a friend after what Margot did to me proves I have let myself become soft — too comfortable.

That is the first thing I must fix.

CHAPTER 27

Sybella

The hardest part of the day's travels is remembering all the things I am no longer supposed to do now that I am headed for France. I do not ride up to the head of the line to speak with Beast, not even when we have to wait for nearly an hour while a felled tree is removed from the road.

I do not draw my weapons as we wait, or even finger my knives. I restrain myself from riding back to the litter to check on Louise and Charlotte and see how they are faring, although I wish to nearly every half hour. Most impressively, I refrain from drawing my weapons every time we pass a village and an entire flock of villagers comes rushing forward, eager to cheer their duchess and throw flower petals and small gifts in her path.

All things considered, it is far more exhausting than a full day of hard riding would have been. By the time we can see the thick stone towers of Châteaubriant castle jutting up against the sky, my soul is exhausted and my body restless.

We circle the moat that protects the outer wall until we come to the barbican, then pass through the tall, narrow space — barely wide enough for the largest of our wagons to fit. It is so narrow that it feels like a trap, and it is all I can do to keep my hands calmly on the reins.

Once we have crossed the bailey and are in the courtyard, the sensation passes.

But too soon. Standing on the castle step dressed in red velvet and a fur-lined cloak is the king's own sister, the regent herself, bane of Brittany's existence.

Unease skitters across my shoulders.

The regent's greeting is gracious and polite; she kisses the duchess upon each cheek. "Be welcome," she says with a pleasant smile.

The duchess returns her smile coolly. "Thank you for your hospitality, Madame Regent." The irony is not lost on her that the regent is welcoming her to one of Brittany's own castles that France's troops nearly destroyed in the Mad War.

"I believe you know my lord husband, the Duke of Bourbon?"

The Duke of Bourbon is soft-looking and somewhat chinless, which balances nicely with the regent. She has plenty of chin for them both. The duke takes the duchess's hand and bows over it. "Welcome, my dear." There is a true kindness in his face. His lack of artifice and his genuineness provide a stark contrast to his wife.

Beside the regent and the Duke of Bourbon stands another man. He is tall, although stooped and thin. His flesh hangs loosely off his face, as if he has been ill. Something about him feels familiar to me, although I cannot place it.

"And, Your Grace," the regent says, "you know well the Duke of Orléans."

Her words have me gaping like a fish, but the duchess's look of joy chases away my disbelief. If she feels the same shock I do at the change in his appearance, she hides it well.

It has been seven years since I saw him, but he has aged at least twenty. He was taller then, square-jawed and renowned for his prowess at hunting and jousting. Now he does not look as if he could manage to hold a lance with both hands.

After he had been captured in the final battle of the Mad War between France and the late duke of Brittany, rumors circulated that he was kept in a cage so small he could not stand and fed naught but bread and water for months on end. I had dismissed them. D'Orléans is next in line for the throne should anything happen to King Charles, and I could not believe either the regent or the king would treat a Prince of the Blood in such a way.

But I was wrong, and every word appears true. Next to him, the regent glitters like a bright red jewel in the falling dusk, and I am grateful she no longer considers the duchess her enemy.

The Duke and Duchess of Bourbon could not have provided a more gracious welcome. The light of a hundred candles sparkles brightly against the silver, gold, and crystal on the lavishly set table. The sideboards groan under the weight of roasts of beef and venison, the savory smell of fine herbs mingling with the sharp, fruity scent of wine.

Throughout it all, the duchess sits between the regent and the Duke of Orléans, talking happily with him, for they are old friends. There had even been rumors of a match between them, but there were too many obstacles, the primary one being Orléans's wife. She is sister to the regent and the king, and the French crown would have fought any attempt at an annulment. His presence is a welcome olive branch.

After a long but pleasant meal, we finally retire to our chambers. Before I have even begun to undress the duchess, there is a knock at the door. She sets her jaw firmly and squares her shoulders. "Enter," she calls out.

The door opens, and Madame Regent steps into the room, followed by the Duke of Bourbon, and the Duke of Orléans. She closes the door firmly behind her. "Your Grace, I trust your accommodations are to your liking."

"They are, Madame Regent."

My mind struggles to guess the purpose of their visit. The regent glances briefly in my direction. "Is there anyone else you wish to have with you?"

"No." The duchess's chin comes up a little higher, and a sense of dread begins seeping into the room. The sympathetic expression on the Duke of Bourbon's soft face adds to my unease.

"Your Grace?" I ask softly, hoping she will inform me what is going on.

The regent spares me a brief glance. "We are here for the premarital inspection. Out of courtesy for her rank and a desire to be tactful, we agreed to wait

until she'd left her own holding and conduct it here, but it *will* be conducted before the wedding can take place."

The force of my revulsion robs me of caution. "The legal contract has already been agreed to and signed," I protest. "Surely this is not necessary."

"This was stipulated in the contract," she answers coolly. "We must determine if she can produce an heir."

As if such things can be ascertained by a public examination. Outrage erupts, burning away the day's fledgling caution. "Did Madame have such an examination prior to her marriage?" My voice is polite and courteous, my words covered in the finest silk.

"Of course not. But it was not my duty to produce an heir for the kingdom." The sharpness in her tone gives me pause. The last thing I want to do is draw unwelcome attention to myself — especially from her.

She turns to the duchess, frowning. "This cannot be a surprise to you."

The duchess is pale, but maintains her regal composure. "No, but that does not make it any more palatable. And I was not expecting such a large audience."

Something ugly, like an eel slithering in the murk of a pond, darts across the regent's face. "There must be witnesses. The matter of an heir is far too important to leave to my judgment alone." Her eyes are overwide, her tone more self-deprecating than the comment warrants. I glance over at the Duke of Orléans, whose stoop is even more pronounced as he tries to make himself nearly invisible.

That is when my wits finally catch up. The regent, profoundly aware of the late duke of Brittany's hope to foster a union between these two, wishes to punish them for it.

Her revenge is so nuanced and diabolical I can scarce wrap my mind around it.

She will punish Orléans for daring to consider putting her sister aside ten years ago. It does not matter that when he was only fourteen, the old king vowed to cut off the heads of his advisors, sew him into a sack, and toss it into a river if he did not agree to the marriage. His mother finally gave in, but Orléans never agreed and has always claimed he was coerced.

The layers of humiliation the regent has woven together are truly astounding. With one brief action, she will remind Orléans of all that he can never have, punish the duchess for her father's grand ambition, and heap further humiliation on her.

By forcing Orléans to be complicit in this degradation, there is a very good chance that their fondness will turn to hate. Or at least mortification, thus forcing a permanent wedge between them. Even though any chance of them marrying has long since passed, the regent is now ensuring they will never be allies, or even comfortable with each other, ever again. These few minutes will bear bitter fruit for years to come, and all out of the regent's spite.

"Now," she continues, "the sooner we do this, the sooner it will be behind you. Disrobe, please."

I clench my fists in frustration. Where are the duchess's great protectors from the Privy Council now? "At least let us stoke up the fire and have a robe ready," I suggest. "Unless it is your goal to have Her Grace catch an ague, rather than simply force her to parade naked before strangers."

For the first time since entering the room, the regent turns her full attention on me. *Careful*, I warn myself. Up until this point, I have been naught but a piece of furniture. The duchess reaches out and gently touches my arm. "That is a good idea to stoke the fire," she says. "It has grown cold in here."

I seethe across the room to the large fireplace, grab the poker, and stab at the lazily burning logs until they erupt into orange and yellow flames. My feeling of helplessness grows as I fetch the duchess's fur-lined robe from the large chest and lay it on the bed.

When I return to the duchess, she presents her back to me. Her grim determination is coupled with a sense of embarrassment so great it borders on shame.

She does not have the emotional armor to protect herself from this vile woman's devious machinations, but I do. I was raised in precisely such a nest of diabolical vipers. I can draw some of the sting from this wound the regent is trying to inflict.

Although by protecting the duchess, I risk alienating the regent. She is not an enemy I or my sisters can afford.

But to truly honor the vow I made to her, I must I lend her my armor until she forms her own. To do otherwise reeks too much of craven self-servitude. I lean in close to the duchess. "It will help if you picture them naked," I whisper as I unlace her bodice.

She emits a muffled gasp. Encouraged, I lower my voice further. "And," I add as I slip her gown from her shoulders, "I believe the Duke of Bourbon's doublet is padded to make his chest appear larger than his belly."

She says nothing, but the corner of her mouth lifts.

When there is finally a ghost of a smile on her face, I pull the linen under-gown over her head so that she stands completely naked in front of these strangers. But at least she is thinking of their nakedness instead of her own.

"She is small," the Duke of Bourbon suggests, almost apologetically. "But soundly built."

"It is the width of her hips that most concerns me," the regent replies, tilting her head. "Turn around, if you please."

To keep from saying something foolish, I grab the duchess's robe from the bed, nearly crushing it in my fingers.

Keeping her eyes straight ahead, the duchess does as instructed.

"Wait. What was that? Did she limp?"

"Yes," the duchess says. "My shoes are made to hide the fact, but it is no secret."

I put my finger to my chin and make as if studying the matter. "Is the length of one's legs known to facilitate breeding?"

The regent casts a cool gaze upon me. "Who are you?"

I sink into a deep curtsy. "Lady Sybella, Madame."

Her attention remains on me a moment longer before she turns back to the duchess. "It is important that no flaws pass to the king's heir."

I press my teeth into my tongue to keep from pointing out that the king's other sister has precisely this type of limp — although from all accounts that is only one of her ailments. It is why the match with Orléans was so devious. By marrying him to a daughter whose afflictions rendered her unable to bear children, the king could ensure the crown had no challenge from the Orléans branch.

The regent orders the duchess to walk to the far wall. With a surprising degree of composure and grace, the duchess begins to traverse the room.

Everyone's eyes are on her: Bourbon's are soft and compassionate. Orléans's are full of apologies, regret, and a desire to be anywhere but here. But the regent's — ah, they are not only cool and assessing, but gleaming with triumph as well.

My hand longs to smack that triumph from her face. I do not want to merely shield the duchess, but to brandish a sword on her behalf. I close my eyes and remind myself of all the reasons I should not. But when I open them again, all I can see is the duchess, head raised proudly, cheeks pink with shame, eyes bright with unshed tears.

I direct a sweet, bland smile to the regent. "Perhaps when she's finished parading before you, you'd like to examine her teeth," I suggest. "I know our master of horse always insisted on seeing those before adding any new additions to our stable."

The regent sends a basilisk glare at me that would turn a lesser woman to stone, and the Duke of Bourbon's chin recedes even further. But I do not so much as flinch. Still staring at me, the regent addresses her words to the duchess. "You may come back now."

I tilt my head and crease my brow with concern. "Tell me, has the king had such an examination?"

Someone — the Duke of Bourbon? — swallows a gasp. The vein in the regent's temple pulses slightly. "Your suggested criticism of the king flirts dangerously close to treason, mademoiselle."

Because I want to spit my words at her like stones, I keep my voice soft and respectful. "On the contrary, Madame. Like you, I wish only the best for the crown of France."

Her nostrils flare in irritation, and I experience a moment of grim satisfaction.

The Duke of Orléans speaks into the tense silence. "I think Her Grace may put her clothes back on now," he says.

Throwing him a grateful look, I step forward and drape the thick robe around the duchess's shoulders, pulling it tightly closed. She is shaking. Although I do not think it is from cold, I draw her near to the fire all the same.

"Have you gotten all that you came for?" I ask.

The regent's lips thin, whether at my implied dismissal or the suggestion that she had complex and ugly motives for this visit, I cannot tell.

"Her Grace is exhausted after her long day's travel," I continue. "If you have everything you need, I would like to see to her comfort."

"I believe everything is in order." The regent's voice is stiff and formal. "We will proceed with the wedding." She turns a disapproving eye to me before nodding at her husband to open the door. As they file out of the room, she pauses. "I am afraid I will not be here in the morning to see you off. There are still many pressing preparations to be made for this most joyous occasion." Her smile of delight is so perfectly performed that I would have believed her with all my heart if not for the last hand span of minutes. "However, there will be an escort of the king's guard to accompany you."

"But of course, Madame Regent," the duchess says. "We can see to ourselves from here. Thank you for your hospitality." She meets the older woman's gaze blandly, disconcerting her, I think.

"Stupid sow," I mutter, once they have all left.

"Lady Sybella!" The duchess's shock is tempered by the illicit thrill in her voice.

I remove her cloak from her shoulders and slip her nightgown over her head. "You are too polite, Your Grace, to ever think or say such things, so as your loyal attendant it is my duty to say them for you."

Her mouth turns up in a reluctant grin. "Your devotion to your obligations is duly noted." Then her formality falls away and she gapes at me like a young girl. "Truly, I have never seen anyone so bold! By my count, you bested her in that exchange at least twice."

"Three times," I correct her, twitching the delicate linen into place around her hips.

She turns around to face me, her expression serious. "But please, do not put yourself in harm's way on my account. If the regent were to take a dislike to you—"

"I think we can safely assume that she has," I say dryly.

"She might encourage me to remove you from my service. Who would cheer me through such travails then? Not that she would succeed," she hastens to add. "I would just prefer to have as few battles with her as possible."

"Forgive me, Your Grace. I did not—"

"Hush." The duchess grabs my hand. "I could not have survived the ordeal if not for your barbed wit. I just wish you to have a care for yourself, that is all."

It is too late for that, I want to tell her. I have drawn both the regent's attention and her ire, and she is not the sort of woman to forget such a thing.

CHAPTER 28

Genevieve

hen I return to the oubliette, I bear not only food, but a plan. If I do not feed the prisoner, he will die, and I am not ready to consign him to that fate. But the secrets I once shared with him in the dark make the edges of my skin curdle with embarrassment. I may as well have left a weapon out in the open and expected no one to use it. I took all those risks, but got nothing out of it. That is about to change. The prisoner will have to earn his keep.

I come in a series of trips, hauling buckets of water, a hook, and extra torches. I also bring a clean set of clothes that I pilfered from one of Angoulême's men-at-arms, leaving a small coin where his pile of clothes had been.

When I have finished all my hauling, I set one of the torches in a bracket on the wall.

"Who's there?" The haunted quality is back in his voice, and I realize I have not visited — or fed him — in over four days.

I grit my teeth. I owe him nothing. I yank open the latch, then hoist the grate open, its rusty hinges screeching like a wounded hawk.

"Water," I call down, lowering the bucket.

"It is *you*. I have been worr —"

"The water is for washing." My voice is harder than the iron bars of his prison. "Once you are clean, there are new clothes." Making an unnecessary amount of clatter so that further speech is impossible, I lower the other bucket, along with the bundle of clothes and a sack of food.

In the thick silence that follows, I feel him observing me through the darkness. After a moment, he begins to rummage through the bundles. A faint shout of triumph that sounds vaguely like the word "Soap!" is accompanied by the splash of water.

Even though I cannot see a thing, I shove to my feet and walk a dozen paces away. I am not squeamish about naked men, but nor do I want to foster the sense of intimacy of sharing a bath.

As he washes, I light one of the extra torches and explore the six rooms that branch off the main antechamber. Two of them have locks with keys and are empty except for a wooden bucket and a thin mattress of straw. The others contain barrels of oil and wine, vats of tallow, furs and antlers from some long-forgotten hunt, old benches, wall hangings, suits of armor, and moth-eaten rugs no longer being used; I quickly lose interest.

As I pace, I run my hands over the weapons I have brought. I have Margot's stiletto, in addition to my own dagger and a short sword a passing man-at-arms traded me for a kiss. Such a mutton-headed trade on his part. Although I suspect he was hoping for more than a kiss.

When enough time has passed, I return to the oubliette. "I am coming down now." I light the third torch and prop it carefully next to the opening. Then I knot the rope at the base of the grate, grab ahold of it, and lower myself into the pit, careful to avoid the flame from the torch.

At first, the opening is narrow enough that I am able to brace my feet against the opposite wall, but it quickly opens up into a larger space so that I am forced to wrap my feet around the rope.

The light from the torch does only a feeble job of illuminating the murk. The oubliette is small, with barely enough room for two people to stand with their arms spread. Even though it is so dark I must squint to see into the corners of the room, the prisoner holds one arm across his eyes, protecting them from the dim light. The lower half of his face sports a matted beard. Behind him is a pile of old, moldy straw and in the far corner is a hole. They have not given him so much as a pot to piss in.

When my feet reach the solidness of the stone floor, I let go of the rope and slip my fingers around the hilt of my knife, although I keep it hidden in the folds of my skirts.

The prisoner is tall, and while thin from lack of food, his shoulders are broad. His exercises and diet of rat have paid off.

Slowly, hesitatingly, he pulls his arm a few inches from his face. His eyes are still braced against the light, but I get my first look at him. His hair is long and wet from its recent washing. The beard obscures the shape of his mouth and set of his chin, but his nose is straight and not overly large.

When his eyes finally adjust, we study each other warily. "So you are the voice in the dark." There is a note of reverence in his words that I do not deserve. "I wondered what you would look like. Wondered if you were even attached to a body."

I lift my chin, my face cold and wooden. "I do not know what you are talking about, but you are wrong. I have never been here before." My voice is as hard as the stone walls that surround us. "Whatever you thought you saw or imagined you heard was likely the product of a mind enfeebled by long captivity. Imprisonment will do that to a man."

The scowl that appears on his face gives him a wild, animal quality. "Surely my enfeebled mind did not produce the food that sustained me for these last weeks. Nor the water, nor the voice that pulled me from the brink of madness."

I steel my heart against his angry confusion. If his wits are fraying at the edges, his memory will be easy to manipulate. "Perhaps your jailors brought you the food, or you simply ate rotted straw and skinny rats and thought them a feast. I know not, but you and I have never met before." As far as I am concerned, our past conversations never happened. Our secrets were never shared. No bond was ever formed. If he cannot accept this most basic truth, we have nothing further to talk about. I stare at him with all the iron I have in me.

He stares back, and I realize he possesses a fair amount of iron of his own.

He looks up at the grate, then back down at his small prison, scanning the whole of it before returning his gaze to me. The faint light from the torch does not reach his eyes.

"If you cannot tell truth from fantasy, there is no point in talking," I say.

"But of course. You are correct. Forgive my mistake."

"I am glad we understand each other. Now tell me why you are in here." My fingers tighten around the handle of my knife. Before we go any further, I must know how dangerous he is.

"Because I fought for the losing side."

"Which side was that?"

"Brittany's."

"That cannot be the whole of it. Not everyone who fought on Brittany's side has been thrown down a hole to rot away in oblivion."

"No," he agrees. "Some were slain on the battlefield."

"You mean killed in battle?"

He adjusts his sleeves. "Yes, that is what I mean."

"Why are you here? Did you commit some atrocity?"

His entire face hardens. "There were many atrocities on the battlefield, but none were committed by me."

"Would you tell me if you had?"

He does not move, but it feels as if he takes a step toward me. "If I were given to atrocities, I would already have overpowered you, strangled you with your rope, and be halfway to . . . Where did you say we are?"

"I didn't." I pull the knife from the folds of my skirt so it is visible.

His eyes shift to my blade. "But, since I am not given to atrocities, I have done none of those things. Besides, I would never cause harm to one who has brought me more comfort and kindness —" He shuts his mouth abruptly, remembering my condition. "Forgive my blabbering, demoiselle."

He learns quickly. I nod in approval. "Now that we are clear, I have a proposition for you." Even though he does not move, I can feel his interest deepen. "I need a sparring partner."

A single harsh croak emerges from his throat. At first I think he is laughing at me, until I recognize he is coughing. To be certain, I point my knife directly at him for the first time. "I will not be laughed at, and certainly not by a sack of bones that is little more than rat bait."

"I was not laughing. It is wretchedly damp in here, and my lungs do not like it. Even so, you must admit it is not every day that a prisoner in an oubliette receives such an offer."

"You are mocking me."

"I am mocking the circumstances in which I find myself. It is certainly the most novel proposition I have ever received from a woman." He folds his arms, studying me in earnest now, taking in my height and the breadth of my shoulders. "So you wish me to teach you swordplay?"

Figs! Are all men truly so lack-witted? "No." In one fluid motion, I retrieve the short sword strapped to my back, whip it forward in a figure eight so that the point of it nicks the back of his right hand, then his left, before coming to rest in the hollow of his throat. "I need someone to spar with."

He eyes the sword. "Clearly, I misunderstood." His manner sharpens with intrigue and . . . mayhap even admiration. "If I do as you ask, will you help me escape?"

Finally he is ready to negotiate. "No, that is not part of the proposition."

He shrugs and begins to turn away, but I know a bargaining tactic when I see it. "You assume that I have the power to give you what you want. I do not."

He tilts his head, studying me. "Who are you that you are allowed access to swords and freedom to roam the dungeons at whim, yet do not have the means to help me escape?"

I smile without humor. "I have a unique position within the household."

He turns his gaze back to my sword, appraising, coveting.

"You will not be given a true sword." I am not so stupid as to hand a battle-scarred prisoner, even one so weakened as he, a real sword and pray that he will not skewer me with it. "But a wooden practice one from the garrison."

"And if I refuse?"

I shrug. "I will leave and not come back. You will have had a bath and some food for your trouble and may return to your slow and tedious dying." My words are harsh and bleak, but they are also the truth. I have nothing else to offer him. Giving him his freedom would put me at even greater risk and gain me nothing. Besides, I have no true knowledge of who he is or whether he is even safe to let loose upon the countryside. This is the limit of my trade. "What have you to lose? You have been thrown down here to rot, forgotten by all except those who are just cruel enough to taunt you with the promise of life."

"Is that not what you're doing?"

His words catch me off-guard. "No! I am giving you a chance, buying you some time. What you will be able to purchase with it, I cannot say."

He looks down at his hands, clenching them, then opening them again. I raise the tip of my sword in case he is considering trying to strangle me.

When finally he looks up to meet my gaze, he gives a single nod. "When you return, bring the wooden sword as well."

CHAPTER 29

Sybella

wo days later, every one of my senses is still on alert, fully expecting the regent to slither out from under some nearby rock despite her claims that she would ride on ahead of us.

But she does not.

I still cannot decide if her actions were in retaliation for the abandoned plan between the Dukes of Brittany and Orléans to set aside her sister, or the opening salvo of a larger, broadscale attack. And is the attack directed at the duchess, or at a potential alliance between her and the Duke of Orléans?

"What is gnawing at you this morning?" Aeva steers her horse alongside mine. While she appears casual enough, the depth of her scrutiny is unsettling.

I glance about to make certain no one else can hear, then quietly tell her of the regent's visit to the duchess's chambers. When I have finished, she gives a disgusted toss of her head. "Women like her are worse than the men they serve. They cling hardest to the very rules that cage them, ruthlessly ensuring that all other women are equally trapped."

Her words ring true. D'Albret's fifth wife was much the same way — more vigilant than d'Albret himself in restricting the women of his household. Especially his daughters.

"A pox on all of them," I mutter.

A shout rings out from the front of the line. *The regent* is my first thought, even though I know it unlikely. I crane my neck, trying to peer through the rows of horsemen to see what is happening.

We are in a gently sloping valley where two riverlets run nearly side by side. Captain Dunois and the French guards in the vanguard have just reached the first bridge. The rest of our party is strung along the road like a trail of goslings: the mounted councilors, including the duchess, who rides pillion with Chancellor Montauban, followed by Beast and the queen's guard, the litters, the priests on their mules, and the baggage train lagging behind.

A copse of trees perches atop the ridge like a dark green crown. The riverlets are swollen with the recent rains, and the sound of their gentle rushing fills the valley, accompanied by the creak of leather harness, the jingle of tack, and the low hum of voices. Nothing appears out of place. Just as I wonder if one of the soldiers fell from the bridge into the river, there is a second shout. Captain Dunois pulls hard on his reins and stands up in his stirrups.

My heart kicks into a gallop as I turn to scan the fields on either side of us, but there is no sign of attack. The trees on top of the slope are far enough away that no arrow could reach us.

Even so, my muscles tense, readying for something I cannot yet see. I press my knees to my horse, urging him forward. Beast, too, has broken from the line and is riding around the others toward the first bridge.

I kick my horse into a canter, trying to catch up to Beast when a third, louder, shout goes up. Captain Dunois places his right hand on his chest and plummets from his horse.

There is a brief moment of stillness, as if we are a tableau frozen by an unexpected winter frost.

Beast wheels his horse around. "To the duchess!" he shouts.

Riding hard for the bridge, I glance over my shoulder to see the queen's guard draw into a tight, fortifying circle around Chancellor Montauban and the duchess. The Prince of Orange and Jean de Rieux draw their swords as well.

My eyes scan the nearby trees again, but no arrows rain down on us, no horses or foot soldiers emerge.

Then I am at the bridge. I leap off my horse, toss my reins to the nearest knight, and break into a run. My feet thud on the wooden planks, nearly drowning out the sound of Dunois's heartbeat.

It is slow, fluttering, erratic.

No. *No, no, no.*

When I finally reach him, I drop to my knees. His face is pallid, his skin leaden, but his heart — his brave, determined heart — still beats.

I reach up and loosen the gorget at his neck in order to ease his breathing. His eyes are open, but unfocused, staring at the sky above him. "Captain?" My hands gently search for a dagger or dart, anything that might have struck him, but they find nothing.

"*My lord?*"

He blinks and turns his head toward me even as his eyes remain focused on the sky above him. He opens his mouth, but nothing comes out.

"What is wrong?" Panic seeps out around my words.

He grunts, and I cannot tell if it is a word or simply an expression of pain. His mouth twists, trying to open, and I lean closer.

"Look." The word tumbles out with a labored breath.

He tries again. "Look . . . to . . . cas . . . tle."

I tighten my hand on his shoulder. "We will get you to the castle right away. Their doctors will be able to take care of you." I motion for the two nearest soldiers to come help. With an uncertain glance at each other, they begin to dismount.

Captain Dunois grunts again, and I turn back to him. His eyes are closed, and he shakes his head in frustration. "Cas . . . sle." The words are little more than a sigh. My own frustration mounting, I place my ear closer to his lips. "What?"

But this time all that escapes is an exhalation of breath. Close on its heels comes a dizzying rush, a jumble of sensations and images — his soul.

A silent wail of despair rises up inside me, but before I can give voice to it, his soul latches on to mine, and I gasp. I am filled with pain. So much pain. His soul is confused by it, his thoughts fractured and incoherent. Like a ribbon being pulled through my fingers, his soul leaves his mortal body.

Dunois's pain is replaced by my own, as if a sharp blade has just scraped out the insides of my heart.

That is when the attack comes.

CHAPTER 30

am still bowed over Captain Dunois when shouts erupt all around us and bodies begin clambering up the wooden rail.

The bridge, I realize stupidly, rising to my feet. They were hiding under the bridge.

They picked their moment well — our train is strung out between the two bridges, and we are distracted by the death of one of our own. As scores of men continue to swarm over the side, the French soldiers assigned by the regent draw their weapons, moving to protect me.

But I do not need their protection. I reach for Ismae's crossbow, slap a bolt into place, and face our enemies.

The crossbow takes out three in a row, surprising the French soldiers as much as the ambushers. "Look to yourself!" I shout, racing to the end of the bridge where my horse waits. Two more attackers come over the side of the bridge and block my path.

With no time to reload, I snatch my knives from my wrists and charge. The first man is still blinking in surprise when I slit his throat. As I spin toward the second man, he is ready for me. Or thinks he is. When he brings his sword up to strike, I duck in low and slam my foot into his knee, snapping it. His leg crumples under him, and I shove my knife deep into his gut, thrusting upward to hasten his death before yanking my blade back out.

I take a step toward the next attacker, stumbling when I must brace myself against the rush of dying souls. Like bright candle flames, they flare briefly, then dim. Some of them head for me, but I have many years hard practice and erect my barriers.

The barriers hold. I can feel the souls, but with my mind shut tight and my heart closed, it is merely like riding through a flock of birds too dumb to fly out of the way.

I run for my horse. She shies but does not bolt. Grabbing ahold of the saddle, I haul myself up, then wheel around to join Beast and the others.

The attackers — there must be fifty of them at least — have raised a blockade, trapping the rear guard on the second bridge along with the litter, leaving only the queen's guard, a score of noblemen, and myself with the duchess.

From behind, more shouts go up, and I glance over my shoulder. Another fifty or so armed men emerge from the trees along the hilltop, swords, pikes, and lances drawn as they rush down the slope toward us.

Merde. There are but thirty of us here to defend the duchess, fifty attackers from the under the bridge, and now this onslaught. My heart sinks.

My gaze searches out Beast. He nods— in encouragement? farewell? — and calls his men to him, the battle fever already filling his eyes with its strange unholy light. Fighting side by side has always felt like an exciting adventure, one that is eagerly greeted. But each time grows harder— especially with so many we care about at stake.

He leaves half the men to guard the duchess and takes the rest with him to repel the second advance. As they gallop up the hill toward the enemy, he gives a bloodcurdling battle cry. The sound of it hangs in the air like a storm cloud before it bursts. Battle-ax in his left hand, sword in his right, he rides straight for the descending soldiers. Captain Lannion pauses long enough to toss me his crossbow before hurrying to catch up to the others.

Once before I stood and watched as Beast took on an army with naught but a handful of men. I cannot do it again. Even those blessed by Saint Camulos are only so lucky.

Besides, the first wave of assailants has cleared the bridge and is upon us. Our one advantage is that we are mounted, but the pikes and halberds will quickly neutralize even that small boon. There is a deafening clash of steel on the hill behind me. I turn from it and focus on the enemy in front of me.

We form two circles around the duchess with the most skilled swordsmen

closest to her to defend against any that breach the outer defense. Aeva and I are part of that, as our bows are more useful at that range.

But Lannion's crossbow has only a dozen bolts.

Even so, I make good use of them.

I shoot the foremost pikeman in the middle of his forehead, reload, and aim for the next. I catch him in the throat, but another man is just behind him. As I frantically reload, a black arrow pierces his chest. Aeva. The deafening clash of steel and soldiers' shouts are joined by the twang of Aeva's bows as she fires off a series of arrows in such quick succession that she takes out three men before I can reload my next bolt.

The valley is awash with frantic racing heartbeats. So many of them! It is like being pelted by a hailstorm.

I glance over at Beast, leading the charge up the hill, his ax and sword cutting through the descending infantry like the bow of a ship cuts through waves.

Between Lannion's crossbow and Aeva's arrows, we are able to thin the number of men the guards must fight by hand. When I am nearly out of bolts, I reach for the rondelles tucked inside my belt. With a flick of my wrist, I send one sailing through the air. It strikes one of the pikesmen just under his jaw, the impact snapping his head back.

The second rondelle goes wide, taking off the ear of its target. The man hesitates, lowering his halberd and giving Châlons enough time to run him through with his sword.

I pause, breathing hard. Châlons is spattered with blood, but unhurt. He nods his thanks. "It helps that they want to take her alive," he says before diving back into the fray.

The sounds of fighting on the hillside have dimmed somewhat. Bracing myself, I look over to see Beast standing in his stirrups, still swinging his ax. His sword is nowhere to be seen.

Men lie all around him like red leaves from an autumn tree.

The attackers — the few that are left, gallop up the hill, Captain Lannion leading a half dozen men in pursuit. I hold my breath, waiting to see if they will ride them down or capture them for questioning.

Just as the attackers crest the hilltop, a score of archers step into view, bows drawn. The pursued men slip in behind the archers just as they release their arrows.

"No!" Beast's bellow of agony echoes through the small valley as Captain Lannion and his men take the full brunt of the volley. Lannion takes three in the chest, the force of them knocking him from his horse.

Instead of advancing farther, the archers withdraw behind the trees. Beast plucks one of the arrows from his arm and continues up the hill. Does he think to take them all on single-handed? Even a man in the throes of battle fever cannot hold against twenty archers.

Alone on the hill, he is also an excellent target. I check to ensure the duchess is no longer in danger, then wheel my horse around so I can lend Beast some cover.

That is when I see what is happening on the second bridge.

Another group of assailants is climbing up the side. A second wave? No, I realize with foreboding. A small, select force. It is headed for the litter.

Merde. Louise and Charlotte and Tephanie have only Tola to protect them.

"Beast!" My bellow echoes throughout the valley, piercing through the din of the battle. He pauses, jerking his head in my direction. "The litter!" I point toward the bridge.

He comprehends immediately. Wheeling his horse around, he races back down the hill. Not sure he will make it in time, I turn my mount toward the bridge and break into a gallop.

There are ten—no, fifteen men crawling up the sides of the bridge. Their absolute silence sends prickles down my spine.

I use Lannion's last bolts to take out the two closest to the bridge. Aeva draws up alongside me and fires her bow at the next two. "I am out of arrows," I tell her.

"It is a good thing we have knives." The grin she gives me is nearly as feral as any of Beast's. Together we charge toward the blockade.

However, if we are to use knives, we will need to get closer. When we reach the bridge, we quickly dismount.

My knife greets the first man over the railing. As Aeva's long curved blade meets the second, an arrow flies out of the litter, catching the third man in the chest and knocking him off the bridge.

Thunderous hooves clatter along the stone shore of the river, followed by a furious splash as Beast plunges into the water. The attackers are strung along the bridge railing like so many rats climbing a wall. Rising up in his stirrups, Beast begins hacking with his ax. Within seconds, the water is churning with blood and bodies.

Six have gained the bridge, safe from Beast's attack. But not safe from me. I smile. As I'd hoped, it unnerves them. Then I stop thinking and simply launch forward, giving myself over to the dark instincts that flow through my limbs as strong and sure as the river below. Every move is swift and sure, not requiring conscious thought but simply doing what I was fashioned by my god to do. That I can still feel his grace in this fills me with joy.

When the cool darkness finally pulls back, I become aware that it is quiet now, except for the rushing sound of the water beneath the bridge and the beating of hearts. I blink. All the attackers are dead, strewn about like broken dolls. Beast stands nearby, breathing hard, ax still in his hand. The river has washed away most of the blood that covered him.

Around us, burghers and courtiers, soldiers and baggage handlers, stare, their eyes wide, mouths agape. One man crosses himself, and another. Some fall to their knees, hands clasped before them, heads bowed.

Uncomfortable with their thanks, I turn my attention to Beast. "How badly are you hurt?" It is all I can do not to go to him and begin tending his wounds.

He frowns at the arrow protruding from his thigh before plucking it out and tossing it into the river. "Naught but a pinprick." He grins, then sobers. "And you?"

I hold out my arms from my sides so he may see. "I am fine."

"Good. I must check on my men to see to the wounded and claim my dead."

"Do we know who they were?"

He shakes his head. "Not yet."

As he heads toward the main group, I wipe my face with the hem of my underskirt, then pick my way among the fallen to the litter.

Inside, Charlotte and Louise are on the floor with Tephanie lying on top of them like a shield. Tola holds her bow, cocked and ready to fire, scanning the horizon for any stragglers. The duchess's attendant, Heloise, grimly faces the other window, a knife in each hand. When she sees it is only me, she lowers her weapons. "Is it over?"

"Yes," I tell her. "The attack has been repelled and the last of the stragglers rounded up."

She nods. "If you don't mind, I would like to go see if I can help with our wounded."

It takes me a moment to remember she serves Brigantia. "I am certain they will be glad of your help."

When Tola hears my report, she lowers her bow and grins. "Well, that was a lot of excitement for one day."

For one brief moment, her fierce joy in the thrill of the fight causes me to forget the pain of Captain Dunois before it closes over me again like a wave over a drowning man.

"Yes, it was. Tephanie?" I ask softly. "Are you all right?"

She looks up, her face sagging in relief. "Is it over, my lady?"

"Yes, sweet Tephanie. It is. You and the girls are safe." When she still seems afraid to move, I continue, "And you may stop sitting on the girls as if they were eggs to be hatched."

That surprises a smile out of her. As she pulls herself up onto the seat, I reach out and grasp her in a fierce hug. "Thank you," I whisper in her ear. "For protecting them with your life."

Blushing, she straightens her cap and skirts. "Louise? Charlotte?" My voice is gentle, coaxing. "It is all right. You may come out now."

Charlotte springs up quickly, straightening her gown and scowling at Tephanie. "You were squashing me."

"She was shielding you with her own body to keep you safe." I motion toward one of the many arrows embedded in the side of the litter. "You owe her your life and your thanks."

Charlotte stares at me a moment, before sighing. "Thank you, Lady Tephanie, for protecting me. Although next time, perhaps you could avoid having stones for breakfast so you will not be so heavy."

My hand itches to slap her. Instead, I pull the arrow from the wall of the litter and hand it to her. "Here. Keep this in remembrance of the woman who loved you enough to save your life, even when you gave her so little reason to do so." I am pleased to see her cheeks redden with shame. Pleased to know she can still feel it. "Now, if you will have a seat over there, I would like to see to Louise."

The younger girl is still hugging the floor, her eyes tightly closed. "Louise, sweeting. I am here. Everything is all right now."

She says nothing but rocks harder and hums louder.

"Louise, come here." I reach into the awkward space and try to pull her up.

"Are you certain they are gone?" Her words, directed at the floor of the litter, come out high-pitched and wobbly.

"Yes, dearest. I am sure." I manage to get a solid enough hold on her that I can pull her up into my lap. Once there, she wraps her arms around my neck and presses her face against me. I rock her back and forth, murmuring comforting words in her ear. After a long while, she finally pulls back and looks at me. "Tola is very good with her bow," she says.

"She is."

Louise is quiet for another long moment. "And Tephanie was very brave."

"I knew she would be."

"Even so," Louise continues, "I think I should like to learn how to use a bow too."

"I think that would be a most excellent idea." I laugh and hug her tight. "Now that I know you all are safe, I have duties I must see to. Not all were as fortunate as us, and I must see what I can do to help."

As is often the way with children, they recover their equanimity quickly, due in large part to Tephanie and Tola's staunch presence.

With another round of hugs and kisses from Louise, and a grudging allowance of a hug from Charlotte, I clamber out of the litter and return to my horse. Our men have lowered the barricade blocking the bridge, and one of them hands me my reins.

With souls lingering in the air like a swarm of drunken butterflies, I decide I might as well see if I can use them to learn who was behind the ambush. I plant my feet firmly in the ground, then open the floodgate.

It is like being ambushed all over again. I am assailed by dozens upon dozens of images and sensations. Pain. So much pain. And anger. And surprise that they have fallen. The next wave is of memories, final thoughts, and regrets. All the small sad stories these men carried with them into battle. A brief remembered pleasure of last night's tupping. Regret over an argument with a friend. A lost dicing game. A wine jug not finished. Some fleeting image catches my attention and I turn my head, trying to better focus on it. A gloved hand holding out a thin sack of coins. A brief flash of the gold and blue of the house d'Albret, and then it is gone.

My eyes jerk open, and I stare out at the field, wondering which fallen soldier these memories come from. But there are dozens of them. The sun is dipping low in the sky, and there is not time to comb through every soul that still lingers. Further, how can I be certain it is a recent memory rather than one from a year ago, when most of these men were likely being paid by Brittany and her allies to fend off the French? It could well be a coincidence — for even Pierre would not risk incurring the wrath of the king of France.

Even so, my hands are shaking and I feel sick inside as I carefully re-erect my mental shields once more.

CHAPTER 31

Genevieve

hen I arrive for our first sparring session, I do not call out a greeting, but let the glow of the torch and the sliding of the bolt announce my presence. With a sack over one shoulder and my knife within my reach, I begin lowering myself down the rope. I descend more cautiously than the first time, mindful of how glibly the prisoner discussed overpowering me, not wanting to give him any such openings.

In the dim light thrown down by the burning torch, I see him waiting a respectful distance away, hands easy at his sides. Good. He is aware of the trust I am placing in him and wants me to know he respects it. "I have brought food and practice weapons." My voice is gruff. "Which would you prefer first?"

"The weapons." His hunger is no small thing, and I cannot help but be impressed by his discipline.

"Very well." I set the bag of food on the floor against the wall behind me, remove the two swords strapped to my back, and hand the wooden one to him. "I have chosen short swords, given the confines of our practice area."

The prisoner balances the wooden sword on his palm, testing the weight and heft of it. Without warning, he grabs the hilt and thrusts it at me, a sharp, quick lunge that I only barely block in time. But block it I do. In spite of my irritation, my heart sings. He has not been imprisoned for so long that he will not be of any use to me. "That was unfair."

He tugs his sleeves down. "But a good way to test your reflexes. You have used a sword before."

"I told you I had."

"True, but you also told me things that made me feel I needed to verify your claim for myself." Before I can warn him that his remark flirts with forbidden subjects, he raises his sword and executes a series of blows, shifting so that he comes at me from alternating sides. For a moment, it is all I can do to meet his attack.

"Why are you still alive if you are only a mercenary?" I am finally able to ask. The dull *thunk* of wood hitting metal accompanies my words.

A corner of his mouth lifts in a humorless hint of a smile. "Can you truly say I was 'alive' when you first came across me?" The moment the words are out of his mouth, he realizes his mistake.

I ignore the transgression as I block one of his blows. "That does not explain why you are here. Surely even a mercenary deserves a cleaner death than this."

"You would have to ask my jailor." He lunges forward, and I step back, my foot slipping on the loose straw that litters the floor. He pauses to allow me to regain my footing. "Speaking of my jailors, how are you getting past them?"

It seems an innocent question. Unless he is trying to learn more about the castle's security. "My relationship with your guards is none of your concern."

"I ask because I have not seen any for weeks." He swings his sword in an overhand, but I grab the lower end of my blade and use it like a stick to block his blow. He gives a surprised nod of approval.

I press my advantage and increase the strength and speed of my blows, trying to force him onto his heels. It takes all of his concentration to keep me from succeeding, and it is his turn to stumble. When he does, I step in under his guard and slap his chest with the flat of my blade.

Instead of anger or annoyance, his eyes glow with pride. "Well done, Lucinda!"

I use the back of my arm to wipe the sweat from my brow. "Lucinda?"

"Bringer of light." He smiles, a quick, unexpected flash of white in the darkness.

I cannot decide if the name annoys me or if I like it. Or it if annoys me *because* I like it. "I suppose you have a name I should call you."

"Maraud."

I scowl at him. "That is not a name."

He shrugs. "It is what my fellow mercenaries call me." He tests the weight of the sword in his hand again. "Where did you get this?"

"From the armory in the garrison. What did your family call you?"

He looks up with a reckless grin. "Jackanapes. Ne'er-do-well. Knave. Take your pick."

Which supports his assertion that he is naught but a mercenary. "Would your company not pay your ransom? Is that why are you being held here?"

"Where is here, if I may ask?"

"You do not know where you are being held?"

"My jailors were not a talkative lot."

I consider his question, but can see no harm in telling him where he is. "You are in Cognac."

His blade whips up, but not as fast as his first blows. "The count of Angoulême's holding?"

We begin a series of slower strokes and parries. "Does that mean something to you?"

"No, but it surprises me. He has always been an ally of Brittany's."

I must tread carefully here. While I do not want to give away too much, my best chance of coaxing information from him will be to allow him to think I am telling the truth. "Ever since the Mad War, the regent has kept him on a short leash." I fall silent as his strokes press me back toward the wall again. I successfully avoid being pinned into place, my parries causing him to grow ghostly pale and beads of sweat to appear along his brow.

"Enough." I put the tip of my sword to the ground. That he has lasted this long says much about both his fortitude and his character. "I've no wish to tire you until you collapse."

"You dream it is so," he says between gasps of breath.

The denial of his obvious exhaustion nearly makes me smile.

"What was that?" He gestures toward my face.

Thinking of all the vile, nasty things that lurk in this pit, I swipe furiously at my cheek. "What?"

"Ah, 'tis gone, and the room is dark once more." He grins, a swift, sudden thing like a bird darting across one's path on a wintry day.

That is when I realize he was referring to my smile. "Jackanapes is right," I mutter. "Give me the sword."

He hands me his weapon, and I shove the sack of food at him. His hunger rises up like a physical thing — his nostrils flare and his jaw clenches. It is even more human than the smile.

I abruptly turn and secure the swords to my back. Even though it is our mutually agreed upon bargain, I feel as if I have just found a worm in my apple. For a moment, I am seven years old and have been walking for what surely seemed like weeks. I am tired and hungry — so hungry — but there is no money for food. I sit on the bank of a small stream, poking at it with a branch and calling it fishing, while my mother lies with a carter in the haystack in the fields behind me. When she returns, her skirts are askew and there are strands of hay poking out of her hair, but she bears a loaf of stale bread and half a wheel of cheese. It is a feast, and I dive into it with abandon, never pausing to think of it as payment.

"What's wrong?" he asks.

"Nothing."

"Your face says otherwise." It is the same voice he used in the dark, the voice I first knew him by. For a moment, one brief, regretful moment, I think back to that time.

Abruptly, I turn away from him and begin to climb the rope. Although I have received only half answers from him, I have learned what I truly needed to know. He will be useful to me.

Who are you? he first asked me nearly a month ago. The more time I spend in the darkness, the more I know the answer to that question. Down here I am exactly who I was raised to be. I do not need to hide who I am or what I think, nor watch my words nor keep my strength in check.

It is the most alive I have felt in five long years.

CHAPTER 32

Sybella

We are a quiet, heartbroken party when we arrive at Angers, bearing Captain Dunois's body on a stretcher fashioned out of spears and a spare cloak, along with the rest of our wounded and dead. A rider was sent ahead to alert our host to our misfortune. Upon our arrival, we are greeted by the Duke of Bourbon himself. I am relieved to learn that the regent is not in residence. I do not think I could contain myself around her right now. Why did she choose not to accompany us? Did she know that nearly every one of the men she left us would die? Plan it, even?

The duke, however, is all solicitousness and sorrow. He knew Captain Dunois from his many years in France and thought highly of him. His grief is comforting, as if, for all our differences, Frenchmen and Bretons alike can agree on what a tragedy it is to lose this great man.

We are shown to our rooms to refresh ourselves. As soon as the seneschal has excused himself and closed the door, the duchess whirls around. "Go," she tells me. "Go to the chapel and use your god's skills to find out what happened to Captain Dunois. I would see those who killed him punished." Her eyes glint with a temper and vengefulness I have not seen before. But beneath the fury is a deep, bruising grief that has left her skin ashen and purple smudges beneath her eyes.

"But of course, Your Grace. I would love to do precisely that."

"Do you need Heloise to help you?"

I blink a moment, then turn to look at the Brigantian nun who is also one of the duchess's attendants. "Thank you, but my work is best done alone." I pause, thinking to check first on Louise and Charlotte, but Tephanie has already anticipated that and is waving me away.

None of the castle servants pays any attention to my passing, which leads me to believe we have been granted every courtesy by the duke. I ask directions twice, but it does not attract any notice.

There are no attendants at the chapel door when I arrive. Upon entering, I find only Beast standing vigil over the body. Hearing my footsteps, he lifts his head, his face set in hard, grim lines. It is a face filled with anger at what has transpired, but with anguish as well. When I reach him, I place my hand on his cheek to let him know I am aware how big a hole this loss has created. "Where are the rest of the dead?" I ask softly.

"In the servant's chapel."

"And the priest?"

"I told him I wished to be alone with the body. He did not see fit to argue."

"Wise man."

We stare at each other a long moment, and then he takes a step back, his hands coming up to scrub at his face. "Saints teeth, Sybella! You scared ten years off my life back there." Even though he has not raised his voice, the force of his words feels like a small windstorm.

"And you scared nearly twenty off of mine, riding with a handful of men into a force nearly five times your numbers."

His hands snake out and grab my head, pulling me close for an urgent kiss — a kiss filled with his fear and the terror he felt on my behalf. The kiss softens, allowing us both to take comfort from it. Slowly, he pulls away and rests his forehead on mine. "Your fighting is a wonder to behold. A thing of terrible beauty. No one can see that and doubt you are an instrument of the gods." His pale blue eyes are alive with intensity.

"It is the same with you," I whisper. "You become lit from within by some invisible light so that every movement, every stroke is full of grace."

He draws me into his arms and holds me fiercely. "Some would call it brutality," he murmurs.

"And they would be fools."

Because I wish to stay like this forever, I force my head from his shoulder. "The duchess asked me to examine Captain Dunois to look for answers."

With a brusque nod, he lets me go. "I assumed you would. I'll stand guard while you do."

I turn to the body. For that is how I must think of it — the body. Not Captain Dunois, the man whose gruff courage and strategic skill had brought us through so much. Not as the man who had been far more father to Beast than his own. Not as the man who was one of the first to believe me, respect me, and value both my ideas and the sum of who I am.

A howl of deep, piercing grief threatens to escape, but I ruthlessly shove it back down, afraid the force of it will shatter me. There is no time for grieving. I must be every bit the daughter of Mortain, a ruthless student of death, in order to find out what has happened and who has taken this man from our midst too soon.

As if sensing how hard this will be for me, Dunois's soul lies hidden and dormant. Or mayhap he is embarrassed by the examination his body must endure. Begging his soul's forgiveness, I remove each item of his clothing, one by one, sniffing them carefully for any traces of poison. Even though he is over fifty, he is still thick with muscle, his body well seasoned with scars from his many battles. It takes over an hour to search among his old, healed wounds for signs of any new ones, but there are no scratches or punctures or any manner in which poison might have been introduced.

"Nothing." My voice is harsh in the thick silence of the chapel. "There are no new wounds. And while some poisons mimic the sort of fit he had, they are not something that can simply be breathed in. They have to have been administered somehow."

"Is it possible he simply died of apoplexy?" Beast's voice is little more than a low grumble. In anyone else I would think it out of respect for both the dead and the church we occupy, but I suspect that for him he is afraid if he speaks too loudly, his voice will betray his emotions.

"What makes you ask that?"

He shrugs. "If he was not struck or shot by an arrow and there are no signs of poison, it is all that is left."

I consider the possibility. "He has been working round the clock of late, and barely stopped to sleep or eat. Nor is he a young man." I feel a chill against my ribs, as if some ghostly finger has poked me for calling him old. "But the timing of his death with the ambush is too convenient."

Beast rubs his face. "I agree."

"It cannot be a coincidence that just as we arrive in France, ready to take up residence in a court we know nearly nothing about, our most knowledge-able advisor, the one who has known every French nobleman and taken their measure over the last four decades, is struck dead. That the brilliant tactician who was responsible for chiseling this path to victory for the duchess has been silenced from ever giving her council again." Not to mention the one man who could point out Beast's father to him will never be able to do so now.

If that is a coincidence, then surely the gods are more enemy to us than the French.

When we emerge from the chapel, a servant waiting nearby escorts us to a private dining room where the rest of the duchess's party are having a small supper. Chancellor Montauban, the Prince of Orange, former marshal Rieux, Father Effram, and the Bishop of Rennes sit around the table, the remains of a meal still spread out before them. As we enter the room, there is a pause — a moment too long — before they call out a welcome. That is when I become aware that they have all been scrubbed clean while Beast and I are still in our bloodstained travel clothes. "Take a seat. Eat something," Chancellor Montauban says. "We are just arguing over the ambush and who might be behind it."

As I slip into the chair that Beast holds out for me, I feel the silent stares of the others on me like fleeting darts. Father Effram gets up from the table, crossing to the ewer on the sideboard. Pulling a cloth from some hidden pocket, he dips it in the water.

"You do not think it Emperor Maximilian?" Beast asks as he takes the seat next to me.

The chancellor rubs his haggard face with his hand. "He is the most logical explanation. They were German soldiers."

"They were mercenaries." The Prince of Orange is barely able to keep a rein on his temper. "German mercenaries are for sale on every road crossing and street corner. It does not tell us who paid them."

Father Effram returns to the table and slides back into his seat, handing the dampened cloth to me. Puzzled, I reach out to take it from him.

He motions to my left cheek. Understanding dawns, and I lift the cloth to my face, wiping at my cheek. I glance down at the white cloth, now covered with a smear of dark rust-colored blood.

"They could also have been German soldiers masquerading as mercenaries," Beast counters. "Just because they were not wearing the Habsburg coat of arms and colors does not mean they were not sent by the emperor. It makes sense he would want to hide his part in the abduction for as long as possible, especially given his daughter's precarious position."

I carefully fold the cloth, closing my hand around it. When I look up, both Jean and Chancellor Montauban look away.

"Which is precisely why I do not believe he was behind it," the prince continues. "He has too much at risk with Princess Marguerite still in the custody of the king."

"But the king would not hurt her." As the bishop speaks, he runs his fingers nervously over his rosary beads. "Everything I have ever heard or seen indicates that he is genuinely fond of the girl."

"Then who?" Jean adds his braying voice to the mix. "Who else has anything to gain by abducting the duchess?"

"England?" the Prince of Orange offers.

"That is absurd," scoffs Jean. "You are simply trying to deflect the blame from the emperor."

The prince narrows his eyes dangerously. "Are you questioning my loyalty?"

Rieux thrusts his head forward to argue further, but the bishop interrupts before they can come to blows. "But to what end?" he asks.

The prince shrugs. "To prevent the marriage."

"But at the cost of war with France?" the bishop asks. "Surely England knew that would be the final result of such an abduction."

The prince reaches for the stem of his goblet. "They have long been looking for an excuse to press their piteous claim to the French throne. Perhaps they see this as an opportunity." He takes a sip of wine. "A better question might be what did the emperor hope to gain?"

His brow furrowed in deep thought, Beast leans forward and plants his elbows on the table, causing the plates and silverware to jiggle slightly. "Did the emperor hope to rescue his wife, or . . ." His next words come more slowly. "To give the accusations he's been making against France the appearance of truth?"

Montauban, too, leans forward. "You mean his accusations that the duchess had been abducted in an effort to delegitimize the union?"

Beast nods, and everyone falls silent.

"So you see." Rieux's voice is smug. "All roads appear to lead to the emperor."

I delicately clear my throat. "I may be able to shed some additional light on the situation, or else muddy the waters beyond all comprehension."

Reluctantly, their gazes turn toward me. That is when I understand that I make them uncomfortable now. They have always known I was an assassin — and accepted it. Or so they thought. But now that I sit here with our enemies' blood splattered on my gown, now that they have seen me kill with their own eyes, they feel differently. Knowing something and seeing it are very different things.

Doing his best to hide . . . not revulsion, but something akin to it, the chancellor leans back in his chair. "By all means, my lady, we would love to hear it."

"One of the last things Captain Dunois said to me was that we should look to the castle."

The bishop regards me as if I am trying to tempt him to evil. The prince is intrigued, but wary, and the former marshal aggrieved. "Did he not simply mean to look to the castle at Angers for refuge from the attackers?"

So much for our bond of mutual trust and respect. Clearly that was only something they were willing to extend to Lady Sybella, not the Sybella who excels in the art of death. "He could have, yes. But do you not find it interesting that we keep crossing paths with the regent? She could not have gotten much of an earlier start than we did. Why not simply travel with us?"

"With a smaller group, she could travel more quickly."

I ignore the chancellor's feeble explanation. "And what of the soldiers she provided? Only one or two of them survived. Did she just happen to leave us France's most poorly trained soldiers, or was that by some design? And Rohan's appointment as governor still bothers me."

Father Effram nods and spreads his hands wide. "What if they are playing a game within a game? As was said before, the king is very fond of Marguerite. Some have even claimed that he loves her. If the duchess were to disappear, Marguerite's original betrothal agreement would still stand. The king would be free to marry the princess and have Brittany by right of conquest."

"Only if he assumes the next in line will not retaliate," the Prince of Orange mutters.

"He knows the next in line cannot raise any more troops," Beast says quietly, and the prince falls silent.

"It is possible," the bishop concedes. "But why not simply press his military advantage when he was encamped before Rennes? Why go through the pretense of a betrothal and marriage?"

A thought, a most disconcerting and unwelcome thought, comes to me. The secret to our victory was the power of Arduinna's last arrow. What if the power of it has worn off? Or what if those powers only work in Brittany, where the goddess still holds sway? This council, and the bishop, are already so uncomfortable with the gods and their hands in the duchess's affairs that I say nothing

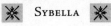

out loud, but resolve to ask Aeva more about her goddess's powers when next we are alone.

The chancellor sighs. "I fear we must at least consider it a possibility. And a most grim one at that."

Father Effram turns to me. "Were you able to learn how Captain Dunois died, my lady?"

The room falls silent at Father Effram's question, except for the bishop, whose rosary beads click even faster as he casts a dark glance my way.

"No." Disappointment makes my voice sharp. "There was no sign of any weapon. No wounds, no entry point, no poison."

"So it was just a coincidence of timing?" The Prince of Orange's voice holds all the skepticism I feel.

"Perhaps you should pray to your god of mistakes," I suggest to Father Effram. "And ask that he look elsewhere for his amusements for a while."

CHAPTER 33

hen we all gather in the grand salon the next morning to break our fast, it is clear that none of us have slept well.

The duchess is nearly beside herself with grief. Of all her councilors, Dunois was the one most closely linked with her father in her mind. It was he who carried her to safety when d'Albret tried to kidnap her. It was he who provided steadfast council and an almost father-like affection for her, gruff as it could sometimes be.

She tries to insist we must take Captain Dunois's body with us to Langeais. It takes Lord Montauban, the Prince of Orange, and the Duke of Bourbon combined to convince her that she cannot arrive at her wedding carting a dead body. Besides, the duke assures her, he and the captain were old friends, and he will make the arrangements as if burying his own brother. And no matter how much I wish to distrust this man, no matter how hard I peer into his face to see some sign of treachery, I find none. Every instinct I possess tells me he is genuinely kind and considerate. This most likely makes him appear weak to others, and may render him weak in many circumstances. But today I am grateful for this much-needed balm to our hearts.

Before we depart, however, the duchess asks me to accompany her to bid Dunois a final farewell. Candles have been lit around the captain's body, and Father Effram kneels beside him, praying. As soon as I enter the chapel, Dunois's soul rises up from its resting place, like a sleeping hound that has been dozing in the sun.

Father Effram smiles as we enter, his face full of both sadness and acceptance. "I imagine you wish to say your goodbyes." He reaches out to pat the duchess's hand before shuffling out the door and leaving us alone with the body.

And Dunois's soul.

All my life I have struggled to ignore the souls that I was able to detect. When I was younger, I thought them simply ghosts that haunted me, yet another sign of my brokenness. When I finally understood the nature of my powers, I was still loath to acknowledge their presence. I did not need their heartache, their emotions, their sense of loss and despair. I was drowning in too much of my own. Later, when I had been the one to kill them, I considered my duty done, feeling no need to acknowledge their dying thoughts and wishes.

But with Captain Dunois, I am grateful to have one last chance to say goodbye and know that he will hear it.

Dunois's soul moves ever so slightly toward me, but not too close. While he is glad to see me, his spirit maintains the faint reserve he had in life.

The duchess clasps her hands in front of her and bows her head in prayer. She stares down at the captain's face, which somehow looks more peaceful than it did yesterday, as if he has accepted this most unexpected interruption to his plans.

With the duchess absorbed in her prayers, I open myself to Dunois's soul, allowing the wall between me and the Otherworld to thin. His presence draws around me like a cloak. Comforting and reassuring, but not touching.

I have no idea how to speak to souls, so I simply form the question in my mind. *Are you at peace now?*

Not yet. I do not know how a soul can feel wry, but the captain's manages to do so.

Do you know what caused your death?

There are no words, but a rush of images and sensations — a feeling that my heart is exploding, followed by pain in my chest, spreading along my arm. As I gasp with the shock of it, the soul quickly shutters the image from me. Perhaps it *was* apoplexy. But there are other answers I seek.

Did you see anything to indicate who was behind the attack?

There is nothing but a vast sense of not knowing and being nearly sick with it.

I am so focused on Captain Dunois's soul that when the duchess places her hand on my arm, I jump. "Are you able to speak with souls, like Ismae was?"

Frustrated by the interruption, it is all I can do not to tell her I was just doing precisely that. "Yes."

"Could you . . . Are you able to tell him how much I have valued him, as well as his counsel? How much I have come to love him, for he has been much like a father to me, even before my own father died. I want him to know that he will always live on in my heart, and in the courage he has instilled in me."

While she is speaking, the soul moves from me toward her. An aching tenderness fills the room, so strong that even she lifts her head and stares in wonder. "Is that him?" she whispers.

"Yes, Your Grace. He has heard your words and returns them in kind."

As the soul continues to hover over her, she bows her head, tears rolling down her cheek.

Lost deep in my own thoughts, I do not realize the soul has moved from the duchess back to me until I feel awash in a love so deep and profound that it reminds me of my own god's love and mercy. In that moment, I feel deep in my bones the truth of Captain Dunois's affection for me and his regard. Afraid I will begin weeping like the duchess, I focus on opening my heart so that he can feel the affection, respect, and, yes, love that I hold for him.

When our souls meet, I am filled with a sense of weightlessness and light. As if my earthly body has been replaced by rays of the sun. It reminds me of the grace I felt when I found myself in Mortain's godly presence. I am stunned, for it never occurred to me that human souls were capable of such things. Dunois's love does not burn with an unearthly heat like Mortain's did, but burns with all that our human hearts are capable of.

In that moment, I also realize the great love that *I* am capable of, that I am sharing right now, and I think, *This*, this is part of Mortain's grace that is still a part of me, still available to me, and mine to give as I choose.

Slowly, Dunois's soul begins to draw back, except for one tendril, which feels for all the world like a hand laid upon my head in blessing, and then that, too, is gone. Now, I realize. *Now* he is at peace.

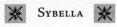

When I finally open my eyes, blinking to reorient myself in this world, the duchess is staring at me.

"Are you well, Lady Sybella?" she whispers.

"Yes, Your Grace. I am."

"You are glowing." Her voice is tinged with awe.

I put my hand to my cheek, wanting to hang on to this moment of grace as long as I possibly can.

CHAPTER 34

Genevieve

eeling triumphant after my successful visit with the prisoner, it is time for me to return to the solar. While I enjoy sewing and like the other women of the castle well enough, it will be the first time I have joined them since Margot's death. But with my newfound resolve to leave, I must maintain a sense of normalcy until I make my move. When I step into the room, my first thought is that they have rearranged the chairs. There is only one empty chair waiting to be filled, not two.

My fervent desire to slip in unnoticed is quickly dashed when Louise herself notes my entrance. "Ah, Genevieve. There you are. Come sit with me."

My heart sinks as she nods to Jeanne de Polignac, Count Angoulême's other mistress, who smiles kindly at me and vacates her seat next to the countess. "I would be honored, my lady." Ignoring the surreptitious glances of the other attendants, I curtsy and take the chair next to Louise. She smiles pleasantly and turns her gaze back to her embroidery frame. It is not until I have pulled my own needlework onto my lap and taken the first stitch that she speaks.

"We have missed you."

"I am sorry, my lady. I fear I would have been poor company."

"You miss her terribly, don't you?"

"Yes." I must shove the single word past the thick lump in my throat.

She leans forward, almost as if trying to peer into my thoughts. "Then why do you not speak of her?"

The beating of my heart feels as if a bird is frantically trying to escape from my chest. "It is too hard, my lady. Every time I think of her, my heart breaks a little more." Anxious to turn her attention from me, I ask, "Is it not hard for you as well?"

I have always wondered how much Margot's relationship with Angoulême vexed Louise. It was bad enough to have to accept that her husband chose a second mistress, but that Margot was one of her oldest friends, as well as her lady in waiting, and managed to get herself with child before Louise must surely have rankled.

She leans back in her chair. "Yes, but you and she were closer and had known each other longer." There is an almost accusing note in her voice.

I look down at my hands and force my fingers to release their death hold on the needle. "Some things are too important to speak of."

"That is true." Her hand wanders to her belly, her expression growing unfocused and far away. It is a manner she often adopts when contemplating her babe, and I desperately wish to know what she is thinking in these moments. While she has always held her own counsel, the tendency grew worse last spring after she had a private audience with the holy hermit who resides at the king's palace at Plessis. Ever since that meeting, she has been apt to wear that smile.

"However," she continues, "you are my attendant, and your role here is to attend upon me." Her voice is pitched low so that only I can hear. "The others are able to manage their grief and still see to their duties."

My grief. As if the enormity of losing Margot can be contained within that one word. "But of course, my lady."

I have always felt sympathy for Louise. She spent years at the palace, having to "my lady" everyone, including a girl little more than a babe who was to be her queen. It appeared to me that her new position caused her to swell with the importance of it. My hope was that one day it would fill her so completely that the constant frown she wears would disappear. But today, I want to poke her with my needle and watch her deflate like a pig's bladder after the fair.

That night when the other women are tucked away in their beds, I make my way up to my own small chamber. When they sent us from the convent, they did not give us many tools. No knives, no garrotes, no thin sharp blades of any kind. We were only twelve and had not yet begun the more rigorous lessons in the killing arts.

The night whispers and hairnet of poisoned pearls were mostly for our own protection, insisted upon by Sister Serafina, who did not care for us to be defenseless among our enemies.

But over the years, I have assembled my own arsenal. My fingers are light, and the soldiers, knights, and courtiers careless around young women with low necklines. Sister Beatriz was right on that point, at least.

A true initiate must have three kills to her name before she can be sent out on official convent business. But that training does not even begin until the age of thirteen, and those assignments are handed out in the fifteenth year. Margot and I had not even been given the Tears of Mortain, which allow initiates to better see His will in this world. The abbess went to great lengths to explain that we were not allowed to kill anybody. We were to sit and observe, to learn and wait.

The abbess had not told us there would be no contact. We knew we weren't to reach out to her, but we also assumed there would be *some* contact through Angoulême or other visitors or envoys from Brittany. They came often enough to the French court, but none of them carried any message or word for us, let alone the crow feather.

I dip a piece of woolen cloth into a crock of goose grease and begin rubbing it on the three-sided blade of my poniard as I once again consider my options.

I could return to Sanson's tavern. For a moment, I let myself imagine how that would unfold. I think of my mother, and Bertine and Yolanthe, of Joetta and old Solange. On the day I left for the convent, all their faces filled with hope for the life I would get to lead — so very different from theirs. Each of them so convinced I was special, that I had some great role to play on life's stage. When I consider returning home, all I can see is the disappointment in their faces.

I set aside the poniard and retrieve my baselard. I hold it up to the candle flame to see if the blade still holds its edge. It does, so I dip the rag in oil and start in on the hammered steel. What would happen if I simply returned to the convent? Has it been abandoned? If so, I could live there for a while, until I figured out what I wish to do. However, it could also have been taken over by the Church, and I do not wish to walk into a nest of sour-lipped, small-minded priests.

I turn the blade over to work on the other side, then pause. Courts and noble families across Europe use assassins and poisoners for their own political ambitions. Surely that is one of my choices, as well. One that my unique background would make me most qualified for.

But am I willing to kill outside Mortain's grace? All the dire warnings from the nuns crowd my head. It is bad enough to be thrust from the convent. Am I willing to risk my mortal soul in order to be allowed to do this work? Have this power? Not only over others, but over my own destiny?

It is a sobering question and one I cannot answer. A soul is as thin and ephemeral as the convent's protection. Will I wall myself off from the most interesting choice in life to protect something I do not even know exists?

I set aside the baselard and take up Margot's stiletto. Testing the edge of it with the side of my thumb, I find it dull, reach for my whetstone, and begin running it along the blade's edge.

It is too bad I do not have a true sword. And I will need a horse. I could steal one from Angoulême, but I fear that would only increase his reasons for pursuing me once he learns of my absence. Besides, Margot and I have our own horses provided to us by the convent, even though they are stabled in Angoulême's other holding. But if I used them, it would take him longer to discover they were missing, if he ever did. And I would not be stealing anything — which I do not wish to do, for that would also bring pursuit. Horse theft is punishable by death.

Even better would be for the count not to pursue me at all, but I am not certain how to manage that.

As I stare down at Margot's stiletto, a thought forms. *What if he did not know I had left?*

What if he thought I had died? He would not try to follow me then.

I set down the whetstone and gingerly test the stiletto's edge. A faint line of red appears along the edge of my thumb. Pleased, I return it to its jeweled case.

I may not know where I am going, but I do know how I will ensure that I am not followed.

Chapter 35

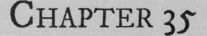

Sybella

ecause of our delayed start, we do not reach Langeais until late. The sun has already begun to set behind the three huge pointed towers that rise up above the grim battlements of the castle. While it is impressive, it is also foreboding.

Upon our approach, outriders meet us on the road, sent to escort us back to the palace. They also inform us that the king is not scheduled to arrive until early tomorrow morning, but the regent is in residence.

When we enter the main foyer, she is standing regally atop a wide staircase. Her bright gown and glittering jewels are in stark contrast to the thick pall of grief that enshrouds our party, and I wonder if she is small hearted enough to have planned that on purpose. She pauses a long moment, forcing us to wait while she descends to greet us, her attendants following her like a flock of sheep.

My gaze passes over them briefly, and I wonder if two of them are from the convent. If so, they have assumed their role well, for they all look equally officious and self-important.

When the regent reaches us, she stops. "Be welcome, Your Grace," she says.

"Thank you for your hospitality." The duchess's head is high, her voice strong, but her sorrow clings to her like the most fragrant of perfumes.

The regent steps forward, deftly inserting herself between me and the duchess.

On my best behavior, I do not so much as glare at her, but simply step back while she takes the younger woman's arm in a friendly manner. "You must be exhausted after your journey. Come, we will get you settled in your chambers so you may rest and refresh yourself for tomorrow."

The duchess does not refuse her arm, but neither does she lean on it. "Thank you. That would be most welcome."

As the regent moves toward the stairs with the duchess, her own ladies are quick to position themselves directly behind the two royals. Beast and the queen's guard fall into step behind them. It is not until they have reached the third stair that the regent stops and turns around to stare at them, raising her eyebrows in question. Beast and the others bow formally.

"Who are you and why are you following the duchess abovestairs?" Her voice is as cool and brittle as the thin layer of ice that forms upon a pond.

"We are the queen's guard, Madame Regent, and have sworn our service and protection to our lady duchess."

A delicate frown appears on the regent's face. "She is perfectly safe here. Our own sentries and guards can see to her protection."

Beast bows again, his face apologetic. "If you will excuse me, Madame Regent, it is our sworn duty to guard her with our lives. We will not leave those duties to another."

Beast's icy blue gaze is well matched to the regent's frigid glare. "It is our vow to see her safely wed to the king, Madame. Surely, you would not ask us to break our oaths."

"The king has personally gone to extraordinary lengths for tomorrow's cere-mony." Her mouth twists with something — disdain? Disapproval? "And I wish for nothing to mar the ceremony. You may guard her tonight, but after that, she will fall under the protection of the king's bodyguards."

Beast meets her gaze steadily. "As my queen wishes it."

For a moment, it is clear she does not know if he is mistakenly addressing her as queen or if he is deferring to the duchess. Unwilling to press the point,

she turns around, dismissing Beast and the others' presence so completely that it is as if they do not exist.

Pleased with Beast's victory, the rest of the duchess's party and I follow them up the stairs.

When we reach the second floor, the regent whispers some instructions to her attendants, then stands aside, looking for all the world like a general surveying his troops, as we file by.

I stare straight ahead as I pass her. My only thoughts are of getting the duchess settled in her room, then ordering both a bath and a hot posset that will help her sleep, otherwise I fear her grief will keep her up all night.

"Lady Sybella." The regent's voice reaches out and snags me like a shepherd's crook.

I stop walking, my heart sinking. What could she want with me? To remove me from the duchess's circle? To haul me off to one of her infamous dungeons? However, when I turn around, my face is serene. "Yes, Madame?"

"You were there."

I tilt my head in confusion. "During the attack?"

The shake of her head is impatient. "When Captain Dunois died."

My heart skips a beat before it speeds up. Has one of the soldiers she assigned to us reported my every move? "Yes, Madame. I was with him when he died."

"Were you especially close with him?"

As her eyes narrow with speculation, I realize she is asking if we were lovers. Or trying to insinuate as much. That would make it easy to have me removed from the duchess's side.

"No, but I have some small skill and training with injuries. When it was clear something had befallen the good captain, I wished to be of service. After all, he is — *was* — one of the duchess's most loyal and trusted advisors."

"He had admirers at this court as well."

I nod in acknowledgment at this faintest of compliments. "Then your grief must also be great."

If she detects the irony that seeps into my voice, she ignores it. "That was most brave of you, considering you were under attack."

"I was not brave, Madame, as we were not under attack yet. That did not come until after Captain Dunois had fallen."

"So he was not killed in the attack?" I cannot tell if her eyes are sharp with interest or something more sinister.

"No. As best we can tell, his stalwart heart simply gave out. Surely the Duke of Bourbon has advised you of these events?"

At my question, some of her sharpness fades. "Yes, but it was brief and lacking in detail." With that, she brushes past me and proceeds down the hallway while I am left wondering what the point of her questions was, for there is no doubt in my mind that there was one. I just have not caught up to it yet.

CHAPTER 36

Genevieve

had not planned to return to the oubliette too soon lest I attract Louise's attention, but I find I no longer care. My hunger for the movement and challenge the sparring sessions bring me is nearly overpowering.

Maraud is silent until I have descended the rope. "I wasn't sure you'd return."

I set the sack of food down in the corner, then hand him his wooden sword. "Why did you think that?"

He takes the sword and shrugs.

I glare at him, trying to determine if he is referring to the time before our sparring began.

He gives the sword a warm-up swing. "You could have been detained by the guards."

In answer, I take up my fighting stance, turning my body sideways to present a smaller target.

"How do you get by them?"

I lunge at him. "Why are you so concerned about the guards?" This is no innocent question. He is trying to glean information for some purpose of his own.

He delivers a short thrust that almost gets through my defenses. "I miss them. They were like family to me."

I allow a faint smile to play upon my lips. "We have an arrangement, the guards and I." I launch a flurry of attacks.

He gets his sword up, but it takes him a moment to recover from the surprise of my onslaught. Before I can gloat overmuch, he barks, "Widen your stance. It will give you better balance. And quit using your sword like a dagger."

I alter my grip. My arms are not used to the heavier weight of the baselard.

"Right!" he calls out, and I swing my sword up to meet his.

"Left!"

Then left again. I block the blow, but the shock of it nearly numbs my arm.

"Right!" he calls out, and I am there to meet his blade.

His words drive me as ruthlessly as his wooden sword until I am breathing heavily and sweat gathers at my temples.

"Your strength has returned quickly," I note as I jump back from a thrust that comes too close to my gut for comfort. Even though it is a wooden sword, it will leave a bruise.

"It is all the food and exercise you have graced me with."

I snort. *Graced* is far too reverent a word for the rough bread and kitchen scraps I have been able to sneak him.

"Get your blade up! Am I forbidden to ask of the duchess as well as the guards?"

"That is a strange question for a mere mercenary to ask," I grit out, my words punctuated by the *thunk* of our blades as he steadily backs me toward the wall.

"Maybe she owes me back pay."

"I will send her news of your whereabouts. Will she recognize the name Maraud?"

He returns to the center of the room, allowing me to do the same. "Of course not. Since when does someone of her rank know the names of the mercenaries who fight for her? The captain of her army, Sir Dunois, will remember, though. You could write to him."

I roll my shoulders. "Perhaps I will." I keep my eyes on his sword, waiting for a surprise attack. "What is it you wish to know about the duchess?"

"How she fares. If she is still duchess of Brittany."

I mentally count the days. "As it so happens, as of today she is the queen of France."

CHAPTER 37

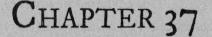

Sybella

he wedding between Anne of Brittany and Charles VIII of France is to take place in the grand salon at Langeais. All the royal guests have arrived, although the special papal dispensation has not, nor even a verbal assurance. In spite of the reassurance of the three bishops who are presiding over the wedding, I know this weighs heavily on the duchess.

The duchess, soon to be queen, is truly magnificent in her gown of intricately embossed cloth of gold. I lean toward her, pretending I am adjusting her ermine-lined mantle. "You are well, Your Grace?" There has not been a moment all morning to catch a word alone with her. The regent's attendants descended upon her chambers at dawn's light to begin the hours-long preparations for her wedding.

She glances at me, her regal, serious expression giving way to a ghost of a smile that does not reach her eyes. "Well enough."

Fiddling with the clasp on her mantle, I whisper, "You have achieved your life's goal, Your Grace. You have secured an enduring peace for your people. Your children will sit on the throne of France. Surely there is much to be proud of."

"You are right," she murmurs. "But I cannot help but think of all those who are not here."

"It is hard not to let our grief over Captain Dunois trail behind us like a long, despondent tail," I agree as I busy myself adjusting the

folds of her gown. "But I know he would not wish you to begin your marriage that way."

"It's not just those I've lost, but all of those I nearly married." She turns to face me. "Did you know I was to be betrothed to Prince Edward of England? And when he was reported dead, then his brother the Duke of York? But for a moment of violence, I would be queen of England.

"It would have taken me even farther from my home, and there is a good chance it would only have made Brittany a staging ground for all the friction between France and England. So I assure myself that this is a better choice, although it ceased being a choice a while ago."

She pauses a long moment. "Or I could be wife to Count d'Albret." There is a faint tremble underlying her voice, as if it still gives her nightmares. "That, too, could have been my fate." She reaches out and takes my hand — her fingers are ice-cold. "If not for your help."

I squeeze her hand before she withdraws it. "In my experience, Your Grace, all victories are bittersweet. It is simply a matter of degree."

Then the trumpets blare, heralding that the wedding ceremony is to begin. I take my position in the procession of attendants in charge of her long train and solemnly follow the duchess into the grand salon.

While I had expected a wedding fit for royalty, the extent of the richness and grandeur causes me to blink. The room is enormous, with a high-beamed ceiling and marble fireplaces on either end. Drapes of Turkish velvet protect the guests from drafts, and a sea of silver and gold cloth adorns the room.

In addition to the royal finery are plaques of walnut upon which the king has commissioned carvings of the ermine of Brittany as well as the lily of France. All the silver that adorns the room, the platters and pitchers and chargers and ewers, have been engraved with delicate flowers encircling the king's and queen's intertwined initials. All the details, large and small, fairly shout a warm and loving welcome to his new queen.

The king has outdone himself, for this is not simply a display of his wealth and royal status, but a far more personal statement. It would seem that whatever rancor his sister holds toward the duchess, the man who arranged for this reception does not share it.

The duchess's procession comes to a stop.

Charles of France is short and somewhat frail, in spite of his well-padded doublet and thick-heeled boots. While he holds himself stiffly, his brown eyes seem both kind and intelligent, if a little too prominent. They have the misfortune of being perched over a royal beak of a nose that is far too large for his face. His long hair is dark and wavy, and his shoulders square, if not broad. But most important is the way his eyes shine as he looks upon the duchess, as if he is in awe of his new bride.

I scan the hall once more, noting all that has been arranged, all the richness that has been put on display, all the ways the duchess has been included in this pageant, and allow myself a sigh of relief. We are in the presence of the king now, not the regent. Not only will the duchess hold a queen's political power and sway, but it appears she will also have a chance to explore the tender shoots of romance that sprang up between them four weeks ago.

We have survived the gauntlet the regent laid before us and reached the safety of the king — not just his protection, but his love and respect. His affection will neutralize the regent's animosity, if she is not soon out of the picture altogether.

I smile and allow myself to enjoy the ceremony.

After the marriage contract has been signed and the wedding mass performed by the Bishop of Angers, some of the stiff formality gives way to the more festive air of a wedding. Music begins to play softly in the background as gathered nobles and dignitaries pay their respects and offer their congratulations to the king and his new queen. The regent hovers at their elbows, standing too close and oftentimes answering questions directed at them.

I, along with the rest of the queen's attendants, wait nearby. To distract from my growing irritation at the regent, I keep one eye on the queen and allow the other to survey the room. It is thick with the stench of French nobility — roses and violets, civet and musk. Sly, speculative glances dart my way. Clearly news of our adventure on the road has reached the court. Whether they include my role in deflecting the ambush or in aiding Captain Dunois as he lay dying, the rumors and whispers about me have already begun.

Beast, standing rigidly at attention with the rest of the queen's guard, is also the subject of furtive scrutiny. I do not know if it is because of his reputation on the battlefield against the French, his recent exploits during our ambush, or simply due to his size and sheer ugliness. He pays it no mind, but it sets my teeth on edge, and I want to clout their foolish heads and tell them to crawl back into their castles and dreary chateaux.

"And I believe you know Count Angoulême." I turn my full attention to the count, who is second in line for the French crown, preceded only by the Duke of Orléans. The king's voice is remarkably neutral, given that Angoulême's relationship with Brittany was primarily in allying against France.

The queen greets him warmly. "I am pleased to see you again, my lord."

"And I you, Your Majesty." He is tall and still bears the vestiges of the soldier he once was, although the effect is tempered by too much indulgent living.

"I hear that congratulations are in order," the queen continues. "Your wife is expecting your first child."

"Thank you, Your Majesty. I indeed feel graced by God for this joyous news." If he feels any rancor at the king's new bride for her expected role in producing an heir and thus removing any chance he might have at the crown of France, he does not show it.

The regent steps forward. "Speaking of the countess," she says, taking the count's arm, "come tell me how dear Louise is faring." The count nods in farewell to the king and queen, and allows the regent to lead him away. We can all stand a little easier without her breathing down our necks. Just as the king turns to speak to the queen, a foppish, self-important man steps forward to offer his good wishes. After a brief introduction to the queen — he is the Italian ambassador — he dismisses her and pulls the king to the side and begins discussing something with him in low-pitched, rapid Italian.

Before I can be affronted on the queen's behalf, she turns immediately to the Duke of Bourbon and drops some of her forced cheer. "Have you been able to learn anything about our attack, my lord?"

The duke glances nervously toward his wife, who is a safe distance away, still talking with Angoulême. "I'm afraid not. We returned to the place of the ambush, but there was not much to learn. They left their dead behind, which should have yielded us some answers, but did not."

"How so, my lord?"

"These soldiers had no personal effects on them. No possessions of any kind that might indicate where they were from. While many mercenaries have little more than the clothes on their back, their weapons, and their horse, there is usually some small, treasured possession from home. A coin, a trinket, or a lock of hair. But these men had nothing. It was most unusual."

"That is an answer of sorts, is it not?"

The duke blinks at my question, but does not dismiss me. "Yes. Clearly they went to great lengths to keep their identities a secret."

"Have you asked the nearby farmers and villagers?" the queen presses.

"I have sent men out to inquire, but I fear that for all intents and purposes, the trail began and ended on those bridges." His mouth snaps shut, and his chin recedes a bit further. The regent is returning. I glance to the king, hoping he will dismiss the Italian ambassador and return to his wife's side, but both men are gone. Furthering my annoyance, the Duke of Bourbon quickly excuses himself and also beats a hasty retreat.

When the regent reaches us, her smile is as false and brittle as spun sugar. "Now that Your Majesty is married in the eyes of the law and the Church, it is time to ensure that the contract cannot be broken."

The queen frowns slightly. "It cannot be broken. We have signed it, attended by witnesses, your own hand among them. The bishop has celebrated the wedding mass."

"Due to your farce of a marriage to Maximilian and the king's prior betrothal, this marriage is most irregular. While we have the blessings and assurances of the bishops, we will not take any chances that a challenge to its validity can be made. Even now, the emperor sends his own petitioners to Rome to argue his case against the pope allowing his marriage to be annulled. Our best protection is for the marriage to be consummated."

"Of course," the duchess answers, blushing. "But surely not *now*."

"On the contrary. What better proof can we offer the pope than a roomful of witnesses to the consummation? They can then carry the tale back to their cities and countries — and Rome — that the marriage is binding and cannot be annulled. It is the best way to ensure that all we have worked for cannot be undone."

I stare at the regent. "You are talking about a public consummation?"

The regent gives a quick shake of her head. "Not fully public, no. There will not be a room of witnesses to oversee the deed itself. But there will be a doctor to confirm that it has taken place, and the guests will await the news of the consummation here in the grand salon."

The duchess has grown as white as one of her linen sheets. What a fool I was to not see that the premarital inspection was to be a road map the regent would continue to follow. "Surely this is not necessary." I try to modulate my voice so that it is well measured and reasoned, but instead it comes out high, almost shrill. "The holy vows have been exchanged. The contracts legally signed and witnessed."

"So have the contracts with Maximilian and Marguerite." The regent leans in closer. "Believe me. This is most necessary. There have been marriages, of royal blood even, that have suffered for lack of attention to such details."

Of course. Her sister and the Duke of Orléans. To this day he vows it has never been consummated. The duchess was but four years old when that scheme was hatched. Why does the regent insist on making her pay and pay for something she had no control over?

But I already know the answer. It is because the duchess is the only one who is powerless enough to be punished. The duke is dead. And in spite of the regent's best efforts, the Duke of Orléans is back in the good graces of the king, his lands and estates restored. There is no one else she can whip for this old sin except the person who is least culpable.

CHAPTER 38

Genevieve

ueen of France?" Maraud rests his sword against mine and shakes his head, almost as if he has sustained a blow.

"I had a hard time with it as well when I first heard. What was the last news you had of her?"

"That her advisors were pressing for a match with Count d'Albret." His voice holds palpable repugnance.

"You did not approve of him?"

"No." His next blow comes at me faster and with far more force.

I parry, then we settle into a rhythm more suited to talking. "Why not?"

"The man — the entire family — has no honor. They serve only their own interests and are ruthless about it."

"You are right about that. D'Albret laid a trap for her, using her city of Nantes as bait. If he had succeeded, he would have married her against her will. Fortunately, help arrived just in time. The duchess escaped to Rennes and found refuge there," I continue. "She married Emperor Maximilian of Austria by proxy, hoping for aid against France that never came."

"Why not?"

My side stroke connects with his ribs, and he grunts in pain. I hesitate, wondering if I have hurt him, but his sword whooshes through the air on the way to my head. I duck.

"His own numerous battles prevented him. She sent out pleas to all her allies and emptied her coffers hiring even more mercenaries, but it was not enough."

His sword stops against mine, and I use the respite to catch my breath. "How do you know that?"

Rutting figs. "I listen at doors. It is a vile habit, but a useful one." I shove his blade aside.

"Who are you," he asks, "that you know the intimate ins and outs of politics, are good with a sword, and are allowed so much freedom?"

I nearly scoff. Freedom. If he only knew how close our situations were. "I already told you I have a knack for listening at doors. I am the only daughter of an impoverished Breton noblewoman whom the count has kindly offered to take into his household. But it is a large household, and all in it are busy with their own interests and pleasures. It is easy enough to slip away unseen." Seeing an opening, I bring my blade in for another side stroke, but he sweeps it aside and grabs my wrist, trapping me.

"The truth is, you are not a noblewoman."

I jerk my arm back. "Let go of me."

"Your reflexes are too fast to have been acquired in a few sword lessons with your brothers."

I glare at him. So that is what the cunning bastard has been up to, why he has driven me so hard. "I never said that was how I learned to fight."

"No, but however you learned, it was not as a noblewoman. What do you really want from me? You clearly already know how to spar."

Even as my secrets stand partially exposed, a part of me is pleased he recognizes that I am far more than a mere noblewoman. "Let us just say I have grown rusty."

"Let us just say I do not believe you." Another pressing attack. "Who really sent you?"

"Who do you think sent me?"

He does not answer, but launches a series of strikes that are so fast and furious, it is all I can do to block and parry and keep my ribs from being broken by his brutal blows. "Maybe my mercenary company could not pay the ransom price, but has sent someone to help me escape."

I am unable to hold my ground and find myself inching toward the wall. "I have not been sent by anyone."

"That you know of."

That is when I realize just how wooly his wits have become with imprisonment. "I would know if someone had sent me."

He shrugs. "The gods are said to use what tools are available to them to achieve their ends. What if you are simply the nearest tool?"

I laugh outright. "Are you suggesting the gods wish you to be freed from this place? Why would they bother themselves with a mere mercenary?"

He shrugs again. "Why do they bother themselves with any of us?"

His words both disturb and excite me, but I do not stop to examine why that is so. Instead, I reach out and rap the back of his knuckles with the flat of my sword. He drops his weapon, and I leap forward to snatch it up. "We are done for today."

He folds his arms, observing me lazily while I secure the two swords to my back. When I begin climbing the rope, he steps toward it, holding his arms out to his sides. "Was it something I said?"

I do not look down to confirm the note of laughter in his voice. Once I have hauled myself up onto the main floor, I let the grate slam shut with extra force.

Who in the rutting hell is he? A mercenary who believes the gods want him free? He is mercurial. Almost menacing one moment, then whimsical the next.

He is not merely a sparring partner, but a whetstone upon which I must sharpen my wits.

Else risk getting cut by his.

CHAPTER 39

nd where have you been all morning?" Juliette is the most annoying of Louise's attendants here at Cognac. Her thin lips curl in an amused smile, as if she is sharing a joke with me, but there is a sharpness to her, a brittleness that is not convincing. She doesn't care if I'm sleeping longer than I ought, dallying with a lover, or simply mourning Margot in my own way. Like a bored cat, she is batting at my absence, trying to see if she can get some sort of tempest stirred up. But this morning, her question plays into my plans perfectly.

"Walking," I say, stepping fully into the room.

"For the last four hours?"

"It was a long walk. I had much to reflect upon." It is easy — so easy — to allow the pain of Margot's death to creep into my voice. It is never far from the surface — I have only to exert the slightest pressure to crack that fragile shell.

"It was raining." She does not let up, her words calling the attention of the others.

I blink owlishly. "Was it?"

That is when Jeanne pats the empty seat next to her. Of all the attendants here at Cognac, I like Jeanne the best. She is genuinely kind, with both a gentle humor and lush sensuality. It is no wonder she is the count's favorite. She is mine as well.

As I take a seat, her eyes are so full of compassion that I fear I will drown in them. I ignore their invitation and busy myself retrieving my embroidery hoop and needle case from my sewing basket.

She leans close to me. "There are better ways to deal with your grief than to make yourself sick with the ague," she says softly. "If you need someone to talk to —"

"I am fine, my lady, but thank you."

My satisfaction at turning the conversation from my own grief is short-lived. "Did the count have an opportunity to speak to you before he left?"

I am so taken aback by her frank question that the needle I am threading slips and pricks my finger. "About what, my lady?"

In answer, she reaches out and gives my arm a reassuring squeeze. "About your position in the household. He is a kind man and will treat you well."

Unable to help myself, I gape at her. There is no guile or ill will in her manner, and I marvel at that. Angoulême set her aside when Margot came to his bed, and now she is encouraging me to follow in her footsteps. "I know that well, Madame, but this is a particular kindness I do not wish."

"It will not ruin your prospects for a good marriage. Chances are, your future husband will not even know."

I do not tell her I have no intention of marrying. "While that may well be true, I don't wish to begin life with a new husband with so big a lie between us."

"You are a very pious girl. You and Louise are much alike in that."

Unable to help myself, I look over to Louise, who sits at the other end of the room, talking with Lady Alinor. "Does that not strike you as . . . odd? That two friends should share one man?" In truth, I do not understand why their arrangement does not bother Louise more, given her own piety and general envy.

Jeanne shrugs, a graceful gesture. "Louise and I are friends. Besides." Her eyes twinkle mischievously. "I think Louise benefitted somewhat from my time with the count."

My mouth quirks at this most practical of benefits. In that moment, Jeanne reminds me so much of my aunt Fabienne that it hurts. She, too, was beautiful and sophisticated, for all that she was a tanner's daughter and worked out of a tavern. She always managed to find something in life to be amused about, whether it was a patron's tastes or the way the tavern cat stuck its tongue out while sleeping.

Seeing my smile, Jeanne raises her eyebrows playfully. "Who is to say that your husband would not appreciate a wife who knew how to please him in bed?"

I see how Louise and the count benefit from this arrangement. "But what do you get out of it?"

She grows serious and purses her lips. For a moment, I imagine I see a look of pain flit across her face, but then it is gone. "What is important is that no matter where his interest moves, once you have been one of his favorites, you will always have a home among his court. You will not want for anything — food, shelter, fine clothes. Any child you have will be taken care of and educated. You will have a powerful man on your side. Your future is assured, and you will always have a place to call home."

So that is what she gains. Even though she is married to someone else, the count mitigates the absolute power her own husband can wield over her. Gives her a second avenue of security. My appreciation for her cunning grows. "Thank you, my lady, for your counsel. I will think on it."

For weeks, it has felt like a net is closing in all around me, trying to bind me to a life I do not want. But perhaps it is not a net at all. The prisoner's claims that I had been sent by the gods to rescue him felt arrogant. But when placed beside my conversation with Jeanne, it begins to feel like a steppingstone.

With the disbanding of the convent, something important and sacred will be destroyed. But more than that, young innocent lives will be irrevocably altered. Possibly ruined.

What if my destiny is to change that?

As I stitch, I think of the king and his invitation to his bed when I was at the French court. Like Angoulême, he vowed to grant my every desire. That I would want for nothing. At the time I thought it but a brash boast of his ability to see to my every physical desire, which, raised as I was, was hard not to laugh at. But when still I demurred, he pressed further, promising to grant any gift or favor I wished for. At the time, there was nothing I wanted that he could give me.

My needle stills and a warm trickle of possibility spreads through my limbs. But now, now there is something I very much wish. Something *only* he can grant. I want the convent to be allowed to continue its existence. It is not even a difficult or expensive wish.

I have always believed I had a purpose, that Mortain planned to use me as an instrument of His will, whether that be weapon or spy. Even now, I am certain there is still some larger role I am meant to play, especially as these tenuous threads of a plan begin to weave themselves together.

I alone among all the daughters of Mortain have captured the interest of the very king who is threatening to destroy His convent and those who worship Him. And I alone have been raised among women whose livelihood is to please men, ease their lust, and see to their desires.

What if *that* is my great purpose? What if I have been uniquely fashioned by both my god and fate to be the one person who can avert this tragedy from befalling the convent?

Could that be the destiny the gods have planned for me? If not sent to the convent of Saint Mortain, I would never have been sent to the French court and gotten near enough to the king to catch his eye. If I had not caught his eye, he would never have promised me my heart's desire.

It has always puzzled me that I attracted his notice and not some great beauty, like Margot. I did not engage in games of flirtation with him or any of the courtiers. He had a carefully selected stable of powdered and perfumed young women just waiting for such an invitation from him.

And yet he wanted me.

What if that is all due to some plan of the gods? What if that is why my path crossed with the prisoner — so he could show me that? For it still makes no sense that I could feel his heartbeat if he was not dying.

Examining the events in that light makes everything of a piece. Almost.

I am also to serve the duchess of Brittany — now the new queen. How does sleeping with the king honor that?

I glance over at Louise, the conversation with Jeanne still buzzing in my ears. Louise does not mind. Indeed, even benefits from it. In truth the queen's own father kept his mistress and his wife side by side. According to the gossip at the French court, the queen's bastard brother was one of her closest advisors. This is the way noble marriages work. The new queen knows that as intimately as anyone.

Besides, she has an obligation to honor the Nine and protect those who follow them. If something has prevented her from doing that, then she will no doubt be grateful to the one who does it for her.

And . . . I realize, my heart beating faster, in saving the convent, I can prove to them how wrong they were to keep me idle all these years. I will have the satisfaction of showing them their mistake in not using me sooner. In not trusting me, in not honoring the contract we made.

By saving them, I will gain their gratitude and their respect. And when they are restored to their former mission and purpose, my name will be first upon their lips.

The idea settles into the hollow place inside me. It does not fill it completely, but it is no longer as empty as it once was. If the size and edges of it do not fit perfectly, surely that is due to my own misguided expectations of what a true purpose would feel like.

Besides, the convent's lessons and guidance are rarely painless, or even comfortable. Why would this be any different?

Chapter 40

Sybella

I am allowed into the bedchamber long enough to help the duchess undress. Tension radiates off of her like a plucked bowstring. In order to give her as much time as possible to come to terms with this new development, I send the other attendants off to fetch the delicate nightshift that has been prepared especially for tonight, and steer the duchess — the queen, I correct myself — to the edge of the bed. "Here, let me remove your headdress for you." She turns, exposing the vulnerable column of her neck. "I must start calling you Your Majesty now."

"I should embrace that title. It is one of the highest offices a woman can possess." Her voice sounds as if it is coming from far away. As if she has already hidden her true self from what will soon transpire. "And yet, I find I am sorely reluctant to give up my title of duchess. In my own mind and heart, that is who I will always be, the duchess of Brittany, only assuming the title of queen in order to protect my people and my land."

I gently tug her hair to loosen it from its coil. "That you have done, Your Majesty."

She nods woodenly. As I begin unlacing her wedding gown, I try to think of something I can say to ease this for her. "Tomorrow morning when you appear in public again, most of these lords and ladies and courtiers will still be abed, sleeping off their wine-filled bellies and late-night excesses. You will likely not have to see any of them again for a long while. At least not until after your honeymoon."

The tension in her shoulders eases. "That is true."

The attendants return, laughing and giggling and bearing a shift of the finest Holland cloth with lace as delicate as a spider's webbing. I fall silent while the others slip it over her head, one of them poking her in the ribs in their haste.

At the queen's gasp of surprise, the young woman falls prostrate on the floor.

The queen and I stare at her in astonishment before the queen says, "Peace. I will not punish you. But perhaps it would be best to see to the readying of the bed. All of you." The grateful young woman rises to her feet and hurries away with the others, more subdued now.

"Oh, well done, Your Majesty."

"I will take a jab in the ribs if I can barter it for a few moments of privacy," she says wryly.

In silence, I brush her hair until it shines in the glow of the candles. I wish — desperately — for something to give her to make this easier — some charm or potion or clever advice, but I have nothing. Instead, I press my lips briefly upon the top of her head as I would one of my own sisters. "You are a queen, born and bred. Your strength, your grace, your love of your people — those are what define you, not this performance the regent demands of you. Tonight will quickly be forgotten, but your child on the throne will be a part of history forever."

She rests her head for a moment against my cheek before motioning to the other ladies that she is ready.

When I close the chamber door behind me, every move is controlled, precise. I calmly fold my hands before me and keep my face arranged in pleasant lines as I move toward the crowd in the main salon. The regent has made it clear — she is no friend to the duchess, but her enemy.

Is the king complicit in this or oblivious? I cannot fathom the doting man who paid court to the duchess, nor even the reserved chivalrous king I saw tonight, countenancing these humiliations, but perhaps he is far more skilled at subterfuge than he looks. Or more fully under his sister's influence.

My stomach churns at how foul a place men have made the world — aided by the women who blindly adhere to their rules. The regent has more power than any woman in France. It would be so easy for her to soften the way for others. That she does not feels like the rankest of betrayals.

My steps bring me to the Breton contingent, gathered among themselves and talking quietly together. As I approach, they look up. Chancellor Montauban sees something in my face and takes a tiny step back. "Did you know?" I demand, my fists clenched.

He wisely refrains from asking, *Know what?* "I am not surprised that they have decided upon this," he says carefully, "but no, I did not have prior knowledge of it."

I turn to glower at the Prince of Orange. "And you?"

To his credit, he meets my gaze, even though it fair scalds him. "I never assumed it would be otherwise. It is precisely the reason the French were able to have the proxy marriage to the emperor annulled. With so much at stake, I never doubted the consummation would be a public affair."

"Then why did you not bother to warn your cousin, dear Prince? For she had no inkling this was coming. It was you who should have been there as she prepared for this public spectacle so you could find the words to ease her embarrassment and humiliation." He looks somewhat taken aback, ashamed even, and a warm glow of satisfaction erupts in my belly.

I step away. "The saints damn you all," I hiss at them. "If you cannot protect your own duchess from these indignities, what earthly good are any of you?" Someone reaches for my hand. There is only a split second to decide whether to punch them or pull away. I am — only just — able to restrain myself, and am glad when I see that it is Father Effram.

He grimaces apologetically. "As odious as it is, my dear, it is truly for the best, and you know I have no love of these customs. But in the end, it will protect our duchess and ensure that the pope agrees with his bishops and approves the marriage."

The fact that he is right does not make it easier to bear. Without another word, I turn on my heel and storm away.

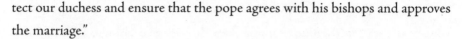

My steps take me out of the grand salon to the main foyer, then out the door to the courtyard. Outside, the celebration continues. Rivers of wine are poured at every corner. Flutes and trumpets, tambourines and raucous cheers echo throughout the night air. I step around a procession of merrymakers and keep walking until I reach the stables. It is quieter here. It is also where the off-duty queen's guard can be found. I want to drink and fight and let my anger spill out into the night until I am naught but an emptied husk.

I do not look for Beast. He will only try to talk me out of it, and I am in no mood for reason. Reason is sitting patiently outside the king's bedchamber, listening carefully for every little grunt or murmur and eagerly awaiting the sight of virgin blood. I will have none of it.

I find the lot of them lounging by the far side of the garrison, drinking wine and talking amongst themselves. When I am spotted, elbows nudge and they sit up straighter.

By the time I reach them, the jug of wine has mysteriously disappeared.

"Good evening, my lady," Sir Roscoff says.

"Good evening, Sir Roscoff." I turn to the others. "Where did the wine go?"

"Wine, my lady?" He turns to the others. "I saw no wine — did you?"

Ignoring him, I hold out my hand and waggle my fingers. "Hand over the jug now, or suffer the consequences. Oh, and a fresh cup." Reluctantly — no doubt concerned about Beast's response — they comply with my request, and the jug reappears. With a look of resignation, Roscoff pours me some wine and hands it to me with an elaborate bow. "Your refreshment, my lady."

I toss it back in one gulp. It barely masks the taste of bitterness and futility that sits so heavy on my tongue. I hold out the cup. "Another."

Feigning concentration to hide his raised eyebrows, Roscoff does as I order. I drink again — this time more slowly — until it is gone. "And one more."

Roscoff cannot contain himself any longer. "My lady? Are you sure this is the best course of action? Perhaps I should find Sir Waroch."

I study him archly. "I did not realize that Beast's handpicked soldiers were the sort to run tattling to their mothers."

Roscoff nearly bobbles the jug, and I hear a stifled snicker from one of the others. Sipping my newly poured wine, I study the men. "What game are we playing, gentlemen?"

One of them shrugs. "Dice, for all the good it's done us. Fortuna is not shining on any of us tonight."

"I believe she has taken the night off," I mutter darkly. "Besides, dice is for green young men afraid to wager anything of importance."

Someone with a beakish nose and a protruding Adam's apple answers. "I have two months' wages that beg to disagree."

I study him. "What is your name?" I ask.

"Poulet, my lady."

I smile in delight, for indeed, he looks much like a chicken. "Truly?"

He bows with a charming flourish.

"Well, Sir Poulet. Let us play a different game — one for higher stakes that will not suck your purse dry," I suggest.

"By all means, my lady. That is the sort of wagering I could warm up to."

"Excellent. Gentlemen" — I set down my cup and retrieve my knives from their sheaths — "how good are you with your daggers?"

CHAPTER 41

nly Sir Gaultier, who has fought by my side in the past and knows my skill, refuses to play. But the others are eager enough. It does not take long for me to beat all but two of them at a dagger toss. "That was too easy," I complain. "Who is up for something more challenging?"

Poulet, to his credit, is willing once I explain the new game to him, and cheerfully takes up position against the barn wall. As I raise my knife, the only sign of his nervousness is the occasional bobbing of his Adam's apple.

"My lady," Sir Roscoff begins, "I do not think this is wise."

I arch one brow at him. "Do you doubt my skill?"

"No. I doubt my good health should Beast learn I have allowed you to use his men for target practice."

"And you would be right," a deep rumbling voice says behind me. Dammit. Usually I am well aware of Beast's approach. Either the game or the drink has dulled my senses. I turn to face him with my cockiest grin. "You know I'll not miss. They will survive intact."

He takes the knife from my hand. "Their bodies, yes, but not their pride."

"You are ruining all my fun." I try to keep my words playful, but they have a whiff of desperation to them. There is nowhere else I can *be* right now. If I cannot stand here, losing myself in the taste of cheap wine and the precision of throwing sharp things, there will be nothing to do but think of the duchess, and that way lies madness. Or something truly reckless.

Much like a parent adjusting a child's cloak, Beast gently slips my knife into its sheath. "The hour is late, and your duties call."

"My duties?" I scoff. "Did you not hear? I have been released for the night."

He leans in close to whisper in my ear, "The deed is done, the proof exhibited, and I believe the duchess would benefit greatly from your company."

I frown in confusion. "The regent expressly told me I was not to return until morning."

He shakes his head in faint exasperation. "And when in the name of the Nine has that ever stopped you before?"

His words are as bracing as a slap to my cheek, chasing away the effects of the wine as well as the taste of defeat. Without another word, I lift my skirts and hurry toward the palace.

"Thank you for your hospitality to Lady Sybella," Beast calls back to the others before catching up to me.

I glance at him. "You cannot accompany me to the duchess's chambers." Embarrassment at my obedience to the regent's order makes my words more curt than I intend.

"No," he agrees. "But I can see you safely to the grand salon and ensure you do not gut some witless Frenchman who is too dumb to steer clear of you tonight."

My lips twitch into a reluctant smile. "You do have your purposes."

"I like to think so."

When I arrive at the queen's chamber, I find her alone in bed while the three ladies in waiting assigned by Madame Regent busy themselves hanging up her cloth of gold wedding gown and being certain none of the seed pearls are in danger of coming loose.

I take one look at the new queen huddled against the pillows with the covers up to her chin, then spring into action. "Where is the bath?" I bark.

The other ladies turn and stare at me. "What bath?" the tallest one asks. "The regent did not order a bath."

"The regent did not just endure her deflowering. Send for a hot bath, with lavender and comfrey." They stare at me a long moment. I clap my hands at them. "Now!" I am shocked at how similar to the regent my own voice sounds.

Finally the featherbrained women begin to move. "And have these linens changed while the queen is at her bath."

"But," a small-faced woman protests, "she will be leaving for Plessis-lès-Tours in the morning,"

I draw to my full height so that I am towering over her. "But she must sleep in them tonight, and surely you would agree a new queen should not have to sleep in her own blood?"

The woman flinches and glances at the queen, finally remembering this is a young woman and not some pawn in a game of the regent's. "Very well, my lady."

Only when they have left and I am alone with the queen do I allow myself to approach the bed. She stares up at me, her brown eyes enormous in her pale face. "Thank you," she whispers. Unexpectedly, she scoots over, making room for me to sit.

"Are you very uncomfortable?" I ask.

She wiggles around a little and grimaces. "Some."

I nod. "A warm bath should help."

She peers more closely at me, wrinkling her nose. "Lady Sybella, did you perchance fall into a vat of wine?"

I wince. "No, Your Majesty. 'Twas but a clumsy Frenchman who stumbled and spilled his wine on my gown."

"Did he, now," she muses dryly.

Just then the door opens and a throng of servants parade in bearing a copper tub, ewers of steaming water, and fresh bed linens. I help the queen into a robe and quickly braid her hair before wrapping it in a coil on the top of her head. When I am finished, the bath is ready and the last of the servants lingers at the door. "Will there be anything else, Your Majesty?"

It takes the queen a moment to realize he is talking to her. "No, that will be all. Thank you."

When we are alone again, I take the robe from her shoulders and she steps into the bath, wincing a bit as the warm water reaches tender places.

I rack my mind for something comforting to tell her. Between my family and my work for the convent, I have far more experience with the unpleasant nature of the intimacies between the sexes rather than the gentler ones. "If he is a kind man, and I think he is, this should be the worst of it."

She glances up, blushing. "I am glad to know it will get better. If it is like that every time, I am not sure how women can ever have any babies."

Babies. My mind shies away from the word, and I abruptly turn and fetch the linen cloths from the washstand. "He *was* kind, was he not?" I dip one of the cloths in the warm water, then allow it to trickle down her back.

"He was, yes. Chivalrous, even, and seemed eager that I should be happy. Considering all the men who have laid claim to my hand, I should be — I *am* — relieved that he appears solicitous. It is just . . ." She shrugs her slender shoulders.

I do not know what makes me so certain what she is keeping herself from saying, but I lean down and whisper, "It is just that you are accustomed to ruling, taking your own council, giving the orders. And now it is hard to know how much of that will be left to you."

She spins around to look at me. "Yes! That is exactly what I fear."

My hand clenches around the wet cloth. The regent's plan to weaken the queen's faith in herself is already taking root. "In most men's lives, there is room for only one woman from whom they will take counsel. We must ensure that woman is you and not his sister."

"But can we do that? She has had his ear for so long. Overseen his education and been governing in his name for years."

I begin scooping up the warm water once more. "And that will work in our favor, Your Grace. No young man — and certainly not a king — wishes to be under the thumb of his older sister. Especially one who made decisions he thought he should have been able to make himself. I imagine that we need only faintly fan those flames of resentment. Besides —" I stop, fearing I am about to go too far.

"Besides what?" the duchess prompts.

"I am not certain it is my place to say some of these things to you." In truth, my upbringing probably demands that I be the last woman on earth to share such things with her.

"Who else will do it?" she asks fiercely. "My dead mother? Madame Dinan, who chose to betray me? The regent, who has only her own interests and love of power?" The duchess laughs, a fragile, bitter sound. "Her ladies in waiting whom she is trying to surround me with rather than my own? Of a certainty, *they* will not tell me."

She is right. "Very well, Your Grace, but know that my view of the relations between men and women is somewhat . . . cynical and worldly."

"It cannot be more cynical than being inspected like a brood mare or prize milking cow."

"True enough. The other advantage you will have is that you are his young, nubile bride." Her cheeks grow pink. "As such, you will offer the king certain advantages that a mere sister cannot. You will also have access to him in his more vulnerable moments, which can work in a woman's favor."

The queen sets her mouth in a resolute line, as if she has just been handed a weapon and is determined to use it to its best advantage.

"And lastly," I continue, "if you give the king a son, he is sure to grant you high favor and indulge you whenever possible. Many men act thusly when presented with their first son, a king even more so."

The water has begun to cool now, so I help her out of the tub and dry her with linen towels. She grimaces. "You were right. The bath did help."

I pull back the clean linens on the bed and she climbs in. Unable to help myself, I tuck the covers up under her chin. "Is there anything else I can get, Your Majesty?" Her new title feels strange on my tongue and will take some getting used to.

"Stay, if you please. The king will not be returning. With my other ladies dismissed, there is no one else, and I would rather not be alone."

CHAPTER 42

Genevieve

nce I am certain everyone is asleep for the night, I rise from my bed, wrap a thick cloak around my night shift, and slip into my boots. My excuse, should I meet anyone, is that I felt a need to pray in the chapel. It is well in keeping with my behavior of late.

In the hallway outside Angoulême's office, I pause to listen. It is as empty as a tomb and just as quiet. Reassured, I quickly open the door and step inside before shutting it softly behind me.

I have searched his study before, but not often. The risk is too great. But there are times, times when my lack of knowledge about my own circumstance becomes so overwhelming that I simply must know more than what he tells me.

It is also a good way to verify he is not withholding vital information. So far, he has been forthcoming with all that he knows.

But tonight I am here to examine his maps. I lift one of the cushions from the bench at the window and lay it along the bottom of the door so no light will leak out. When that is done, I go to the fireplace, strike the flint, and light a brace of candles.

His maps are carefully rolled and stacked in a stiff leather canister. I pull out the first one, carefully unrolling it. It is of Flanders and the surrounding area. I put it back and reach for another. It is the fourth one I find that shows the roads of France.

The wedding between the duchess and the king took place in Langeais. Louise told the other attendants that the royal couple would spend a month at the king's castle at Plessis-lès-Tours, which is north and to the east of Cognac. I can travel north to Angers, then follow the Loire River to Plessis, but there is no main road, only a series of lesser ones that crisscross through the small towns and cities between here and the Loire.

Or I can travel east from Cognac to the city of Angoulême, where a main road runs directly north to Tours. The main road is faster. And my horses are in the city of Angoulême. With Angoulême and his men away until the new year, I do not have to worry about being recognized in that city. The main road is also more well traveled, making a lone traveler stand out less.

My route decided on, I try to etch the roads and rivers and towns upon my mind.

When I am certain I have the route memorized, I roll the map up and return it to its tub. As I turn to leave, my gaze falls on the intricately tooled leather box that Angoulême uses for storing correspondence. My fingers itch.

What if it holds additional correspondence from the convent? Or information on the puzzle that calls himself Maraud? It would be foolish to leave without searching it.

Inside is a thick stack of letters and messages. I set them on his desk, paying careful attention to the exact order and placement I found them in. The first message is from the king, announcing his intention to marry the duchess of Brittany. The second is from a General Cassel, reporting on the situation in Flanders. There is one from Viscount Rohan, inviting the count to his holding in Brittany. Indeed, there are dozens and dozens of letters, none of which has any bearing on the convent or the prisoner.

When I am nearly the bottom at the box, the big bold strokes of the regent's handwriting catch my eye. I lift the parchment gently by the corners, noting that it is not signed. But the writing is most definitely hers. There is only one reason she would she send an unsigned letter.

Because she did not wish anyone to know it was from her.

With regards to your questions of the prisoner, he is to remain in your possession. Due to a shift in the political winds, it will be better if he is never released. It would be best for everyone concerned if he were simply forgotten. The king, especially, would be distraught to learn of his existence or the nature of his confinement. I cannot guess how the king would react if he knew you were the one to have treated him thus. Since he is in your custody, it behooves you to be certain the king never finds out.

Do not write again of this matter.

It does not mention Maraud by name, but the date, the circumstances, and the instructions all fit with what he has told me. Indeed, it is nearly as cryptic as his own story, but verifies his claims to some degree. I wonder if he knows it was the regent's orders that landed him in the oubliette? Or that the king would be distraught to learn of his very existence? Surely the king would not be distraught over a simple mercenary being treated in such a manner.

While the letter does not contradict anything Maraud has said, neither does it shed further light on the subject. So far, he has kept every promise he has made. Honored every condition he has agreed to. And yet . . . and yet I feel there is more to all of this than I can see. If he is doing those things, it is because it serves his own purpose. Whether that purpose is merely to stay alive one day longer or something else altogether remains to be seen.

Chapter 43

Sybella

am awake before the regent's attendants come in to wait upon the queen — but just barely. My head feels as if it is inhabited by a dozen goldsmiths' hammers, and my mouth tastes like something from the bottom of a watering trough. I have only just straightened my hair and gown and am assisting the queen from the bed while trying not to retch when they descend upon us; a loud, brightly colored flock of birds chirping and twittering, their beady eyes everywhere at once.

The tiny hammers in my head swell to the size of a blacksmith's mallet. Fortunately, we do not have time to linger, as the queen would like to bid her council members farewell. They are not to travel with us any further, but will remain here and avail themselves of the king's hospitality before they return to Brittany.

It is a hard goodbye, made even harder by the keen, inquisitive scrutiny of the regent's attendants. I hang back somewhat, as I have still not forgiven the councilors for the indignities the queen has had to suffer. Chancellor Montauban, the Prince of Orange, and the Bishop of Rennes all stand soberly as their new queen approaches them. "I cannot thank you all enough." She speaks in a low voice that frustrates the attempts of others to overhear. "For all that you have done to get me here. I am only sorry I cannot bring every one of you with me."

The chancellor takes her outstretched hand and bows low over it. "It is my most fervent wish that you will not have need of us in your new life, Your Majesty."

The queen smiles. "Your counsel and loyalty will always have a place in my life, my lord."

When she turns to the Prince of Orange, he astonishes us all — himself included — and pulls the queen into a quick embrace. "Take care, dear cousin. You are queen of France, and no one can naysay you now."

She nods at him, then turns to the short, red-robed Bishop of Rennes. He clasps her hands in his. "Take care, dear child. Remember to trust in God and say your prayers, and all shall be as He wills it."

It is all I can do not to roll my eyes at his words. Every step of the way he has claimed that God willed it, never mind that it was the saints — and their followers — who wrested this victory for the duchess in the end.

To my great delight, I learn that Father Effram will be traveling with us as the queen's personal confessor. His eyes twinkle as he informs us of this, and I cannot think of a more compassionate, morally nimble confessor to have interceding on one's behalf.

And then the regent arrives, sweeping into the courtyard like an ill wind in a long, ermine-lined riding cloak. When it is clear that she is alone, the queen frowns, perplexed. "Where is the king?"

"I am afraid he had to leave earlier this morning, Your Majesty."

Chancellor Montauban eyes the regent unhappily. "He will not be escorting Her Majesty himself?"

She dismisses his question with a cool glance. "As I said, he has already left."

"Surely, after the attack . . ." Father Effram ventures.

The regent turns a gimlet eye upon him. My bilious stomach and pounding head are grateful that it is he who has asked the question this time and not me. "She will be perfectly safe."

"It is fortunate, then, that she travels with her queen's guard." The chancellor refrains from pointing out it was the very one the regent tried to dismiss. Which is no doubt why he is chancellor and I am not.

The regent's gaze goes immediately to where Beast waits along with the eight other guards, resplendent in their chain mail and white tabards. She wants to argue. But why? And how in the name of the saints will the king and queen have any chance to establish affection for each other, let alone trust, with this interfering woman following them on their honeymoon, sticking her long nose between them at every opportunity?

The interfering woman gives an elegant shrug. "They are welcome to ride with us."

Beast does not argue. He does not need to. His implacable will and enormous bulk are argument enough.

Even though we are traveling along the Loire, in the heart of France owned by the king, I cannot relax and enjoy the morning's ride. My glance darts to the surrounding woods, wondering who might be hiding there. I hold my breath every time we cross a bridge, bracing myself for another ambush. And every few minutes, I must seek out those I love, counting them like a farmwife counts her chickens, needing to be certain they're still safe.

I am so busy watching for danger that I do not see it when it slips up next to me on a white palfrey. "Why so ill at ease, Lady Sybella?"

The regent's voice at my elbow causes my shoulders to tense, as if waiting for a blow. "I am sorry, Madame, I did not hear you approach."

"I daresay," she murmurs wryly. "You were too busy gaping at every leaf that rustles in the wind. I would like to know why."

"It may have something to do with recently being ambushed." My voice is tarter than verjuice.

"You Bretons do like to harp on that, don't you? Does your queen's guard not make you feel safe? If not, what use are they?"

"They are the only thing that gives me peace of mind."

The regent's nostrils flare, but she lets the matter drops and abruptly changes the subject. "Who are the two young girls riding with the other attendants?"

Her words land like heavy rocks in my already queasy stomach. "They are two young women the queen has agreed to foster at court."

Her brows arch faintly at this. "Yes, but *who* are they?"

I consider — briefly — lying, but it is too easily disproved. There is no choice but to tell her the truth. "They are my sisters."

Her casual curiosity sharpens into keen interest. "Why are they not with their father?"

I tighten my fingers on the reins and stare at the space between my horse's ears. "He took a mortal injury and is not able to provide for their care." My voice is cool and distant, signaling it is not a subject I wish to discuss.

It does not work with her. "What of his sons?"

I glance at her. "My eldest brother is the king of Navarre, which keeps him quite busy."

"But what of Sire d'Albret's other sons? Why are they not providing for their sisters?"

It has not taken her long to piece together my family's name. It was inevitable that she would learn at some point, but I do not like it all the same.

"They have," I patiently explain. "By placing them in my care. Besides, what better way to provide for them than have them fostered by the queen of France? I believe you yourself have set this example, have you not? You have taken scores of girls under your tutelage and protection."

The words are the nicest I have uttered about the regent. They feel false and unfamiliar on my tongue. Her nostrils flare with pride. "I have always believed in providing a solid foundation for girls and women to follow." She sniffs, eloquently conveying her doubt that the queen is up to the task. "I will be sure to advise the queen in this matter. Molding young minds is not to be taken lightly."

I do not know if it is my pounding head or her own consummate political skill, but whatever I say, whatever direction I try to steer her in, only captures her interest further. "Your generosity knows no bounds, Madame."

When she lifts her reins and returns to the head of the column, I am left with the uneasy sensation that in revealing my sisters, I have just handed her a weapon.

CHAPTER 44

Genevieve

s there an upcoming tourney you are training for? Why are you pushing so hard this morning?" Maraud's back is pressed against the wall, the tip of my baselard at his throat.

"That is twice now I have had you cornered." I try to keep the lilt of victory from my voice, but I do not succeed.

He shoves my sword aside with his forearm. "You will not always be so fortunate as to do your fighting in a rabbit warren," he mutters. "We have practiced all the close-quarter maneuvers scores of times. We are too limited here."

"And what do you suggest?" I ask, knowing full well what will come next.

"I suggest we begin using one of the rooms where they first held me prisoner, rather than this hole."

"You weren't always down here?"

"No. I was in a cell above for the first months of my stay. Given daily food and water as well." He smiles ruefully.

I lift my sword again, making sure he sees the point aimed at his heart. "And what did you do to earn being flung down in this pit?"

"You are as tiresome as a yapping dog with that question."

"Answer it."

His gaze meets mine, as open and earnest as a babe's. "I do not know. One day they wrapped a gag around my mouth, bound my hands, and shoved me down here."

I cannot help but think of the letter I discovered in Angoulême's study. "You are not bound or gagged now."

"No." His smile is one of grim triumph and puts me in mind of a wolf.

Why would his circumstances change so? "When was this?"

"That is hard to say. Accounting for time is difficult down here, but it was before Michaelmas."

"Not so very long, then."

He raises a dark brow at me. "I would beg to differ."

"Touché."

He brings his sword up to tap my blade. "Which brings us back to the point at hand. We need a larger practice area."

I snort. "What will we do in a larger cell?"

"You will back me into a corner even faster."

Unable to help myself, I laugh. "It would be most convenient if I were to trust you to return to the oubliette like a dutiful sheep to its pen once we had finished our practicing, but I am not a fool, Jackanapes. Especially since your story has more holes than a beggar's cloak."

"What do you mean?"

"I mean, your concern for the duchess is most unmercenary-like. The captain of her armies knows your name. You have not been killed nor ransomed. And you are such an ardent follower of Saint Camulos that you believe he would send someone to help you. If you have such a heightened sense of your own importance, why shouldn't I?" I do not tell him of the letter. I am not ready to reveal what I have learned.

He comes at me fast, pressing hard in a flurry of blows that take all of my concentration to block. "Mayhap the confidence you speak of comes from knowing that whatever life throws my way, I can wrest some sort of victory from it."

He is so concentrated on pressing his attack that he creates a small opening for me to duck and spin to the side, allowing me to get out from under his guard. "That may very well be true," I say, "but I also know that when one strikes too close to the truth, people react defensively. Your own fury gives away your secrets."

"Your keen sense of observation only enforces my conviction that you are not who you say you are. But to answer your *incessant* question, I am the fourth son of an impoverished minor Breton lord who sold my services as a mercenary."

I want to crow with satisfaction. I knew it! "Why would you fight as a mercenary and not under your family's coat of arms?"

A sour smile twists his lips. "Clearly you have never met my family."

For some reason my mind goes back to our conversations in the dark, conversations I have forbidden him to speak of, and think of the heart wounds he spoke so knowledgably about. "So it was not your mercenary company, but your family that refused to pay ransom?"

He shifts to his right and tries to find an opening on my left, but I block it. "If there were any ransom demands sent, that would be the most likely reason it was not paid." He picks his words carefully.

"Why did they not simply kill you once the ransom price was refused?"

He hesitates, and in that hesitation, I can feel all the lies he is considering. "I do not know why I was chosen for such hospitality."

That is a lie. It has the shape and feel of truth, but smells off in some way. "Why are you really here?"

"I already told you." His eyes meet mine, challenging me to remember.

"No, you didn't."

"I did. Before. In the dark. On your third visit here."

"This is my third visit," I tell him through clenched teeth.

"Ah, perhaps I am mistaken." He smiles smugly, and I want to smack it off his face.

Instead, I begin a new attack, backing him against the wall. "Since you dreamed that you already told me, you should have no trouble repeating your answer now."

There is a long moment of silence except for the rapid tapping of metal on wood. Finally, he speaks. "I saw something. On the battlefield. The commander overseeing the route and subsequent surrender summarily executed two nobles to whom he had given quarter. That is the only reason I can think of that I have been imprisoned. But why he did not just order me killed, I do not know."

And there is the truth. I can feel the hum of it in his words. My mind reels. "But that goes against all I have learned about how the game of war is played among the powerful."

"Precisely. And why not just kill me and be done with it? Furthermore, who would take a mercenary's word against the king's general?"

"It is a mystery within a mystery within a mystery," I murmur.

"You are wise to be mistrustful," he says, his voice serious. "But I would have you know this. I would never endanger the only person who has shown me kindness and humanity in the last twelvemonth."

His words are as surprising as they are sincere, and catch me unawares. Surely that is the only reason his wooden blade is able to slip inside my guard and rest ever so gently against my collarbone.

My heart quickens. Even though he holds a rough practice weapon, he is also a seasoned soldier and could undoubtedly use it to kill me. It would be ugly, and far more painful than a sharp metal blade, but it would do the job. As I stare into his shadowed face, I become aware of all the things in this room he could kill me with—his wooden sword, the knotted rope, even his large, powerful hands. Furthermore, he is willing me to see that he could have overtaken me at any time and has chosen not to.

Well, he thinks he can overtake me, but he does not know who or what I truly am. I whip the stiletto from its hiding place, intending to bring the point of it up to rest against his throat. But he is quick—far quicker than I guessed—and knocks the knife from my hand so that I am left defenseless with his wooden blade still pointed at my gullet.

We share a long moment of silence. "It seems we have come to an impasse."

"No impasse, my lady." He removes his sword and takes a step back. "Simply an understanding. Here. Let me show you how to recover from such a move." He retrieves my knife from the floor, hands it to me, then spends the next half hour showing me how to send my knife spinning into my other hand with a mere flick of my wrist.

I am impressed, in spite of myself. "Do you have more tricks like that you can show me?"

"A dozen, at least."

He could not have dangled sweeter bait in front of me. The allure of having an array of such tricks and skills at my disposal to demonstrate to the convent just how ready I am, or to use in the service of the new queen, is irresistible. Besides, moving to a larger room — increasing the risk he presents — will be excellent training for the road.

CHAPTER 45

ow that my destiny is calling me, it is nearly impossible to sit still. I am eager to be away from here — on the road to my greater purpose.

But the open road is a lawless place traveled by bandits, vandals, and roving bands of mercenaries. Even though I am skilled with weapons, my training with Maraud has reminded me that so are many men. A lone woman presents a ripe target. Indeed, all the attackers must do is shout "whore!" before their attack, and their actions are no longer breaking the law or even considered a sin by the Church. There will not necessarily be time to get to my weapon, or even trust that I can deliver a killing blow.

So tonight, I carry the two hairnets over to the small table against the wall and carefully remove the wax pearls. All told, there are nearly three dozen of them. Some are slightly shrunken and dry, but others are round and plump with poison. I slip my needle case from my pocket and study my collection of needles.

The two largest are best for picking locks, so I leave those alone. The smaller, finer ones are too light to be of any use, which leaves the four midsize needles. I remove them from the case and knot each of them with a short piece of red thread so I will know which ones I have altered.

I am so pleased with this idea of mine that, for a brief moment, I cannot wait to tell Margot of it before the memories come rushing back.

My hand holding the needle trembles slightly, so I brace the butt of my palms on the table and press hard against the wood. I will not think of her. I will not.

When my hands are steady again, I take one of the red-knotted needles and the fattest pearl, then slip the needle into it so that the point is immersed in the poison. I leave it there to soak and repeat the process for the other three needles. As they steep, I turn my mind to the matter of my own death. How best to fake that?

The part of me trained by the convent has all sorts of clever ideas. But all of those would require a body, and I will have need of mine. Because of that, I settle on drowning. The current of the Charente River, especially swollen with winter rain, would easily carry away the body of anyone who fell into its depths.

After a quarter hour I withdraw the needles from the poison and place them along the table so that their tips hang over the edge while they dry.

Now. Now I am ready to risk sparring with Maraud in a bigger room. If he is planning to overpower me, or attempt an escape of any sort, he will have a surprise waiting for him.

CHAPTER 46

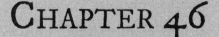

Sybella

he great towers of Plessis-lès-Tours come into sight just as darkness begins to fall, their pointed turrets thrusting up from the surrounding forest like four raised spears. The walls are of the blackest stone, the crenellations as wide and gaping as a giant's teeth.

The late king of France, the Spider they called him, was well known to live in fear of plots and schemes and treason that might be planned against him. That is what happens to evil spiders; they are so used to weaving webs, they believe they will be caught in one as well.

But only if they could get to him, I realize as I take in the full scale of Plessis-lès-Tours's fortifications. We must first cross a moat, then are met by an outer wall, after which we pass through another trench that is edged with palisades of iron topped with sharp clusters of spikes. I do not know whether to thank the saints for the extra protection or curse them for commending us to a prison. Of a certainty, no one will be able to breach those defenses. Not even Pierre.

When we finally gain the innermost bailey, there is no one to greet us in the courtyard. Not so much as a steward — and certainly not the king. I glance at the queen, whose face is shuttered and pale. Once we have dismounted, we are not even taken to the grand entrance, but instead are ushered to a side door, where we follow a back passageway.

"It is faster this way," the regent says at the queen's questioning look.

When at last we reach the queen's apartments, they are grand enough, but they are also as cold and uninviting as humanly possible. Where is the king's lavish welcome now? Or was that all merely a show for the attending nobles and guests rather than the queen? That thought sends an icy finger trailing down my spine. What pressing duties could he possibly have that would prevent him welcoming the queen to her new home?

Or is this the regent's doing? A way to intimidate the queen and imply how unwelcome she is?

The regent claps her hands and orders the fire and candles to be lit. Within minutes, hard-pressed servants swarm us, making every effort to see to our needs.

Next come a veritable army of the regent's ladies in waiting, scuttling out of their hiding places like beetles from under a rock. They surround the queen and nudge her own ladies aside so efficiently that it must be by design.

I turn a baleful glower upon the regent, but it is too dark for her to see it.

"I am not certain the room will hold all of us." The queen's voice can barely be heard from behind the wall of bodies that surrounds her.

The regent motions a lingering servant out of the room. "Of course not. You will be served by my ladies now that you are part of the French court."

The queen firmly steps around two of the regent's attendants blocking her path. "That is most kind of you." Her words are covered in frost. "But I am accustomed to my own attendants and intend to keep them with me." There is a clash of silence as the two women's wills test each other. Not looking away from the regent, the queen says calmly, "Elsibet and Heloise, you will stay with me tonight. The rest of you are no doubt exhausted from our travels, and I am certain Madame Regent's attendants can serve me well enough for one night."

The regent's nostrils flare, but she says nothing. Perhaps she thinks she has won, but by the queen's expression, the matter is far from settled.

It quickly becomes clear that it has always been the regent's intention to separate the queen from her ladies, for there are a number of chambers set aside for our use. My assigned room is small and on the uppermost floor, far removed from the queen's apartments — or the regent's. By silent agreement, Aeva and Tola accompany Tephanie and me and the girls.

The room contains a bed large enough for four to sleep abreast, with thick brocade bed curtains to help block out the chill. There is a fireplace, a begrudging scrap of a rug, and a small chest. I immediately cross the room to examine the two narrow windows on the far wall. I do not open them, but place my nose against the thick glass and peer down. It is a long, sheer drop to the courtyard below. Only a mouse could climb that.

Assured that my sisters' physical safety and needs are adequate, I turn to Louise, who is marching. "Is something wrong, my sweet?"

Louise scrunches up her face. "My backside is sore from all the sitting."

I suppress a smile. "And you?" I ask Charlotte. She stands against the bed, her fingers lightly running over the coverlet as if assessing precisely how old and worn it is and how that translates into our status as guests.

"It is a small room," she says at last. "And dark."

"Yes, but we have it to ourselves, which is a luxury."

Her gaze finally meets mine. "Why do you care that we have it to ourselves? You will hardly even be here. You have more important things to do than tend to us." There is no heat in her voice, no emotion at all. Which is how I know it is bothering her. Although the reason it is bothering her is unclear, as she has shown little enough preference for my company.

I reach out and lift her fingers from their examination, then hold them firmly in mine. "I do have other duties that I must see to, but you and your sister are the most important duty I have. All other duties serve that. Never doubt it, Charlotte."

She snorts. "You don't protect us. Aeva and Tola do. Even Tephanie protects us more than you."

Behind me, I hear Aeva take a step toward us, but I hold out my hand. "Safety is not only about preventing a physical attack. There are many ways I see to your protection, and some of them keep me from your side much of the time. That is why I take turns with Aeva, Tola, and Tephanie. Besides"—I reach out and tweak a strand of her hair—"surely you do not long for my company."

Her eyes flash with annoyance. "I *don't*. But you told Pierre you would see to our safety. You claim that is why we are here. But it was only under your protection that I have ever been in danger."

Her words find their target as effectively as any booted foot or clenched fist, and I let go of her hair. It is better to tell her the truth? List for her all the ways she would be in danger if she stayed?

Do I tell her that I was younger than she is when Pierre first kissed me? Younger than she is when I gave him the scar across his eyebrow when he tried it a second time?

That I was only a year older than she when he first came scratching at my bedroom door? Of the terror I felt in those moments? Or the extreme measures I took to deter him? Measures that haunt me still.

No. I will not rip away the few remaining shreds of her innocence from her eyes.

"I can understand why you would think that. But as you yourself saw, even being the duchess of Brittany cannot guarantee safety from attack. As you also saw, your safety was adequately provided for, as you and Louise both survived the encounter."

"And we got to go to the wedding." Louise's voice is tentative, eager to soothe.

Charlotte spares her a scornful glance. "We did not *go* to the wedding. We watched from the gallery above. It is not the same thing at all."

"And yet," I remind her, "you were the two youngest allowed anywhere near the ceremony."

She shrugs one shoulder; whether that means *true* or *who cares*, I do not know.

She is at a hard age, stuck in the body of a child but poised on the verge of womanhood, and all of that further muddied and made more turbulent by the nature of our family and her upbringing. When and how far this small green apple falls from the family tree is anyone's guess, but I will not give up on her.

Not yet. "But, you are right," I say briskly. "I should do more to see to both your comfort and your safety now that we have arrived. And your lessons," I add.

She glares at me.

"Ah! Do not be so quick to complain! This is one lesson I think you'll enjoy." I take the small knife from the chain at my waist and hold it out to her, praying she does not grab it and poke me with it.

She stares at it, her eyes both wary and greedy. "What am I to do with that?"

"Learn how to use it," I tell her. "You're of an age when you can begin learning to see to your own safety. Aeva and Tola can show you how to use it when I am not here."

Louise eyes the knife anxiously and retreats to Tephanie's side. "Do I have to have one?"

"No, sweeting. Not until you are old enough and want one."

She frowns. "Does Charlotte want one?"

I turn back to Charlotte, waiting.

"Yes," she says at last. "I do."

"Very well." I lower my voice to naught but a whisper. "The first rule is that if you ever use it on Louise, I will make you sorrier than you can even imagine."

It is the first time I have ever threatened her, or even promised punishment. She looks at me, her chin set at a defiant angle, but something in my face convinces her that defiance in this matter is unwise. "Of course I won't."

I nod. "Of course. But it is always best to be certain."

❧

The king's absence eats at me. I want — *need* — to know where he is, what excuse he could possibly have for not being here.

I want to know if I — and the queen — have been duped by the warm welcome he provided at the wedding or if he is simply thoughtless.

Or perhaps there truly is some urgent matter of state. If so, I would like to know that as well.

Because the royal couple's time together at Plessis-lès-Tours is meant to be a chance to get to know one another away from the demands of the full court and affairs of state, the castle is relatively empty.

With so few people about, it is much easier to sense heartbeats and choose a path that avoids the gaggle of the regent's ladies bustling in and out of the queen's apartments. I head purposefully in the direction of the king's chambers, wanting to ensure the regent did not simply lie. But as I pause outside the ornate double doors, it is clear there is only one heartbeat and it is that of a sleepy, patient valet, waiting to undress the king when he returns.

I retrace my steps through the palace, following the same route the regent used to usher us in. At the foot of the stairs is a door that leads to the courtyard in which we arrived, and a second short passageway that, by the sound and smells coming from it, must lead to the palace kitchens. I edge carefully forward, wrap myself in the deepening shadows, and listen. From the activity level and casual conversation, it appears the king did not dine here tonight. Nor does the kitchen staff seem put out by this, so clearly his absence was expected. Someone is giving instructions to the cook for tomorrow's dinner when a page arrives announcing that the king has returned.

My heart quickening, I pull back into the shadows and wait to make sure no one from the kitchen comes this way before retracing my steps back to the courtyard. I find a dark corner, tuck myself in, and wait.

After nearly an hour of waiting, I finally hear the steady clop of a large group of horses. When the clattering of their hooves ceases, the steward hurries forward to greet the king. "I trust you had a pleasant ride, Your Majesty."

"Yes, I have. Has the queen arrived?"

"Yes, Your Majesty. She and her party arrived over an hour ago and have been made comfortable for the night."

Their voices shift as they move away from me, closer to the palace's main entrance. I turn my attention to the rumble of talk from the rest of the party as they dismount and relinquish their horses into the care of the stable hands. I have little patience for stealth and spying. If I had my preference, I'd slip up behind one of the king's men, place the edge of my knife against his throat, and demand he tell me where they have been and why, instead of lurking in dark corners like a rat begging crumbs.

A number of men follow immediately after the king, but a few of them linger. Once all the others have dispersed, their tone changes from deferential to almost mocking.

"Now, that was a fool's errand."

"Nonsense. That was chivalry at its finest." The claim is followed by a round of laughter.

"That was a guilty conscience, that was," a dour voice interjects.

"I haven't heard that much weeping and wringing of hands since that troubadour from Paris was here last winter."

"And that was before the Princess Marguerite started talking!"

Another round of guffaws.

The dour voice speaks again. "Eh, they should return the girl to her father and be done with it. It's bad enough his feelings for the queen caused him to break his vows to the princess. It is even less honorable to string her along like this."

There is the sound of a thump as someone claps him on the back. "This is politics, man! The princess is a most excellent pawn in the disputes between Maximilian and the crown. You can't expect them to hand over such a useful tool without maximizing its advantage."

"So much for chivalry," the dour fellow mutters. "The princess deserves better than that."

"Hush! You don't want anyone to hear you talk like that. Go sleep it off and be ready to greet your new queen tomorrow."

The knot of five men passes but two arm lengths in front of me. I hold my breath and press myself closer to the wall at my back, giving thanks for the deep shadows.

It is only when they have safely passed and entered the palace that I let myself absorb the full meaning of what I have just heard. Marguerite has still not been returned to her father. Which gives Maximilian even more reason to retaliate against France, perhaps even attempt to abduct the new queen to ransom for his daughter.

And that is the least disturbing news I heard. The king was visiting his former betrothed. On the very night he should be welcoming his new bride.

That cannot bode well. Does his heart still belong to Marguerite? Or is it simple regret? Or something far more sinister that speaks to an intricate plot that could end up doing great harm to the queen?

A heartbeat behind me scuttles my thoughts. My knife is out of its sheath and in my hand before I turn around.

"Usually you can tell it is me." Beast sounds slightly put out.

"I *could* tell it was you."

He glances pointedly at the knife.

"After I drew," I concede, returning it to its sheath.

He looks to the right, then the left, before taking my hand and pulling me into the shelter of the stable wall, where we will not be seen. "What are you doing out here?"

"Answers as to why the king was not available to greet the queen will not come knocking on my chamber door. I must seek them out."

He stares down at me a long, hard moment. "Please don't tell me you were spying on the king."

I lean up against the wall of his chest. "Very well. I will not tell you that."

He closes his eyes and appears to be counting. Or praying. I cannot tell which. "Would you like to know what I have learned?" I offer, trying to distract him from that line of thought.

He scrubs his face with his hand. "Yes, but only so if they hang you for treason I can know whether or not the information was worth it."

"My, you are in a dark humor tonight."

"Yes," he says heavily. "Yes, I am."

I am instantly on alert. "Why? Have you learned something more?"

He throws his hands out to his sides. "Do we need more? We've lost Captain Dunois, Captain Lannion, and a half dozen other good men, the regent

threatens us at every turn, and the queen's new home looks more like a prison than a palace. I'd say that warrants a foul humor."

I grimace. "You'll get no argument from me. Where are you and the queen's guard assigned to?"

"The garrison."

"The garrison? How will you protect the queen from there?"

"My question exactly. For now, we will be posting two of our guards at her door until we can find a way to settle this matter. Even if I have to take it to the king himself," he mutters. "Speaking of which, what did you learn about his whereabouts?"

"He was not here to greet his new queen because he was off visiting the former dauphine, Princess Marguerite."

"You mean she has not been returned to her father?"

"No. She is less than half a day's ride away."

"To what end?"

"I do not know if she is still here because of the king's affection for her or as a political advantage meant to keep Maximilian from retaliating over the marriage."

"Or perhaps they are reluctant to give up her dowry. It was a great deal of land, and the French are greedy in that regard."

"Or," I say more slowly, "could they still be holding out hope that Marguerite will one day be queen of France? With this latest revelation the king could easily have been behind the ambush and Dunois's death in a desperate move to acquire Brittany while still honoring his betrothal to Marguerite. Just how far are they willing to go to see that happen?"

Beast shakes his head. "I cannot believe it of the king, Sybella. Or that the Duke of Bourbon would agree to such a plan."

"Not willingly, no. But I have yet to see him stand up to his wife." There *are* other explanations, I assure myself. Some of them even benign.

CHAPTER 47

Genevieve

araud regards me quizzically. "You want me to do what?"

We are in a bigger room, surrounded by the light of three torches rather than the feeble dribble from a single one. We are not here because Maraud asked, but because he is right — the oubliette is far too small to be of much use. We have practiced every move and strategy that I could employ in such close quarters. "Hold your wrists out so that I may secure them."

In the additional light, I can see that his eyes are not only large, but fiercely intelligent, his lips well-shaped, and beneath the beard, his cheekbones sharp and defined.

"And this will improve your swordsmanship how?"

"Today we are working on something other than swordsmanship." I do not like that he is getting precisely what he wants. It feels like a fool's bargain, and I am no fool. We will use the bigger room in a way he does not expect. I have not brought my short sword with me, and no weapons for him at all. We will be practicing a different kind of fighting, although it is tricky. He is larger than I, and a more skilled fighter. Practicing the moves I wish to practice means getting physically close to him.

"Give me your hands, please."

He hesitates.

"I will not hurt you, if that is what you are afraid of."

He snorts.

While he is weaponless, I carry four knives, a thin piece of wire, a thick piece of rope, and my needles. He will only know about the rope. The rest are insurance. Should he try anything other than what I tell him to, he will quickly learn about the other weapons — in a most painful way. "If you do not wish to cooperate, I can find better things to do with my day."

He looks at me, a faint, pained accusation in his gaze. It is all I can do not to squirm under that look. There is no rule that says I must play fair. In fact, there are not any rules for this situation.

Besides, it will make a most excellent test. If he obeys the rules of today's game, he will have come just that much closer to proving to me that he is a man of his word. And if he does not, I am well prepared for that.

After a long hesitation in which I hear every word of his silent protest, he slowly raises his arms. I slip the rope from my belt, intending to loop it around his wrists, then stop. "What are those?"

He tries to tug his sleeves back down. "Manacles. I told you they had bound me."

"Yes, but I thought you'd meant with rope." Not these thick iron bands that encircle his wrists. Wrists that are rubbed raw and red. My gaze springs back to his face. "Why did you hide them?"

He shrugs. "I didn't hide them so much as use the sleeves to buffer the chaffing. The darkness of the oubliette did the rest."

He is right. The one time his wrists were close enough to see clearly, I was distracted by the wooden blade he held at my throat.

"Besides, displaying my manacles did not seem as if it would earn your trust."

"Well, hiding them hasn't helped. Where is the chain?"

He waves vaguely toward the oubliette, the iron band slipping down to bump against his hand. "On the floor down there."

I remember his feral smile when I commented that he was no longer bound. "How did you get it off?"

He runs a hand over his head. Unable to help myself, my gaze follows the manacle. I cannot unsee them. "Where the chain attaches to the cuffs is the weakest link. I used a small piece of stone, or rock, or bone — whatever I could find — and just tapped and hammered and pried until it came loose. There wasn't much else to do."

Such determination! What drives a man to such patience and persistence — to eat rats, to exercise his body even as he grows thin from near starvation, to chip away at the impossible?

"I can make you a salve."

"What?"

Not sure who is more shocked by my offer, I gesture to his wrists. "For the chafed spots. Now," I say gruffly, "give me your hands."

I can feel the heaviness of his gaze on me as I tie the rope to the manacles — his wrists are too raw — but I keep my attention on the knot I am tying. "There." I step back. "Clearly it will not hold you for long, but that is not the point of this endeavor."

He shrugs one shoulder. "You are the one making up the rules."

I take a deep breath, savoring the feel of that. "Exactly. Now" — I pull another length of rope from my belt and wrap an end of it around each of my hands — "today we are going to —"

"Strangle me?"

"I like to pretend it is a garrote, but yes, that is the thrust of it. I have not practiced these moves in quite a while and need to refresh myself on them."

He folds his arms. "And why does a supposed noblewoman need to practice how to garrote a man?"

I widen my eyes. "Why, to defend herself, of course. You know how eager men are to prey on helpless women. What choice have I but to learn to fend off an attack of any sort?"

He lifts a finger. "But the one holding the garrote is usually the one attacking."

I wave away his point. "Not always. Sometimes in close quarters, a garrote is the easiest weapon to get into place."

He continues to study me, his fiercely intelligent eyes mulling me over as his mind gnaws on the puzzle I present. He steps away from the wall with a sigh. "What am I to do?"

"Stand facing me as if we are having a conversation."

"What are we talking about?"

"That doesn't matter! It is just the position you are to assume."

"Very well." He squares his body, feet slightly separated in a well-centered stance.

I nod. "Perfect." I glance up at his face. "Although, if you wanted to talk about something, you could tell me why the captain of the duchess's army would know a mercenary's name."

As he opens his mouth to respond, I step in close, use my elbows as leverage, and come up behind him with my rope tight against his neck. Yes! This is exactly how we did it in practice at the convent. In the next moment, however, there is a swooping sensation deep in my belly, and before I know it, I am airborne, passing over Maraud's shoulder toward the floor. The only things that keep me from landing flat on my back and knocking all the air from my lungs are Maraud's hands.

"*Rutting figs.*" That is precisely what Sister Thomine did whenever I put too much weight on my front foot. When I open my eyes, I find Maraud peering down at me.

"Captain Dunois made it a point to know the men who fought under his command."

I ignore his outstretched hand — and his answer that tells me nothing — and spring to my feet. "Let's try again."

It takes me three turns at being airborne before I finally manage to center my weight correctly and anchor myself with my back foot. When I get the rope around his neck the fourth time and he is unable to budge me, I crow. "Ha!

He glances over his shoulder at me, slightly out of breath. "You are nothing if not persistent." He smiles, his face full of good humor and admiration. In that moment, I become exquisitely aware of my arm still around his neck, his heart beating just under my elbow. Damp heat rises from his body. No doubt a similar heat is rising off of mine. Our position is far closer to an embrace than a fight.

I scramble to untangle myself from him, stepping away as quickly as I can — but not so quickly that he will suspect why. "It is time for me to go."

He says nothing, but raises one eyebrow at me so that I want to smack it clean off his face. "Hurry." I start to yank on the rope, then bite back a huff of annoyance as I remember the manacles. "I have spent too long down here already, and I will be missed."

When we reach the oubliette, I untie his wrists so that he may climb down. When he has reached the bottom, he starts to say something, but I slam the grill shut, the loud clang of it drowning out his words.

My heart beats too fast and not, I think, from exertion. I can still feel the weight of Maraud's hands on my body, the heat of him through the fabric of my sleeves. Still feel the dampness of our sweat.

Of all the times for lust to rear its vexing head, surely this is the most inconvenient.

I probably smell of him as well. Which means I will need to slip up to my room and wash before I join the others in the solar.

That realization has me quickening my pace, not wishing to be gone any longer than I already have.

Just as I emerge from the dungeons into the antechamber at the base of the stairway, I stop, shocked to see Louise herself halfway down the stairs. Her eyes widen as I emerge from the hallway. "There you are!"

"My lady." I drop into a deep curtsy, wanting a moment to compose myself.

"Genevieve." Her voice is filled with both affection and annoyance. She stops before me, her solemn gray eyes combing over my appearance, taking in my flushed, heated face, the state of my clothes. "I fear I have come to the end of my patience with you." She reaches out and takes my arm in hers, tucking it into the crook of her elbow. While it is a friendly gesture, there is a steely possession in her grip that makes it clear that it is not friendly at all. "It is not healthy for you to be down here this much. It is not calming you, but agitating you further. You must stop coming here and return to your place at my side. I will not be ignored in this, do you understand?"

"Yes, my lady."

"Good." She sniffs. "Although I do think a bath is in order before you join us."

CHAPTER 48

Sybella

he next morning I am abruptly awakened when the door to the queen's chamber is thrown open. Hands reaching for the knives at my wrists, I wrench into a sitting position just as the regent walks in.

She is followed by a long line of her attendants. As the queen sits up in bed, blinking and trying to sort out what is going on, I stifle a yawn and glance at the thick curtain covering the window, wondering how early it is. It feels like the night has been far too short for any of us to have gotten enough rest.

"Good morning, Your Majesty." The regent's greeting is brisk and pleasant. "Your staff is here to assist you with your morning toilette."

Merde. Can these French not even manage to wash without creating a pompous ceremony to go with it?

The queen glances around at the sheer number of people filling her chamber. "I am quite certain my own ladies can help me wash and dress, Madame Regent. They have been doing so for years and are quite practiced in it."

The regent gives the queen a stiff, cool smile. "Ah, but they have not been trained in the ways at the French court. Your morning bath, indeed, your every move, must be up to the French court's standards so you do not shame the king." My heart plummets. We will never be free of this harridan.

"I am not sure the order in which I dress can shame him," the queen says tartly. "But," she adds, "I would be interested in seeing how it is done so my own ladies may learn."

The regent's smile stays frozen in place, but she motions her women forward. They pull back the covers and hold out a robe for the queen, who rises to her feet and shrugs into the proffered garment. She turns to the regent. "I do not know how it is done here in France, but my first commitment every morning is to pray to the Almighty, and I would not set aside my duties to God for ceremony."

I hide a smile, for even the regent cannot outdo the queen in this regard. My only regret is that, as her lady in waiting, I, too, must kneel in prayer, something I rarely do.

The regent does not miss the rebuke, and her nostrils flare in irritation. "Nor would I want you to. Of course that is your first duty here as well."

The duchess smiles sweetly. "How lovely that we are aligned in our deference to God. Best that you watch me pray to be certain I am doing it in accordance with your standards."

A hush falls upon the room. As we quiet ourselves for prayer, a wave of hopelessness threatens to engulf me. The regent has no intention of allowing the queen to establish her own household, let alone take her rightful place at court. She has cunningly laid all manner of traps and snares.

But she will not prevail. I have survived a lifetime of Count d'Albret's schemes and torments and bested him in the end. I defeated Pierre and his henchmen — singlehandedly. I have faced Death himself — three times — and come away the victor. This snake of a woman, no matter how formidable she may be, has nothing she can throw at the queen that is greater than what I have already endured. She will not win this battle.

The queen's prayer is a long one, longer even than normal. She will not have her piety questioned by anyone, least of all this most un-Christian regent. Unaccustomed to such long prayers, Madame shifts more than once before the queen is finished.

When the queen finally rises, a well-dressed woman steps forward bearing a finely wrought silver basin. A second woman dips a soft cloth in the water while a third removes the robe from the queen so that she is stripped bare before the entire group. Surely the regent must lie awake at night, plotting to find ways to force the queen to stand naked before others. For her part, the queen does not flinch, but holds her head high, her chin tilted at a proud angle, staring straight ahead as if she is alone in the room.

When that is done, another series of women begin dressing the queen, one article of clothing at a time. They move around Heloise, Elsibet, and me as if we are naught but pieces of furniture. When one of them elbows past me, it is all I can do not to stick my foot out and send her sprawling to the floor. Instead, I force myself to memorize every detail of their ministrations so we will be able to do it ourselves and prove to the regent that the queen's own attendants are more than equal to the challenges of the French court.

Once the queen is dressed, it is time for us to attend the morning mass. Instead of groaning in dismay, I vow to use it to my advantage. Somehow.

"Will the king be attending?" the queen asks as we proceed down the hall.

"Yes," Madame answers, "but the men of the household worship in the main chapel, while we women use a smaller one."

I cannot help but wonder if this has always been the case or is a new development meant to keep the king and queen apart.

Since all the ladies of the household are expected to attend mass, Aeva, Tola, Tephanie, and my sisters arrive with the rest of the Breton ladies in waiting. Louise smiles at me and I wink. Charlotte's eyes are everywhere but on me — taking in the number of finely dressed ladies present and the opulent trappings of the royal chapel.

With consummate skill, the regent maneuvers things so that those of us who arrived with the queen find ourselves relegated to the back of the chapel.

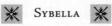

That suits me perfectly, however, for it is the best place to observe the others and have those observations go undetected.

As the priest drones on in his melodious Latin, I examine the heads of the women in the front of me. Between the questions raised by the king's visit to the princess and the regent's determination to maintain her stranglehold on power, we are in desperate need of insight to both the king's intentions and the regent's strategy. Who better to provide that than the convent's own moles?

All of the women's hair is covered, but with their heads bowed, it is possible to see a few tendrils at the nape of their necks. Margot's red hair should be the easiest to spot. Only one woman has hair with the faintest tinge of red to it, but I cannot tell if it is truly red or merely the effect of the light coming in through stained glass windows. Either way, there is only one possibility for Margot.

And what of Genevieve? Which one of these ladies could be her? A handful of women have dark blond hair, but the bulk of them have brown. And a twelve-year-old's hair color is the flimsiest of hints to go on. How will I sort through all the possibilities?

There is also no guarantee that either of them are among the attendants the regent has brought with her on the honeymoon. By all accounts, the regent has more than a hundred women to attend her, and Plessis-lès-Tours is supposed to be a small, intimate court. What if they are not here?

Despair threatens to raise its head again, but I drown out its voice by uttering a fervent prayer to Mortain to help me find his other daughters.

The rest of the day is spent in a blaze of pomp and ceremony that the king has arranged for the queen. Whether it was planned all along or hastily put together to make up for his absence last night, I do not know. It is the welcome she should have received yesterday, and as far as I am concerned, being late tarnishes the gesture greatly.

But the queen is pleased, glowing with pleasure, so I cannot begrudge her that.

The king takes the opportunity to allow the queen to present her attendants and courtiers to him. When it is Beast's turn, the steward announces, "Sir Benebic de Waroch, captain of the queen's guard."

A faint crease appears upon the king's brow as Beast bows deeply. It does not disappear once Beast stands. "Why is there a queen's guard?"

At his question, the queen stares at him a moment, and I imagine all the various disappointments she is feeling.

"If I may, Your Majesty?" Beast's deep voice rumbles into the silence.

Both the queen and king nod their heads in permission.

"The queen's guard was appointed by the duchess and her Privy Council in order to see to her safety."

"We have a king's guard for that," the king says, waving vaguely to the captain of his guard who stands a few paces behind the throne.

"While this is true, Your Majesty, the attack on our traveling party outside Angers shows that one can never be too careful when the queen's safety is at stake. We had twenty of your men with us, brave men, most of whom gave their lives to keep her safe, but it was very nearly not enough."

The king looks incredulous. "An attack? Upon the queen?"

Beast, the queen, all of us, are taken aback. "Has no one informed Your Majesty?"

He grips the arms of his throne. "No, they have not." And he looks none too pleased about it.

The regent slips forward. "You've been so busy, sire, there has not been time to fill you in on Her Majesty's journey."

He considers his sister coldly. "There has not been time to fill me in on an attack on my own queen?"

This, I realize with a sharp thrill of recognition. This is the regent's weakest link in her strategy. This blind spot the brilliant tactician cannot see from her vantage point of older sister.

And if there is a weakness, I can drive a wedge into it.

"Please, Your Majesty. It is being taken care of. The Duke of Bourbon himself is looking into the matter."

"May I ask what he has learned?" Beast asks.

The regent does not spare him a glance and instead addresses the king. "There has been little enough to discover. The force was comprised of German mercenaries —"

"Was it Maximilian, then?"

The regent gives a single shake of her head. "Not that we have been able to confirm, sire. That is why we have had nothing to report."

The king waves her back and turns to the queen. His cheeks are faintly flushed. "I am deeply sorry that you were endangered on your way here. I will see the attackers found and punished."

"Thank you, my lord husband." The queen's cheeks also pinken, but in relief, I think, rather than embarrassment.

The king turns back to Beast. "I still do not think that warrants a separate queen's guard. Her safety will fall to the royal bodyguard now that she is my wife."

I watch him closely, trying to discern whether it is a surfeit of confidence that has him wanting to disband the queen's guard or some more sinister purpose.

"I am certain Your Majesty's bodyguards will take the queen's safety as seriously as your own," Beast says. "However, as king, you will travel often and she will not always be able to join you. Should she not have a guard dedicated solely to her safety? Did not the Princess Marguerite have her own guard?" he asks quietly.

It is a dangerous gamble, mentioning the princess, but it works.

"That is true," the king says. The regent makes a move as if to speak, but the king waves her away. "Very well. The queen may retain her guard, but you will not be needed inside the palace itself. Whenever she leaves or travels, you will accompany her."

It is not the full support that we were hoping for, but it is not an outright dismissal, either.

"Thank you, sire." Beast bows. "I am honored to serve your queen in whatever way you see fit."

As he steps aside, the king calls out, "Wait!" He leans forward on his throne. "Do I know you, Sir Waroch?"

Anticipation shoots through me, and I wonder if Beast realizes the implications; while the king has never seen Beast's face before, he has no doubt seen his father's.

Beast looks discomfited, no doubt trying to avoid mentioning the times they may have met on the battlefield. "Perhaps you saw me at Langeais?" he suggests. "I have traveled with the queen since she left Brittany."

"No, I mean before then. Your face is familiar to me."

I watch Beast carefully, but there is still no reaction. "No, sire. I have never had the pleasure of meeting you before today. But perhaps you caught a glimpse of me when you visited Rennes."

That is when it hits me. Beast does not know. For whatever reason, Captain Dunois did not have an opportunity to tell him. Beast is still in the dark. I look out at the nobles around us, searching for someone as tall and broad as he, but I see no one.

"Which one of them are you planning to kill first?" I glance over to find Aeva smirking beside me.

"All of them, if I had my way." But as soon as the words are out, I recognize them as a lie. Killing them has not once crossed my mind. I want to know their plans and intentions, and neutralize them, but I have no desire to kill them. Not even the regent.

"Are you listening?"

"I'm sorry, what?"

Aeva folds her arms and leans back against the wall behind us, not minding that she is crushing the Turkish velvet wall hanging. "I said, you'd best start with the regent. Cutting off the head of a snake is the only way to kill it."

My mouth twitches. "The followers of Arduinna have a delightful way with words."

She lifts one broad shoulder. "I don't trust her one bit. I don't trust anyone here."

"Tell me, what do you think of the king?"

The corners of her mouth turn down as her gaze seeks him out. "Not much. He looks less like a king and more like a junior cleric that the rest of the clerks enjoy harrying."

I wince at the accuracy of her description. "Can you tell if he is still under the effects of Arduinna's arrow?" For that is at the heart of what allows us to wrest victory from defeat — the magic in the last of Arduinna's remaining arrows.

She tears her gaze from the king and frowns at me. "What do you mean?"

"Calm yourself, it was not meant as in disrespect, but rather a theological question." I briefly fill her in on what I have learned about the Princess Marguerite. "And so I am trying to determine if the effects of the arrow have worn off now that we are in France. The genuine love and admiration the king displayed toward the queen in Rennes is no longer evident. Perhaps the magic only works in Brittany."

"No," Aeva says softly. "He loves her still, as much and in such a way that he is capable of. Arduinna's arrow can only guarantee a person's love. If a person's capacity to love is meager, Arduinna's arrow cannot fix that — only ensure that meager love is directed toward a particular person."

And that is precisely the answer I feared most.

CHAPTER 49

Genevieve

hen next I return to the dungeons, it is in the early hours of the morning before everyone else is up. Because of that, my forage through the kitchen does not yield much of a meal, but it is all I can manage at this hour. It has also occurred to me that I probably should arrange for another bath for the prisoner, but that will take a fair amount of planning and stealth and so will have to wait for a different day.

When at last I reach the dungeons, I use my torch to light the others in the sparring room, collect the swords from their hiding place in the storeroom, and head for the oubliette. "Are you awake?" I call down.

"Should I not be?"

I set my torch down and slide the bolt loose. "It is early," I tell him as I open the grate.

I can almost hear him shrug. "I have no measure of time here."

"Fair enough." I toss the rope down, then draw my baselard as I wait for him to climb up. I have chosen swords today as I prefer the distance they put between us.

Maraud's head emerges from the dark hole, followed by his arms. As he levers himself up onto the floor, I am startled to see that both of his hands are bound in rags. I forgot to make him the salve I promised. "What happened to you?"

He swings his legs up and out of the oubliette, shrugging sheepishly. "I have not held a weapon for over a year. My hands have lost their calluses and grown soft. When I descended the rope yesterday, it scraped the blisters open."

"Will you be able to hold a sword?"

He sends me a mocking look as he rises to his feet. "So now you are my nursemaid as well as my sparring partner?"

"Hardly. I only want to make sure our session is worth my while. Now, if you are done whining, let's get to work."

His lips twitch as I motion for him to proceed me into the room. Once there, I toss the wooden sword at him, watching carefully when he catches it. He winces, but only slightly. "Back to swords?"

"You said you had more tricks to teach me, and I would like to learn some of them today."

He raises his sword, and I raise mine. "I have in mind to show you how to compensate for both your smaller size and shorter reach. Both will be vulnerabilities in a true fight." He parries, quickly altering the direction of his sword from left to right to left again. "Your footing is a disadvantage. My lunges and strides are half again as long as yours. You must move faster and quicker, taking two small steps back for every one of mine, or you will soon find my blade against your nose."

He is right, I think. We could never have trained for this in the smaller room.

Even so, I block his attack easily. "My reach does not seem to be an issue here."

"No?" He pivots and attacks my blade with a series of diagonal swings. It is all I can do to keep him at bay.

Because I must extend my arm farther, it will tire before he does. I feint to the left, then leap to the right, creating an opening for me to get inside his guard.

But he is prepared for that and blocks my blow hard enough to cause my teeth to clack.

Irritated now, I grab my sword with both hands and use all my force for a downward strike on his blade, close to the hilt.

As I'd hoped, the force of it causes him to drop his blade, although I am certain if his hands were not injured, he would not have done so. With satisfaction, I bring the point of my sword up to rest against his heart. Our eyes meet. "And now what do you think of my reach?"

He grins, almost apologetically, then grabs ahold of the blade. Before I can so much as gasp in surprise, the point of my own weapon is turned toward me and rests upon my heart. His eyes are expressionless.

"Well done," I concede, although I am loath to admit it. "Now what trick do I use to get out of this position?" For some reason, my voice sounds thin, thready.

"You don't." His voice is soft and apologetic. My heart plummets down to my feet, my body somehow understanding what is happening before my mind can absorb it.

His hands were never injured at all. The bandages were to protect them from the sharp edge of my sword.

"Don't go for your dagger," he orders. With his free hand, he pulls a knife from some hiding place. It is made of bone — bone from one of the meals I fed him — and has been carefully sharpened against the stone of his prison until the end is a wicked — if rough — point.

"I need you to drop it onto the floor." There is true regret in his voice, as if this pains him in some way.

Fury sits in my throat like a hot coal, but I have no choice but to do as he asks. I reach for the stiletto up my left sleeve. While his eyes are focused on my knife, I slip my fingers into the cuff inside that same sleeve to retrieve the needle case hidden there. Moving suddenly, I toss the stiletto onto the floor. As I'd hoped, it draws his eye long enough for me to hide the case in my palm.

"Is this some new trick you are teaching me?" I ask to further distract him. "If so, I do not care for it."

"No. Not a trick. I am leaving, and you are coming with me."

My fingers fumbling with the needles grow still. "Coming *with* you? Am I to be your hostage? I assure you, no one will pay a centime for me."

His face curls in disgust. "Not my hostage. We will escape together. You yourself said you were a prisoner here." His voice is low, urgent, and as seductive as when it first rose up out of the oubliette to greet me.

And that voice now holds a sword at my throat. It is such a huge betrayal that fury lashes through me. I lean forward, using the movement to conceal my hand behind my skirts. "If you wanted to escape together, you could at least have included me in your plans."

"I thought about it," he admits. "But wasn't certain you would agree and couldn't risk showing my hand."

My fingers unfold the supple leather of the case. "Just how long have you been planning this?"

"A while."

That spark of fury crackles along my skin. "How long is *a while*? Ever since I first brought you food and water? Ever since I saved you from starving to death? Or was it after that? When I brought you news of the outer world. Trusted you — trusted your word."

He takes a step toward me. "I have been planning my escape for over a year. It is the one thing that kept me alive. Kept me from giving up. I was planning it long before you stumbled upon my prison. You just happened to be the first opportunity that presented itself."

His words are like the blade of a knife — I was never anything but an opportunity to him. "So you were planning it before we even came to our sparring agreement?" When we were naught but voices in the dark, easing our loneliness? My fingers count along the tops of the needles until they reach the ones with the knots of thread.

"Yes," he says softly. "But that does not mean that any of what I have said was not true. It was and is. I still have no wish to harm you or put you in danger."

"You have an odd way of convincing me." There! The needle is firmly grasped between my finger and thumb, the point of it a safe distance from my own skin.

"I proved it all the times I did not move against you."

I shake my head. "That was not honor. That was stringing me along on a line, hoping I would lead you to a bigger fish. And I have! By trusting you enough to agree to this room, I have given you a much greater chance of success. Do not pretend it was anything other than you trying to set up the best opportunity for yourself that you could. At least be honest about it."

"Until you have been shut in a hole for months on end, with no food, no light, little water, and even less hope, do not lecture me about honesty. The only thing that kept me going was my vow to find vengeance for those wrongly slain before my very eyes. That vow comes before all others I have given."

His face grows soft again, and he lowers the sword slightly to take half a step toward me. "But now is your chance to be free. You are not happy here. You hope for adventure or you would not be training as you do. We can find it together, once we are away."

My attack will not require much movement. If he is trying to persuade me to escape with him, he will hopefully not run me through due to a flick of my hand. Even so, it is a risk I must take. "With me doing what, precisely? Being your lightskirt? Your laundress?"

His eyes widen in offended surprise. *Now!* I whip my hand out, jam the needle into his forearm, then quickly yank my hand back to my side so he will not think I am trying to wrest the sword from him.

"Ouch!" He frowns in both pain and annoyance. "What was that?"

"That, O False One, is a trick of my own."

He blinks rapidly as his vision begins to blur. The arm holding the sword starts to tremble slightly.

"What kind of trick?"

"The kind I wore up my sleeve in case you turned out to be as false as you are. I wish you sweet dreams."

"Dreams? What are you talk —" His voice stops abruptly and the sword clatters to the floor. His eyelids flutter and his body loosens, like a puppet cut from his strings.

Realizing I will be in trouble if he hits the ground — he is far too big for me to carry — I leap forward and wedge myself under his shoulder just as he goes slack.

"Wha haf you done ter me?" he slurs.

"There, there, now," I assure him as I get my arm around his waist and steer him toward the door. "It is just a bit of poison."

"Poyshum!" The garbled word is filled with alarm. Fortunately, the poison has not reached his legs yet and I am able to clumsily guide him out of the sparring room toward the oubliette.

"Ewe poyshumed mme." His lips have grown numb and are tinged with blue.

"It isn't enough to kill you. Or it shouldn't be, at any rate. With luck, you will just sleep for a bit."

"Can't schleep. Mussht eshcape." When we are only halfway to the grate, his entire body stiffens briefly, then grows utterly limp and begins to slip to the floor.

Figs! He is too heavy for me to hold up. I have no choice but to let him fall.

As I fold my arms and stare down at his motionless form stretched out on the stone, a dark swirl of emotions writhes inside my heart. I cannot believe what he has done. Cannot believe that, once again, I have allowed myself to be lulled into trusting someone.

Resisting the urge to kick him, I get down on my knees and roll his unconscious body toward the grate. The only thing keeping me from feeling like a fool is that I have always known this was a possibility and prepared accordingly. It is that very planning that has stopped him today.

It is the hollowest of victories.

By the time I reach the oubliette, I am hot and sweating and angrier than ever.

I briefly consider going down first to make sure his pile of moldy straw is directly beneath the grate to soften his landing, then scoff at myself. He held a sword to my throat and was going to escape — after all I'd done for him and the assurances he'd given.

I study his sleeping face, trying to see if the signs of his treachery are written upon it. If they are, I cannot see them, even now. I have half a mind to pry open his mouth and inspect his tongue to see if it is forked. Instead, I place my hands on his shoulders and hips and roll him into the opening of the oubliette.

He folds in half and disappears down the hole, followed by a solid thunk as he hits the floor.

I sit on my knees a moment, breathing hard, then stand up, slam the grate closed, slide the bolt in, and lock it. Our sparring sessions have come to an end. And I was the one who emerged victorious. Now all that is left for me to do is leave.

CHAPTER 50

Sybella

e give it a week before we make our move — enough time for the household to fall into a recognizable rhythm. Waking, mass, dinner with entertainment. In the afternoon, the king pays a visit to the queen. Inevitably, the regent contrives to be there just prior to his arrival.

But this morning when the regent and her retinue arrive to oversee her toilette, the queen is already out of bed, washed, and dressed. I stand on her right, Aeva on her left. Heloise, Elsibet, and the others stand behind us, a solid phalanx. "Good morning, Madame Regent. Would you care to accompany us to the chapel?" The queen's invitation is delivered in the most dulcet tones, as if she would like nothing more than for the regent to accompany us.

The regent's mouth crimps in annoyance. "But we shall be quite early if we leave now." Her faint note of dismay nearly makes up for the extra time I will be forced to endure chapel.

The queen gives her a sunny smile. "That will give us all the more time to pray." She nods cheerfully to us, and we fall in line behind her as she leads the way. The regent has no choice but to follow or be left behind.

The next morning, the regent arrives even earlier, but we have anticipated this and are dressed and waiting for her. This time, she gets the message, and when mass is over, we are all yawning our fool heads off. The queen is so tired from our early mornings that she falls asleep immediately after lunch before the king has even come for his daily visit. Disgusted, the regent collects most of her ladies and leaves. As she passes me, she pauses. The spiteful gleam in her eye has my fingers itching for my knife.

Her hooded gaze sweeps over me. "The queen takes great strength from you, doesn't she, Lady Sybella?" Before I can respond to her observation, she sweeps out of the room. Moments later, the king arrives for his afternoon visit.

Heloise offers to go wake the queen from her nap, but he stops her. "No," he says. "Let me. I have always wanted to wake a sleeping princess." The women smile at this bit of romantic foolery as they quietly open the door for him.

He does not emerge from her room for the rest of the afternoon, which gives me plenty of time to wrestle with the regent's words — were they an acknowledgment that we had won the rout, or a threat?

During our first week here, I have had time to identify a handful of attendants who might have come from the convent. They are of the right age, with hair that could possibly be described as Genevieve's was. But that is so little to go on. I do not even know if they are using their real names or have taken different ones.

Instead, I have had to look for contradictions or inconsistencies. Women who keep to themselves, or those who allow themselves to be separated from the group and thus provide opportunities to be approached, have ended up on my list. I have also noted those who seem most interested in the queen, or those who feign exaggerated disinterest — as both could indicate a spy's strategy.

This morning as everyone files out of the chapel, I wait for one of the regent's attendants who is exceptionally devout, outpraying even the duchess.

What better way to keep attention from inconsistencies in one's own faith?

She also wears an elaborate rosary that reminds me of the one the convent made for me when I was first sent out, its heavy ornate cross easily able to serve as the hilt for a hidden dagger.

Her name — Honorée — shows possibilities as well. It is a sly choice for one who has been sent to spy. And Mortain knows we could use a spy's insight to the regent and her plots.

When she finally rises from her knees to follow the others, I slip out of the last pew where I've been waiting. As I fall into step alongside her, she draws back slightly, trying to put space between us.

I give her a warm smile of greeting, but all I receive in return is a cool nod. I press on. "Forgive me for intruding, but I have been admiring your rosary. It is exquisite, and I wondered if you might tell me where you had it made."

She clutches the string of beads in her hand as if fearing I will take it from her on the spot. "It has been in my family for well over two hundred years. I would not even know where to suggest you look for something of comparable quality."

My initial disappointment is quickly overtaken by annoyance. "That is too bad, as it has drawn the queen's eye. But thank you for the courtesy you have shown me. I shall be certain to report your kindness to the queen." The smile I give her is warm enough to melt butter, but I make certain it does not reach my eyes, wanting the sharp-tongued shrew to stew in the knowledge she has just landed on the wrong side of the queen.

CHAPTER 51

Genevieve

t does not take long for my conscience to poke at me. I decide to check on the prisoner to be certain he did not break something in the fall and has recovered from the poison. Even in small doses, it can be unpredictable.

Besides, I feel I should tell him I won't be returning. Not that he deserves even that much.

There is no call of greeting or noise of any kind as I approach the oubliette. I pause for a moment and listen in the darkness to see if I can feel an extra heartbeat, wondering if I have miscalculated the poison. But no. There is no heartbeat except mine inside my chest.

When I reach the iron grate, I set my sack of food down and kneel to unlock the padlock. "Are you dead?" I put a healthy dose of cheer into my voice. He need never know how much his betrayal stung.

A deep groan of misery rises up from the darkness. "I wish it were so," he mutters.

I slide back the bolt and hoist open the grate. Instead of lowering myself down into the hole, I gather my skirts and sit the floor, allowing my legs to dangle into the oubliette as if it were a cool stream on a hot summer day. "What hurts?" I ask. "Your stomach or your head?"

"Everything," he growls.

"Yes, but which hurts *most*? I don't know if you broke any bones when I dumped you back into your hole. If your skull is cracked, it might be best if you don't eat quite yet."

There is a faint whisper of movement as he checks his head. "I don't feel any lumps or cracks. And everything moves more or less as it ought to."

"Well, that is good news." I take a pear from the sack and bite into it, letting the fragrant juice drip down into the oubliette.

"What happened? What did you do to me?"

"I stabbed you with a poisoned needle. But don't worry. It wasn't a fatal dose. You'll feel sick for another day or so and then be back to your normal, treacherous self."

My own voice is jovial, happy even, as if his actions have had no impact on me. "Are you hungry?"

He groans again. "Yes. No. Maybe. My stomach feels ungodly empty, but it also roils like a boiling pot. I'm not sure I could eat."

"Very well. I will enjoy this picnic all by myself. It is too bad, though, because if you could get food in your stomach, it would soak up the last remaining dregs of the poison and draw it from your system."

"Did you just come down here to torture me?"

"But of course. What other fate would you deserve after betraying me?"

"I told you." The words sound as if they are being forced out between clenched teeth. "I was not betraying you. I was going to take you with me. Rescue you, even."

I laugh. He does not know me well enough to know it is forced laughter. "And yet here we are."

"If you are done gloating, feel free to leave anytime."

"Ah, but I did not come to gloat. Or not *only* to gloat."

"Then why are you here?" His voice is tinged with, not anger, but something bleaker than that.

"I have come to tell you goodbye."

The stillness that follows is so thick I could slice it with my knife. "Goodbye?"

"Yes. I am leaving." Even though he does not deserve it, I speak the words softly to gentle the blow.

That announcement is met with another silence, this one filled less with bleakness and more with interest. There is a loud rustling as he sits up. "If you are leaving, take me with you." The fierce longing in his voice causes it to tremble slightly.

"Unfortunately, I cannot take you with me as I can no longer trust you. But I did bring you one last meal before I leave." Teasing him was supposed to feel more satisfying than it does.

"Food!" He spits out the word. "What do I want with food if I am to remain shut away in here?"

I take another bite of the pear, being sure to slurp the juices loudly. "You once cared very much for food."

"That was when I had hope and a plan. Both of which you have taken from me."

"Taken from you?" My voice grows hard. "And what of the trust and sense of safety that I have had taken from me?"

"I will swear on anything you ask."

"There is no oath you can swear that I will believe. If I was wrong to trust you in the enclosed space of a dungeon, how much more foolish would I be to trust you on the open road?"

"If I was on the open road, there would be no need for trust. I would have what I wanted!"

"That is a good point. And if I trusted you, I would believe it. But this is not just about me. I have important things I must do. People who are counting on me and whom I will not jeopardize with misplaced trust."

He takes a step closer to the middle of the room. I casually pull my feet up out of the hole and fold them under me.

"As do I," he says.

"You?" I frown down into the pit. "You have languished down there for nearly a year. What important tasks could possibly await you?"

"I told you, I witnessed a crime on the battlefield. I am the only one who can see justice done for those who were wrongfully slain."

At the urgency in his voice, I set down my pear and wipe my fingers on the sack. "I am sorry." All the teasing is gone from my voice. "Your cause sounds noble, but my task involves saving those who are still alive. Your revenge will have to wait."

"I could help you save them before I pursue my vengeance."

Surely that smooth, reasonable voice is the same one the serpent in the garden used in the stories favored by the Church.

My own voice takes on a mocking tone. He will never know it is directed at myself for wanting to believe him. "That is a gracious offer, but the sort of saving I will be doing does not require strength or mercenaries."

"I will die if you leave. No one comes down here anymore."

I shift on the hard stone. "You can't know that. Opportunity presented itself once. Who is to say it will not again?"

He snorts. "The gods will not roll the dice in my favor twice. Better to have been left alone than to have fed me hope, only to snatch it away."

His words have the force of a punch, for I suspect in my heart they are true. "I did not know when I began this that I would be leaving."

Now it is his voice that takes on a mocking tone. "How did you see this playing out? Keeping me like a child keeps a pet? Or would you eventually have become skilled enough with your sword that you no longer needed me, and we would have said goodbye then?"

"I did not think that far ahead," I admit. "I have only been putting one foot in front of the other, praying that a steppingstone would appear in time to carry me forward. And this newest steppingstone leads me away from this place." I rise to my feet and pick up the sack of food, knotting it before holding it out over the oubliette. "Here." I let go. "A parting gift."

There is a dull thud as it lands in the straw. I grasp the grate and lower it back down over the hole, but slowly, so it does not clang loudly like a funeral bell. As I slide the bolt into place, he calls out, "Wait."

I pause.

"If you are feeling charitable, consider leaving me the rope."

Even though I had planned on leaving him the rope, I do not answer. Instead, I turn to leave, but a thought occurs to me, causing me to stop. "Who are you really?"

"Will it matter once I am dead?"

"If you have any family, surely it will bring them some peace of mind to know what became of you."

He considers for a long, hard moment. "My name is Anton Crunard," he says at last.

I can scarce believe the name I am hearing. "Crunard," I repeat.

"Yes. The fourth son of the chancellor of Brittany."

My mind reels at all the implications crowding into my head at once. "Why has he not paid your ransom?"

"I told you, we are not close. I was the prodigal son."

He does not know, I realize. He does not know that his father is no longer chancellor. He does not know that his father betrayed Brittany.

And that he did so in an attempt to save Anton — Maraud.

I think of him, and his honor, honor that would not allow him to overpower me, no matter how many unwitting opportunities I gave him. It is said the apple does not fall far from the tree, but in this case, I think perhaps it did.

"Thank you for telling me," I say at last. "And I will think about the rope."

⁓❧⁓

I take my time making my way back to the main floor of the chateau. My footsteps drag as my mind races. Maraud is the son of one of Brittany's most noble families.

Or at least, what was once Brittany's most noble of families. War and politics have taken their toll on the Crunard name, with three of the sons — Maraud's brothers — killed in the conflict between France and Brittany. But it is the stain his father brought on the family honor that will leave the deepest scar. The man betrayed the duchess — and all of Brittany — right into the hands of the French regent. Or tried to. His plans were discovered in time.

That is why Maraud's ransom wasn't met. The regent held him hostage, with treason as his ransom price. And even though the chancellor paid the required price and betrayed his country, the gambit failed. And apparently Maraud was not freed.

But why keep him hidden now, if Brittany and France are truly allies? Should he not be returned to his family? Is there some risk to having him back among the living, telling of his treatment at the hands of the French crown? The way he has been treated goes against all the rules of engagement and chivalry. For the king, chivalry and honor are everything.

I think of the letter in the study. Or . . . My steps slow even further. Is the whole affair too dishonorable for the regent to admit to?

The faint simmering in my gut tells me that this changes things. It is as if Fate herself has rolled the dice for me and landed on a new number.

I can use Maraud's identity to my advantage.

I *can* take him with me.

Not because of any misplaced sense of obligation or fondness, or because I feel he has drawn a miserable lot, but because his identity could prove useful on many fronts.

My plan to return to the king after a long absence and collect on a promise he made over a year ago is risky. His tastes and desires may well have changed. There is no guarantee he will still want me with the same fervor he once possessed.

But arriving at court with Anton Crunard in tow is like slipping poisoned needles up my sleeve. If my first gambit fails, I have something else to bargain with.

It is clear the regent has worked hard to hide Crunard's existence from the king. There are only a few reasons she would do that. And whatever the reason, the king will likely be angered by how Maraud has been treated and will embrace the chance to fix the wrong that has been done him. It is even possible he has been looking for him. If so, I will be doing the king a service.

I turn the puzzle over in my mind again to see it from another side. It is also possible that the queen will want revenge on the Crunard family for what the father did to her. While that is not nearly as pleasant an option for Maraud, it still puts me in a position of having done the royal couple a service. With the war between France and Brittany now over, the king could give the prisoner to the duchess as a gift — to release or punish as she saw fit. Either way, there is a good chance that someone at court will be grateful and reward my efforts.

And surely that is one more roll of the dice than Maraud has right now. It is not precisely what he wanted, but it is an opportunity. Surely that is something.

My head is still spinning by the time I reach the upper floors. Not wanting to join the others in the solar just yet, I stop to glance out the window. A flutter of movement and color catches my eye. At first, what I am seeing makes no sense. Leaning closer to the glass, I realize it is a group of mummers, heading for the castle, their long, brightly colored ranks strung out along the road like the ribbons on a maypole.

But of course. Today is winter solstice, and while not part of the Church's Advent celebrations, it is the day the mummers — who belong to a much older tradition than the Church — begin to make their rounds. By custom, they start in Cognac, then travel to the count's residence in Angoulême city, before looping back to arrive in Cognac by Epiphany Sunday.

There are easily thirty of them, or more. They come pushing carts, half dressed in their costumes, with their masks tucked under their arms. The castle guards pay them little mind, except to smile and wave them through.

Like a ripened apple dropping from its branch, a plan comes to me. A bright, shiny, colorful plan.

I think I have found my way out of the castle.

Chapter 52

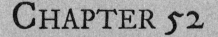

Sybella

fter the midday meal, the women of the court gather in the solar. The queen has relegated all the regent's attendants to the far end of the room so she can write her correspondence away from their prying eyes. Aeva and I sit to either side of her. I pretend to be embroidering, while Aeva does not pretend so much as simply stab her unthreaded needle into the fabric when it occurs to her.

I send a sidelong glance to the other end of the room. Honorée is not stitching but reading a book of hours. Another of the attendants, Katerine, seems more interested in the queen than the others. She also works hard to blend in — another sign she might be from the convent. I think I will approach her next

"I am asking Duval to look into the matter of the ambush." The queen speaks softly, her voice barely audible over the scratching of her quill. "Perhaps he or my cousin, the Prince of Orange, will be able to gain some insights."

"Mortain knows no one here seems to be able to," I grouse at my embroidery.

She looks up at me, lowering her voice even further. "Has Beast learned anything?"

"Not much. He and the other queen's guards have assimilated as best they can in the garrison, training on the field with the others, dicing and drinking and trying to earn their trust. He has put out a few inquiries regarding Crunard's son, but to no avail. No one appears to have even heard of him, so if he was being held hostage, it was not something that was done openly.

"He asks the marshal daily if there is any word of the attackers, so much so that the marshal heads in the opposite direction when he sees Beast coming. He has toned down his questions for now, lest they draw too much attention his way."

The queen sighs in frustration as she sprinkles sand on her letter so it will not smear. She sets it aside to dry and retrieves another piece of parchment. "I am also writing to the Princess Marguerite." At her name, my fingers grow still. "I wish to extend a hand of friendship and attempt to repair any ill will that may exist between us."

Studying my stiches more intently than I have all morning, I ask, "Do you know where she is currently residing?" I have not had the heart to tell the queen that she is but a league or two from our own location.

The queen's quill pauses. "No. I had assumed Amboise, or perhaps Bourges." She taps the quill on her chin. "I suppose I should confirm that before I send the letter."

"And best to do it without the regent learning of it," Aeva adds darkly.

As if the warning has called her, the regent herself steps through the solar door. She glances at her ladies, relegated to the far corner, then heads directly for the queen.

The queen pretends to be so absorbed in her correspondence that she does not see the regent. When she reaches us, Aeva and I have no choice but to stand and curtsy. That is when the queen looks up. "Oh, Madame Regent! Good morning. Is there something I may do for you?"

The regent's lips curve up in a smile that lacks any hint of warmth. "On the contrary, Your Majesty. I had heard you were working on correspondence this morning and thought to see if there was something I could help you with."

I glare at the knot of attendants at the opposite end of the room. That news did not take long to travel.

"That is most kind of you, Madame, but I have the matter in hand."

"Do you not seek my counsel in these things? Surely you do not wish to risk offending or embarrassing the king in such matters after all that he has done for you?"

The queen lifts her chin and narrows her eyes. "After all that we have done for *each other*, Madame. Never forget that I have brought much to this marriage, land as well as peace, and I will not be set aside to embroider. I will be an involved queen and do honor to the king. Besides, I have been writing to heads of state since I was seven years old. Please be assured that I am quite capable at it."

The regent's face sours around the edges, but before she can speak again, the queen changes the subject. "Speaking of correspondence, has the king received any word as to who might have been behind the ambush on our traveling party?"

The regent's smile returns now that she has something the queen wants. "I fear there has been no news on that front, Your Majesty."

My hands itch to slap the false regret off her long face.

The queen sets her quill down with an audible click. "That is unacceptable. One of my dearest and most trusted advisors was killed in the attack."

"We do not know that, Your Majesty. He may have simply died of apoplexy."

"Perhaps," the queen says, unconvinced. "Has there been any word from the pope yet on the dispensation?"

The regent's moue of disappointment is as false as her earlier regret. "Not yet, no. But the bishops continue to assure me that all is in order and it is simply a matter of the paperwork to be completed and delivered."

"Let us hope you are right. And speaking of Church matters, has the Princess Marguerite reached her father's holdings yet? I wish to write to her and was not certain where to send my message."

My stitching forgotten, I study the regent's face closely. She does not so much as twitch an eyelash. "I do not believe she has reached him yet. But you may give your message to me, and I will see that she gets it."

"That is a very kind offer," the queen says, although she has no intention of taking the regent up on it. With well-disguised relief, she turns her attention to a flutter of commotion at the far end of the room. The king's chamberlain enters, bows to the attendants, then makes his way over to our end of the room, where he bows to the regent and then the queen. "Your Majesty, the king requests that you join him for a walk through the palace gardens this afternoon."

The queen's face brightens at the invitation. "Please tell His Majesty I would be honored to join him."

As the chamberlain leaves to take the queen's response to the king, the queen glances up at the regent. "If you will excuse me, Madame, I must get ready for my lord husband."

Unable to interfere with a request from the king, the regent inclines her head in acknowledgment, but not before I see how very much she hates this intimacy between the king and queen that by its very nature excludes her.

CHAPTER 53

Genevieve

efore I leave the castle never to return, there is someone I must say goodbye to.

With my heart thudding in my chest, I head to the nursery. Two women sit near the fire, a small child just learning to walk toddling on the carpet between them. The child points and makes an unintelligible sound. One of the women turns her head.

Jeanne's face softens when she sees it is me. "Genevieve." She rises gracefully, steps around her young daughter, and comes to greet me. "I am glad you're here," she says simply. No questions or remonstrations for not having come sooner. She takes my hand gently in hers, and I let her. She gives it an encouraging squeeze before leading me to a spot on the other side of the room where a small wooden cradle sits, just beyond reach of the fire.

My heart beats louder, my mouth growing dry.

"Here she is," Jeanne says softly, squeezing my hand again before withdrawing. She scoops up her daughter and shoos the nurse out of the room.

I am alone with the babe.

I look down in the cradle, for the first time laying my eyes on Margot's daughter.

The infant is asleep, her long lashes lying against a round cheek that looks impossibly soft and pink. On her head is a smattering of fuzzy down, the same dark red as Margot's.

A sharp pain lances through my chest. For so long, I've felt nothing but a hollow, aching emptiness where she used to be. But seeing this small creature who already has so much of Margot to her is like lifting the heavy iron grate to the oubliette and letting all the pain come flooding out.

Breathless with the ferocity of it, I kneel on the floor, careful not to jostle the cradle and wake the sleeping babe. But I must gasp, or sob, or perhaps it is something inside the babe herself that causes her to open her eyes just then.

Margot's eyes.

For a moment — an all too brief and dizzying moment — Margot and I are twelve again and snuggled up in bed, the thrill of our new adventure keeping us from sleep. Indeed, we are so giddy with it, it is all we can do not to giggle and wake the others.

The babe blinks her big solemn eyes, and it is clear she is not Margot at all, but her own self. Her mouth starts to pucker, and her small hand flails. Without thinking, I reach down and hold my finger out. She grabs it with a grip that is surprisingly strong for a three-week-old babe. "Good girl," I whisper fiercely. "Take what you want." I know she has been christened and baptized in the Christian faith, but Mortain's blood also flows in her veins.

Would Margot want her to know Mortain? For all that she turned her back on Him, she was desperate for the blessings of the Nine near the end.

Yes.

The answer comes up from deep in my gut, as swift and sure as an arrow. I open my mouth to promise to come back for her, then stop. I do not know if that is a promise I can keep.

But it is all the more reason to ensure the convent is still there when she is ready to learn about those parts of herself.

I squeeze her fingers. "I will come back for you. Someday. At least long enough to tell you who you truly are."

I surprise myself — and the babe — by leaning down to place a tender kiss upon her brow. "For all the ones your mother would have placed there — had she lived. For I've no doubt she would have showered you with them."

And with that, I shove to my feet and hurry from the room.

It takes no time at all to arrange my own death. The Charente River runs just outside the palace gates. Making sure the sentries see me leave, I follow the wall to the first bend, which is just out of view of the guard tower. It is a small strip of bank, not nearly large enough to launch an attack from, but just the right size for sitting morosely and staring into the dark water as it rushes by.

I bring an old cloak, a nearly empty jug of wine, and a large, flat stone. When I am out of sight of the guards, I use the stone to flatten a spot along the mushy bank so that it looks like something — a body — slid down into the water. Next I lay the jug on its side and leave the cloak in a heap, anchoring it in place with the stone so it will not get washed away before it is found.

There. I step back and admire my handiwork. They will wonder if it was an accident or choice. A shiver dances across my shoulders, and I say a short prayer for the Genevieve who has fallen in the river. The Genevieve who, despondent over the death of her best friend — her only friend — has allowed herself to be swept away.

That is when I realize yet another way Maraud can be of use to me. The regent gave Angoulême clear instructions to keep the prisoner hidden. She implied she would place all the blame for his treatment squarely on the count's head. Angoulême could end up in a great deal of trouble. Well and good. If he wishes to meddle in my life, then I have found a way to meddle in his. And he will not like it. Not one bit.

But it is the least he deserves for leading Margot to her fate.

CHAPTER 54

Sybella

he queen takes great care with her appearance for her outing with the king. She tries not to let her excitement show — mostly so as not to give the regent's attendants any fodder to carry back to their mistress. When the king calls upon her, they walk toward the palace doors trailed by a small flock of her ladies and his retainers.

We have no sooner reached the garden than the regent emerges from a door in the south wing of the palace, followed by two of her own ladies. *Merde.* She is as relentless as the tide. "Oh, look." My voice is both welcoming and loud enough to reach the king and queen. "The regent is joining us as well." One cannot let a serpent slip silently into a garden.

The queen's face falls slightly, and even the king looks annoyed. The regent sends me a cutting glance, but continues to the royal couple's side. When she reaches them, the king inquires coolly, "Is there something that requires my attention?"

I nearly crow with delight. She has overplayed her hand. What man paying court to his new wife wishes his older sister to trail along? The regent quickly hides her disconcertment. "I thought only to enjoy this welcome bit of sunshine, like everyone else."

The king sighs, his expression somewhere between fondness and exasperation. "Dear sister, do you truly not trust me to walk with my wife on my own?"

I must bite my lips to keep any trace of triumph from my face. The regent tries to laugh off his rebuke. "Do not be silly. It is simply rare enough for us to have sunshine in the dead of winter, and I thought to enjoy it. However, if you are forbidding me to do so . . ."

"You are welcome to enjoy all the sunshine you like, I only question that you must do so here. I wish to spend some time with my queen."

"But of course. I will walk somewhere else."

It is all I can do not to cheer as she picks up her skirts and heads in the opposite direction, her two ladies trailing uncertainly behind her. She takes but three turns of the lawn before returning inside, her purpose snatched from her.

Once she has left, the king and queen stroll away, and his men wander off in small groups. Uncertain what we are supposed to do, I observe the French ladies in waiting. They take a seat on benches and begin talking amongst themselves.

I glance at Aeva. "I do not feel like sitting, do you?"

"Saints, no!" Keeping a surreptitious eye on the royal couple, we begin strolling among the carefully cultivated bushes and trees. For the most part, they chat politely, the queen smiling often, and the king as well. At one point, he plucks a winter rose from its branch and hands it to her, which can only be a good sign.

"What wouldn't I give to be a little bird right now," I mutter.

Aeva raises a questioning brow. "You wish to hear their conversation?"

"But of course I wish to hear their conversation. How else can I parse what is going on between them? The king's affections run hot and then appear to cool. He welcomes the queen with great spectacle and fanfare, but spends very little time alone with her. He is polite, attentive, even charming on occasion, and yet I can see his eyes often wandering."

"And you think he is confessing his reasons for that by that bush?"

I nearly punch her. "No, you goose. But what he says, how he says it, what he doesn't say — are all clues that can be used to help better understand him."

Her face clears in understanding. "All you needed to do was say so." She takes one, two, three steps back until she is standing among the trees that encircle the garden. Even as I watch her, the next minute, she is gone. I blink, my mouth hanging open. No. Not gone. There. I see a faint movement in the shadows. But she makes no sound, and even the leaves do not so much as twitch with her passing. I quickly lose sight of her as she moves silently toward to the king and queen.

I turn my back to the trees and stare out at the garden, acting for all the world as if I am here alone. After a few moments, I see that Aeva's disappearing trick has not attracted any notice, and I allow myself to breathe somewhat easier.

While Aeva is masquerading as a tree and eavesdropping on the king and queen, I return my attention to the ladies in waiting. Katerine is watching the royal couple nearly as intently as I am. She has also chosen to separate herself from the other attendants somewhat, which provides a window of opportunity. Perhaps she has even planned it that way.

That possibility propels me across the lawn. When I reach her, I smile in greeting. "Are you enjoying the gardens, Lady Katerine?"

She hesitates a moment before answering. "It is a pleasant change from the solar. And once winter is here, it is rare enough to have a chance to enjoy them."

Does she put extra emphasis on the word *winter*? It is often referred to as Mortain's own season. Her face gives nothing away as she watches the king and queen. I curse myself for not having brought a crow feather with me, but I did not know this opportunity would present itself. "Have you been to Brittany?" It is an innocent enough question — preamble for further discussing gardens or winter weather. But it also provides an opening if she needs one.

"Brittany!" She laughs. "Why would I go to Brittany?"

Her laughter sours my budding hopes. "Many French noble families have holdings there," I reply sharply. "I thought perhaps yours might as well. It would explain your interest in the queen."

Her gaze snaps round to meet mine. "I'm sure you are mistaken, Lady Sybella. I have no interest in the queen. Good day." And with that, she rises and returns to the others. The taste of my disappointment is so bitter that I must clasp my hands tightly together to keep from making a rude gesture at her departing back.

I try to take comfort that the queen's outing is going better than mine, but

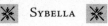

as I watch her, something shifts. She is talking earnestly, but the king's gaze is impassive. She grows more impassioned. His gaze remains on hers for a moment before he looks away, turning his shoulder slightly to her.

Her face creases in concern, and she places a hand on his arm.

He ignores it and points to a flowering shrub. After a long moment, she acknowledges the bush. He offers her his arm again, but it is stiffer this time, held farther away from his body than it was when they first started walking.

I glance frantically around for Aeva to see if she has returned — and can explain what has happened — but she is still hidden somewhere in the trees.

Instead of completing their circuit around the park, the king walks the queen back the way they have come, the winter rose she had been holding now dangling listlessly from her fingers. My heart dips at the wooden expression on the king's face, and the poorly hidden distress on the queen's. When the king reaches us, he bows. "My ladies, I hope you enjoy your time in the garden. I am afraid I have pressing matters I must attend to now." And with that, he takes his leave, the queen doing her best to blink back tears.

Fortunately, the other attendants are so absorbed in their own gossip and enjoyment of the day that I am able to quickly step to the queen's side, take her arm, and begin walking in a direction away from the king. "What happened? It seemed that everything was going so nicely."

She stares straight ahead, a pleasant expression pasted on her face. "It was. It was going so well that I felt comfortable with him. As if we were truly a husband and wife come together to talk of our mutual interests. He mentioned something about Brittany, which I said reminded me that I had been meaning to ask him about his appointment of Lord Rohan as chancellor, as Chancellor Montauban was doing a fine job in that role."

"And what did he say to that?"

She looks down at her hand, her face bleak. "That matters of government were his prerogative and he did not wish to discuss them. And then he left."

It is her worst fear made real. He has no intention — if ever he had — of relinquishing any power to her or even allowing her to govern Brittany. I feel sick, both for her and my sisters.

She shoves the flower at me as if she can no longer bear to hold it. But it is too delicate to withstand yet another human touch. As I take it from her, the petals separate and the winter rose comes apart in my hand.

Later that afternoon, with my heart heavy in my chest, I slowly climb the five flights of stairs to my room. When I reach the landing, I see that the door to our chamber stands open. Concern prickling along my scalp, I pick up my skirts and hurry the rest of the way.

Drawing closer, I hear voices coming from inside. When I reach the door, the sight that greets me brings me to a stop.

The regent sits in a chair by the fire. Louise is on the floor at her feet, looking up at her. Charlotte sits perched on a second chair, wearing her most polite and attentive expression.

"Lady Sybella!" The regent's voice is warm and welcoming.

"Madame Regent." I dip into a deep curtsy.

"I was just getting to know your sisters."

Her words are friendly, but my heart begins to thud hollowly in my chest. "So I see, Madame."

She smiles down at Louise as she rises. When she is standing, she lifts her gaze to mine. "They are charming girls." There is no malice in her words or on her face, nor even the hint of a threat, but I can feel it all the same.

"Be well," she says, and takes her leave.

It is all I can do not to slam the door and bolt it shut. I try to reassure myself that she would never harm two young girls. Then I think of the queen, and know that is a lie. There are infinite ways to hurt someone, and the regent is more resourceful than most.

CHAPTER 55

Genevieve

hen I reach the oubliette, I throw back the bolt on the latch, not caring how loudly it echoes through the stone corridor, then heave the grill up so hard that I nearly wrench my shoulder.

Not bothering with a greeting, I toss the rope down into the hole. "Hurry," I call down to Maraud.

His head appears in the opening. He eyes me warily, taking in the metal breastplate I wear, the vambraces and chausses. "I thought you were leaving?"

I ignore his question. "You once said the gods would not roll the dice in your favor again. What if I told you they were?"

"You would have my complete attention."

"Are you of a mind to bet on them today?"

His gaze latches on to mine with the force of a lance blow. "Yes."

Good. He knows it is only a chance I offer him, and that there is risk involved. "Then you are coming with me. And we are leaving now."

There is risk for me as well. By bringing him along, there will be no turning back. I could lie my way out of the faked death (*I wondered where I had left my cloak!*) or even claim to have been overtaken by a fit of melancholy. But by freeing a prisoner I should not even know about — who should by rights be dead by now — I have not only shut the door behind me but burned the bridge that leads to it as well. "You have until the count of ten. One . . ."

He scrambles out of the hole that has been his home for months. When he reaches the landing, he regards me quizzically. "I thought I had lost your trust."

"You have."

"But something caused you to change your mind."

"For the moment at least. You must do exactly as I say. No questions asked. Will you swear it?"

Our gazes clash as he tries to peer past my face into my very head and untangle the convoluted web he knows I have woven. "If it is one step closer to freedom than where I currently sit, I will swear it."

But of course, that is not enough.

I have thought long and hard about how to ensure his cooperation on our travels. While his honor once proved impressive, I am not sure how well it will hold up once true freedom is within his grasp. "Good. But just to be sure, I need you to drink this." I hand him a small vial.

He stares at it. "What's in it?"

"Poison. If you wish to be free of this place, you must drink it." It is his first test. If he cannot obey, he cannot come.

Maraud gapes at me, an unreadable expression on his face. "You already poisoned me."

"That was something else altogether. This poison is different. It is slow acting and has an antidote. An antidote that I will feed to you each morning. As long as you take that, the poison will not harm you."

"But I gave you my word." His voice is accusing, almost hurt.

"And we all know how well that turned out," I say dryly. "I can leave nothing to chance. This is the way it must be."

He lifts the small glass bottle to his nose and sniffs. "Of all the ways I dreamed of my release from this place, it never came with a dose of poison." His gaze lifts to mine. "Before I drink, will you at least tell me who you are? If I am to place this much trust in you, I have a right to know."

If he places that much trust in me, he is a fool. But it is as good a time to tell him as any, and may help ensure his continued cooperation. "I am an initiate of Saint Mortain. I was sired by Him, taken to His convent, and trained in His arts."

The reaction dawns slowly, and if I were not in such a hurry to be gone from this place, nor so conflicted about bringing him with me, the emotions that flit across his face would be amusing. "You are one of Death's daughters?" His voice is filled with caution and reverence and a tiny bit of disbelief.

"Yes."

"But what are you doing here in Cogn —"

"We do not have time to discuss this. You wished to know who I am and I told you. Quit bleating like a nervous sheep and drink the poison. Or not. But I am leaving either way."

He tosses the contents into his mouth. "Now what?" he asks.

"Now we get you ready." He returns the vial, and I tuck it into the pouch at my waist as I motion for him to go in front of me. "Take the fifth door on the right."

He pauses in the doorway. "This is a storage room."

"Your wit is as sharp as ever. It holds the clothes you will need. But if you continue to drag your feet, I will toss you back in your cell and leave without you."

He shoots me a pained glance as he enters the room. "Do we have a schedule we must adhere to?"

"Yes, actually. There is a troupe of mummers arriving to perform for the household. After tonight, they will move on to Jarnac, then to the city of Angoulême. We will be going with them."

"Wait, let me be sure I understand. We are going to parade in front of the very people you — we — are trying to escape from?"

"No," I scoff. "We will wait in the shadows and join them as they come out of the grand salon, slipping in among them as easily as smoke up a chimney. Two lone travelers, even under the guise of messengers, would be noted leaving the city — especially if they were not seen delivering any messages. This way, we will hide in plain sight. The guards at the tower can see the road for nearly a mile, there is no way to get by them unnoticed. Believe me, I have spent much time thinking on this. And if I must tell you to hurry one more time, I will put you back into your hole."

This spurs him to action, and he hastily begins undressing. "Use the water for a quick wash. You may be dressed like a wolf, but there is no reason to smell like one. There is also a salve for your wrists, and linen strips to wrap around the iron so it won't chafe."

He emerges a few minutes later, smelling faintly of the balsam soap and dressed in the simple clothes of a peasant, which fit well enough, considering they were part of a costume junk pile. Even though his wrists are now wrapped in linen, I am pleased that the sleeves are long enough to fully cover his manacles. "It will do. Your beard adds a nice touch."

He grimaces and reaches up to tug at it. "But will it be enough to disguise me?"

"We will not be relying on that alone. Here is the rest of your costume." I pull a great wolf skin from the open chest and shake it out.

He stares at it, faint admiration mixed with equal parts horror. "I am to wear that?"

I look at it, inordinately pleased with the thing. "It is perfect. We will be dressed as Saint Brigantia fighting off the wolves of war." I glance up at him. "You know the story? How Brigantia tricked your god and averted a war that would have—"

"Yes, I know the story. But . . ." He reaches for the wolf skin. "*How* am I to wear it?"

"Look, it has been fashioned into a mask and will fit over the top of your head. You can see out of it."

He settles the snarling wolf's head over his own, tugging and adjusting until I see his eyes behind the two holes. "It smells of old wolf." His voice is hollow, distorted by the mask. That is also good, in case he has to speak.

"It makes the disguise all the more believable. Now for the last part." I hold up a heavy loop of chain.

He rears back, looking for all the world like a hound resisting a leash. "You already gave me your poison." Faint sparks of temper lurk in his voice.

"It is part of the costume, and while you have given me your word, you have also betrayed me once. Bringing you with me is a big risk."

"Why?" he asks. "Why are you taking such a risk to help me?"

"Mortain knows," I mutter. "Now stop flapping your tongue else we will miss our chance."

He heaves a great sigh and lowers his head so I may slip the chain over it. After giving it a quick tug to make sure it is secure, I reach for the helmet that will complete my own costume. I settle it over my head, roll my shoulders, then grip the chain firmly in my hand. "Time to go."

CHAPTER 56

ully disguised by our costumes, we cautiously make our way through the long winding corridors of the dungeon. When we reach the landing, I peek out to be certain the coast is clear before we hurry up the three flights of stairs to the main floor. Once there, we lurk in the shadows, waiting. Faint strains of quiet music drift out of the great hall. That isn't right. The music should swoop and swirl and be accompanied by laughter and applause as well.

I motion for Maraud to stay put and edge forward, drawing closer to the hall. There is still nothing but quiet voices and the plucking of lute strings.

"Where are they?" Maraud's voice at my ear nearly causes me to jump.

"I told you to stay put."

"You also told me we'd be joining a parade of mummers, and yet —"

Voices approach from the opposite side of the causeway. Maraud and I leap back toward the landing. By the smell that reaches us, it is a pair of servers bearing the fish course.

". . . can't believe she wouldn't let them perform." It is a man talking.

"She's a somber one, she is," grumbles the second voice.

"But does she need to spoil it for the rest of us?" The voices disappear into the main hall.

"Rutting figs!" I whisper. "Louise canceled the performance." My mind is buzzing like a nest of frantic hornets, replaying all my options in my head. We will have to go with a second plan, then, which is not nearly as safe. As I open my mouth to explain just that, rapid footsteps, quick and light, come down the stairway.

Before we can do so much as move, Lady Juliette appears in front of us, her haughty gaze widening in surprise before narrowing in suspicion. "Why are you skulking in here?"

Lady Juliette with her sharp eyes and prickly disposition. But even she cannot see through an iron visor. Or so I pray.

I look down at my feet, allowing my shoulders to slump. When I speak, my voice is pitched low so that my words are broad and flat. "We were told to meet in here, my lady, so we could perform for the count and his household."

She looks briefly to Maraud, her lip curling. "Not tonight. The count is away, and his countess does not like for the mice to play." She smiles at her own jest, and I wonder how much wine she has had. "The countess does not approve of mummery. Now be off to the stables with the others, or I'll have to assume you are here to steal the silver and have a footman throw you out."

"No need to do that, my lady! If you'd just show us the way . . ."

She points to the staircase.

We quickly bow our thanks and scramble toward the stairs. When we reach the door, the porter opens it for us, loudly complaining about stragglers as he shuts it firmly behind us.

Maraud turns to me, his wolf jaw leering in the light of the torches. "That went well."

"Shut up, or I will rip off your mask and shove you back inside."

He pauses, his mouth open. "I do not think any of them would know who I was." He smiles. "They'd still just think me a lost mummer trying to steal the silver."

"People hang for less than that." I tug on his chain. "The stable is this way."

As we cross the courtyard, we keep close to the walls in an attempt to draw as little attention to ourselves as possible. I pause silently at the cluster of guards on the gate tower, then again at the sentries patrolling the battlements, wanting Maraud to see for himself why we could not just walk out of here.

When we finally reach the stable, it is full of a colorful collection of fools, men dressed as maids, and two kings. Someone dressed in a black cloak with a crow mask tucked under his arm talks to a man wearing stag's antlers.

We fit right in. Someone — the steward perhaps? — has provided jugs of wine and rough bread and cheese — appeasement, perhaps, for the canceled performance.

Luckily, everyone is so busy either grumbling or swigging wine that we are able to slip in unnoticed.

Or so I think.

Two steps inside the door, a hand reaches out and grabs my arm. I freeze.

It is Alips from the kitchen. A thick, solid woman, tonight she is dressed in the dark green and gold of Dea Matrona, a wreath sitting crookedly atop her head. "Don't worry, dearie. All of our welcomes won't be like this." She leans in close, close enough that I can smell the wine on her breath. "No one saw you slip in among us. The others won't even know you're missing. We always lose a few this time of year. Just be sure and be back by the day after Epiphany, and no one will be any the wiser."

She thinks I am one of the castle servants who plan to join the mummers in their revelries. "Very well, ma'am."

She gives Maraud a long appraising look before winking at me in approval. Then she turns to a yellow-costumed fool who is arguing with one of the red-and-black-masked hellequin. We are forgotten.

Even though others have begun to remove their cumbersome masks and the bulkier parts of their costumes, Maraud and I leave ours on until we reach a remote corner of the stable. The stall is as far away from the door — and inquiring eyes — as possible. "We'll sleep here." I hold up a finger. "And not one word. Not one. We are out of the chateau, and that is what matters."

He says nothing.

I shrug. "You can take off your mask, if you wish."

He tilts his wolfish head at me, then reaches out and jiggles the chain.

He watches me closely — too closely — as I detach the chain from around his neck. When I am finished, I quickly step back.

He lifts the mask from his head and runs his fingers through his hair. "Sweet Jesu, it's hot in that thing."

When I go to remove my own helmet, he is still watching me, so I turn my back to him and lift it from my head, grateful for the cool air on my hot cheeks and scalp.

"Is your ability to alter yourself so completely one of Mortain's arts?" he asks.

I frown. "What do you mean?"

"When we stepped out of the stairwell tonight, you lowered your head, your shoulders drew in, your whole body shifted. It was like watching someone bank a fire. But when you are sparring, or fighting, or yelling at me, your shoulders are straight, your head and chin are up, daring the world to be so foolish as to overlook you." He tilts his head, studying my face. "Even your eyes. I do not know how you do it, but the vividness of them recedes when you choose it."

I nearly laugh. It is not Mortain's art at all, but the survival skills of a whore's daughter who must move in a sea of nobles without being detected. "Hush your prattle." I dump my helmet on the floor. "We have a long walk to Jarnac tomorrow, and you will need all your strength to keep up."

I kick the straw on the floor into a lumpy pile, then lie down, stretching out my full length. A moment later, Maraud does the same, although to my great annoyance, it is closer to me than I would like. His very existence is demanding small intimacies I've no wish to share.

There is a rustling in the straw a few stalls over as a furtive coupling takes place. A whispered argument between two voices slurred with drink. There are even, when the other noises are quiet, the sounds of horses, stomping an occasional foot or whinnying softly at all the unfamiliar activity.

"How much longer until I need the antidote?" His question comes out of the darkness, as offhand and casual as if asking how long until the planting season might begin.

"Not until late morning. You are fine."

"Must I take it forever?"

"No. Only for a month. After that, the poison will have worked its way out of your body."

"I gave you my word," he grumbles as he pokes at the straw to soften the prickliest parts.

"And we both know precisely how much that is worth."

"I never promised you I would not try to escape."

Is that true? I fold my hands under my head and cast my mind back over all our conversations. "I did not ask you to say the words out loud, no, but I explained escaping was not part of our bargain, and you agreed to that. Therefore, your word is tarnished in my eyes."

When he says nothing, I remove my hands and turn to my side, pillowing my head with my arm as I make myself comfortable.

It's hard not to question my decision to bring him along. He has betrayed my trust, proved that he is ruthless, and taken me for a fool. I owe him nothing. I made clear that his freedom was never part of the bargain. He is an extra assurance, much like the poisoned needles I wear inside my sleeves. That is all. That is the only reason I have brought him.

It is not because I have grown fond of him like one does a cat. Or because of all the times he could easily have overpowered me but chose not to. It is not because he wished to rescue me as well as claim his own freedom.

He is a valuable negotiating tool. Nothing more.

Something hot and sharp stabs at me. The hay, which had seemed so comfortable only moments ago, now feels prickly and pokes roughly through my tunic.

"What are you worried about?" Maraud asks.

"You should be sleeping. It is more than ten miles to the next town. If you cannot make it, I will not be able to carry you."

He shrugs. "If I have to drag myself by my arms, crawl on my hands and knees, or tie myself to a passing cart, I will keep up. I will not go back into that hole." He says this so simply that it would be easy to miss the underlying note of ferocity that runs through it. He turns to look at me again. "I owe you a debt I can never repay."

It is all I can do not to flinch under his gratitude. "We shall see."

CHAPTER 57

hen I open my eyes in the morning, the first thing I see is Maraud. While I am pleased he did not try to escape during the night, I am not pleased that his head is propped on his elbow and he is watching me.

I squint against the morning light spilling into the stable and scrub my face with my hands, using the movement to check that I was not drooling. "What are you staring at?"

"Until the sun rose this morning, I had never truly seen your face."

For a moment, vanity rears its head, and I want to protest that sleeping on the floor of a stable does not work to my advantage. Instead, I force myself to shrug. "It is just a face." Still not looking at him, I shove to my feet, push my hair out of my eyes, and adjust the belt at my waist so my chausses do not fall down.

"Ah, but that is where you are wrong." He stands up, his movements smooth, quick, and graceful. "I have never seen the face of the daughter of a god before."

"Mind your tongue, wolf," I growl. In the stalls around us there is the low rumble of voices and the sound of someone pissing.

"They cannot hear us any better this morning than they could last night."

I do my best to ignore him and begin collecting my things, but he continues to study me — much the same way the count's illuminator did when contemplating who would sit for his paintings. "We need some charcoal or a bit of ash from last night's fire."

I stare back at him stupidly. "What?"

"You have a distinctive face. We don't want any of the castle servants to recognize you. I'll be right back." And with that, he turns and strides from our stall. My heart slams against my ribs in alarm. He can't think to simply walk out of here. "Don't forget to return for your . . . physick!" I say in a loud whisper.

He gives a wave of his hand to indicate he has heard before stepping out of sight. A brightly dressed fool emerges from a nearby stall just then, clutching his belled cap in one hand and his stomach in the other. I nip out of his way as he hurries past me to retch up the sour remnants of last night's wine.

Distinctive face? What is that supposed to mean? I snatch up my breast-plate and try to peer at my own reflection, but the steel is not polished enough. Disgusted with myself, I shrug into the piece of armor and fasten the straps at my shoulder. Just as I am buckling the sides, Maraud strolls back in.

"I was about to leave without you."

"But you didn't. Hold still." He gently grips my face, the warmth and weight of his fingers shocking me into momentary silence. When I open my mouth to tell him to remove his hand or risk losing it, he talks over me. "You cannot keep that helmet on the entire time." His other hand also reaches toward my face.

I flinch away. "What are you doing?"

He laughs, enjoying this far too much. "It is only charcoal."

I glare at him, but hold myself still. "Look up," he says, adjusting my chin.

I jerk my head higher in an attempt to minimize his touch. The glance he gives me is unreadable. "Close your eyes so the dust won't get in them."

I sigh heavily so he will know how tedious I find all this, but I am also willing to accept whatever can be done to alter my appearance.

With quick, feather-light strokes, he brushes the charcoal along my eyebrows, darkening them and drawing them so they are closer together. Next he smudges a bit onto his finger and rubs it in a thin line from my nose down to my mouth. His final touch is a smudge under each eye. He steps back to survey his handiwork. "There. You look older, less fair, and much more tired." Unsettled by the small intimacy of his ministrations, I scrunch my nose against the feel of the dirt on my face. "Now we can go," he says.

I hold up my hand. "Not so fast." I remove the vial from the pouch at my waist.

He eyes it with revulsion and relief. I pull the stopper and lift the bottle. He is taller than I, which makes administering the drops awkward. I am tempted to ask him to kneel, but the idea of making him kneel at my feet to receive an antidote he doesn't deserve is too much like a mummer's farce. Instead, I reach up and hold it out to him. Needing no instruction or encouragement, he bends his knees and opens his mouth.

I allow three small drops to fall onto his tongue. "There," I say, not meeting his eyes. "You are good until tomorrow." I tuck the vial back into my pouch, feeling as if I have managed to regain control.

⁂

It is easy to attach ourselves to one of the small groups of mummers leaving the castle yard. Behind me it feels as if all the windows of the castle are watching. My shoulders itch, and I hope it is only the hay that I slept on.

When we pass through the barbican, I draw my first easy breath of the morning. By the time we reach the main road, I allow myself to look up into the sky, to feel the fresh morning air on my face. The clouds have disappeared during the night, but the air has grown colder, leaving a light dusting of frost so that everything sparkles in the sunlight.

My gaze seeks out Alips, and I wonder if the charcoal dust will fool her in broad daylight. To my relief, she is not among our group of travelers. I recognize some of them from the village — Blavot the chandler, as tall and thin as the candles he makes. Herbin the butcher and his wife, Jacquette. The miller's wife, Matilde, is among us, wearing a furred tunic and carrying a bow and arrow. As is Rogier the stonemason, who has been working on the chateau remodels that Angoulême has undertaken. But no other household servants that I can see. Best of all, no one's gaze lingers overlong on me or Maraud.

It is an easy group, talking and laughing as they walk. Some carry bundles attached to their backs. Others have their masks tucked up under their arms. The stonemason pushes a handcart full of casks and drums, while Herbin drives a wagon pulled by two oxen. A handful of matrons sit on the back end, their feet dangling over the side. A various assortment of children tag along, like a long, wiggling, giggling tail.

A number of them take great sport in following Maraud, the terrifying wolf's head of his cape hanging down his back, leering at them upside down. Occasionally one grows bold enough to run forward and tug at his tail before quickly darting away with a squeal of terrified laughter. I glance up at Maraud to see how he is taking this, my words shriveling before I can utter them.

It is the first time I have seen him in good light. This morning, even as he gazed at my face, I avoided his. Besides, the sun was streaming in through the window directly into my eyes.

In spite of his overlong hair and his beard — which should be bushy and matted from his time in captivity but instead manages to accentuate his strong features — he is . . . *Rutting figs!* There is no word for it but *handsome.*

He turns to me just then, our gazes meeting. "Can you feel it?" he whispers.

"Feel what?" Mortified at being caught, the word comes out hoarse, croaked.

He leans in closer, and the lips I have just been admiring form the word: "Freedom."

Released from my embarrassment, I huff out a breath. "Yes. I do."

He smiles at me, a flash of strong white teeth against the darkness of his beard, then grows serious. "And for that, I thank you."

His sense of indebtedness sits as uncomfortably as a nail-studded shirt. "Perhaps you have simply traded one prison for another," I say lightly.

He looks at me as if he knows better — as if he knows *me* better — than that. Ignoring my provocation, he pulls his wolf skin closer against the crisp chill of the morning. "So," he lowers his voice. "*Were* you sent to rescue me?"

Now that I know who he is, the question makes more sense. "Assassins don't rescue moldering prisoners."

An odd expression appears on his face. "Were you sent to *kill* me?"

I stare back at him. Was I? Was that why I heard his heart beating that day? Should I have grabbed a torch and examined him for a marque? The thought never crossed my mind at the time. It was too far outside what the abbess had instructed us to do. "You're still alive, aren't you?"

"Well, yes. There is that." He grins. It is wide and welcoming, inviting all who see it to be drawn into his net. Surely it is as dangerous as his sword arm. "Perhaps my charms swayed you from your purpose and you chose to rescue me instead."

Does he truly think me so weak and softhearted? Fool. It is just my luck to have stumbled upon the one mercenary lacking in cynicism.

"If you must thank anyone," I tell him, my words as tart as an unripe apple, "it should be the god of mistakes, for surely it was Salonius himself who led me to you."

He blows on his hands, then rubs them together. "Maybe the god of mistakes wishes me to live."

I slip my own hands inside my sleeves to keep them warm as a thought occurs to me. "Are you a bastard?" It would explain his earlier comments about his family.

"No." His face grows hard. "Not a bastard."

"And yet you joined the mercenaries rather than fight with your father's men." Another thought occurs to me. Did he suspect his father's honor was in question, even then?

He shrugs, but the movement is stiff and wooden. "By the time I was born, my father already had three sons to carry on his good name. A fourth was merely one more mouth to feed, one more youth to train and supply." He grins, mostly to himself. "He wanted me to join the clergy. I refused." That explains his deep faith in the Nine. "Since he would not teach me the art of soldiering, I ran off to join the ranks of mercenaries."

"How old were you?"

"Twelve."

The same age I was when I was sent to the French court. "Why so eager to fight?"

He looks puzzled by the question. "Because I am good at it. With three older brothers steeped in the arts of soldiering and warfare, I presented a useful target. By the time I was twelve, I had acquired most of their knowledge, along with a burning desire to learn what they could not teach me so I could use it against them."

Before I can even smile at his confession — it is so like my own thinking — his face shifts again, growing somber as he falls silent. That is when I remember that all his brothers are dead.

He stares unseeing at the road ahead of us for a long moment before speaking again. "Does Angoulême know you are an assassin?"

My relief at seeing the shadows disappear from his face is replaced by annoyance. I would be happiest if I never had to think of Count Angoulême again. "You should conserve your strength for the long walk ahead."

"I told you, I will keep up. Why are you evading the question?"

"No," I lie. "Angoulême does not know I am an initiate of Mortain." He has coaxed too many answers out of me already. "I am simply a ward, entrusted to his care."

"Will he come looking for you?"

"He would if he knew I was gone, but he will be at Blois until Epiphany."

Maraud frowns. "Surely someone will notice you are missing."

Rutting figs, he is persistent. "No. I . . . made arrangements."

He stops walking so suddenly that one of the young boys trailing behind bumps into him, squealing in delighted terror. "What sort of arrangements?"

I bring my arms closer to my body, wishing for a thicker coat. "It's no concern of yours."

"I beg to differ. If they come looking for you, they will find me."

I squint into the distance and study the nearby fields. "I faked my own death."

His regard feels heavy against my skin. "Will that not cause them heartache?"

I think of Louise and Juliette. Of Count Angoulême and the babe who is not mine. "No more than your disappearance caused your family."

It is unkind and not even true — his father betrayed Brittany in an attempt to rescue him — but it has its desired effect, and he falls silent. He shifts his gaze to the north, toward the faint roar of the Charente River in the distance.

"So you never had a sister?"

The question catches me like a kick to the gut. It not only knocks the air from my lungs, but rips off a scab that has only just begun to form. I use every ounce of will I possess to resurrect the thick walls around my heart. "My sister is — was — real."

Something warm brushes my shoulder, bringing an unfamiliar sense of comfort. I look down to see Maraud's hand. He gives a brief squeeze of compassion before removing it. I do not know what surprises me more — his touch or that the sense of comfort remains long after his hand is gone.

CHAPTER 58

Sybella

y sisters' presence seems to cheer the queen somewhat, reminding her of her own sweet Isabeau. She is in desperate need of good cheer right now, for the king has not visited her since their disastrous walk in the garden. It casts a pall over the winter revelry. Even the king appears out of sorts.

In truth, it is only the regent who seems merry. I do not know if the king told her of what transpired in the garden, or if she simply sees there has been a breach between them and that is enough for her.

As we draw near the week mark with no visit from the king, my unease grows. Will he ever return? Is he seeking comfort elsewhere? With the Princess Marguerite? How easy to seek comfort in the company of someone who has been raised to be his wife since she was three and trained to reflect his own glory back at him. She would never dare to place demands or ask to govern a duchy. She would never dare to be a person separate from him or his be-damned crown.

All of these questions give more urgency to my search for the convent's moles. Since it is Advent and the rest of the castle is caught up in the celebration of the Christmas season, I am able to de precisely that.

The most reliable factor I have to go on is age. However, most of the regent's ladies in waiting have small, shriveled souls, so it is hard guess how old they are. Especially since they do not take kindly to the

queen's attendants trying to infiltrate their ranks, or even chatting with them in a friendly manner. While I do not adopt a friendly manner often, when I do, it nearly always manages to charm. That these stick-faced women are impervious to it just adds to my conviction that the regent has stolen their hearts and holds them locked away in stone jars.

But today, one of the women has been sent by the regent to deliver a message to the steward, and I have decided to follow.

Martine is a compact woman with a thin face and deep brown eyes. While her hair is brown, it does have glints of red when the light hits it. She is somewhere between sixteen and nineteen, with an aloof manner and keeps herself somewhat apart from the others. While it could simply be her nature, it could also be the reticence of someone who does not feel she can let down her guard.

If she is going to the steward's office, she will pass through this same hallway on her way back. My plan is to place a crow feather someplace where she will see it and observe how she reacts. If she is looking for one — her reaction will tell me much. If she has no knowledge of the convent, she likely will not even notice it.

There is no way to guarantee she will see it but to leave it on the floor so that it is directly in her path. Provided no servant wanders by and removes it before then.

Fortunately, there is an alcove further down the hallway. If I press myself into it, suck in my stomach, and do not move, I will not be visible.

Luckily for me, Martine is an efficient woman and does not take long with her errand. The rapid clack of her footsteps alerts me to her return. Then an abrupt silence. Has she spotted the feather?

The silence is followed by a huff of irritation accompanied by more hurried steps leading back the way she came. Unable to help myself, I peer around the lip of the alcove in time to see her yank on a rope to summon a servant. I pull back into my alcove. Did she not see it after all?

Moments later a young maid hurries from the far end of the hall toward Martine. Her voice is slightly breathless, eager to please. "Yes, my lady?"

"Are you in charge of seeing to this part of the castle?"

"Not personally, my lady, but —"

"Find whoever is responsible."

"But of course, my lady. Should I request they bring anything in particular to be of service?"

"Can you not see what is before your own face? Look!"

There is a long moment of silence. "Look at what, my lady?" the maid finally asks.

"That . . . filthy, dirty feather right here where the regent or the king himself could see it. The regent will not tolerate such slovenliness in her household, and I want to know who is responsible so that they may be held to account."

Cursing Martine for being a shrew — the regent's household! — I step out of the alcove and walk briskly toward them as if I have just come from the solar. I put my hands to my cheeks. "Oh, dear! There it is."

Both women look at me as if the feather could only have come from my brain.

"This is yours?" Martine finally asks. Her brow is creased, making her eyes smaller and meaner.

"Not exactly." I give an apologetic smile. "I found it outside and meant to give it to my youngest sister, who likes to collect them. It must have fallen from my pocket." I bend over, scoop up the feather, and hold it out like a prize. "Thank you so much for finding it. I know it will delight her." And with that, I hurry back down the hall.

Merde. That did not go at all how I had hoped.

CHAPTER 59

Genevieve

y the time we reach Jarnac late that afternoon, our group has grown. Much as rivulets run together turning into little streams, which in turn come together to form small rivers, so too have the villagers from Cognac, volunteers from nearby chateaux, and stray travelers joined with the mummers until we are a sea of performers. The people of Jarnac have eagerly awaited our arrival, and the guild hall in the center of town has been set aside for our use.

The hall is large, and I head for a secluded corner in the far back. No one has given me any additional notice, but it is wise not to push my luck. I select a quiet corner, pull my pack out from under my breastplate, drop it to the floor, and lie down next to it, my legs grateful for the rest. A moment later there is a whomp and a thud as Maraud does the same.

"Why are you tired?" I ask without looking at him. "You haven't had to walk since before noon." When Herbin's wagon got stuck in a rut on the road, Maraud was one of the first to lend a hand. He was offered a ride in the cart by way of thanks.

"There was room for you if you had asked." My eyes are closed, but I can hear the smile in his voice.

"I did not need to be carted in a wagon."

"*You* have not been confined to a cell the size of a large tankard, with no exercise for nearly a year."

"Your offer of help was very well timed."

When he says nothing, I open my eyes. His gaze rests on me with a faint air of disappointment. Guilt pokes at my gut. I adjust the hood of my cloak to better cushion my head. "Even so, it worked out well. You could not have walked the entire way. Although," I amend, "you have done far better than most would have."

He grimaces good-humoredly. "Do not be too impressed. I am now ready for a nap."

Within moments, he is breathing deeply, asleep already. I marvel at how easily he shrugs off both insults and embarrassment. In my experience, either one is enough for men to puff up like a peacock or draw into a wounded silence. But not Maraud. He is as resilient as a piece of gristle.

It would be so much easier if he would puff up or lash out in anger. He would not be so likable then. And I cannot afford to like him. No more than a farmwife can like the goose she is fattening up for her dinner.

I roll over on my side, trying to get comfortable. Even though I have just walked miles, my limbs still twitch with the need to move, to run, to exercise my newfound freedom.

To forget the pain of Margot's death, the comfort of Maraud's touch, and the vague sense of emptiness that lingers even though I have discovered my destiny. I give a grunt of frustration and sit up. Maraud is still asleep, but there are scores of people — colorful, warm, easy people — with which to distract myself.

Thus resolved, I go in search of the men who are passing around the wine jug.

⁂

An hour later, Maraud finds me sitting with a group of mummers near the front of the hall. "Ah! Here is the wolf now!" Herbin, the wagon driver, pours a cup of wine, hands it to Maraud, and lifts his own in salute. "Thanks for you help today. You know your way around an axle."

314

Maraud shrugs at compliment but takes the offered refreshment. "Drink up," Jacquette urges. "It was a long day and will be an even longer night."

As Maraud folds himself down onto the floor among us, Jacquette leans forward, a speculative gleam in her eye. "So, do you work at the same tavern Lucinda does?"

Maraud slips into the lie I have told as easily as a fish into water. "No, but I visit often."

This elicits a round of laughter and a refill of his glass. One would never guess he was from one of the noblest families in Brittany. His years with the mercenaries have rubbed away some of his polish.

A man from Jarnac appears bearing hot, fat sausages on sticks. He hands one to Maraud and Jacques. "Eat up. We begin shortly."

When he tries to hand one to me, I nod my head toward Maraud. "Give it to him. I had two already." It is a lie, but the wine has filled my stomach. And besides, Maraud has much catching up to do as far as meals go.

As he eats, I introduce him to my new friends. "This is Denic, a weaver of wool here in Jarnac. And this is Jarnac's village priest, Father Innocent. Although," I say in a loud whisper, "with his wandering eyes and sneaky fingers, he is anything but."

Father Innocent blushes, looking abashed as the others laugh. I smile to soften the barb in my words. I do not begrudge him his pleasures, simply the sneaking of them. "And this is Marie, whose husband's fine wine we are drinking. Herbin and Rogier you already know from this morning."

Maraud nods at each of them, lifting his cup in acknowledgment. In order to maintain the pretense I told the others — that Maraud and I are "friends" from a tavern in Norvaigne, I lean against Maraud's arm. "Denic will be dressed as the king tonight, and Father Innocent will be performing as the Green Maid."

Maraud lifts his cup to Father Innocent. "A lovelier Green Maid I cannot imagine."

As the men laugh at his joke, I wonder briefly if my act of being nobly born is ever discovered, can I plead it was naught but a Twelfth Night frolic gone on too long? It is the one time of year when the world turns upside down and peasants may dress as kings and kings play beggars and fools.

And here I sit, a peasant pretending to be a noble pretending to be a peasant. It is absurd enough that my laughter joins with that of the others.

Maraud looks at me, a single brow raised. "What was that?"

"What?"

"That noise you just made."

I place my hand on my chest and look offended. "You are mistaken. I made no noise." I hiccup, for good measure, and the others laugh.

It is surprisingly easy to simply *be* with these people. It is as natural to me as breathing. Surely that is why I giggled and exchanged a quick smile with Maraud. Before I can make a further fool of myself, Rollo — the round jester who seems to be in charge of the entire operation — appears. "Places, everyone." He claps his hands and rubs them together. "The fire has been lit, the people gathered. It is almost time to begin." As he speaks, his face is transformed, and his eyes take on a purposeful gleam. For the first time, I wonder if he is perhaps a true follower of Salonius.

As we prepare for the performance, the jug of wine is passed around again. I take a swig because doing so draws less attention than refusing, then hand it to Maraud. I secure the sword at my hip and lower my helmet, careful to ensure my hair spills out beneath it so the audience will know I am Brigantia taming the wolves of war.

Once Maraud places the snarling wolf's head over his own, I step closer, holding out the chain. Our eyes meet and something both warm and dark passes between us. Unsettled by the nature of it, I secure the chain around his neck with more force than is strictly necessary, as if binding him will somehow control my own wayward feelings.

We are two people in costume using each other to escape our circumstances. There is nothing more to us than that.

CHAPTER 60

s I step out into the night, my vision is momentarily dazzled by the huge bonfire and scores of torches. For a moment, I feel I have gone back in time and am reminded of just how old this tradition is.

The mummers have been tasked with telling the stories of the gods since long before there were written words to record such things. They told of their exploits, their victories, and their defeats. When the new Church crowded out the Nine, it fell unto the mummers to keep the memories of the old gods alive in the minds of the people.

A drumbeat sounds, a deep pulsing that feels as if it comes up from the bowels of the earth itself. A trumpet blares, cymbals clash, and a flute begins its haunting melody, and like a single serpent made up of many parts, we all move to take our places.

Perhaps we all move as one because we float on a surfeit of wine, or perhaps it is the gods themselves who command our movements as we honor their existence. Whatever the reason, I feel more my own self than I have in years.

Within moments, the music is pulsing deep within me, the rhythm of the other performers a perfect accent to my own. Step, step, face Maraud. He raises his arms and bares his teeth. I raise my sword. He ducks. I swing to the left. He ducks again.

The music builds.

He lifts his face to the sky and snarls, raising both hands overhead as if coming in for the final attack. I raise my sword, thrusting it to deliver a mortal blow.

As the sword finds its target, the frantic drumbeat stops. In silence, the crowd watches Maraud the wolf flail in the agonies of his death throes, a flute picking up the final notes of his dying.

A moment later, the music begins again, cheerful and upbeat, fools come tumbling by, and Maraud and I advance a quarter circle around the bonfire to begin our performance once more. Our bodies are in perfect accord with the music, the crowd in perfect accord with us. There is little thought, no room for remorse or guilt or worry. Simply the dance and the surrounding night. The dance grows — encompassing musicians, performers, and crowd alike — holding us in its arms, carrying us away from our own smallness.

Again, step, step, stop. Face Maraud. As he rears up snarling, his eyes find mine, the impact of them as potent as a slug of the strongest wine. Our eyes locked, I raise my sword. He ducks, his dark gaze fixed upon me, never wavering, reading my body for the next move. I swing to the left, willing him to look away, loath to be the first to do so for if I do, it feels like I will have lost some silent challenge he has issued.

And so we continue, thrice more around the bonfire, each time our bodies and movement more in tune until it feels as intimate as a pair of lovers. On the final build of the drum, I thrust my sword in the space between his arm and his ribs. When he writhes, clutching the sword, I finally look away. As my eyes scan the rapt faces of the crowd, I find I am no longer certain as to precisely what struggle Maraud and I are performing for them.

In silence, we return to our small corner of the hall. Even though he says nothing, I can feel his presence behind me, as unrelenting as the night. When we reach our things, I turn away from him to remove my helmet, desperate to break free of the spell that has settled over us.

I am so tired that my limbs feel as useless as wet straw, but my skin, my senses, are wildly, painfully awake.

Behind me there is a grunt of frustration. Before I can stop myself, I glance over my shoulder. Maraud's head is tilted up, his fingers plucking in increasing agitation against the leather ties at his neck. "It is in knots," he says in disgust.

Part of me, the wise part, thinks, *Good*. Let him choke on his costume all night if need be. But another part, the wild, painfully awake part, takes a step toward him. "Here. Let me do it," I say, hoping the note of impatience hides the breathlessness I feel.

He comes closer, exposing the thick muscled column of his throat. Such trust! And so poorly placed. Just a quick stab with a small knife, a stray nail, or even a needle, could end his life.

The most disturbing part is that what I actually want to do is to run my tongue along that vulnerable length of skin, taste the salt of him, nibble my way up to his lips, and lick them. Once. Twice. Then slowly ease them apart with my own. Would he savor such pleasure? Or would he take over, forcing his way in with his tongue before we had fully explored each other's lips?

Such thoughts only make me more clumsy. No matter how quickly I try to untangle the leather ties, they do not budge. As I continue to struggle, Maraud's eyes rest on me. Heat rises in my cheeks, and my fingers become nearly useless. "Perhaps we should just cut the things," I mutter.

"But then I would be unable to wear it."

I glance up at him to make a withering remark, the words drying up when I see his eyes watching my mouth. I resist the urge to lick my lips and instead allow my gaze to rest on his. They are parted slightly, and finely shaped.

His head begins to move closer to my own. In surprise, I glance up. He stops, meets my eyes. I wonder if the wine we drank will taste the same on him as it does on me.

"You're drunk," I finally tell him, a last effort to put some distance between us.

He raises his eyebrows. "Of course I'm drunk. Not on wine, but on freedom. Don't tell me you don't feel it too."

He is right. The effects of the wine have passed. Somehow, instead of repelling me, his honesty draws me closer. "I feel it." Almost as if aided by some wise god, my fumbling fingers finally find purchase and, like magic, the snarled ties untangle. Reason returns and I step back so quickly I nearly stumble. "We've an early start in the morning."

Without looking at him further, I lower myself onto the floor and busy myself with taking off my boots and folding my tabard into a pillow before stretching out.

Beside me, I can hear Maraud do the same. I turn my back to the room and settle onto the floor as best I can, then pull my cloak over my shoulders and try to sleep. But I cannot.

The victory of this newfound freedom fizzes through my veins, like water tossed on hot coals. I shift positions, trying to get comfortable. I hear a rustle off to my left and know that Maraud, too, is restless.

I peer over my shoulder to see if he is pretending to be asleep. He is looking at me, eyes unreadable in the dark.

"We are free," he whispers.

"We are," I whisper back.

"I never thought to be so again."

"Nor I." Surely that is why my heart is so full and my skin feels too tight on my bones.

He rolls up onto his side and props his head on his elbow. "We should celebrate." His voice is naught but a whisper.

I turn around to face him, propping my own head on my hand. "I am fairly certain all the wine is gone."

"There are other ways to celebrate." He does not move a muscle. He simply waits.

There is a tug deep inside me, like being pulled by some invisible chain. This desire I feel is not because of Maraud, I tell myself, but because I am free. My body and my heart are once again my own. I roll to my hands and knees and crawl across the space between us, slowly, like a predator might stalk his prey. "Are there." But it is not a question, and he knows it. He simply continues to wait. When I am close enough to touch him, I stop. What sort of lover will he be? Will his soldiering side take over? All quick thrusts and parrying and speed?

Will his wit and sharp humor make an appearance? Or the coaxing seduction of that first voice in the dark?

I toss my hair over my shoulder and slowly lean down, my eyes never leaving his. As I draw closer, he shifts his elbow so he is flat on his back, and I am hovering over him. It is meant to be a gesture of submission, and yet it is not that at all. Merely an agreement that strength and power will remain in check.

The force of my desire causes my belly to tighten.

I want this.

Slowly, with our gazes locked, I slide one leg over and across his stomach so that I am straddling him. My hair spills forward, brushing against his chest.

His jaw tightens.

"Is this the sort of celebrating you had in mind?"

He nods, whether because he cannot find his voice or does not wish to break the spell, I do not know.

"Very well, then." I reach for the hem of my tunic and slowly pull it over my head.

My nipples pucker at the cool air and a rush of goose bumps spreads across my skin.

I lean down to press my lips to his.

Ah, they are warm and firm and fit perfectly against my own. He allows me to explore his mouth without rushing, lazily exploring mine in return. His hands come up, and the warm, callused feel of them sliding along my skin causes me to shiver with pleasure.

He cups my head, pulls me closer, and opens his mouth as my tongue licks his lower lip. I feel the heat of him through his breeches, the urgency of it causing my hips to rock slightly against his.

He runs his hands down my neck, cupping my shoulder, exploring it with his palm before moving down to my back. I shiver again and he pulls away slightly. "You are cold."

I shrug. "It is a cold night," I whisper against his lips.

His hands grip me tighter, tucking my body close to his. With a dizzying roll, he switches our positions so that I am beneath him, cushioned by the soft wolf skin, still warm from the heat of his body.

And even though he is on top of me, he makes it clear that I am in control. He waits for my hips to move against his, for my arms to pull him back down. With that final permission given, it is as if a dam has burst and his mouth is softly probing mine, his hands exploring, his rough palm pressing against the soft skin of my stomach, moving up, up, up until it brushes the underside of my breast.

I arch into him, silently begging him to continue.

He complies, moving his hand so that it brushes over my nipple once, twice, then finally his palm closes over my breast, encasing it in the heat of his hand.

My own hands have found their way to his chest. Frustrated by the rough woolen tunic that lies between us, I shove my hands beneath it and run them up the hard planes of his stomach. Sweet saints! The ridged muscle is like a washing board, his nipples flat and — his breath hitches — sensitive. I smile against his mouth. As urgent as both our movements are, there is no rushing, only hunger, a hunger to feel this and explore that. When at last he dips his hand inside my breeches and eases them down my hips, I nearly shout with joy.

This, I think, with my last coherent thought. *This is what I want.* My arms come up around his shoulders and my legs wrap around his waist, pulling him closer and closer until we are nearly one, and a rhythm as ancient and sacred as that of the mummer's dance captures us both.

CHAPTER 61

Sybella

he next morning, Father Effram gets word to me that Beast has something to report. When pressed, he does not know if it is good news or ill, but he has arranged for us to meet in the servants' chapel near midnight.

It has been days since I have seen Beast except across a crowded hall with fourscore of the French court and household attendants between us. Nearly twice as long since the night we last spoke together in private.

I did not think it would be this hard — to see him, but be unable to speak with him. In retrospect, we were all woefully naïve and underprepared for how hostile the regent would be to the queen and her interests. How foolish we were. How foolish was I! I know better than to believe in happy endings.

When I am only two corridors away from the chapel, I become aware of another heartbeat, drawing closer. At first I think it is Beast, but it is too light and rapid and not at all familiar. I search for a hiding place, my only choice a thick Flemish tapestry that decorates the wall. I slip behind it, praying the person is in such a hurry that they are not looking at the floor in hopes of discovering feet protruding from unexpected places.

The footsteps are light and graceful — a woman, then. But quiet also, as if she does not wish to be discovered any more than I do. Curious now, I place my finger on the edge of the tapestry and push it aside just enough to peer into the hallway.

She is walking away from me, but all my mornings spent studying the backs of the women's heads pay off. It is Katerine. Interesting. I let the tapestry fall back into place. She so thoroughly rebuffed my overture in the garden that she has fallen off my list of potential fellow initiates. Perhaps this midnight visit of hers could change that.

I wait a hand span of minutes before continuing down the hall. There are fewer torches here, and the flickering glow from the candles in the chapel beckons me inside, where a familiar heart beats.

Beast kneels near the front, head bowed. His is the only heartbeat in the room. The realization that we are truly alone brings to mind all manner of longings — most of which are twice as sinful if contemplated inside a church.

At the sound of my approach, he stands and turns to face me. "Sybella."

The chapel is empty, and small, and the gruff whisper feels loud and heavy in the stillness. Heavy with the weight of all the words we are not allowed to share while others are watching.

For one hopeful moment, I think he will draw me into an embrace, but he has too much discipline for that.

Beast nods his head toward the confessional. In the shadows of the chapel, his face looks careworn and tired. I want to take my hand and smooth the furrow from his brow. Instead, I follow him toward the stall. He opens the door and waits for me to enter. My heart gives a beat of joy when he does not enter the priest's half of the confessional but follows me into the penitent's side.

It is not meant for two people, especially when one of them is as large as Beast, but the closeness is most welcome. I can even pretend it is an embrace. "Is there word on the ambush?" I ask.

Beast gives a curt shake of his head. "None. But I have heard from Duval." The faint rumble in his voice tells me this will not be good news.

"And?" I prompt.

"Crunard has escaped."

I gape at him. "What? How?"

Beast shrugs, further straining our tight quarters. "He does not know. The old fox was simply not there one morning when the guard went to feed him."

"Which means he must have had inside help. Again." A thought that has long niggled in the deep recesses of my mind surfaces. "The timing is interesting, is it not, that Crunard tried to escape the day before Rohan arrived in Rennes? Could he have known he was coming and planned to hide until he arrived?"

"That is what Duval thinks." Beast's arm twitches, as if he longs to run it over his head, but there is not enough room.

"The question is, was Rohan committed to helping Crunard find his son, or was there some other factor at play?"

Beast shakes his head. "Both have lost sons. Perhaps he feels for the man."

We are quiet as we try to sort out what hidden game is being played. "Have you any word on Anton?" I ask.

"None." He smiles grimly. "I did not claim to bear good news. However, the general who was on the field the day he was taken by the French has been recalled from Flanders to attend upon the king. Perhaps he will know something."

"You would ask him outright?"

"If we have no more answers than we do now, I will have to. Has the queen given any more thought to simply asking the king?"

I bark out a laugh and tell him of the disaster when she asked about Rohan's appointment. "And she has not seen him since. So not only is she uncertain of his answer, but she must worry that another question will drive him even further away."

Beast swears, then falls silent again. The small compartment grows thick with our joint frustration. *Now,* I think. *Now that he is contained in a small space and cannot go anywhere.*

"Beast," I murmur, wrapping my arms around him and pressing my cheek against the soft wool of his doublet. "Did Captain Dunois talk with you about . . . about someone you might run into here at the French court?"

Beast pulls away — or tries to, but there simply isn't room. "No."

Sweet Jesu. I press my cheek more firmly against Beast's chest, fair burrowing into him so that he has no choice but to put his arms around me.

"Why? What did he say?" His voice is thick and rough with his grief over Dunois's loss.

"He wanted you to know that your father" — Beast's entire body grows rigid —"is still a part of the king's inner circle. He wanted you to know that you might one day run into him."

"I have no father." Beast's voice is like two rocks rubbing together.

"Captain Dunois was not talking about Lord Waroch, but the man who sired you." My voice is as gentle as I know how to make it, but a thick wall begins to grow between us. "He meant to tell you himself," I rush to explain. "But you were out looking for Pierre, and once you returned, it was time to leave for France. He simply ran out of time. But he didn't want you to run into the man at court and be caught unaware."

"How could he have been so certain?" Beast's voice is achingly hollow. "My mother claimed she did not even know his name."

Such an easy lie to tell a child. "Dunois said the man was not shy about speaking of the ravages of war he had visited upon the lady of the manor. And that there were physical similarities that might stand out."

Beast stares at the confessional wall. "He cannot be uglier than me."

"Dunois did not say that he was. Only that you were of the same height and build, and that some of your features were similar."

A low growl erupts from Beast. He tries to pull away, but our small quarters give him no room. The ugliness of what he is feeling seeps into the air around us. I can sense his withdrawing from me, like an animal wishing to be alone to tend his wounds, but I grab him and hold fast.

I open my mouth, but before I can speak, he brings his hand up between us, angling it toward the votives that light the confessional. "Do you see this scar?" He indicates the large, shiny red patch on the back of his wrist. "I gave it to myself the day my mother marched me to the paddock and forced me to watch a stallion covering a mare in heat. 'That,' she whispered with her sour breath, 'is what your father did to me.'"

I want to place my hand over his mouth, to halt the words that I know are causing him pain, but I do not. "Your mother was a vile woman."

"She was gravely wounded — and it festered. That was the day I vowed to cut all traces of my father from me, like mold from a cheese."

Unable to help myself, I run my finger along the shiny red patch. It looks like a burn.

"It turns out one's lineage is harder to remove than a cheese rind. My sister found me and stayed my hand."

I close my eyes and say a silent prayer of thanks to Alyse. Just one of many I owe her. I take Beast's face between my hands and force him to meet my eyes. "Dunois told me all this so that I would be ready should you try to distance yourself from me. I will not let that happen." His be-damned honor is so great, it would be just like him to do such a thing from some misbegotten sense of nobility or desire to protect me. "If you even try something so dumb-witted, I will have to stab you to prove that however monstrous you think your past might be, mine is every bit as much so."

Tension radiates for a moment longer, then, like a thunderhead blown away by the wind, recedes. As he places his forehead on mine, a realization hits me with all the force of one of Arduinna's arrows. It takes far more courage to love than it does to hate. And even more courage than that to have faith in that love. "If you are allowed to love a monster," I whisper, "then so am I."

※

On my way back to my room, I come face-to-face with the king himself. I do not know who is more surprised. I'd thought the heartbeat I sensed was Katerine's again, but I was wrong. "Your Majesty." I fall into a deep curtsy.

"My Lady . . . ?" His face is relaxed, pleasant even, and his manner friendly.

"Sybella, Your Majesty. I am Lady Sybella."

"Ah, and what are you doing roaming the halls at so odd an hour?" He sounds more curious than suspicious.

"I fear I am a restless sleeper, made worse when cooped up too long. I walk the halls late at night to avoid driving my fellow ladies in waiting to distraction."

The smile he gives me is bland, but his eyes speculative. "We have been poor hosts indeed if we are forcing ladies to wander the halls looking for sport." I cannot tell if he is flirting or even aware of all the possible meanings his words have, but if so, it does not show on his face.

"I bid you pleasant walking, Lady Sybella." And with that, he bows and moves past me, leaving the faint scent of lilacs and musk trailing in his wake.

CHAPTER 62

Genevieve

 sleep so deeply that when I open my eyes the next morning, I am disoriented. A moment later I jolt fully awake when the memory of the previous night falls on me like a hammer.

Lust was not a part of my plan. It is a decidedly bad idea. Even worse, this morning I feel as if a thin, complex web now connects the two of us more firmly than before. As if what we shared *mattered*.

My heart skitters in my chest. It cannot matter. I do not want to be connected to him any more than a farmer wishes to be connected to the sheep he is leading to market. Unwilling to face him until I have my wits and armor firmly in place, I glance over to see if he is still asleep.

His space is empty and panic spurts through me. Was it all a ruse? A way to lull me into lowering my guard? With frantic hands I reach for the pack that holds the antidote, relief pouring through me as my hand closes around the vial. He won't have gone far. Not without the antidote.

Around me, the hall is still littered with sleeping bodies. A few industrious souls wander among them, nudging them awake. Ignoring the others, I rise and begin to dress. Just as I am pulling on my boots, a tall figure slips in from outside, moving purposefully toward my corner.

It is not until the man is a dozen paces away that I realize it is Maraud, and his beard is gone. When he sees me, he gives a rueful grin and reaches up to stroke his newly shaved cheek. "It itched."

His hair, too, is wet. He must have risen early and found a bath house or barber. When I realize I am staring, I give an uninterested shrug. "That is too bad. It worked so well with your costume."

"The wolf's head covers most of my face, and what is not covered is cast in shadow."

It does not matter that he is right. The bearded Maraud was rough and unkempt, a convenient reminder that he was — *is* — a prisoner. This beardless Maraud looks leaner, sharper, the fierce intelligence on his face even more plain. His rich brown eyes are even more commanding without the dark beard to distract from them.

The man has never been easy to ignore — not from the moment I first felt his heart beating in the dungeon — and this . . . this will not help matters. Surely the gods are testing me. Or punishing me. Or simply finding amusement at my expense.

I grit my teeth and reach for the vial of antidote. "Before you wander off again," I say too sharply. "Let's not forget this."

His expression never changes, except perhaps for the left corner of his mouth, which twitches faintly, in amusement or disappointment, I cannot say. Surely if there were any connection between us, I would be able to tell such a thing.

We are a quiet group when we set out for the city of Angoulême. For one thing, the dark clouds have returned, and the day's journey will be longer. But mostly, everyone has had too little sleep and too much wine.

Everyone except the children, both those who belong to the mummers and those from Jarnac who are tagging along for the first portion of our day's travel. They leap and frolic and chase one another. It would be amusing if they were not so very loud and energetic.

Maraud handles the children good-naturedly. He is just approachable enough that they are able to work up the courage to try to tweak his wolf tail, but not so friendly as to rob them of the thrill of terror they derive from doing so.

This good humor of his is nearly as annoying as his pretty face, and it makes me want to stab something. Mayhap during our next performance I will be less careful with my sword. That thought makes me smile.

My hope that he is as eager to put last night behind us is soon quashed. When he looks at me, there is an unnerving warm light in his eyes. Twice he tries to break the silence between us, but I successfully rebuff both attempts.

I need time to reason with myself, to wrestle my mind back under control. My body has been too long deprived of such pleasure and is simply being greedy, that is all. Not to mention that Maraud himself has not been with a woman in, what — a year? Surely a goodly portion of his skill was simply due to pent-up demand.

Any thread that connects us is merely having lived through a shared escape. We are joint survivors of narrowly averted disaster. The intensity of my feelings is nothing more than still being slightly drunk with my newfound freedom. Surely that is all there was to our coupling. To think it was anything other than that is to make the same mistake all the noblewomen at court make — to think that it *matters* only leads to broken hearts, tears, and unwanted babes.

With my thoughts untangled, I breathe deeply and look around, taking in the utter emptiness of the countryside. There are no buildings, no nobles, no one watching. There are no demands to pretend I am something I'm not. Just gently rolling green hills, a wide open gray sky, and an empty road. Yes, I am awash in an intensity of feelings, but very few, if any, have to do with Maraud.

That is when he decides to break my hard-won silence. "Don't worry." He speaks quietly. "It will not happen again unless you wish it to."

I stare at him in horror, but his face is resolutely on the road before him. My need to shout that I do not have maidenly qualms is tempered only by the knowledge it would simply make things worse. Every other time I have taken a lover, we have both moved on immediately. That was no accident. But now I am stuck with Maraud for several more days. Several more nights with an attentive, skilled lover rather than a rutting bore, lying just within arm's reach. There is only one way to end this.

When I reply, my face is utterly blank. "What?" I ask. "What will not happen again?"

There is a brief flash of disbelief on his face — incredulity that for a second time I am denying something we both know to be true. His jaw tightens, and he turns his face to the road.

Remorse crashes through me like a wave, but I harden my heart against it. His feelings, my feelings, are not what are important. The convent, the younger girls, the older nuns — they are what is important. That is why we are riding side by side. He is a weapon in my arsenal, a bargaining piece. Nothing more.

Shortly after noon, thunder rumbles through the air. I look up into the thick gray clouds overhead, but they do not have the appearance of storm clouds. And there is no rain.

It is Maraud who understands what is happening first. "Riders," he shouts. "Get off the road."

There is a moment of inaction as everyone tries to make sense of what he is saying, then we all begin scrambling to make way for the company of mounted knights barreling in our direction.

They are visible now, a standard bearer riding in front, the blue and gold banner he carries streaming behind him. At least fourscore mounted knights follow.

"They're not slowing down," Herbin says uneasily as he tries to steer the oxen to the side of the road.

"They won't." Maraud grabs the head of the closest ox to shove him along. "They have the right of way and these knights in particular will take their due and more."

The two women next to me both carry sleeping children. While I rack my brain to remember which house bears the blue and gold standard, I reach out and steady their elbows so they can cross the deep ruts and reach the safety of the side of the road.

Two of the children eager to see the horses slip from their mothers' sides and edge back toward the road. I let go of the women, grab the children by the hands, and haul them back to safety. The riders are coming fast now, recklessly fast. The road is full of deep ruts that could easily trip one of their mounts and cause it to break a leg.

But they do not slow or check their speed. The churning hooves turn up small clods of dried mud, sounding like a smattering of hail along with the thunder of their stride.

Just as they are nearly upon us, one of the straggling children clambers over the berm back into the road. Perhaps he thinks it is a game. Or he wants to see the knights more clearly. Perhaps he thinks he is quicker than the oncoming horses or that he is small enough to dart between their legs. Who knows what thoughts children have in such moments? But now he is on the road with four-score mounted knights bearing down on him and none of them — not one — is breaking stride or slowing in the slightest. The sight of them strikes all reason from the child's head, and he freezes with terror. And still they do not slow. They will simply run him down.

"Stay here!" I thrust the children next to me farther from the road. Before I can run out to snag the boy, Maraud launches himself from the ox cart like an arrow from a bow. His long arms reach out and snatch up the child, curling his body around the boy as the momentum from his leap carries them both to the far side of the road. There is a loud thud and then the riders are upon us.

Unable to do anything but watch the streaming knights and flailing hooves, I grab the children's hands again and hold them tight. My heart beats so hard I fear it will break one of my ribs. Is it Maraud's and the child's heartbeats I feel? Or simply my own? The thunder of the passing horses reverberates so heavily from the earth through my legs to my chest that it is impossible to tell.

I glare in impotent fury at the riders. Their visors are down, their spurs lowered, their horses covered in sweat. The knights' armor is dark, their faces hard and cruel-lipped. That these men can ride down others with no consequence to themselves causes my stomach to twist into a seething knot.

When at last they have passed, there is a muffled sob as one of the women dashes across the road to Maraud and the child.

With the sound of hooves still ringing in our ears, a small voice calls out. "Get off! You're squishing me!"

A near hysterical laugh escapes me, and I squeeze the two boys' hands before letting them go check on their friend. I am halfway across the road before I realize I have even moved. The child wriggles out from under Maraud, bouncing up like a spring rabbit and running to his mother, complaining that the wolf threw him down on the dirt.

Jacquette grabs him tightly to her bosom, then clouts his head and tells him to be grateful because that big wolf just saved his scrawny life.

When I reach Maraud, he is still lying on the ground, staring up at the sky. His face is deathly pale. No, no, no. I will *not* go through this again.

I drop to my knees as my frantic fingers begin gently probing his body for signs of injury. "Are you all right? Can you speak?"

He turns to look at me, the expression on his face both distant and disturbing. "You care," he says, almost offhandedly.

"What hurts?"

He answers with a hollow voice. "It is just a bruised rib."

I nearly reach out and clout his head in relief, like Jacquette. "Then why do you look like Death?"

He blinks, turning to stare back up at the clouds. "Because those knights are of the house d'Albret, and riding at their helm was Pierre d'Albret. Every one of those men knows exactly who I am."

CHAPTER 63

he city of Angoulême comes into sight just as dusk is beginning to fall. As we approach the gates, Maraud puts a hand on my arm, drawing me back to the edge of our group.

I glance at his hand, and he quickly removes it. "So now that we are here, I need to know what our plan is. We are entering not only your enemy's territory but, with d'Albret's arrival, mine as well."

I want to ask why they are enemies, but instead say, "Will d'Albret and his men spend the night in the city?"

He glances up at the darkening sky. "Most likely. It is a convenient stop on the way to his holding in Périgord." He is silent a long moment. "Why are *we* spending the night in Angoulême? I thought you were escaping. It makes no sense to run to one of the count's strongholds."

"Is there another way to reach the route north?"

His eyes scan the poplar trees that line the road like upright soldiers. "Where north?"

"Poitiers. And we will need horses to get there." Poitiers is only a stop on the way to Plessis-lès-Tours, but I do not want to share our destination with him. He has traveled these roads far more than I have, and I do not wish to give him so much information that he thinks he can begin plotting against me.

He tilts his head, thinking. "There are not any horse markets in Angoulême this time of year."

"We do not need to buy them. They are already mine."

His eyes narrow as he begins to sense where this is leading. "Where are these horses of yours stabled?"

It is hard not to squirm under that gaze. Obtaining horses has always been one of my greatest challenges. "At the count's stables in Angoulême."

Maraud stops walking and gapes at me. "Are you mad? Surely that is too dang—"

"Is it any less dangerous than stealing a horse? When the punishment for such is death?" It is hard to explain why I do not want to return to the convent —or face those who used to run the convent—empty-handed. To have lost Margot, to have achieved nothing in five years, and to have abandoned the few tools they gave me feels like too great a defeat.

"But the count—"

"Is not in residence. I told you, he is spending Christmas with the Duke of Orléans and will not be home until after Epiphany. No one at his castle in Angoulême knows me."

"So how do you plan to collect these horses of yours?"

"It is simple. In exchange for their entertainment, the mummers are given hospitality in the castle's lower halls or stables. Tonight we'll make our way with the other mummers to the castle, settle ourselves into the stable, and wait. The best time for us to leave the city will be during the performance. All eyes will be on that. If anyone does see us, we can claim to be latecomers or part of a surprise ending act."

Maraud considers this. "Will the count's stable master not think you are stealing his horses?"

I send him a scathing look. "No. They bear the convent's brand, proving they are not his."

"Yes, but will that be enough for him to let you take them?"

"I do not intend to ask permission," I mutter.

"This isn't Brittany." Maraud's voice is gentle. "Not everyone even knows of the Nine or Mortain, other than as something from stories long ago. I think we should find horses another way."

"How? Do you have a bag of gold on you that you have not told me about?"

He shrugs. "I have a few coins from our performances."

"As have I, but not enough to buy decent horses."

His face brightens. "I could find a dicing game. I'm good with dice."

"Good enough to turn a handful of coppers into the funds needed to buy two healthy palfreys or rouncies?"

"Given a day or two, yes."

"We don't have a day or two. We have tonight and tomorrow, then we must leave. Besides, do d'Albret's men not frequent taverns and gaming houses?"

Maraud's face falls. "Yes. And their games of dice often turn to much worse."

"As you said earlier, there are no fairs with horses for sale or marketplaces for such." I gesture at the city around me. "Where do you propose we buy them?"

He rubs his hands over his face. "So we steal them."

"If we are caught in the act, we will hang," I remind him.

"So we do not let ourselves get caught."

I shoot him a look. "I am not a thief."

"But you are an assassin," he points out.

"That is entirely different." While I *have* been light-fingered in the past, I have always taken from those who had plenty — or who helped themselves to things that didn't belong to them. "Stealing a horse from someone like Herbin or Jacques could easily threaten their livelihood. The only one who can afford the loss of two horses is the count. And since I already have two in his stables, there is no need to steal from him.

"Truly, my plan is as sturdy as a three-legged stool," I tell him. "No one at the palace knows or has ever seen you. I have only been there for one brief night over a year ago, dressed in finery at the countess's side. No one will know us. There is no disadvantage to stealing from the palace, except that it is not stealing."

"Except for the palace guards. And d'Albret."

"But d'Albret will never see you! We won't be performing. Even if we were, you'd have your mask on the entire time."

Recognizing the superiority of my plan, he sighs and changes the subject. "How will we get out of the city gate?"

"I was planning on using the sally port in the east wall."

"Isn't it guarded?"

I shrug. "By only two men, not an entire gatehouse full."

The first leg of my plan crumbles just as we enter the city. The guards greet us cheerfully as Rollo has already plied them with japes and jests. He himself waits for us just inside the gates, motioning us to gather around. "There has been a change in plans." Maraud shoots me a dark look. "We will not be staying at the palace." As my heart plummets to my stomach, Rollo reassures us. "They have given us the guild hall. It is much nicer than the one in Jarnac."

I should keep quiet, but staying in the stables is such a core part of my plan that I cannot. "But why?"

Rollo shrugs. "The knights that nearly ran us down have called upon the castle's hospitality, and they have granted it."

"Clearly," Maraud says grimly as Rollo walks away, "they know better than to refuse."

CHAPTER 64

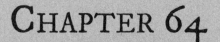

Sybella

hree days after my midnight run-in with the king, the queen and her attendants received an invitation to go hawking with him.

The queen's hand shook with relief as she wondered how on earth she was to breach the wall that had sprung up between them.

Dressed in scarlet and gold and green, our gay party mills eagerly in the courtyard. The horses stamp their feet, impatient to be on their way, their breath visible in the early morning air. I search among the crowd for the regent, but unless she has altered her appearance significantly, I do not see her. Not even when the horn is blown and we all mount up.

As I settle myself in my saddle, Beast approaches. "My lady, I do not think your girth strap is tight enough."

"If you would be so kind as to tighten it, sir, I would be most appreciative."

He comes closer and takes the leather strap in his hands. "What are you looking for?" he asks under his breath.

"The regent," I mutter. "It makes me uneasy when I can't see her."

My saddle now secure enough to satisfy him, he flashes me a grin. "She isn't coming. I heard the king tell the grooms when they were readying the horses."

"Well, that is most welcome news. Although now I find myself wondering why." *What trap is she setting for us back at the palace? What new humiliation is she plotting for the queen? And other innocents. I have not been able to get the image of her sitting with my sisters out of my head.*

While the others may be hunting for pheasant, I will be hunting for a mole. Three possibilities remain, two of whom are on today's hunt. Symone has caught my eye due to the jewelry she wears. Her heavy gold cuff reminds me very much of my own garrote bracelet. Furthermore, she sports two rings, one on each hand, with stones large enough to conceal a hidden compartment. While nearly all of the ladies have fine jewelry, none wear any similar to this.

But she seldom leaves the others' sides, and today may present a chance to speak with her alone.

The other attendant I have my hopes set on is Perrette. She is more athletic than the others and appears indifferent to the queen, which would be a good way to keep her true intentions hidden. She is also, I note as we ride, an excellent horsewoman.

The huntsman leads us through the woods surrounding the castle, and I give myself over to the pleasure of being out of doors with a hawk on my arm. It has been over a year since I have gone hawking, and along with hunting, it has always been my favorite sport.

When we reach the designated spot, the beaters move forward into the bush, thrashing their sticks and making noise. It does not take long. There is a deafening flapping of wings as a bevy of pheasant take flight. I release my hawk, admiring her as she soars into the air. She picks a target, and plummets back to the ground, intent on her prey.

But another hawk gets there first, Perrette's. My falcon screeches in protest, but Perrette's hawk hunkers over the pheasant, spreading its wings wide to defend its catch.

I whistle, but the frustrated hawk ignores me and climbs back into the sky. She circles once, twice, then a third time before something catches her notice and she plummets toward the ground again. *Merde.* Has Father Effram trained this bird? Keeping my eye on the spot where she disappeared into the trees, I steer my horse in that direction.

As my mount picks his way through the underbrush toward the stream, I spy my hawk on the bank, squatting over her prey and hissing at something.

Except, her prey is not a pheasant flushed from the underbrush, but a deer with its stomach lying open. Gored by a boar, perhaps. The overwhelming scent of it must have attracted my hawk. But when I am closer, I see it is no ragged gouge, but a clean slice to the creature's belly.

A man did this. And not a poacher. If a poacher had been stupid enough to enter the king's forest, he would not leave his prize behind. A chill breeze scuttles along my neck. I reach for the small crossbow concealed by my skirts.

That is when I feel a heartbeat somewhere behind me. I whistle once more to the hawk, but it is feasting and ignores me. Using my knees to guide the horse, I slowly turn it toward the direction of the heartbeat.

I cannot see anyone through the thick trees, but I can feel them, and the beating of their heart is growing louder as they draw near. Something deep inside me screams *Trap!* even as my mind insists I have interrupted a sloppy poacher before he could remove himself and his prey.

"I know you are there." My voice is calm, conversational even, as if I am coaxing a lover who is playing hide-and-seek.

"Do you, now?" The voice that rumbles back is deep and carries a faint note of challenge.

"I do. And since I have found you out, I think it only fair you show yourself. Is that not how these games work?"

"Indeed, it is, my lady." He steps out from behind a tree, and my worst suspicions solidify. He is dressed in good-quality riding leathers, a boiled leather tabard, and a fine cloak. His chain mail is black, as are his thick leather gauntlets. His woolen cloak is pulled low, shadowing his face. No peasant, then. While he bears no visible weapon except the long knife at his waist, he comes bearing the scent and feel of death. I tighten my grip on the concealed crossbow, slowly bring it up, and aim it directly at him.

"Is that, too, part of this game, my lady?"

"I know not. You are the one who has set the game in motion."

He is not marqued, of course. It is only long years of habit that has me checking.

That is not true. I check because I am an eternal fool, hoping against hope that Mortain will still be able to reveal his will to me.

"It is not some game, my lady, merely a man beset by misfortune. My horse went lame, and I have become lost looking for the king's palace at Plessis. Can you point me the way?"

"Is that why you gutted the deer? You were trying to divine the way to the king's palace with its entrails?"

"A man grows hungry, my lady."

"And yet I smell no cook fire."

"I was out gathering wood when you arrived."

"And yet your hands are empty." I keep my voice light and teasing, but my hawk, having filled herself on the deer, has turned her attention to the tense undercurrent between the man and me. She shifts on her feet and spreads open her wings, letting out a screech. I tilt my head and smile. "My hawk does not like you."

I should kill him. I should do it now and be done with it.

But some small part of me wishes to be absolutely certain before I release my bolt. Besides, a bolt will scream murder, and possibly lead to too many questions. There is a subtler way to achieve the same end. Keeping my eye and my aim firmly on the stranger, I slowly dismount so that I am standing on the ground, facing him. I give a sharp whistle, and the hawk launches herself to land neatly on my arm.

The man tilts his head, a faint smile playing about his lips. "How will my lady shoot her bow with only one hand?"

I smile. "It is a small crossbow, especially designed so that the trigger requires only a finger to release it. Besides, I do not think I shall waste a bolt on you."

This causes his eyebrows to raise in faint surprise.

Now!

I launch the hawk at him. He doesn't shout or raise his hands to protect his face like any normal man would, but reaches for his knife. *Merde.* I have no choice but to use the crossbow.

I squeeze the trigger, releasing the bolt. It pierces the man's woolen cloak and embeds itself in the hollow above his breastbone. Even as his hands scrabble at his throat, I close the distance between us and slip around behind him. Fortunately, he is not tall. I grab his head in both my hands, then wrench it to the left, breaking his neck.

I prefer a knife. It is cleaner and faster. But this way when they find his corpse they can assume he fell from his horse.

His soul bursts free of his body, shocked and angry. It rushes for me, as if it still has the power to harm. Instead, it swirls impotently around my head, filling me with his final thoughts. I force myself to remain open to them. A bag of coin. A voice giving my description. The order for my death.

My actions vindicated, I shove the body to the ground. An assassin. And I was his target.

Working quickly, I search him for any indication of who has sent him, but there is nothing — no messages, no seals, not even so much as one of the coins he was paid. Next, I hunt through the bracken for a stout twig, pull the bolt from his neck, and jam the twig into the remaining hole. Not only has the poor man broken his neck in a fall, but he has had the misfortune to land on a sharp stick.

Grunting with the effort, I drag him toward the bank. With the recent rains, it has swollen to nearly the size of a small river. I give him a final shove and he disappears for a moment before bobbing back up as he is swiftly carried down current. By the time he has reached the bend in the stream, his clothes are heavy with water and have begun to pull his body below the surface.

If the gods do not like it, they can take it up with those who keep attacking me. It is the best I can do for now. Besides, if I do not hurry, the others will come looking for me.

Beast is waiting just behind the queen, scanning the trees. When he sees me, the tension in his face eases, and I smile to reassure him that everything is fine. For it is. The threat has been identified and addressed. The shaking and sickness I feel in my stomach is merely the dregs of the surprise of it. While I have killed often enough, it is rare that I find myself a target.

I have taken so long that everyone is flush with pheasant, and it is time to head back. The heavy weight of Beast's regard is on me for the entire return trip. I can feel the sheer effort of will it takes for him not to pull me aside and demand to know what has happened.

We are met in the courtyard by squires, stable hands, and falconer's attendants who are eager take the reins or retrieve their beloved falcons. Beast shoulders aside the squire trying to assist me and helps me dismount himself. "What happened?"

"It is handled," I utter under my breath. "Meet me later tonight, and I will tell you what transpired."

Displeasure radiates from him like heat from a smoldering fire, but there is naught he can do about it with others watching. "Midnight," I promise him.

When I emerge from the stables, the regent and her party are just riding into the courtyard. Two of her attendants are with her, as well as six of the royal guard. I slow my steps, giving the groom time to help her so she is off her horse by the time I approach her.

"Madame Regent, we missed you on our hunt today."

At the sound of my voice, her shoulders flinch, and she slowly turns around to face me. "Lady Sybella. I am sorry I couldn't make it. Was there good hunting?" Do her eyes shift ever so slightly, or is that merely the scudding clouds reflected in them?

"It was fine hunting," I say. "And you?"

She gives a fluid shrug that says both everything and nothing. "I wasn't hunting, I was paying a visit." She begins removing her riding gloves. "Since I can feel your curiosity from here, I will put you out of your misery. I was visiting the Princess Marguerite."

While I am pleased to have an answer, I am also perplexed that she would share it with me. "And how was she?"

"Very well. And how have your charming sisters entertained themselves with you out hunting all day?"

Her question is as effective as holding a knife under my throat. "By tending to their sewing and their lessons, Madame. I will tell them you were kind enough to inquire after them."

"Yes, please do." She sends me a smile that is as lovely as it is false, and I am left wondering why she was willing to tell me where she had been.

CHAPTER 65

Genevieve

he second leg of my plan crumbles shortly before the mummers are scheduled to perform, right after we reach the palace courtyard. As we mill about waiting to enter, Maraud and I drift toward the edge of our group. When we are on the very outskirts of the mummer troupe, we pause. To the right sits the smithy, the fletcher's hut, and the kennels. The stables are on the left. "Best we approach them indirectly," I tell Maraud under my breath. "Once the courtyard is clear, we can make our way to the stables. And avoid the kennels lest we set the dogs to barking."

He nods in agreement. We check one last time to see if anyone is watching, but the mummers are all making last-minute adjustments to their costumes and whispering among themselves. I give the signal, and we take a step away from the crowd.

No one so much as blinks.

We take another cautious step, then another. No voices raised in surprise, no one urging us to come back. Everyone is thoroughly involved in their own preparations and merriment.

I nod again, and this time we walk with purpose, heading in the direction of the smithy. Just as we reach it, an enormous man with a black beard down to his belly comes around the corner, fastening his trousers, nearly running into us.

We stop and stare at each other. It is the smith, I realize, taking in his bulging arms and leather jerkin.

He is the first to recover. Scowling, he lifts one beefy hand and points. "The palace is that way."

There is nothing for it but to try to step into the hole he has created. "Oh, we know, monsieur," I say breathlessly. "But our chain!" I grab for Maraud's chain and hold it up for the blacksmith before quickly dropping it again. "Two of the links are coming loose, and we wondered if, tomorrow before we leave, you could fix it for us?"

He stares at me from beneath his bushy brows, the tip of his nose suspiciously red. He smiles. "Be glad to. Good luck to help a mummer!" He claps one large hand on each of our shoulders and begins walking us back to the palace. "And who are you dressed as, demoiselle?"

"Brigantia and the wolves of war," I tell him.

His face breaks into a huge grin. "I never liked that story as a boy. Always wanted the wolf to win. But tonight? Tonight I'll be rooting for you." He winks and chucks me under the chin. "Here we are now, and here's the rest of your troupe. I'll keep an eye out for you."

I smile and cheerfully wave goodbye as my insides wilt. Beside me, Maraud shifts, but before he can speak, Rollo appears. It is time to begin. I sigh. "We will have to separate from the others once we are inside," I tell Maraud. "And find our way back out later."

"Won't your smith friend miss you?"

"With luck he'll be too drunk to notice." And if not, well, hopefully we'll be long gone by then.

⁂

The castle at Angoulême is far different than the chateau at Cognac. It is of an earlier time, a true fortress designed and erected for defense purposes. As such, its rooms and furnishings are more imposing, the ceilings higher, the walls thicker, the windows smaller. That is not to say it is not furnished with richness and grandeur, only that the effect is that of a harsh mistress rather than a comforting one.

It is also full of people. There are bodies everywhere — lining the hallway, pressed three deep in every entryway and vestibule. "How are we to sneak away with so many watching?" Maraud mumbles in my ear.

"Hush! I'm thinking." Although fighting off panic is more accurate. There is simply no place where there are not at least a half dozen pairs of eyes on us. With Count Angoulême absent, the entire town has gathered to watch the performance. "I don't think we have any choice but to perform," I finally whisper to Maraud. "There are too many people. Even so, no one will know we are not simply two more mummers."

From behind the slits in his wolf mask, his eyes glint with skepticism.

"There is no one who would recognize us," I insist as the music begins. Rollo claps and the line of mummers, with Maraud and me trapped among them, move toward the salon. I wipe my palms on my tunic at least twice. Performing in the grand salon will be no different than performing in Jarnac, I assure myself.

However, it is in the grand salon that the third leg of my plan crumbles so completely that the entire thing collapses. The enormous room is not the problem. Nor are the hundreds of people filling it. The problem sits on the dais, watching the performance with bored, lazy eyes.

"I thought you said Count Angoulême was away!" Maraud hisses, his wolf whiskers tickling my ear.

"I did! He was!" But for some inexplicable reason, he is here in the city a full two weeks earlier than expected.

"Even better," Maraud's voice drips with sarcasm. "That is Pierre d'Albret on his right."

Of course it is. Why should my plan merely collapse when it could go up in flames instead?

D'Albret is thickly built with a face that would be handsome if not for the cruelty that lurks there. His eyes scan the room with barely concealed impatience, looking as if he would tear the wings off of everyone else's happiness simply to relieve his own boredom.

I am so unsettled by the magnitude of this disaster that I draw my dagger from its hilt and hold it in the same hand as Maraud's chain.

Then I secure the visor more firmly in place and shift the contours of my mind. I am not Genevieve from the convent, or one of Louise's attendants, but Gen, a girl raised in the upper room of a tavern who has spent her entire life among people such as these performers. A girl for whom the highlight of the entire year is a chance to frolic and perform in such a way.

Three brightly colored fools tumble by, our cue to enter the circle. I take a deep breath and step out into the hall, brandishing my sword in one hand and Maraud's chain in the other.

My body does not lose itself in the rhythm of the music. There is no feeling of moving in time with the gods or even my fellow mummers. There is simply need, raw and primitive, to stay hidden from those who seek me.

I do not look at the audience. I most especially do not look at Angoulême. I focus on Maraud. Our steps are as precise and well timed as one of the rare clocks that sits in the town square.

We have taken three turns around the room and have only one more left to go when we have our first misstep. One of the tumblers misses his footing as he executes his tumble, and his wrist connects with Maraud's ankle just as my sword arcs down for a blow. Off balance, Maraud flings out his arms to keep from tripping. In doing so, he knocks my sword from my hand.

A few in the crowd gasp, as if it is part of the act. Without missing a beat, I give my dagger a twisting spin — just like Maraud taught me — flipping it from my left hand to my right, and step in close to hold it at his throat.

The audience *oohs* in appreciation. Maraud grabs his neck, writhes as if in agony, then slumps forward and grows still. The music stops, the audience claps and hoots, and coins rain down upon us. Angoulême's presence is as heavy and suffocating as a shroud. Is it because he is watching me? I refuse to look and risk drawing his attention. Not when we are so close to being free.

When the applause has begun to die away, we finally begin to file out of the grand salon. "Hold," a deep voice calls out.

It is not Angoulême, but Pierre d'Albret. He sprawls in his chair, staring at me. "You there, with the long hair and helmet."

I point my finger at my chest.

"Yes, you."

I take a step forward, but say nothing, afraid Angoulême will recognize my voice.

D'Albret lifts his goblet, eyes shrewd and thoughtful. "Where did you learn that trick with the knife?" He takes a sip of his wine, then looks at the wolf at my side. "I have only known one man to use that before."

A deep note of alarm clangs inside me. Having have no choice but to speak, I pitch my voice slightly higher hoping to keep Angoulême from recognizing it. "I don't know, my lord. I have traveled with mummer troupes since I was a child and picked up many tricks in that time."

D'Albret's gaze turns languidly to Maraud. "And what of your wolf?"

"What of him, my lord?"

He plants his elbows on the table, his lips growing slack as he leers at me. "Is he one of the tricks you picked up?"

All the men at his table, and a number of the lower ones, laugh at his jibe. Next to me, the muscles in Maraud's neck grow taut in anger, but he keeps the rest of his body loose.

"La, my lord! He is much too heavy to pick up. I will leave him to haul his own sorry carcass around."

The men laugh again, this time at Maraud's expense. A page appears to refill d'Albret's goblet just then. With a wave of his hand, he dismisses us. As I turn toward the door, I allow my gaze to flit to Count Angoulême. He is deep in conversation with the woman on his left. Even so, it is not until we are free of the grand salon and filing into the lower hall that I allow myself to breathe.

"Rutting saints, that was close!" I shoot Maraud an accusing glance. "You did not tell me your knife trick was so easily recognized."

"No, but I did tell you that coming here was a bad idea. I just didn't realize how bad."

❧

There are a few pockets of soldiers in the stable yard, but most seem to be heading toward the castle or the garrison. I motion for Maraud to follow, and we step from the shadows, walking purposefully, but not so fast as to draw attention to ourselves.

When at last we reach the shelter of the stables, there are no torches and only a few lanterns — the muted light as welcome as a mother's arms.

My relief is short-lived, however, when I see just how many men are loitering in here. More men — travel-stained and loud — swagger into our path. Without a word, Maraud turns on his heel and disappears down a row of stalls so that I am left facing them alone.

Coward, I think to myself. I stride forward, keeping my steps confident and frowning as if I am in deep thought.

The ploy works. The men spare me but a passing glance. I wait until they are at the main door before slipping into the second-to-the-last row of stalls. There are no soldiers or stable hands here. When I reach the sixth stall, I stop, press myself against its door, and give a soft, low whistle. Two black ears swivel in my direction. She remembers!

"Hello, Gallopine," I croon softly.

The horse swings her head around and swishes her tail as I let myself in. She whickers softly, nostrils fluttering as she takes in my scent.

I step forward and give her a firm rub along her back. When she does not object, I move my hand up to her forehead, and her ears flop out to the side. "I've missed you." I let my words blow gently against her nostrils. She butts me gently with her head.

"I am sorry I have not been able to visit, but you and I are going on a trip now." I give her a final pat, then go to the wall and lift her harness from the hook.

Wondering what is taking Maraud so long, I loop the harness over her head and fit the bit into her mouth. I do not want to waste time searching for him, but it is a large stable and he didn't see which row I turned into. With a grunt, I lift the saddle off its stand and turn to place it on Gallopine's back, nearly dropping it when I see Count Angoulême himself, standing in the doorway, two men at arms at his back.

Chapter 66

enevieve." The count's voice is deep with authority and laced with annoyance, his face unreadable in the faint light.

Rutting goats! "I thought you were spending Christmas up north," I say.

"I was, but was worried about you and Louise and changed my mind." Of all the times for Angoulême to be struck by consideration for others.

I force a laugh as I carry the saddle over to Gallopine. "Is that why you need reinforcements?" Uneasy at the sudden tension in the room, Gallopine stomps her foot and raises her tail as I settle the saddle onto her back.

"When I saw you with the mummer troupe, I was uncertain you were with them by choice."

I toss him a scornful glance. "You believe a handful of mummers could force me to perform against my will?" I shake my head. "Have no worries. I chose to travel with them." *None of the choices you offered me held any appeal,* I almost tell him, then stop as another idea takes root. "Actually, I was coming to find you."

"What?"

"Louise and the babe are not well. Louise did not want to bother you, and your men would not let me leave on my own. This was the only way I could think to fetch you."

There is a whisper of movement, a rasp of sound behind him, but I keep my eyes on his face. He takes a step into the stall, stopping when Gallopine lifts her rear leg. "What is wrong with the babe? Has a doctor been sent for?" His eyes narrow with suspicion. "And why didn't you wait in the hall to give me this news?"

"I did not say it was the only reason I am here."

There is a second movement, this one loud enough that Angoulême turns around, reaching for the weapon at his hip.

But too late. An arm crashes down, bringing the hilt of a sword to connect solidly with the back of Angoulême's skull.

The count's eyes roll up in his head, and he crumples into the straw. Behind him, his two companions are similarly laid out on the ground. I glance up at Maraud. "I thought you were hiding."

"I was. That last group we passed were men I'd fought with before. Didn't want them to see my face." He reaches down and relieves one of the soldiers of his belt and sword and fastens them around his hips. Then he kneels down to retrieve a second sword from the other unconscious guard.

"Two?"

"I've been without weapons for a year. I will not pass up any I find lying around."

I shake my head and turn back to Angoulême's crumpled figure. I feel nothing. No, that is not true. I feel relief. "Is he dead?"

"Saints, no!" Maraud sounds insulted. "He is just out for a while. Although, depending on the thickness of his skull, it might not be for very long."

"Then let's quit talking." I nimbly step over the fallen bodies and lead Maraud to the next stall. "This is your horse — Mogge."

At the sound of my voice, Mogge's head swings around. I put out my hand, her velvet nose taking in my scent. She keeps snuffling, her muzzle swinging to my left, looking for someone else.

Understanding comes like a blow. Looking for her mistress — for Margot. Just when I am certain my heart is fully protected, some new sliver of pain finds its way in.

Maraud reaches around me to let Mogge sniff at him. Interested in this new scent, Mogge steps closer and lets him whisper something in her ear as he rubs her forehead. The quickness with which she takes to him stings a little. "Her tack is on the wall. Get her saddled so we can leave before Angoulême wakes up."

Back in Gallopine's stall, I retrieve my pack and fish out one of the small silver boxes I carry. Just a tiny bit to ensure the count sleeps until we are well away. I take a pinch between my fingers, lean close to his face, and blow. I hold my own breath and quickly step away, moving on to his two fallen guards to do the same. Just as I am putting the lid back onto the silver box, Maraud emerges from the stall, leading Mogge. He glances from my hands down to the soldiers. "You poisoned them?"

"Only a little. Just to ensure they cannot raise an alarm until we are well clear of the city."

He shoots me one of his piercing looks that are as effective as any arrow in exposing my weaknesses, then takes Mogge's reins and leads her toward the end of the row. I stuff the night whispers in my pack, take Gallopine's reins, and follow. Or try to. When I reach the end of the stalls, Mogge comes to a complete halt. Next to her, Maraud is still as stone.

Scowling in annoyance, I start to step around him, but am halted by a newly familiar voice. "Well, Anton Crunard. I was right. It was you who taught the mummer girl that trick."

Figs! We are having Salonius's own luck tonight.

"I have taught many girls many tricks, as have you." Maraud's voice is different — deeper, louder.

Pierre d'Albret laughs, growing more at ease. "That is one of the things I have always enjoyed about you, Crunard. I never know what will come out of your smart mouth."

He does not mean smart as a compliment.

I inch my way to the other side of Mogge, trying to peer around her into the main corridor. Pierre d'Albret's head is tilted at an arrogant angle, his hand resting on the hilt of his sword. His gaze flicks in my direction and runs the length of my body. It feels like a snake has just slithered down my spine. Four men-at-arms stand just behind him. "Why are you cavorting with mummers? Though it has been a while since I have seen you, I would never have guessed you'd fall that far."

"It's been since the battle of Saint-Aubin-du-Cormier, I believe. Although, come to think of it" — Maraud tilts his head and rubs his chin with the back of his sword hand — "perhaps it was even longer than that, because I never did see you on the field there." The challenge in his voice is unmistakable.

Pierre's face tightens. "Careful, Crunard," he says softly. "I would hate to have to teach you manners. Especially in front of the girl."

In the tense silence that follows, I wonder if I can reach for the night whispers without calling d'Albret's or his men's attention to my movements.

"Come, Pierre." Maraud's voice is more jocular now. "You know I have no manners. You cannot have forgotten that much about me."

D'Albret laughs and takes a step closer. "Where have you been? First I heard you had fallen on the battlefield. Rumor was you'd been taken. But here you are, cavorting with mummers and stealing horses."

Maraud shrugs. "I was taken. Now I am free."

Pierre glances at me once more. "And looking for more suitable employment, surely. I have work that you will be most interested in."

"As you can see, I already have a job."

"I think you'll find mine to be of personal interest to you."

I can almost feel Maraud's hackles rising. "What personal interest is that?"

"It is far too sensitive to speak of in a stable, but we could use a man of your skills."

"As I said, I already have a job, but I'm honored that you thought of me."

D'Albret's eyes darken as he weighs a score of ugly options. "You have always been saddled with that damnable family honor." I hold my breath, wondering if d'Albret will throw Maraud's father's treachery in his face, but he does not.

"As soon as you have finished this job, if you're still alive, come find me. I promise you, you will be most intrigued. If not for your own sake, then for your brothers'."

Maraud grows completely still, the stillness of a predator before it attacks. Surely he cannot think to take on all five men. Even so, I ease my hand down to my belt and unbuckle the leather strap on my sword.

"I will be in touch," Maraud finally says, his voice tight. "You may rest assured." The words are no promise, but a threat.

Pierre nods, his reactions as much a part of some silent dance as our mummery. "I look forward to it." He steps aside, motioning for his men to do so as well. With our way finally clear, Maraud does not move. Saints! He does not know the way out. "To the left," I murmur.

D'Albret and his men remain in place, silent and threatening, while Maraud leads Mogge toward the back of the stable. By the time we reach the door, my entire body is drenched in nervous sweat. Once we get it closed behind us, I lean against the thick wood, relieved to have something solid between us and d'Albret.

I have not taken but three paces into the cool air when Mogge comes to another abrupt standstill, this time rearing back and pulling sharply on her reins. I leap to the side. As I struggle to steer Gallopine clear of her flailing hooves, Maraud shoves Mogge's reins into my hand. "Stay here." He draws his sword and turns, launching himself forward.

Still fumbling with the reins, I crane my neck in time to see Maraud drive his sword into the chest of a man whose own sword is raised high in attack. My heart's rhythm shifts, racing in time with the dying man's. He is one of five men blocking our path. Maraud places his foot on the impaled man's stomach and pulls his sword out in time to run a second attacker through.

My heart lurches like a drunken man, beating more erratically. Gut wounds are a long, ugly way to die.

The third man is upon Maraud, holding his enormous broadsword in a two-handed grip. Distressed by the smell of blood, the horses neigh and pull on the reins. Swearing, I drag them toward the nearest post.

When I look over my shoulder, the third man is down, but a fourth comes at Maraud, swinging a mace.

Maraud grins maniacally. Just as the man swings, he crouches low. While the mace is still mid-arc, Maraud thrusts his sword high, trapping the chain. It whips once, twice around the blade, then Maraud yanks it out of the other man's hand. As his attacker reaches for his own sword, Maraud draws the second one from his hip and runs him through with it.

My chest feels as if it will explode as it is filled with yet another heartbeat, and my fingers work frantically to secure the reins tightly enough that the panicking horses cannot bolt.

The fifth man is upon him now, this one bearing a battle-ax. Maraud grabs both the blade and the hilt of his sword, using it to block the bone-jarring blow. A blade cannot hold long against such force. I jerk on the reins with all my strength to assure the knot cannot be pulled loose.

A sixth man appears — where are they coming from? — walking purposefully toward Maraud, a sword in each hand. Maraud's back is to him, but even if he could see, he has his hands full keeping his current opponent from splitting his skull.

I snatch my dagger from my left sleeve. It has been months since I have practiced so I do not let myself think, but simply throw and trust that years of training will hold true.

The dagger whips through the air and catches the sixth man on the side of his head. He ducks and swears, dropping one of his swords as his hand comes up to stanch the gush of blood.

There is a long single moment when everyone — Maraud, his attacker, and the man now missing his ear — is surprised, and immobile with it.

Maraud recovers first. He grabs his hilt with both hands and drives it into the faint hollow just above his attacker's collarbone.

The man drops his ax and falls to his knees, the movement releasing the sword from its bloody scabbard. Maraud spins around to face the one-eared man and finishes him off with a quick, clean thrust between his ribs.

Surely my heart was never meant to beat with the rhythm of so many dying men. It feels as if an entire herd of galloping horses is trapped inside my chest. With Maraud's gasping and the thundering heartbeats, it takes a moment to register the sound of clapping behind us.

I whirl around to find Pierre d'Albret leaning in the doorway, applauding.

Maraud wipes his brow, leaving a bloody smear. "Why?"

Pierre shrugs. "I needed to see if you'd lost your edge. You haven't. When you are finished here" — he glances at me — "find me. Do not make me come looking for you."

With that, he and his remaining guards disappear back into the stable, leaving Maraud and me surrounded by the groans of his dying men as we try to catch our breath.

"It was an ambush?"

Maraud nods. "With that particular snake, you must always check for two heads."

"Is he truly allowing us to leave," I ask, "or merely waiting to stab us in the back?"

"We'll know soon enough."

Once we clear the sally port, I can no longer feel the heartbeats of the dying men. Have they passed from this life into the next, or am I simply out of range? Just one of a dozen questions I have.

We ride in silence, grateful to be free of the city and eager to put as much distance as possible between us and d'Albret. As we gallop down the hill toward the valley below, we startle a flock of crows from the branch where they've been sleeping. As one, they spread their black wings and rise up into the night sky. It is not a crow feather, but an entire flock of them. Surely it is a sign that the Nine smile on this venture.

As disastrous as our escape was, it did not cost us too much time. "How long a ride is it to Tours?" I ask.

"I thought you said we were going to Poitiers?"

"I lied."

"Of course you did," he mutters. Then, louder, "Five days' hard ride — with luck and the weather on our side."

"Very well." I put my heels to Gallopine's flanks and send her cantering down the road.

There is barely enough moonlight to see by, but the road is straight, and our mounts are fresh. Besides, it is Christmas night, so we have it to ourselves.

Twice, Maraud steers us off the road to wait among the trees. I say nothing the first time, but by the second time, my desire to keep moving makes it impossible to hold my tongue. "This is costing us too much time."

"And I wish to get there alive."

"You said d'Albret was headed to Périgord. You think he will follow us instead?"

He reaches down and gives Mogge an absentminded rub. "If it suits him."

"Why does he want you to join him so badly?" If the animosity between them were not so thick, I would worry they were involved in some plot.

"I don't know. But if d'Albret is involved, I want no part of it."

Gallopine paws impatiently at the forest floor beneath her hooves. I allow her to inch forward, hoping Maraud will take the hint. "He insisted it would be of personal interest to you."

"He was wrong."

I almost ask if it could be about his father, but do not have the stomach for breaking that news to him. Not when he has finally gained a measure of freedom. There will be time enough for him to learn that ugly truth.

"What of Angoulême?" he asks as Mogge draws alongside me. "Will he follow you?"

"Not with the news about his babe."

Maraud's gaze is piercing. "Was it true?"

There is no one on the road behind us, so I allow Gallopine back onto it. "It was necessary. He needed a pressing reason not to follow me. Now he will hurry to check on his wife and unborn child instead. Why so concerned about Angoulême's babe? He was letting you rot in an oubliette."

"I'm not concerned about the babe. I'm trying to ascertain the extent of your ruthlessness."

CHAPTER 67

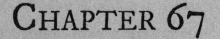

Sybella

hen I reach the servants' chapel, Beast is already there. "What happened?" His voice is rough. Others might think it anger, but I know it is fear that has been gnawing at him since we returned.

"There was an assassin."

His brow furrows, as if he cannot quite fathom what I am saying. "On the hunt today?"

I nod. "Waiting for me in the woods."

He takes me by the arm, the solid warmth of his grip grounding me, and pulls me deep into the chapel so that we are standing in the corner farthest from the door. "How do you know he was there for you?"

"Because . . ." I didn't, I realize. "I didn't know he was there for me until I had killed him." *You are a d'Albret. You lie like one. You kill like one.* Pierre's words echo inside my head, as sharp and clear as a bell. Those words keep me from looking into Beast's face. From taking comfort in the familiar lump of his nose and the scar across his cheek. I am unable to meet his eyes. I fear if I look at him, he will see the truth of Pierre's words. He will understand just how easily I kill. I square my shoulders. "Not until he was dead and his soul was laid open to me." My voice is steady, but colored by the bleakness I feel.

"There was no god guiding me in this," I whisper. "Only instinct. He did not strike first. I did."

Beast puts his hands on my shoulders. "You do not know that there are no gods guiding your hand in this. You only know that you did not see Mortain's marque."

I start to ask him what he means, but he talks over me. "We have had this discussion, you and I. I cannot fathom why the god of death would not grace you with killing to protect the innocent. Perhaps there is no innocence or guilt when death is concerned. But other gods, other saints, do sanction killing to protect innocents. Saint Arduinna, Saint Camulos. And make no mistake. Not only is this war, but you and your sisters are innocent in this."

I snort. "I was never innocent."

Beast shakes me — gently, but a shake nevertheless. "Don't say that," he growls. It is the closest I have ever seen him to being angry with me. "You are a survivor who has done precisely what she needs to in order to survive. You are not even close to what your brothers or father are, any more than Charlotte or Louise is."

Even though I don't think he is right, I allow myself to believe his words, just for a moment — much as one might step briefly into a church to snatch a passing moment of grace. "This is a war, isn't it?"

"Yes. Someone was sent to kill you. How could you tell he was an assassin?"

I explain the trap that he'd laid with the dead deer, his dress, his manner. "But mostly," I say, "it was simply instinct." The same inner voice that told me what to do with the dying guard. "Once he was dead, I saw that he was told to look for me. Given my description."

Beast grips my shoulders tighter. "By who?"

I look up and meet his eyes. "I do not know. The hand that held out the bag of coins was wearing a leather glove. I could not tell if it was a man's or woman's or if it had a fresh scar across the back of it as Pierre's would have. But," I say slowly, "the glove was similar to the one I saw handing money to one of the mercenaries."

Beast's face is almost comically blank. "What mercenaries?"

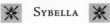

"After the ambush, as the field was awash in souls, I caught a glimpse of the d'Albret coat of arms."

"And you did not tell me." He does not raise his voice, but suddenly the room feels much smaller, as if he has somehow grown to take up all the space.

"It was one of the many things I have been meaning to tell you — when next we had the time." I lift my chin. "Besides, it was one soul among dozens. I had no way of knowing who it belonged to or how long ago he had seen such things. And we had more pressing things to deal with, such as our own dead and wounded."

He stares at me a long, taut moment. "Is there anything else you've neglected to tell me?"

I cast my mind back, trying to remember.

"You must think about it?" His whisper feels like he is bellowing.

"I wish to give you an honest answer!"

He shoves his hands onto his head and walks three paces away. "So you think Pierre sent the assassin?" His voice is calmer now.

"Or the regent. By now she has as much reason to hate me as he does. And," I point out, "she picked a most interesting day to suddenly be absent from the palace."

I watch as the implications of that spread across Beast's face. "I can't believe . . ."

I take a step toward him. "You can't believe what? That she is that ruthless? That she will kill to advance her hand? Tell me." I tilt my head. "Have you heard anything about Crunard's son yet?"

He winces as the point of my arrow finds its home. "No." His voice contains the acknowledgment that I am right.

"But what if it hadn't been your hawk to wander afield?" he asks. "It could have been anyone's falcon who did that."

I shrug. "Mayhap he would simply have stayed hidden until I showed myself. He likely had a number of plans on how to gain access to me. We saw only the one that worked."

He sighs. "What of the body?"

When I explain, Beast's mouth quirks up and his eyes shine with admiration. "I admire a lady who can think on her feet."

I shake my head. "Be serious."

"I am. What of the horse?"

"If there was one, I never saw it. He must have left it behind somewhere."

Beast nods. "I will send Lazare to check." He is quiet a moment. "My biggest worry is how long will it take whoever sent this man to realize he has failed?"

"My bigger worry is that if Pierre thinks I am out of the way, he will feel free to make another attempt on the girls."

"Then he will be most surprised, won't he, when he faces not just you, but the rest of us protecting them as well. When do you think the queen will be able to ask for the king's protection on your behalf?"

"Not until she is assured of her own," I tell him glumly.

CHAPTER 68

Genevieve

e reach Ransle just as the heavy gray clouds above us open up and release the rain they have been threatening all day. We stop at the first inn we pass, a plaster and timber building with an arched gate between it and the road.

Grateful for shelter, I step across the threshold, the rain dripping off my cloak onto the wooden floorboards. Maraud is close on my heels. The low-beamed room is lit by the fire and filled with the smell of tallow candles mixed with old wine and cooking. There are trestle tables set up, but only a handful of travelers.

"You'll be wanting a meal and a bed?" the innkeeper asks. "And stabling for your horses." I can see him adding up the sum in his head.

"That's right."

"Can you pay?"

In answer, I pat the small purse at my belt.

With a shrewd eye, he judges it full enough to bear the costs and motions us to one of the three empty tables. He hollers over his shoulder to some unfortunate lad to come see to the horses.

We have barely shaken the rain from our cloaks and taken a seat before the innkeeper returns with a platter of food, a wine jug, and two cups. My mouth waters as Maraud reaches for the knife and divides the braised coney in half, placing one portion on my trencher and the other on his. Following his lead, I rip the loaf of coarse brown bread in two and hand one of the sections to him, then turn to our meal. The rabbit is a little tough, but the sauce is flavorful and the bread is warm.

The quiet talk of the inn's other patrons is interrupted by a rap on the door. Maraud sets his food down and slides his hand under the table toward his sword. I shoot him a questioning look, but he simply shrugs. Whatever he knows about d'Albret must be truly vile to keep him on edge.

Blissfully unaware of Maraud's concerns, the innkeep hoists himself to see to the door. Raised voices follow. My pulse quickens as I worry Maraud was right — d'Albret *has* followed us — but realize the voices are too good-natured for that. "Let us in, old man!"

The innkeep grumbles something about mercenaries always taking and never paying.

"Yes, we'll pay! In advance."

"Besides," a deeper voice says, "if you do not let us in we will drown, and our deaths will stain your eternal soul and you shall have to do penance."

"Lots and lots of penance," the first voice agrees.

"Very well, but you'll have to leave your swords here." A round of protest goes up. "Those are the rules for mercenaries. I'll not have you slashing my place to ribbons when you're done with it. Now hand them over or drown, it's no difference to me."

More grumbling is followed by a clatter as swords are removed and handed to the innkeep. I reach for the jug and pour myself some wine. "Good thing you're not a mercenary, else you'd have had to remove yours as well." We are dressed as messengers, my hair braided and tucked under my hood to alter my appearance somewhat.

"Good thing," Maraud agrees dryly. When he glances at the newcomers, a look of stunned recognition appears on his face and he shoots me a rueful expression.

A voice hails him. "Maraud? Is that truly you?"

"Jaspar?" Maraud's smile is warm. "What are you doing in this part of France?"

While I am glad these aren't d'Albret's men, mercenary acquaintances of Maraud's could pose nearly as great a threat to my plans.

"Me? *Me?* You are the one we thought dead for over a year now."

The four men — no, three men and a woman, I realize — reach our table. "Truly." The man's voice is somber. "We thought you died at Saint-Aubin." He has the dark skin of a Moor and is dressed in riding leathers, a leather jerkin with a surcoat of chain mail, and a pair of muddy riding gloves tucked into the belt at his waist.

"You should know it takes more than a blow to my thick skull to kill me. Come. Sit with us." I kick him under the table, but it is too late.

The man, Jaspar, sits next to Maraud, his gaze flickering briefly to me. "It wasn't the blow I was worried about, but the pike."

Maraud grimaces. "That *would* have finished me off if I'd lain there and waited for it."

My appetite shrivels as two of the men sit on either side of me. The woman takes the free spot next to Maraud. She bumps his shoulder with her own. "You are thin."

He smiles at her. "And you are blunt." It is plain that she has a hundred questions she wishes to ask him. "Valine," he continues, "this is Lucinda. Lucinda, these three brutes are Jaspar, Andry, and Tassin." Does he place special emphasis on my name? Would it mean something to them?

My nod is more wary than pleasant as I try not to feel crowded and outnumbered. It was foolish to allow myself to be caught in the middle. Tassin on my left is a stout fellow with short hair, a bushy beard, and thick brows. His nose has been broken multiple times. If they chose to overpower me, they would win.

Jaspar leans across the table. "Do not mind Tassin. He is not much of a talker."

"No, we save all the talking for you," Valine says dryly, motioning the innkeep for wine.

On my right, Andry is paying little attention to the rest of us, his eyes roaming restlessly over the room as his fingers rub two thin coins together. "I still don't know why we're wasting money on this."

Valine stretches her legs out under the table. "Because we are not as miserly as you and did not wish to drown in our sleep."

Maraud smiles and raises his cup. "I've missed you miscreants." By the note of joy in his voice, these are not casual acquaintances, but friends. This is worse than I thought. If Maraud chooses to enlist their aid so he can escape, they could easily overpower me. I might possibly fend off Jaspar, and maybe Valine, but not Tassin or Andry, and certainly not Maraud. Not all at once.

The innkeep appears with a fresh jug of wine and four more cups. "I'll be back with your food in a moment. No need to be shouting clear across the room."

"Thank you," Valine tells him. She lifts her cup to Maraud. "Here's to learning that you are alive."

"So, where *have* you been?" Jaspar asks.

Will Maraud trust them enough to tell them the truth? "Here and there," he says. "I spent some time down near Périgord."

Something inside me relaxes a bit. Andry's coins grow still and he swings his head back to Maraud. "That's where we're headed. They say d'Albret is hiring."

Maraud carefully sets down his knife and spoon and pushes his plate away. "I've heard."

Andry's interest sharpens. "Then why are you here and not there?"

The look Maraud gives him is unreadable. At least to me. "I already have a job."

Jaspar sighs and shakes his head. "That's where Andry wants to go next. We've been hoping to dissuade him along the way. Maybe you'll have better luck."

"Why do you want to work for d'Albret?" Maraud gives Andry a probing look.

The other man peers down at the coins in his hand. "He's hiring, and he pays well," he says, then tosses back his wine.

Maraud does not look away. "There is a reason for that. You know what he's capable of."

Andry shrugs, but does not meet Maraud's gaze.

"And you?" Maraud turns to the others. "Do you want to work for d'Albret as well?" It is as much a rebuke as it is a question.

"Not me," Jaspar says around a mouthful of braised rabbit. "I'm thinking of returning to Brittany."

"More's the fool, you," Andry grouses.

"Brittany?" Although Maraud's voice does not change, his face grows alert with interest. "I thought all the mercenaries had been paid and dismissed."

Jaspar raises a shoulder in a careless gesture. "Word is there's new work to be had, and I've a mind to visit home again."

A deep, rumbling voice comes from my left. "Place is crawling with English troops." It is the first time Tassin has said anything all night. "Don't like the smell of 'em," he says. "They're watching the borders, minding the ports — why?"

Valine arches a brow in amusement. "They're looking for someone, of course. It does not take a scholar to discern that."

"Yeah, but who? And why?" The bulky man rolls his shoulders. "They failed us twice now when we needed 'em. A pox on them all, I say." He drains his cup and falls silent again.

The awkward moment is quickly replaced by another when Valine turns to me. "And who are you?"

There are many answers I could give, but the truth will serve me best and be a warning to them all. "An assassin."

Maraud chokes on the mouthful of wine he has just taken, and four disbelieving faces turn my way. It is the first time since they arrived that I have had their full attention. "Well played, Lucinda!" Jaspar says with a low whistle. "No one would ever suspect it."

"That is the point, is it not?"

Valine turns a speculative gaze on Maraud. "So you're an assassin now?" Her question is careful, the words weighted with some meaning I can sense but not fully discern.

Maraud folds his arms and tosses a smile at her. "Not me. I'm just the hired help."

Tassin tilts his head, his chin at a belligerent angle. "If you are an assassin, why do you need him?"

"Although I know a hundred ways to kill a man, I am still a lone woman, which makes me an easy target on the road. His job is to get me there. My job is to kill." Our gazes remain locked for another moment before he finally turns away.

The innkeep comes over to remove the last of our dishes. "I'm bolting the door and putting out the candles. If you want to see your way to your beds, you'd best come along now. If not, you're welcome to stumble your way to 'em in the dark, just be sure you mind the stairs. They're steep and narrow."

"Well I, for one, am off to bed," I tell the others as I rise from the table. I glance meaningfully at Maraud. "You should be too. We have an early start in the morning."

Chapter 69

lie on the lumpy straw mattress, breathing deeply, as if asleep. Exhausted as I am from our ride out of the city, there will be little rest for me tonight. There are far too many ways Maraud could use his friends against me.

The pouch with the antidote is under my pillow, along with two daggers. My baselard is snuggled on the mattress next to me. They cannot steal the antidote and sneak away. Nor can they catch me unaware and try to wrest it from me. At least, not without a fight. And if it comes to that, I have the case with my poisoned needles hidden in my cuff.

It takes so long that I very nearly do fall asleep, but the faint rustle of someone rising from their bed jolts me fully awake. There is another rustle, and another. I curl my fingers around the dagger handles, careful not to change the rhythm of my breathing.

The floorboard at the foot of my bed creaks. More creaks follow, but they are the faint padding of bare feet, not boots. Not leaving, then.

After another hand span of minutes, I silently rise from my own bed. I slip one of the daggers back in its sheath but keep the other in my right hand. Moving even slower than they did, I pick my way to the door, then stop, pressing myself up against the wall. When I am certain they have not heard me, I slowly peer around the doorjamb.

And jerk back when I see them sitting in the hallway right outside. My heart thuds loudly in my ears. Did they notice me? When no one moves or calls a warning, I inch closer to the door.

"I still can't believe you've been in a dungeon this whole time." It is Jaspar who speaks. "Did you tell them who you are?"

Maraud's *no* makes it clear the subject is closed.

Valine's voice is easy to pick out among the others. "But why would —"

"I saw something. Right after the surrender. France had just captured the Duke of Orléans, and our side had agreed to terms. Two . . . noblemen offered their swords to General Cassel. He told them he had been ordered to keep d'Orléans alive, but had no such orders for them. He accused them of treason against the king and beheaded them where they knelt. I think it is he who was having me held."

Vile oaths erupt all around. "Ride with us in the morning, and we'll find out," Jaspar proposes.

"I must finish this job first. But I want to know where Cassel is."

"Flanders," Jaspar says. "He has been overseeing the campaign in Flanders."

Maraud swears. "That will make him hard to get to."

"Hard, but not impossible," Valine points out. "Is that where you're headed?"

"After I finish up with the assassin."

"What do you want us to do?" Jaspar's offer drives home the full extent of their loyalty to Maraud.

"I want Andry and Tassin to find out why d'Albret is raising troops. I need to know what he is planning."

"Why?" Tassin's deep voice is calculating.

"He was most insistent that I join him. To the point of detaining me. Said the campaign would be of deep personal interest to me. I want to know what that means."

Andry snorts. "Does he know you're the most idealistic mercenary ever to ride with a company? Every campaign becomes of deep personal interest to you."

There is a soft thud followed by an *oof*. Maraud's elbow connecting with Andry's ribs is my guess.

"Very well. What of Jaspar and me?" Valine asks.

"I want you to return to Brittany as planned. Find out who is putting out a call for troops. Join them if you need to, but find out why. And I would like to know who the English are searching for."

"Is there anything else, my lordship?"

372

"Here." Another *oof*. "You can polish my boots while you're at it."

Valine interrupts their snickering. "Why not go yourself?"

"As I said, I am escorting the assassin north. Once I've done that, I'll join you."

"Is she truly an assassin?" Andry asks.

"Yes."

"Can't be much of one," he snorts. "We snuck by her, and she hasn't so much as stirred."

I step into the hallway, a dagger loose and easy in each hand. "On the contrary."

Five heads snap up to gape at me. Well, Maraud is not surprised. They sit at the end of the hall, much as they might around a campfire. A leather flagon of wine dangles forgotten in Andry's hand. "I heard you all lumber by me like a flock of drunken geese and have been standing here the entire time." I tilt my head and study Andry pointedly. "I have to wonder just how good you are at soldiering if you can be so unaware of your surroundings as to miss me."

There is a flash of white as Valine smiles broadly, then digs her elbow into Andry's ribs. Her eyes meet mine from across the hallway, and she takes the wine from Jaspar and raises it in salute. "Care to join us?"

For a moment, the desire to sit with them is so strong it is akin to hunger. I want to hear their story. How did they come to be so close? How did Valine end up a mercenary? If she can do such a thing, who is to say that I cannot?

I adjust the grip on my knives. Hunger or not, that is not where my destiny lies. The convent needs me. "What I would like is to catch a few hours of sleep before dawn."

I have only just gotten comfortable in my bed when I hear the rest of them troop back into the room. I do not fall asleep until their breathing and snoring assures me that they have.

⁂

I am the first one up in the morning and none too quiet about it, eager to be on my way. As we all trudge toward the stables, I take Maraud's arm and pull him behind the corner of the inn where we will not be seen by the others. "Here." I hold up the antidote.

He nods curtly, then opens his mouth. I let three drops fall on his tongue before tucking the vial back in my pouch. Maraud studies me with such intensity that it is all I can do not to squirm. "What?" I finally ask.

"We could help you. My friends and I. We could help you with your mission to save those people you spoke of."

I busy myself with securing my pouch to my belt. "I told you, it is not that kind of job. Besides, I am certain it doesn't pay well enough for Andry's liking."

Since we are going in the same direction, we ride for a short way together. Maraud looks over his shoulder far less frequently. Whether because he is no longer believes d'Albret is following us or because he has four trained soldiers at his side, I do not know.

When we finally reach the crossroads, it is time to part ways. With few words, Andry and Tassin turn their horses to the southeast. Valine and Jaspar take the west fork.

"Join us when you can," Jaspar calls out.

"When I am ready," Maraud calls back. "I will take the road west from Sainte-Maure." I do not know if he truly feels as confident as he sounds or if it is a pretense for his friends.

Jaspar swivels around in his saddle. "Where shall we meet?"

"At the sign of the bone and cross. I will send word when I am there."

Jaspar raises his hand in the air, turns back around in his saddle, and gallops down the road to catch up to Valine.

As they depart, I remind myself that my plan for Maraud is a good one. A necessary one.

If that is true, a little voice whispers in my ear, *tell him so he can join you freely.*

But I do not. Not now. Not when he is still smiling from the time with his friends who once thought him dead.

CHAPTER 70

e spend the next two days slogging our way through a sea of muddy road, occasionally broken up by a dark, smoky inn, a tepid meal, and a dirty straw mattress. Now that it is only two of us again, Maraud has resumed his habit of constantly looking over his shoulder.

By noon of the third day, my nerves are pulled tight and my patience frayed. When we draw near a bridge, Maraud reins Mogge in and calls out, "Hold up."

"No one is following us," I snap. "Stop wasting time traveling in twists and turns."

"We need to get off the road," he says tersely.

I open my mouth to argue, but he is already using Mogge to herd me off to the side. "Why?"

"Mounted horsemen. Lots of them." He points behind us, and I squint down the line of his arm. Approaching the bridge from the east are well over a hundred men on horseback. "Can you make out their standard?"

"They're not carrying one. They're mercenaries."

"How can you tell?"

"The lack of standard for one, and no colors. The armor is plain, and they do not ride in formations so much as a mob. See? There are pikesmen amongst the mounted soldiers, archers among the lances. A battalion marching under a house banner would be more orderly. Remember how d'Albret's men rode in formation? These men are not doing that."

He is right.

"Come." His voice is filled with quiet urgency. "I want to reach the bridge before they spot us."

"But surely you are one of them. They would not do you any harm."

"I think the friends of mine you met in Ransle have led you to mistake the nature of mercenaries. Most are like Andry and Tassin. Even more are like d'Albret's men. And there are close to two hundred of them. Two hundred bored, hungry soldiers spoiling for a fight or at least a little sport. I do not want to be that sport."

The full implications of his concern finally register. I press my heels along Gallopine's flanks to urge her along.

Luck, or mayhap the gods, appears to be on our side, and the clouds above us drop lower to the ground, turning into a thick, drizzling mist. Between the heavy fog and the trees, we are able to reach the bridge without being seen.

At the river's edge, we dismount and lead our horses up the bank to where the bridge is built into the ground. We can hear them now, a loud steady clop of hooves. They are close.

Maraud whips off his cloak and wraps it around Mogge's head, muffling her senses. I do the same. And then we wait. The first clop of hooves strikes the wooden planks of the bridge and is quickly joined by the thunder of dozens and dozens of horses making their way across. Just under the nearly deafening noise of the hooves is a faint metal jingle of harness and tack, weapons and spurs, and occasionally a man's voice or a laugh.

They clear the bridge, but still we wait. When we can no longer hear any sounds of them, I start to edge out from our hiding spot, but Maraud grabs my arm and gives a quick shake of his head. When I nod in understanding, he releases my arm and we wait some more.

We wait for nearly an hour after they pass, our horses growing bored and restless. At last Maraud hands me Mogge's reins before crawling up the embankment to see if the road is clear.

"They are gone," he says when he returns. "And no stragglers remain behind. But I don't like that they are traveling the same road we are. Any town we stay in will either be overrun by them or will have locked their walls until they've passed."

"So we must sleep out on the road? Will that truly be any safer?"

"Only if we find a spot now and choose one that gives us the best advantage. It is early enough in the day that I do not think they will retrace their footsteps this far back to camp for the night. But neither would I bet either of our lives on that."

By the time we set out again, the faint drizzle has turned into a light rain.

We had hoped to reach Vivonne by nightfall, but it is clear by the numerous hoof prints in the mud that the mercenary company has gone that way. To avoid them, Maraud chooses a small cart track that leads off the main road. Just when I am convinced he has led us down naught but a deer path and we will be forced to sleep on the ground, a small village comes into view.

It is hardly more than a handful of cottages, and rundown ones at that. The entire village is still and quiet. At first I think the rain has driven everyone indoors, but none of the houses have so much as a wisp of smoke coming from their chimneys, or a dog or chicken roaming the yards.

"Do you think they are hiding from the mercenaries?" I ask Maraud.

"No. This place was abandoned long before today. A plague. A poor crop. Sick livestock. Take your pick." He reins Mogge in, then dismounts, and I do the same. Together we survey the village. No one has come out to greet us or chase us away, which only heightens the sense of desertion.

The cottages are simple ones, with thatched roofs and lime wash. A common well sits near the center of the village. Just beyond it is a small church.

Maraud ties Mogge to one of the nearby fence posts. "I think it is deserted, but better to make sure." He draws his sword. "I'll take the houses on the left. You take the right."

I nod and draw my own sword. As I creep forward, all of my senses are heightened. The door of the first house is ajar, and it is easy enough to see that its one room is utterly empty. The second house has a thick oak door with iron hinges that creak as I open it. Inside there are a bench and two wooden hoops hanging from the wall, as well as a tripod for cooking. I draw my toe through the straw on the floor. It is old, but dry. No one has likely occupied this house for days.

I move on to the next house, and the next, each of them equally barren. When I am finished, I return to the horses, where Maraud joins me. "They've been gone a month," he says. "Maybe more than that, but not much more."

"I agree they've been gone awhile, but why do you think as recently as that?"

He flashes me a grin. "Because there are feral chickens behind one of the cottages. I say we pick a cottage and I will go hunt for our dinner."

I stare at him, my mind consumed by the image of him stalking feral chickens. Unable to come up with any semblance of a reply, I simply say, "Very well. The second house on this side was sturdier than the others, with a thick door that locks. There's also a small barn in back."

"That will do."

I leave him to his adventure and lead our horses to the barn. When I return to the cottage, I remove my damp cloak and begin poking around, happy to find half a sack of large gray peas and two onions. I lift the patched iron pot from its hook on the wall and go outside to fill it with rainwater from the barrel. In addition to the rain barrel, there is a large stack of firewood within easy reach of the door.

Once I have set the pot on the hearth, I return to collect some wood to start a fire. With a brief plea to Saint Cissonius, the patron saint of travelers, I search the stones near the hearth, looking for flint and tinder, and am pleased when they are there. Maraud returns just then, triumphantly bearing a plucked chicken in his left hand.

I raise my eyebrows. "You think it safe to start a fire?"

"I think the company we saw earlier is too far away by now to see any smoke. Besides, the cloud cover and darkness of night should mask it well enough."

"Excellent." I nod to the pot, then to the spit iron standing leaning against the hearth. "Do you want to stew it or roast it?"

He glances at the chicken. "Which is faster?"

I cannot help it. I laugh. "The pot, I think. Also, it is most likely a tough old bird and could use some stewing."

After putting the chicken in the pot, he kneels to start the fire. I have finished chopping the onions, and he steps aside so I can toss them into our stew. As I look up, he smiles — a smile that reaches straight into my chest and squeezes my heart so tightly I can scarce draw breath.

There is so much . . . trust in that smile. Trust and warmth and satisfaction in having found shelter, food. Maybe most impressively, there is no hint of expectation or assumption. The smile pierces my heart like a fisherman's hook — bearing twin barbs of guilt and regret. Regret that things cannot be easy between us. Regret that we cannot be lovers again or even take pleasure in this simple shelter we have found.

Well, I cannot, anyway. "Peas and onions make for a thin stew," I say abruptly. "I will go forage to see what the other cottages might offer up."

Maraud takes a step as if to come with me, but I stop him. "I don't need help." Before he can argue, I grab my cloak, throw it around my shoulders, and step outside.

I lift my face to the deepening twilight, letting the soft rain wash the heat from my cheeks. Back in Cognac, my plan seemed so sound. Fair even. Maraud would at least have a chance to plead his case before the king and not simply rot like a forgotten slab of meat.

But I have lost the taste for the bad bargain I made on his behalf. My weakness shames me. What would my aunts say, they who traded men for a night's lodging, a sack of wheat flour, or a meal without so much as a sigh of regret?

What would my mother say — she who was able to trade her daughter for a sack of coins?

No, I remind myself, not simply a sack of coins, but to give that daughter a better life than hers.

Even so, she didn't look back. Not once. I know because I waited and watched and prayed that she would, that there would be one last goodbye between us, even if it was silent.

But there wasn't. She did not look back, nor hesitate. That I should do so now, when the entire convent's future is at stake, embarrasses me. The better life my mother envisioned for me did not entail becoming soft or weak.

CHAPTER 71

fter combing through the cottages and their gardens, I acquire two blankets, a handful of leeks, a wilted cabbage, and two somewhat leathery turnips. Even better, hanging from the ceiling of the last house in the village was both a bundle of rosemary and a chunk of salt pork that someone was in too big a hurry to collect.

It is nearly full dark when I reach our cottage. A thin line of smoke oozes out of the chimney. As I approach the yard, the back of my neck starts to itch, slowing my steps. I quickly glance for any signs of others, but there are no horses, no people — it looks as deserted as when we first arrived.

And yet . . . I roll my shoulders but proceed cautiously, placing my feet so they make no noise. When I step inside the yard, my heart starts to race. No.

Not my heart. Someone else's.

I drop my bundle of goods, draw my sword with my right hand and my long knife with my left, then hurry to the window with the broken shutter to peer inside.

Three men face Maraud, whose back is to the hearth. They are tall and well armed, their cloaks embellished with braid, their boots of excellent quality. One of them, with a thick mustache, holds Maraud's own sword at his throat. The other two men's hands rest on their hilts but have yet to draw them. Their voices are low, the words fast and guttural.

". . . here first. It is ours."

"You were nowhere to be seen for the last two hours, so forgive me if I doubt your claim."

"Doubt all you want, but we will be sleeping here tonight."

Through the window I can see that the door is not only unlatched, but slightly ajar. I silently back away from the broken shutter. Which of them should I attack first? If I take out the one wielding the sword, can Maraud get to his other weapon in time?

If he can't, I have seen for myself how good he is at disarming an opponent. What I do not know is how quickly he can disarm two.

By the time I reach the front door, my heart is hammering so fast I can scarcely think. The men are still facing Maraud, their backs to me. One takes a step closer to Maraud. "Who sent you?" I ease my sword arm into the room, pausing long enough to be certain I have not been spotted. Then I suck in my breath and squeeze through the narrow space.

"How long have you been following us?"

Should I kill them? Will Mortain consider this self-defense? The weapons are not pointed at me, but they would be if they knew I was here.

"Did you pick up our trail in Le Blanc?"

I glance at Maraud. To his credit, he does not look at me, but moves his finger — only slightly — at the man talking. My heartbeat kicks into a gallop.

I lunge forward, using the full weight and force of my body to drive my blade through the back of the intruder holding the sword at Maraud's throat. The momentum shoves him forward, but Maraud is able to leap aside and avoid being skewered. Using my foot for leverage, I yank my weapon from the body as my chest is filled with yet another heartbeat, lurching and careening against my ribs. I pivot, then drive the blade into the second man just as he rushes at me.

The intensity of his own attack drives him into my sword with such force that I must use both hands to hold my position. With his body impaled on my blade, our eyes meet, his widening in surprise before his hand spasms and lets go of the hilt.

I glance over in time to see Maraud drive the spit from the hearth into the remain—

I gasp. A shocking and unfamiliar . . . presence . . . fills me, stretching the contours of my mind and rubbing against my soul.

It is both the most intimate of connections and the most galling violation.

"Lucinda?" Maraud's voice comes to me as if from far away. "Are you hurt?"

I try to make my mouth answer his question, but a second presence crashes up against me, a thundering wave of new sensations, followed closely by a third.

I look down at my hands, my arms, fearing that I am bursting out of my own skin. A moment passes, then another, and then the intensity, the sense of overfullness, begins to recede. I can breathe again and feel my heart beating.

But I am not alone.

Images fill my head — things my own eyes have never seen, my hands never touched, my heart never felt. Faces. An ocean crossing. A dowager duchess with a steel spine. A fair-haired man.

Souls, I realize, after a long moment. These are the souls of the men we've just killed.

As if that very thought agitates them, they writhe within me, already growing cooler than the shocking heat of their initial presence.

Should I thrust them from me? *Can* I thrust them from me?

Or is this some weight we of Mortain must bear, to forever carry the souls of those we have killed?

Lessons from the convent quickly take over. Three days. That is how long souls linger near their bodies after they die.

I must endure this — this violation, for three days?

No. The knowledge rises up from my very bones.

"Begone!" I say.

"Who are you talking to?" Maraud asks in a whisper.

I shake my head. The pressure of the souls lessens, as if they are considering my command. It is that hesitation that allows me to see more clearly. No matter who the men were, their souls are confused, cut adrift from the bodies they have lost.

It is life they hunger for, not me.

Begone, I say again, although this time silently.

To my surprise, they do what I ask, although reluctantly, like sullen children.

I am touching a miracle, I realize, a shiver running through me.

As I come back into my body, the first thing I am aware of is the warmth on my cheeks. Puzzled, I put my hand up and am surprised to find Maraud's hands cupping my face.

"There you are," he murmurs, quickly removing his hands.

I am struck by two things at once — the grave concern writ so plainly on his face, and that as soon as he knew I was no longer in danger, he stopped touching me. He not only hears the messages I have been sending him, but respects them. Except when my safety is at stake.

That brings a jumble of new emotions that threaten to sink my wits altogether. "I am fine," I reassure him.

"You are not only fine, you are wondrous!" He takes my hand and, just as I fear I have reached the wrong assessment of him, pulls me over to the fire before letting go. "That was as impressive a rescue as anyone could ever hope for."

I blink up at him, half my mind still consumed by the souls — who now hover in the corners of the room. "You were hoping for a rescue?" I ask stupidly.

He snorts. "I didn't spend all that time sparring with you so you could leave me to a band of rapacious bandits."

His babble, for that is what it is, helps anchor me in my skin and tether me to my bones. I can once again feel where my own soul begins and ends, the boundaries firmly back in place.

"Here," he says. "You are cold." He throws his cloak over my shoulders and pulls me even closer to the fire.

"I am not cold," I protest, and yet I am shivering slightly. But not with cold. Not even with fear. But with the enormity of what just happened.

I can see dead men's souls. Indeed, they are drawn to me in their moment of death. By some strange gift, they are able to share pieces of themselves, their lives, with me. And for all that these three men wished us ill, it feels miraculous. I have — finally! — experienced the fullness of my gifts from Saint Mortain.

But those gifts are weighted with both responsibility and gravity. I have never, in all the five years I've been gone, more fervently wished for someone from the convent to speak to. To explain to me what just happened. To let me know what it means, what we are to do with it, if anything.

"Lucinda?" Maraud's hand reaches out, his fingers lightly brushing my cheek. "Don't go away again. I don't know how to bring you back."

I look up into his eyes, which seem nearly black in the shadowed light from the fire. Such concern shines there, such caring.

Perhaps it is my befuddledness at what just occurred, or perhaps it is simply basking in the gravity of my new gifts, but I don't shrug from his touch nor slap his fingers away. "I am fine," I tell him. "Truly."

"But something just happened." His deep voice is low and soothing.

"Yes."

He runs a hand over his head. "I felt like I witnessed something." His voice grows deeper still. "A miracle, I think."

It is the respect and reverence in his voice that allows me to speak of it. "You did. I told you that I was an initiate of Mortain, but what I did not tell you was that I hadn't yet killed a man." I glance over at the bodies on the floor. "Until tonight."

Without realizing he is doing it, he reaches out and gives my shoulder a reassuring squeeze. "It is a hard thing, the first time. A shock, no matter how much one has trained."

"You're right," I tell him slowly. "But it is more than that. There are gifts that Mortain bestows upon those of us sired by Him. And I"— I take a deep breath —"I have never experienced the fullness of those gifts before."

"That is where you went? Into the realm of Mortain?"

"Yes," I say, realizing that is precisely where I went. "In their moment of death, I am able to experience men's souls as they leave their bodies. I am able to . . . speak with them, although not with words. I know that they are here on the orders of a dowager duchess. A Lady Margaret, perhaps? And that they also serve a younger fair-haired lord."

Maraud stares at me. "That is quite a gift. All I was able to determine was that they were trained soldiers from Burgundy and wanted to kill me."

I laugh, as he no doubt intended, and in that moment of laughter feel wholly myself once again.

Albeit with a wondrous new awareness and appreciation for who and what I am.

After the bodies have been removed and our dinner eaten, we stretch out before the dying fire. It is dark except for the faint glow of the embers. "What has Saint Camulos gifted you with?" I don't know what prompts me to ask such a question — the sense of awe that still fills me? The darkness? I remember his impressive fighting back in the city. "Are you possessed by battle fever?"

"Me? No. That is truly rare. I have only ever met one man who possessed it, and he would tell you it's no gift." Maraud puts his hands under his head and stares up at the timbered roof. "His name was Beast, and he could easily slay a dozen men — twice that when the fever was upon him. But it was a great burden to him as well."

"Is that the only gift Saint Camulos bestows upon his followers?"

He shrugs. "I can see men's weaknesses. Like a mason sees fault lines in stone."

I turn on my side and prop my head in my hand. "What of those who attacked us? Could you see their weaknesses?"

"One was arrogant, too certain his weapon gave him an advantage over me. The second preferred to act on orders rather than his own thinking, and the third was too cautious, giving himself too much time to calculate the risks before making his move."

It all fits with what I saw with my own eyes and gleaned from their souls. "What of me?" My voice is almost a whisper — I am desperate to know my weakness so I may pluck it from me, but afraid of the answer as well.

Maraud turns his head so that he is facing me. "Trust," he says. "Your weakness is your inability to trust."

And just like that, the spell is broken. "Trust," I snort. "Trust is a fool's game, and I stopped playing it long ago."

There is a creak just outside the cottage door. Before I can react, the door bursts open. A half dozen armed men pour in, their weapons drawn and pointed straight at us.

385

CHAPTER 72

Sybella

 t will be easy enough to verify that the regent was visiting Princess Marguerite. Indeed, I find myself with a number of questions I would like to ask the young princess. I think it is time to pay her a visit.

I do not tell Beast. He will only try to stop me. Instead, I tell Aeva in case something should happen and I don't return. And while she does not try to prevent it, she does insist on coming with me. "You will be traveling at night. It will be safer to travel together."

"But I want you watching the girls."

"They will be safe enough. It is you I am worried about."

"I am perfectly capable of taking care of myself."

"I am not saying you aren't, but there is no shame in having someone watch your back. Especially when venturing into unknown territory where someone may be conspiring with your enemy."

She is right, dammit.

"Besides." She tilts her head and smiles knowingly. "Have you given any thought to how you will get past the traps and snares placed in the surrounding woods? You will not be able to venture out on the road, which leaves only the forest."

I sigh heavily, as if her suggestion greatly inconveniences me. "Very well. If you insist."

Dressed as men, we sneak to the stables. As we saddle our horses, Aeva works some Arduinnite magic to keep the others from growing unsettled by our presence and giving us away to the grooms. When we are done, we also take the time to wrap our horses' hooves with burlap sacks before leading them out onto the cobblestones in the courtyard. It is not until we reach the palace garden that we remove the cloth and mount.

We have not gone a hundred paces before Aeva puts out her hand. "Hold." She backs up her horse in order to cut a wide swathe around a patch of bracken.

"What was that?" I whisper.

In answer, she reaches up, breaks a small branch off the closest tree, and throws it into the spot she has just avoided.

A loud, metal crunch ruptures the silence, and I find myself staring down into the closed jaws of a steel trap. "How did you know?"

She shrugs one shoulder. "I can smell them."

"A gift from Arduinna?"

She snorts. "No. A gift from living in the woods all my life and being able to recognize the stench of iron."

At her words, a new realization comes to me. The assassin would have needed to avoid these traps as well. Which means he was either someone from the palace or someone shared that knowledge with him.

Aeva peers at me. "Are you all right? I will find them all. You needn't worry."

I stare at the other woman. Should I tell her of the assassination attempt and this newest discovery?

I know it is the smart thing to do. She could easily be a target as well — simply for being with me. That is what finally forces me to tell her.

When I have finished, she grimly shakes her head. "I cannot decide if trouble seeks you out or you merely attract it to yourself as the moon attracts a moth."

"I do not seek it out," I protest. But she has already ridden ahead.

She finds two more traps and one snare before we finally clear the forest. I do not bother to thank her, as my openmouthed awe at her skill is gift enough for her.

When we reach the princess's castle, Aeva waits in the nearby trees as I silently make my way to the palace walls. Marguerite's bedchamber is likely near the solar — the room placed to receive the most sunlight and therefore having the largest window. I find that large window, with a smaller one on either side of it. I pick the right side, as it is in a corner with a chimney and the most promising spot, then quickly begin scaling the wall.

When I reach the window, I slip my knife in between the two panels of glass, gently lift the latch, and push one of the panes open, praying it will not squeak.

It does not.

Inside the room, four figures sleep in cots set up on the floor near the fire, while a large canopied bed occupies the opposite wall.

I inch my way to the bed, then slowly pull back the curtains.

A young girl sits there, wide awake. "Are you here to rescue me or assassinate me?"

Her question causes the fine hairs along the back of my neck to stir. "Why would you think someone has been sent to assassinate you?"

She wraps her arms around her knees. "I do not know what to think anymore. Everything I've been promised has been swept aside by politics. What I once thought was certain and safe holds nothing but doubt."

"I am acquainted with that feeling," I mutter.

"I no longer trust any promises that have been made, not even those regarding my personal safety."

For all that she is an indulged, pampered princess, she is not lacking in wits. "You're wise not to trust anyone, but I am not here to kill you. I wished only to see you with my own eyes and ascertain whether you were safe."

Intrigued, she scoots herself to sit up against her pillow. "Who are you?"

"I am no enemy, that I promise. I am merely trying to untangle an ugly knot of truth and lies."

"It's too bad you wear that hood so I cannot better determine your sincerity."

"It is too bad," I agree. "But I cannot risk being recognized later."

She puts her finger to her chin and studies me. "*Have* you been sent to rescue me? I must admit, I was expecting a troop of mounted knights with my father at their head, but you will do."

It is all I can do to keep from smiling. "Do you need rescuing?"

She makes a delicate sound that in anyone else I would call a snort. "It has been well over a month since my betrothal was cast aside like day-old bread. I do not want to molder away in this castle forever."

"Has the king or regent indicated they have planned such a thing for you?"

"The king? No."

"But the regent has?"

She shrugs. "I have not spoken to her since she bid me goodbye nearly two months ago. She has not shared her plans with me."

And there is one of the answers I came looking for. "But you have spoken to the king?"

She settles back against the head of her bed, making herself comfortable. "Yes. He feels guilty. Not just for breaking our betrothal agreement," she explains. "But for his claims of love and devotion that have turned out to be as meaningful as dust."

It would be easier to feel sorry for her if she wasn't so clearly sharp and full of wit. I am not sure that she hasn't received the better end of that bargain. Even so, I am sorry for the pain that Arduinna's arrow caused her, for all that it must be weighed against the cost of war. "Do you find it odd that the regent has not been to see you?"

She purses her mouth, thinking. "She has always treated me with great affection. A daughter could not have asked for a better mother. But now, now I do not know." It is the first time I hear a note of true loss and confusion in her voice. She feels more betrayed by the regent than the king, I think.

"The regent has always been a complex woman." I turn and look at the princess's attendants, sleeping on their cots. "Did you know she often bribes the closest associates of her enemies? How long have your ladies in waiting been with you?"

"Why? Do you think one of them could be spying for the regent?"

"It is possible." But that is not my reason for the question.

She turns her gaze toward the sleeping women. "Two of them came with me from Austria, and two I chose myself from among the regent's ladies."

My heart quickens at that possibility. "Why did you pick them?"

"One lacked the power of speech or the ability to write. The regent used her lessons with the younger women to shame her, and I thought it poorly done."

My admiration for her grows.

"The second one found the constrictions the regent placed upon her to be too confining. Not that she was ever improper," the princess hurries to add. "She was simply too full of life for someone as dour as the regent." After a moment of silence, she adds. "Another girl, Margot, was the same way."

Everything inside me grows still. When I speak, I am careful that my voice does not change. "Margot? Is she still with the regent?"

"No, she and Genevieve were sent with Louise when she married. Although I must confess, I feel sorry for them because Louise is every bit as serious and pious as the regent."

"Where was Pious Louise sent?" I ask.

"She married Count Angoulême and now resides in Cognac."

Cognac. Over a hundred miles away. My limbs grow heavy with disappointment. That is it, then. They are both too far away to be of any help.

"So," Marguerite continues, "while it is possible the regent could have one of my ladies spying for her, I don't believe she does. Besides, I have no secrets from her. Well," she amends. "Except you. You are my first secret." She hugs her knees. "A most delicious one."

"Thank you for all that you have shared. You owed me none of these explanations."

She looks up at me, and for all of her intelligence and wit, I am struck by how young she is. "With all that has happened in the last weeks, not one person has asked me what I think or what my opinion on the matter was. You are the first to ask."

A slow familiar anger fills me. A young woman to be plucked or snatched or tucked away at anyone's whim. "Well, Princess, I am most grateful for all that

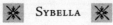
you have shared. And while I can make no promises, if I am ever in a position to help in any way, I will do my utmost to see that I can."

Now she is the one to look surprised. "Thank you, but why would you do that?"

"Because you are not a plum," I whisper. While she is still gaping at my answer, I take my leave.

CHAPTER 73

Genevieve

n the dark, it is hard to make out anything except that there are five of them. And they are large and well armed. My sword lies on the floor next to me, but I do not reach for it. Not yet.

The tallest one speaks first. "You owe us three lives." His words are shaped by the same Burgundy accent as the men we killed.

"We owe you nothing." Maraud's voice is hard as flint. "We defended ourselves against an attack."

"We got here first. You trespassed on our shelter for the night."

"But when we arrived," I point out, "the whole town was empty."

After a moment of astonished silence, five heads turn to stare at me. "You are a woman!"

"Who killed two of your men," Maraud reminds them. "So do not underestimate her."

"As we searched the village," I continue, "you made no move to show yourselves or stake your claim. How were we to know?"

The man shifts. In the dark, he is impossible to read. "We could not risk showing ourselves until we knew your purpose here."

Maraud scoffs. "Purpose? We wanted shelter for the night. What other purpose would we have? And as I told your other men, there were plenty of cottages for all of us. They chose to attack instead. You cannot fault us for defending ourselves."

"No, but you did not have to be so very good at it," a man in the back complains. "There were three of them."

"Next time send better men if you want to win."

A new voice speaks up, trying to smooth over the growing animosity between Maraud and the other man. His voice is young, his words shaped differently. English, I think. "Those men carried a huge weight on their shoulders. They could not risk divulging their purpose to you."

"They did not have to divulge anything. They simply needed to leave us alone."

One of the men in the back growls. "Watch your manners around his lordship. You are in no position to demand answers from him."

"Gentlemen," I interrupt. "Surely fighting over shelter in an entire village full of empty houses is a waste of everyone's time and energy."

Maraud frowns. "Unless you are the reason it is empty in the first place."

I can feel rather than see the other man's scowl. "It was deserted when we first came upon it."

"Then why are we fighting to the death over it?"

Silence follows and the men exchange glances. "We have only your word that you simply seek shelter." His voice is less certain than it was before.

"What else would we be doing in this godsforsaken place?"

The tall man's chest thrusts out like a rooster's. "Following us. Noting our movements and reporting back to others."

"His lordship" steps forward to place a restraining hand on the taller man's arm. "Perhaps some explanation is in order."

"Perhaps," Maraud agrees.

"Tomas, go stoke up the fire so we may have some light. I think everyone would be more at ease if we could see each other."

One of the men steps over us to the hearth and kneels down. Moments later, flames spring to life, casting a bit more light into the room. "Are there candles?" his lordship asks.

"None that we could find," I tell him. He nods to the man on his left, who slips outside, then quickly returns with two torches, and dips them into the fire.

With enough light to see by, I experience a hard jolt of surprise. I recognize his lordship from my brush with the souls of the men we killed. "This is Jorn," he says, indicating the one acting like an angered cockerel. He is shaped like a barrel and sports a bushy beard. "On his right is Crespin, and to his left is Brion. And you know Tomas over there by the fire."

Maraud pulls his knees up and rests his arms on them. "I am Maraud. She is Lucinda."

The man eyes me curiously, still discomfited that I am a woman. He is younger than the others, and dressed more finely, wearing English boots and a Burgundian cape. The other four are taller and broader, clearly the muscle of whatever operation this is.

"Now," his lordship rubs his hands as if warming them. "Let us start at the beginning. We are on a mission of critical importance. A mission many wish to keep us from. When so many are after us, it is easy enough to presume everyone is. Safer, as well."

Maraud scoots back far enough to lean against the wall. Not for warmth, I think, but so he cannot be surrounded. "You will be relieved to know that neither of us has any idea who you are or where you are going." I think of Valine and Jaspar's talk at Ransle and realize that is not completely true. I have a suspicion.

Jorn shrugs. "We have only your word on that."

"So you'll run us through right now just in case we might tell someone something that we don't even know?" I try to catch Maraud's eye, uncertain what his strategy is here.

"Forgive Jorn," the leader says. "He has served my family a long time and his loyalty often overtakes him."

Jorn speaks again, his gaze never wavering. "I think instead of running you through, we shall take you with us. You have cost us men. We need to replace them. That is how you can repay us for their deaths."

Two of the others exchange a glance, and Maraud laughs outright, which while satisfying, seems unwise. "You would force us to travel with you in the hopes that we would fight *for* you? What makes you think that we will not simply turn our swords against you instead?"

Jorn takes a menacing step forward, looming over us. "Because we outnumber you more than two to one."

"Perhaps we should say 'persuade,' rather than force," his lordship murmurs.

"Ah, now. Persuasion is something I well understand," Maraud says. "I am a mercenary and not so very hard to persuade. As long as the price is right."

"We must get to Brittany as soon as possible." Jorn's words are stiff, as if it pains him to give even that much of an explanation. "My lord has a ship to catch."

"Oho!" Maraud's voice is so full of glee that even I believe he is happy to hear this. "Now we are talking. That is where I am from. Where in Brittany?"

Jorn crosses his arms. "Why do you want to know?"

"Because I have traveled between here and there more times than I can count. If you wish to avoid other travelers, I can direct you to the least-used roads." He could not have dangled sweeter bait.

Jorn's eyes sharpen with interest. "Do you know how far it is to the coast at Nantes?"

Maraud tilts his head. "Four days' hard ride with good weather and no washed-out roads. Five or six if you run into bad weather or a big storm."

"Or more soldiers," Tomas mutters.

"Or more soldiers," Maraud agrees. "Why do you think soldiers are following you?"

This time when his lordship speaks, there is an unmistakable hauteur in his voice. "I am a person of some importance — Richard of Shrewsbury." He pauses, waiting for some response from us, but his name means nothing. At least to me.

Or Maraud. "And I am very pleased to meet you, Richard of Shrewsbury, but I'll need more than that if you're expecting me to go eight days out of my way to help you."

"I thought you said you were from Brittany?"

"I did, and I am, but I am here in France for reasons other than your convenience."

Shrewsbury rises up on his toes slightly. "I am the rightful claimant to the throne of England."

My mouth gapes open, as does Maraud's, though he recovers first. "I believe Henry the Seventh sits comfortably on that throne."

"But it is not his," Shrewsbury says vehemently. He begins pacing. "You have heard the story of the princes in the Tower, yes? How their evil uncle Richard had both of them put to death so they could not claim the throne?"

We nod.

"Well, they were successful in murdering my brother, Edward, but a loyal guard smuggled me out of the tower before they could kill me. I am on my way to Ireland to meet with those who would support my bid for the crown."

After a few moments of stunned silence, I finally speak. "My lord, we both wish you well in your endeavor, and we are truly sorry for the misunderstanding with your men over the cottage. But we have urgent business of our own — matters that affect a number of lives — and cannot be turned from our course."

"You said you were mercenaries. We could hire you. Not only for your knowledge of the roads, but because you are good in a fight."

"That is a tempting offer," Maraud concedes. "But we have pressing business of our own." When Jorn puts his hand back on his sword, Maraud continues. "However, since our road goes in the same direction for the next two days, we could travel together for greater safety and discuss it further."

Shrewsbury looks at Jorn, who nods. "We'd like that very much. Now we will all get some much-needed rest before resuming our travels tomorrow. Tomas will take the first watch. You have my word you will not be harmed tonight."

"Yes, *that* will allow us to sleep well," Maraud grumbles.

CHAPTER 74

Sybella

n the way home, my disappointment draws around me like a shroud. They are gone. There is no one from the convent to help us.

There is no one to give us insight into the regent or the king. We are on our own. That was always a possibility. The truth is, I allowed myself to believe I would find them because I wanted to. It was a weakness. An indulgence. Like telling Louise she is perfectly safe, when she lives in a world that is not.

Merde.

Not only have I lost hope of finding help at court, but I've learned that whoever wishes me dead has more allies there than I do.

We are just leaving the stable after tending to the horses when Beast steps out of the shadows. "Where have you been?" The only reason I do not jump is that I felt his heartbeat while we were still rubbing down the horses. Aeva does not so much as twitch in surprise. She must have nerves of iron.

"I went to pay Princess Marguerite a visit."

"You did what?"

"You see? That look right there? That is precisely why I did not tell you."

His eyes flame blue before he closes them and takes a deep breath. When he opens them again, he appears more in control. "Sybella. How can I keep you safe if you will not even tell me where you are going?"

Aeva keeps walking, pausing only long enough to reach out and pat Beast's cheek. "Don't worry, Angry One. I insisted on going with her, and she was perfectly safe."

This seems to appease him somewhat. "Thank Camulos someone has the sense the gods gave a turnip." While Beast's anger has faded, it is replaced somewhat by hurt. As if my not telling him has wounded him in some way.

"The only reason I did not tell you," I rush to explain, "was because I was afraid you would try to stop me."

He stares at me, eyes beseeching me to see reason. "And I would have."

"Tried."

He stares at me a beat longer. "How am I supposed to face Charlotte and Louise — especially Louise — if I must tell them something happened to you? Something you did not even trust me enough to tell me you were doing?"

His words are like a bucket of cold water and make me feel small. "Nothing happened."

"This time," he points out. "But surely even you recognize you cannot always be so lucky." He opens his mouth to say more, closes it again, then shakes his head and walks away.

On my way back to my room, I pause on the floor of the king's apartments. I can see the large double doors to his bedchamber from the landing. With thoughts of Marguerite heavy in my mind, I cannot help but wonder what sort of man he must be. A confusion of chivalry and noble ideals wrapped up in a lack of confidence and a need to assert himself. But only able to truly do so with those who are on an unequal footing with him. An eleven-year-old princess. A queen he has stripped of all power. It is an unattractive collection of traits, and yet he

does not feel evil or cruel. It is more that he is unsure of his own abilities, and until he becomes confident, we will all suffer.

The door to his bedchamber opens, followed by light feminine laughter and the lower rumble of a male voice. I duck back into the shadows in time to watch a woman emerge from the room. Katerine says something over her shoulder, then lifts her skirts and makes her way down the long hallway to the queen's apartments.

Katerine from the garden, who held Brittany in such contempt. Katerine, who claimed to have no interest in the queen, yet watched her closely. Now her interest makes sense. She is having an affair with the king. Of course she would want to pay close attention to the queen's comings and goings. And no wonder he visits the queen so infrequently.

I cannot help but feel as if the Nine themselves have all decided to piss right where I am standing.

CHAPTER 75

Genevieve

n spite of Maraud's dire prediction, I manage to catch a few hours' sleep. When I wake in the morning, Tomas and Crespin have added some of their own supplies to the remains of our pottage from last night and are heating it for breakfast.

There is little opportunity for Maraud and me to talk, but I manage to pull him aside when we go to saddle our horses. "How do we get rid of them?"

"I don't know that we do."

"We don't have time to be haring off on their behalf. Every day I linger, more innocents are at risk. I will poison them. That is the only answer."

"All of them?"

"What choice do I have?"

"We wait. We're traveling in the same direction as they are. Once we're out on the open road, our options will be greater. Besides," he adds. "There is safety —"

"In numbers. Yes, you've said. Here." I slap the vial of antidote in his hand. It is impossible to administer it without the others seeing.

He stares at it for a moment. "How I've longed to hold this very thing." His gaze flits briefly to our captors. "And now that I finally do, it is useless to me." He takes a quick swig, then hands it back.

"Not useless," I point out, tucking it back into my pouch. "It still keeps you alive. You just can't grab it and run."

"Hurry up," Jorn growls at us. "There's enough light to ride by."

"We're ready," Maraud calls back.

I lean in close. "If they are still holding us back once we clear Poitiers, I am poisoning the lot of them, the English crown be damned."

"I am sure Henry the Seventh would reward you most handsomely," Maraud says wryly.

The next two days' travel is relatively uneventful. And Maraud is right, there is a certain sense of safety when traveling in such large numbers. We even make better time because Maraud is no longer looking over his shoulder.

We spend the second night in Poitiers at an inn just inside the city gates, and I am grateful for a true bed, even one of lumpy straw. At dinner that night, Maraud is able to convince the claimant's party to continue northward with us for two more days. While it was four days' ride straight to the coast from the abandoned village, to reach the coast near Nantes will take longer. By traveling north with us, then cutting over to the coast at Sainte-Maure, they will be using a much less conventional route and will therefore be better able to avoid their enemies.

After giving Maraud his antidote the following morning, I slip all of my poisons — the night whispers and the few remaining wax pearls — out of my pack and set them in the small pouch I carry at my waist. I also secure the poisoned needles up my left sleeve. I do not wish to cause these men harm. They are committed to a cause they believe in, and I admire that. But I will not allow them to divert me from a cause I believe in just as fervently.

CHAPTER 76

Sybella

t takes me a few days to decide how I want to handle the issue of Katerine. I could approach her directly, but there is a chance she would not heed my warning to leave. And if I do what I must to convince her, well, it would be easy enough for her to report such actions back to the regent, who would be only too glad to use such accusations against me.

Besides, the more I think upon it, the more I wonder if the regent herself isn't behind this. If she cannot share pillow talk with her brother, what better than to have a loyal attendant fill his bed and report back to her?

It will be a most delicate conversation, one best had away from listening ears. So when the morning's mass is over and we all begin to file out of the chapel, I linger behind, waiting for the regent and her party to pass. "Madame Regent."

She peers down her nose as I slip into place next to her. "Lady Sybella, to what do I owe this pleasure?" Frost drips from her words.

"If it pleases you, I fear I have learned of something, and believe you are the most qualified person to guide me on the matter."

The disbelief on the regent's face is matched only by her curiosity. She glances over her shoulder at her maids of honor, motioning for them to precede her. "Pray with me," she offers.

We turn back toward the front of the church. Because I hold the cards in this game for once, I decide to stir the waters a bit.

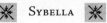

"I was surprised to hear that Princess Marguerite was within riding distance. I had assumed she would return to Austria to be with her father."

The regent looks straight ahead. "Her father has not yet arranged for her transportation."

"Surely he would be eager for a chance to see his daughter after so many years?"

The regent looks at me. "I am sure that he is, but the travel arrangements and logistics are complex. Now, what is this problem you wished my guidance on?"

I kneel before the altar and stare at the cross that hangs above it. With a sigh, she does the same.

I fold my hands, as if praying. "There is no way to sweeten this, so I will just say it straight out." I turn from the cross and look directly at her. "One of your ladies in waiting is having an affair with the king."

Her face grows immobile, as if she has just been turned to a pillar of salt. "Who?"

"Katerine."

"That is a most serious accusation to make. Why do you think this is the case?"

"I saw her coming out of the king's bedchamber, straightening her gown."

The regent's mouth purses in annoyance. "Have you been following the king?"

"Indeed no, Madame. I merely happened to be coming down the stairs while she was emerging from his room. The door is visible from the landing," I remind her.

She is quiet a long moment. "That is not proof."

I shoot her a reproachful glance. "Madame, it would be enough to ensure the dismissal of any lady of court."

She sighs then and shakes her head, as if weary. "Men have different needs, needs that a woman of your young and noble sensibilities cannot be expected to understand."

It is hard — so hard — not to laugh outright at this. "I'm sure that is true," I concede.

"And kings, even more so."

I must tread carefully here. "While serving the king in any capacity is an honor, does not the queen's honor bear some consideration?" Before she can answer, I continue. "The ladies surrounding the queen, indeed, the entire royal family, must be above reproach. Are those not the ideals you have instilled in countless young women?"

"Of course." Her voice is terse, like a piece of ribbon pulled too tight.

"It is hard to imagine what the families of all those girls would say if they learned—"

"You have made your point. What is it you want?"

"The same thing that you want, Madame Regent. To ensure the power and legitimacy of France. I think we can all agree that the sooner the queen is with child, the better for all concerned. Surely providing an heir is the best way to ensure the pope delivers the much-needed dispensation? The pope would never allow the dauphin of France to be called a bastard."

She stares at me a long, hard minute. "You're right, Lady Sybella. I appreciate the discretion you exercised in bringing this to my attention. I will be certain it is addressed in an appropriate way." She stands, taking a moment to straighten her skirts. "Does the queen know of this?"

I rise to my feet as well. "No, Madame. I felt that if the problem went away, she need never know. I see no sense in hurting her with such information."

She looks at me, a faint glimmer of approval in her eyes. "Good. It will be taken care of. Now, if you will excuse me, I will leave you to your prayers."

I do not think she would be so willing to leave me to my prayers if she knew how many of them involved asking for deliverance from her.

CHAPTER 77

Genevieve

n the afternoon of the fourth day of our travels with Shrewsbury, Maraud draws his horse to the side of the road and points. "There." Up ahead is a crossroad marker. "The west fork leads to Brittany, the north to Tours."

"The west, of course," Jorn says.

As we draw nearer the fork in the road, I realize the marker is not a sign, but a cross made of ancient knobby wood, polished white with age.

The road that curves west has a steam running along the south of it. Gallopine, thirsty, makes for the water's edge. I dismount to let her drink, and the others do the same. While the brook burbles cheerfully enough, a thick silence lies over the small valley. On the northern slope are two granite outcroppings. No. Not outcroppings, but ancient standing stones. I look back over my shoulder to the cross in the road, staring at it more carefully. It is not made of wood. The realization scuttles along my spine like a tiny spider. "What is this place?" I ask Maraud in a low voice.

He glances up to see if the others are within earshot. "One of Saint Camulos's old shrines." His gaze moves over the stones, the wood grove, and back to the stones. "The French might not recognize him any longer, but his shrines and old altars are still known to some.

It is also why the road is less traveled. It is an old, old road from a much earlier time."

That explains why the air feels not only heavy, but thinner as well. As if just on the other side of it, the gods sit watching. It is most unsettling, yet wondrous as well. I look back at the cross. "What sort of bones are those?"

Maraud regards me steadily. "You already know the answer to that question."

Just then Jorn comes barging over. "How far to the coast from here?"

"Three days."

"I don't know how long the captain will hold our ship, so after your horses are watered, let's move out."

"Actually," Maraud says, "this is where Lucinda and I part ways with you."

Jorn takes a step closer. "That was not our agreement." His ire draws the attention of the others.

"If you'll remember, we never actually agreed to anything besides traveling with you as long as our roads went in the same direction. Here is where they do not."

Jorn crosses his arms across his chest and plants his legs wide, as if he is some barrier we dare not pass. Shrewsbury hurries over, his casual arrogance giving way to dismay. "Surely you don't mean that? Your knowledge has been invaluable to us."

"You don't need it anymore. I've saved you two days' travel time and steered you clear of those who would follow you. That is more than enough compensation for the men you lost, especially since it was self-defense."

Jorn glowers at Maraud. Neither man blinks. Slowly, I slip my hand into my pouch, nudging aside the vial and the wax pearls until my hand closes around the silver box. "We will make you come with us. Tie you to your horses if need be."

Maraud laughs. "What will that gain you? Do you think I will happily call out directions while chained to my horse?"

Jorn's face reddens with anger, but Tomas calls out. "Cease your bickering and come look at this." He points back to the road.

In the far distance, a party of mounted knights approach. Jorn whirls on Maraud. "I told you we were not free of our enemies!"

Ignoring him, Maraud hops up on a boulder, shielding his eyes from the glare to get a better view. "I don't think they're after you."

My head snaps up.

"Then who? You?" Jorn scowls. "You brought danger upon us?"

Maraud hops back down from the boulder. "Didn't mean to. Besides, you waylaid me, remember?"

"D'Albret?" I ask under my breath.

Maraud nods, too distracted to boast that he's been right all this time.

Shrewsbury frowns. "How many are there?"

"Twenty. And they're approaching fast."

"We are seven against twenty!" Shrewsbury's voice goes high with concern. "Can we get off the road and let them pass? Surely that will be the fastest way to get rid of them."

"Except there are no good hiding places nearby. They will see you before you reach the trees."

"What do we do?"

"Fight or run," Maraud says.

"This is *your* fight, mercenary," Jorn says. "Not ours. We will not be dragged into it."

Crespin says more calmly, "Our first duty is to our lord. We must protect him at all costs."

"Then you'd best get going. These men will not care about your loyalty if you are in the way of what they want."

"But what of you?" Tomas looks faintly uneasy.

"I'll run. And when I can't run any longer, I'll fight."

Just as I wonder what he thinks I will be doing this entire time, he shoots me a long, intense look. "But take Lucinda with you."

"What?" I stare at him in horror.

Jorn and Tomas exchange a glance, then look to Shrewsbury, who nods his agreement.

"You hay-wit! Just because those cowards are leaving you to fight alone doesn't mean I will."

Maraud grabs me by the arm and walks me away from the others. "Stop it." He gives my arm a shake. "D'Albret wants me. Not you. They may hurt me, but they'll keep me alive because their lord wants me alive. I can't guarantee they'll grant you the same courtesy."

I will not accept this. Not accept that I am powerless to help.

"Lucinda, these men are capable of terrible cruelty. You've seen them fight. You've seen how little they care for fairness or honor. I assure you, they are capable of many vile things. Things I could not bear any woman to suffer, especially not you."

I open my mouth to argue, but Maraud tightens his grip on my arm and thrusts me at Jorn. "Take her away from here. Now."

He strides over to his horse and vaults into the saddle. "Hurry," he says. "They are almost at the fork. Best if they don't see you. If they do, they might not be able to resist giving chase."

That spurs the men to action. Jorn picks me up, carries me over to Gallopine, and dumps me in the saddle. Tomas has already mounted and draws alongside me. "You know he is right about this," he says. "Can we trust you to come of your own accord, or must I take control of your reins?"

"I'll come willingly," I promise even while plotting a way to get free. Not because I am stupid—Maraud is right. I do not want to imagine the cruelty Pierre could inflict. But it is my fault he must face them at all. I may have freed him from the oubliette, but I also put him in d'Albret's path.

He also did not ask for the antidote, which disturbs me. Does he not intend to be taken alive?

Fortunately, Shrewsbury's men are focused on getting their lord to safety and their allegiance to Maraud is slim. A quarter mile down the road, when I turn Gallopine and head back, there is only a halfhearted protest.

Tomas alone rides after me—hoping to stop me, I think. Until he unhooks one of the crossbows from his saddle and holds it out to me. "Here. You will need this."

As I take it from him, he gives me a nod, then turns to catch up to the others.

CHAPTER 78

'Albret's troops are not yet in sight, so I steer Gallopine toward the grove of linden trees and use them to hide my approach. By the time I reach their cover, d'Albret's men are at the fork. The bulk of their party advances down after us, but a smaller group keeps riding north. Are they heading to Tours on other business? Or planning to surround us?

I rein Gallopine in, slip silently from her back, and tie her to a nearby trunk. Taking Tomas's crossbow and my sword, I use the trees to conceal my movements and work my way back to where I last saw Maraud. He did not stand still as we rode away, but turned off onto the verge and headed north, making for the granite stones. Best to face one's enemies with something solid at your back. Or mayhap he knows it is a strategy of theirs to attempt to surround their quarry and thought to neutralize that possibility.

I pick a spot well hidden among the trees, drop to the ground, and remove the four bolts attached to the crossbow's frame. Opening the pouch at my waist, I grab a handful of the wax pearls. I am a good enough shot with a bow, but it takes an excellent shot and a good dose of luck to make every shot a killing one. It will not hurt to increase my odds.

I stab a pearl onto the point of one of the bolts, then smear it over the tip, careful to avoid getting any on my fingers. When I glance up, d'Albret's men have reached our watering spot and Maraud's trail. I hastily grab three more pearls, smear the rest of the crossbow bolts, then snap them back in place.

Over a dozen hoofbeats thud along the dirt. Under the cover of their noise, I leap to my feet, crossbow cocked and ready, and weave my way toward the clearing.

With a suddenness that is so unexpected it feels shocking, the churning hooves come to a stop. Thick silence follows.

"Gentlemen." Maraud's jaunty voice cuts through the menacing silence. "To what do I owe this pleasure?"

"He said you'd be expecting us."

"He was wrong."

As they talk, I resume my creeping. I am nearly in position. And once I can see them, I can shoot them.

"He also said there'd be a girl with you."

"She and I parted ways back in Poitiers."

"And yet you rode out from Poitiers with a party of six."

Figs! They've been tailing us that long.

"How brave of you to make your move when I am alone."

At last I reach the second row of trees before the valley. Maraud and Mogge are up against the granite drop with twelve — no, fifteen — mounted soldiers in front of him. They are in a V-shaped formation, with three men facing him and the rest lined up behind them.

"It is only you our lord wants. You should feel flattered."

"As a rabbit feels flattered when surrounded by a pack of jackals."

"Watch your tongue."

What is Maraud's strategy? He must have one in mind rather than simply inflaming their tempers.

"Can you tell me what this job of your lord's entails? I've many offers for work and would like to weigh them all carefully."

As the leader opens his mouth to answer, Maraud draws his sword and charges, catching the knights off-guard.

But I am ready. Using the distraction of his charge, I fire the first bolt, aiming for the man closest to me. It catches him in the shoulder. Not a killing blow — except for the poison.

I get a second shot off, this time hitting my target in the chest. The fall from his horse calls the attention of the others from the fight in front of them to the downed knights.

My third shot pierces a soldier's thigh and someone calls out a warning. Nearly out of time, I fire my fourth bolt, striking one of the men in the arm. He plucks it out and turns his horse toward me before the poison takes hold.

I must leave. Now. I have increased Maraud's chances — it is only one against eleven — no nine, he has already killed two himself — instead of one against fifteen.

Three of the soldiers break out of formation and head for the trees behind me, trying to cut off my escape route. I quickly calculate how long it will take to reach Gallopine — too long. I swear in annoyance and draw my sword and dagger.

The first of d'Albret's soldiers is upon me. He raises his sword, then stiffens, falling to the ground, a crossbow bolt protruding from his back. A second bolt embeds itself in the next closest man. I only have time to wonder if Shrewsbury and his men returned before a third bolt finishes off the last of the men headed my way. That shot is followed by a jubilant whoop as four soldiers emerge from the stone — no, not the stone but a narrow passageway — brandishing swords and pikes like the furies of the gods.

"What took you so long?" Maraud calls out, then it erupts into a melee — churning horses, shouts, and cries, and the nearly deafening sound of sword against sword.

And heartbeats. So many hearts are beating within my chest that I must press my hand over it and sit down for fear it will explode.

The pounding of my heart continues to grow and multiply as those around me draw close to death, but the sounds of battle begins to fade. Forcing myself to my feet, and keeping one hand tightly on my sword, I creep back to the clearing. Someone — a woman? — drives a sword into a fallen man's chest. It is the last of d'Albret's soldiers. The rest lie dead or wounded, their blood staining the floor of the small valley.

The first of the souls leaves its body just then, a whoosh like a bat swooping down from the sky. It is followed by another and another until the entire valley is awash in souls — vile souls with fleeting images of deeds and thoughts that almost make me retch.

Utter stillness follows as the last of them dies, and once again, it is only my own heart beating in my chest.

Finally able to look up, I see Maraud grinning at Jaspar and Valine. Tassin and Andry are slowly making their way toward the others.

"What in the name of Camulos's teeth took you so long?" Maraud swipes his forearm across his brow. He is wounded, but doesn't seem to notice.

"We thought they were planning to surround you, so we went to head them off. Turns out they simply had someplace else to go."

I stare in stunned silence. Maraud was *expecting* them?

There is only one meaning I can glean from this, and I do not like it at all.

Maraud sees me just then, the humor leaching from his face, leaving it gray and haggard. "What are you doing here? You were supposed to be safe."

Is that concern he is feeling? Or dismay that his plans have been discovered?

"I returned to help."

Valine claps a hand on Maraud's shoulder. "It's a good thing she did. She picked off four waiting for their turn to get to you. Not even you could have taken on nine men at once."

"You were supposed to be safe with the others," he repeats stubbornly.

"And you were supposed to be taken by d'Albret's men. Not all goes according to plan."

He struggles with whatever emotion he is feeling — anger? fear? regret? — then casts it aside and grins. His smile is so wide and inviting and full of joy that it is all I can do not to forgive him everything there on the spot. "Well, you are safe, and you saved my hide, so I can't help but be glad."

But his smile does not reach the cold place in my heart. The place that realizes he arranged for this — all of this, as far back as Ransle. He told his friends to meet him here. Whether because he was certain of d'Albret's pursuit or because he always intended to overpower me, I do not know. Not yet, anyway.

CHAPTER 79

he horses and weapons will fetch a pretty penny," Andry says. I cannot place what is different about him — ah! He is smiling. The first time I have ever seen him do so. "We'll get more for them than we'd have gotten fighting for d'Albret."

"Those we won't want to keep for ourselves," Tassin grunts.

Maraud slaps Andry on the back. "You may both stand here and count your stacks of coin if you wish, but I'd like to make camp before nightfall."

"Where?" I ask, having no desire to sleep in this valley tonight.

"Up there." Maraud points to the small ridge behind the granite outcroppings that overlook the valley. "But first, I need to wash some of this blood off in that stream."

By the time we have collected all the horses and Andry and Tassin have retrieved everything of value, we must scramble to make camp and secure the animals in the quickly fading light. But these soldiers are old hands at it, made even more efficient by their many years together.

I do not say much, allowing the occasional chatter of the others to swirl around me like sparks from the campfire. Everyone is quieter tonight, far more so than when we were in Ransle. Whether it is due to the bodies we left behind or some other reason, I don't know. Maraud volunteers for first watch.

As he disappears down the path toward the watch post, Tassin casts me an unreadable sideways glance. "You came back for him."

"I did," I say simply.

He nods his head and grunts in approval.

❧❀❧

Some time later, I find Maraud leaning against a boulder, his long legs stretched out in front of him, looking down over the valley even though it is too dark for him to see. His hair is still damp from his dip in the stream.

"You're supposed to be on watch."

He glances over at me and grins. "That is the beauty of the high ground. I can sit in comfort and survey everything below me."

"Not many would consider cuddling up to a boulder to be comfortable."

"Try it." He shifts to the side, making room for me to stand beside him.

I remain where I am. "What is that place, truly?"

"Camulos's Cup." He plucks a strand of grass from where it grows in the crevice of the rock. "It's not only one of his old shrines, but a place where a few can take on many. And win."

From this vantage point, it is clear to see. "The entire valley is the altar, and the dead you leave there are his offering."

He runs the grass through his fingers. "Trust one of Mortain's daughters to recognize the stark truth of it."

"So if d'Albret's men hadn't come along, was Shrewsbury's party to be the sacrifice? Or me?" I don't truly believe that, but this whole day has turned my beliefs upside down.

"Saints, no! Why would you even think such a thing?"

"Because you clearly planned this. Planned for them to meet us here. You arranged it back in Ransle."

"Yes, but not so I could sacrifi—"

"You betrayed me!" No worse than I have planned to betray him, a small voice reminds me.

"No! I sent the others on ahead because I was afraid d'Albret would pursue us. And I was right."

414

Some of my anger leaves me. "I think that you planned this all along so you could overpower me and make your escape."

He stares at me a long moment, not certain he has heard me. "I was hoping I could persuade you to let me — let us — help you, but I would not have forced you."

In that moment, something stirs within my chest. Something as nebulous and fragile as the blade of grass he holds in his fingers. As small and tentative as it is, it terrifies me. "You can't help. Only one is required for what I must do."

"God's teeth! Even assassins need help sometimes — and you do. I can tell by how it gnaws at you."

"You couldn't be more wrong. Don't you get it? I never needed your help. I only needed something to trade. I was going to hand you over . . ."

"Hand me over to whom?"

I look down over the ridge toward the valley. "I hadn't figured that out yet. There are still too many unknowns. Especially given the matter of your identity." My voice softens. I have started this boulder rolling downhill, but I have no wish to flatten him with it. "You are Crunard's son, and there is a reason he is no longer the chancellor of Brittany."

Beside me, Maraud grows very still. "What are you saying?"

"I am saying that your father betrayed his country." I lift my gaze back to his. "He very nearly delivered the duchess into the hands of the French."

Instead of showing shock or anger, Maraud smiles bitterly. "I know."

His confession takes a moment to sink in. "You *knew?*"

"The guards at my first prison told me, wanting to be certain I suffered as much as possible."

"Did they tell you why?"

"That he threw aside his honor — his family's honor — for the one who has always been a thorn in his side? Yes, they told me." The piece of grass now lies shredded in his palm.

"The regent coerced him. He was not the only one she got to. Many of the duchess's most trusted advisors were being paid by her." Annoyed that I am comforting him, I return to the matter at hand. "Regardless, I never required an escort for my safety. I was never *rescuing* you. From the moment I first threw back the grate on the oubliette and told you to come with me, I have only ever had one purpose in mind. And that was to take you directly to court and trade your freedom for that of others."

His face remains impassive, only the tightening around his eyes showing my words have stung. "Tell me of these innocents you need to save."

"It is official convent business, which I am forbidden to speak of."

"I will happily exchange myself for those innocents, if I can bring Cassel to justice first."

I gape in disbelief. "Why would you do that?"

"Because my father's actions are a stain on my name and honor as well as my family's. One of us must shoulder that burden and I am the only one left. Besides, I told you I seek justice for the crime I witnessed on the battlefield. What better place to find answers about the king's general than with the king himself?"

As I stare into his determined eyes, a faint sense of panic fills me. "This is not your sin. You shouldn't have to pay for it."

Maraud's face grows hard. "It is a wrong my family committed. That is how honor works. But there was also a wrong committed against my family, and I would avenge that first."

"What wrong?"

His lips flatten, and he returns his gaze to the valley below us. "Remember the nobles I saw slain? One of them . . . one of them was my brother. Ives."

The ghost, I realize. The one that he spoke of back in the oubliette.

"I had been fighting beside him when he was taken — the pikeman knocked me to the ground before I could reach him. I started to get up, to go after him, but Ives motioned me to stay silent. He knew, I think, what a weapon my name could be in their hands. But in the end, when the sword swung down on his neck, I couldn't help myself. I called out. That's when they realized I was still alive, and who I was."

"And you were taken."

His eyes — normally so full of good humor or keen wit — are haunted before he quickly shutters them. "And I was taken."

It doesn't matter. I will not hand him over to the king to answer for his family's crimes. Only my life, my body, is mine to trade. I realize now that some part of me decided this a long time ago, the same part that understood that if I did that, I was no different than the abbess handing me over to Count Angoulême to do with what he would. Making that sort of bargain, no matter how well I come out of it, feels like I lose something more important than I am willing to pay.

"Yes," I tell him. "You must see to justice for Ives. And your father."

"My father?" He shakes his head, disgust plain on his face.

"It would be a poor father who was not tempted by the offer to save his only son," I point out. "It was the regent who dangled that in front of him. It was the regent who ordered you thrown into the oubliette. There is vengeance to be had there, and you must see to your family's justice. I will see to mine."

"But how? You won't have me to trade?"

I laugh. "That was only one of my plans. I have many options up my sleeve. Have no worry on that account."

"I don't like this." His voice is edged with an anger I do not fully understand.

"I don't care."

After a long moment he looks back over the valley, the entire landscape varying shades of gray in the feeble moonlight. While his face is impassive, I can feel the turbulence of his emotions, shifting the night air as surely as a breeze. It is hard, but I give him time to come to terms with all that I have just told him. Time to realize he is not coming with me.

When he turns back, his face is impassive. "And what of the poison?"

And there it is. He has just given me the perfect weapon with which to drive him away. There is even a story they tell in the new Church, of one of the Christ's disciples denying him three times. "What poison?"

Maraud glowers at me, his face harder than the granite at his back. "The one you've been feeding me the antidote to for the last ten days."

I reach for the pouch at my belt, pluck the small vial from its depths. "You mean this antidote?" As he nods, I remove the cork and dump the contents on the ground.

Reflexively, he lunges forward, then stops himself. He looks from the damp spot on the ground back to me, his jaw clenched.

"There is no poison. And no antidote. It was nothing but a ploy. Water flavored with bitter herbs to make you believe it was real. I have never poisoned you. I only needed a way to ensure your cooperation."

He reaches out and grabs my chin, forcing my gaze to his. The look of utter betrayal in his eyes guts me. Good. That will make this easier. I jerk out of his grasp, but do not look away.

"I gave you my word." He is angry. Angry that I doubted him. Angry that I questioned his honor.

"And I didn't trust you." But I did. I have. In so many other things. "You yourself said it was my weakness."

He grits his teeth in frustration. "I will not let you face this alone. Just like you would not let me face d'Albret alone."

"Don't put too much importance on that. It was simply guilt. After all, I was the one who put you in his path to begin with."

"That was sheer bad luck! You are also the one who freed me."

"So I could turn you in."

"And yet," he says softly, "now you are now telling me I am free to go."

Frustration roils inside me, nearly choking back all the words I need to say. "Very well." I nod brusquely. "You are right. It is your choice, after all."

He is stunned at my quick capitulation, but I have had enough. He is a fool, and he can live with the consequences. I peer at the horizon. "How long until dawn, do you think?"

As he turns around to glance at the sky, I reach for the pouch at my waist.

"Three hours. Maybe four." When he turns back to ask why, I hold my cupped hand up between us.

"I am sorry," I whisper.

He frowns. "For what?"

"This." And then I blow.

CHAPTER 80

t first, nothing happens. He looks from me to my hand and back again, opening his mouth to ask a question. Before the words can form, his eyes roll back in his head and his entire body goes slack.

I leap forward, catching his shoulders and easing him onto the ground.

I lay his head gently on a tuft of dead grass, straightening his neck so that he will not awake with a crick in it. I try to arrange his body as comfortably as I can, but he is heavy, and it is like trying to arrange a pile of stones.

When I am done, I lean close to his face to make certain he is breathing, then lift one of his eyelids to check his reaction to the night whispers. He is large, and I used only a small amount. I reckon he will sleep four hours, maybe five, but enough for me to put some serious distance between us.

I stare down at him, refusing to indulge in guilt or remorse or any of the dozen feelings running through me. He has already created more complications in a hopelessly complicated situation. The convent must come first.

Even so, I allow myself one last indulgence. I lean in close and press my lips to his. They are as soft and warm as I remember. *So*, I think, as I pull back, *that is what true honor tastes like.* I press my hands to my lips to seal the memory, and say a quick prayer to Camulos to guard him as he sleeps. Now there is nothing to stand between me and my duty to the convent.

When the eastern sky finally begins to lighten enough that I can ride, I return to the camp where the others are still sleeping. I search out Andry and kneel down to shake his shoulder. He comes awake immediately. "I wasn't able to sleep, so I took the last watch. I must continue on my way, but Maraud will be traveling with you. Well"—I grimace—"once he has slept off all the wine he drank. Good luck to you all," I tell him, and mean it.

He will need it once Maraud awakens and realizes what I've done.

CHAPTER 81

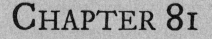

Sybella

onight's dinner in the grand salon has been a quiet affair. The king is relaxed, almost bored, his gaze wandering aimlessly among his guests. He has spoken politely to the queen the few times she has ventured to speak to him, but he does not seek out her conversation. More and more messengers have been arriving, and he spends longer with his advisors attending to matters of state. This short month they had to get to know each other is drawing to a close. It has been hard enough to cultivate any intimacy between them. How much harder will it be once we are at the full court?

I glance around the hall, looking once more to be certain I haven't missed Katerine. But no, she is not at supper. Has Madame sent her packing already? If so, that was an easy victory.

And suggests that she wasn't planted by Madame. Who is also not here, I note.

A page appears at my shoulder, offering to refill my goblet. With the matter of the king's affair attended to, I allow my mind to circle back to the moles. I cannot travel to Cognac, but what if I called them into service from here? Would they come if they simply received a letter containing a crow feather and a single word naming where to meet?

Yes. They are convent trained and have been waiting for this for years. As initiates of Mortain, they are resourceful. The hardest part would be getting the message to Cognac, but surely the king corresponds with Angoulême regularly. What if I could sneak it into that courier pouch without his knowledge? Or the regent's.

A slight commotion at the door draws my attention, my heart sinking as the regent appears. Can the woman be summoned by one's thoughts like some gorgon from the oldest of hearth tales?

Beside her is a man I've not seen before. He is tall and pleasant enough of feature, except for his eyes, which are both calculating and contemptuous. It does not bode well for whatever business he has with the crown. My gaze is drawn back to the regent, who wears a faint satisfied smile. It is so imperceptible that I almost miss it. Until she looks at me. The smile deepens.

My stomach sours, and all the food I have just eaten turns to lead. Unease snakes along my shoulders, and I allow the fingers of my right hand to dip under my sleeve for the reassuring feel of my knives.

A hush falls over the room as the regent and her guest make their way to the dais. The king straightens in his chair, looking faintly annoyed.

Whatever the regent's purpose, it is not entertainment. I am as sure of that as I am that the sun will rise in the morning.

When she reaches the high table, she curtsies. "Your Majesty."

"Dearest sister." His voice contains a sour note. Is he wroth with her over his banished favorite? Maybe this guest is someone she plans to use to get back in his good graces. "Who have you brought before us?"

"This, my dear brother, is Monsieur Simon de Fremin, and he comes to you with a most urgent matter."

"Urgent enough that it must interrupt my honeymoon? Not to mention my dinner?" I take heart at his growing annoyance.

The man himself — Monsieur Fremin — steps nimbly forward, ignoring the regent's quelling stare. "It is imperative that I speak with you at once, Your Majesty. As for interrupting your dinner — and your honeymoon — both my liege and myself regret that deeply, but the matter pertains to those here at court with you, Your Majesty."

Interest piqued, the king shifts forward. "And who is your liege, Monsieur Fremin?"

"Pierre d'Albret, Viscount of Limoges."

His words clamp around my chest, forcing all the air from my lungs. Pierre. The regent is working with Pierre. Truly, I cannot draw breath.

It should not surprise me — it was Pierre who negotiated with the regent to hand Nantes over to France. But I never dreamed he would appeal to her on such a personal matter.

My heart resumes beating — but too fast. I grip the edge of the table and force myself to take slow, deep breaths.

The king is frowning. "What possible urgent business does the Viscount of Limoges have with us?" he asks.

Fremin's eyes flicker ever so briefly to the queen, and I wonder if he knows she was once the house of d'Albret's most sought-after prize. "It is a matter of utmost importance and speaks to the sovereignty of a man over his own household." A hush goes round the salon. This is far better than a mere troubadour's tale or minstrel's tune.

The queen glances in my direction before reaching out and gently touching the king's elbow. When he begrudgingly turns to her, she speaks in low tones, looking meaningfully at the door behind the dais, hopefully suggesting this would better be handled in private. But Pierre's lawyer is a master of showmanship. Before the king can agree, Fremin continues speaking, his voice pitched perfectly so all in the room can hear.

"Lord Pierre d'Albret respectfully requests that you return his sisters, whom you now hold in your possession, to his custody as soon as possible."

A number of curious eyes turn toward me, but I keep my attention politely focused on the dais. The king scowls in confusion. "You are mistaken. I do not harbor any of d'Albret's family here."

The regent leans forward. "Oh, but you do, Your Majesty. Lady Sybella d'Albret is one of your queen's ladies in waiting."

At my name, a faint expression of surprise flickers across the lawyer's face — surprise and a faint note of alarm. He was not expecting *me* to be here, only Charlotte and Louise.

So there is my answer as to who sent the assassin.

The king turns to his wife. "Is this true?"

The queen sits straight and tall in her chair. "It is true that Lady Sybella has served loyally as one of my ladies in waiting for quite some time. She is one of my most valued attendants and here at my request."

The king leans back in his chair, his face clearing. "Well, there you have it. Surely d'Albret's sister can receive no greater honor than serving as attendant to his queen?"

The king's blithe dismissal catches Fremin off-guard, for it is true that serving the royal household in such a fashion is a great privilege bestowed upon very few. That is no doubt one of the reasons they wished me conveniently buried in the forest somewhere. He must tread carefully here. As must I. Every muscle in my body is corded so tightly that I fear they will snap.

"I am sure Lord d'Albret is beholden to you for bestowing such great distinction upon his house. However, as you know, daughters are meant to be married to forge new alliances and strengthen a family's political ties. With so many recent deaths in his family and the loss of lands that had been promised to him —" He risks a glance at the queen, for it was her lands and hand in marriage that had been promised to him. "He is forced to create these new alliances as soon as possible."

The queen's lip curls in contempt, and even the king's mild humor dissipates at the reference to Brittany, brought under his rule at such great cost to so many.

Seeing his misstep, the lawyer changes tactics. "Besides, two of the girls are far too young to serve as attendants to Her Majesty. Lord d'Albret respectfully requests their return so he may arrange for their education as well as suitable marriages."

The king turns to the queen. "We have the younger sisters, too?" He sounds slightly aggrieved, as if what once promised to be of mild interest now demands a true hearing.

"We do," the queen says calmly. "Since their mother died some time ago and their only sister serves in my household, I agreed to take them in as wards and see to their education. However, Your Majesty, I believe these are family matters and best discussed in private."

"Very well." He turns to the lawyer. "We will discuss this further with you tomorrow. Until then, please accept our hospitality." It is a tepid offer — a mere formality and not a true welcome.

The man starts to protest, but the regent knows when to quit the field and motions for the steward. Fremin is taken by the elbow, turned around, and escorted from the hall.

While everyone's attention is focused on the retreating figure, I slip silently from my seat like a wisp of smoke and drift to the side door used by the servants.

I must see if anyone accompanies Pierre's lawyer. If he is traveling alone, then he is only pressing a legal claim, a simple enough problem.

When I reach the balcony above the anteroom that the steward uses for those awaiting entrance to the king's presence, four men linger there. Even though I have not seen them in more than two years, their presence sends shards of ice down my spine. Yann le Poisson, Maldon the Pious, the Mouse, and the Marquis. I clench my fists in an effort to stop the trembling in my limbs. When it does not work, I press my back against the solid stone wall behind me.

This is no mere diplomatic mission. He intends to take the girls by force if necessary.

⊶⥈

I mount the stairs two at a time, racing for the east tower. With every step, I assure myself that my sisters are safe. Aeva and Tola and Tephanie are with them. The d'Albret henchman have only just arrived, and I saw them with my own eyes loitering in the gallery.

But what if those were not the only men who accompanied the lawyer?

When I reach the fifth floor in the east tower, I force myself to walk more slowly. It will not do to burst into the room and terrify my sisters.

The corridor is empty but for myself, so that is good.

Before entering the chamber, I pause, shaking out my hands in an attempt to stop their trembling. I straighten my shoulders and pinch my cheeks, knowing that fear has leached all the color from them. Only then do I allow myself to open the door.

Tola and Tephanie look up from where they sit on the rug in front of the fire, their heads close together, shoulders touching as they play with Louise.

"Sybella!" Louise calls out joyfully. "Come play with us!"

"Perhaps in a minute, sweeting," I tell her as I close the door behind me.

Aeva looks up from where she is sitting in a chair with a piece of linen in her hand. Charlotte stands just behind her, watching. As I head for the window, I glance down at the square of fabric Aeva holds. "When did you take up embroidery?"

"When I feared I would begin slapping my fellow ladies in waiting out of sheer boredom." She stands, tosses her embroidery to the floor, and follows me. "Something is amiss." She keeps her voice pitched low.

I glance at the others. They have returned to their games, except for Charlotte, who pretends she is watching the others play even as her eyes follow Aeva and me.

When we reach the window, I lift the heavy velvet curtains and peer outside. Using the curtains to muffle my words, I tell Aeva what has happened. She gives a sharp nod, then looks out the window as well. "The wall is steep. I do not think they can get in that way."

I squint my eyes. I had been certain only a mouse could climb that wall, and that is who Pierre has sent. I let the curtain drop back into place and move to the second window. The view out of it is much the same. "They will likely come through the door," I tell her. "But we cannot rule out an attempt to climb the wall."

Tola becomes aware that Aeva and I are not discussing the weather and hurries over to join us.

"What are you looking at?" Louise asks, but Tephanie, also realizing something is amiss, distracts her by capturing one of her game pieces on the board.

"For now, I want you two to stay with Tephanie and the girls at all times. The queen will not object, I am certain. I will talk with Beast, and we will come up with a plan. I think it will be best if you and the girls are gone from here as soon as possible."

Aeva looks out the window at the impossible climb, then back at me. "If you think it best, I will not argue."

Something inside me relaxes. I had feared she might make light of my concerns or, worse, mock them. Before I can thank her, Charlotte appears in front of me. "I have my knife," she says. "Tephanie and Tola have been teaching me how to use it."

As I look down at her, I cannot help but remember how she hesitated in the garden, uncertain if she would follow Pierre or stay with me. I bring my face down closer to hers. "But would you use it against Pierre's men?"

Charlotte pulls the knife from the silver chain at her waist, studying the point of it. "Yes," she says at last, a strange light in her eye. "I would." Her voice is flat, emotionless. Aeva and I exchange glances. Charlotte looks up at me, fully meeting my gaze. "Especially to protect Louise."

Chapter 82

e do not need to go anywhere." Beast's voice is calm and steadying. It makes me want to scream.

"I'm not going to let them take my sisters. If you will not come with me, we will leave without you."

"Stop." He places his large hands on my shoulders, as if holding my body in place will cease my racing thoughts. "Pierre's lawyer will not take your sisters without the king's permission, and we do not know yet if he will give it."

Not wanting him to feel the trembling I cannot control, I shrug his hands off and continue pacing. "He will if the regent has her way. How did I not foresee this unholy alliance?"

"Is it possible she just found him cooling his heels in the gallery and thought to use him to her advantage?"

I snort. "I am not certain *she* did not reach out to Pierre directly. After all, they conspired once before when the French took Nantes." I stop pacing and turn on him. "Why do you not think it is so?"

He runs his hand over his head, his eyes bleak. "Because I do not want to believe the regent is that ruthless or evil." He shakes his head. "She cannot know the truth about the d'Albret household."

I consider this a moment. "You are likely correct," I concede grudgingly. "Few paid any heed to the rumors. There is a good chance the tales of his wives' fates did not make it to the regent's ears."

"Do you think it would change the regent's position if she knew —"

"No. She would not allow herself to believe it — not if it meant seeing me in a different light. Besides, someone gave the assassin the means to navigate the traps set in the forest. It was clear that the lawyer was surprised to see me."

"So Pierre sent the assassin." His hands flex, as if longing for a neck to wring.

"Yes. With me out of the way, the legal case is clear-cut, and there is no question a decision would be in Pierre's favor. It may still be after he speaks with the king. Besides, it will not matter. Pierre has sent his henchmen as well as a lawyer."

Beast grows utterly still even as I feel his heart begin to beat faster. "How do you know?"

"Because I saw them in the antechamber."

"How can you be certain they are not simply his travel escort?"

"Because I know them — Yann le Poisson, as cold as the fish he is named for. Maldon the Pious, who plays the penitent after his killing is done. The Marquis —"

"All right. I take your point." He shakes his head. "It is hard to believe he thinks to simply snatch the girls from the king's palace."

"That is precisely what he intends to do if the king's decision does not go his way."

"They will at least wait and hear what the king's decision is before acting, will they not?"

"I believe so. But they did not count on my still being alive. I don't know how that will affect their plans."

"Let's at least wait and see what direction the king is inclined to go in. If he decides in your favor, it will be the highest level of safety and refuge available to you and the girls."

"If." It is all I can do not to snarl. "Do you know how many men in positions of power have offered my family protection when we most desperately needed it?" Even as our mothers grew unaccountably ill, or fell down stairs, or had hunting accidents? "None. Not a single one came to our aid or offered us protection." Even when my true father, Mortain, finally came, it was many years too late, and he was here so briefly that it feels like naught but a dream. A cruel dream that echoed all the cruel dreams that came before. Despair, as insistent as a jilted lover, pulls hard on my sleeve. "There is no reason to believe the king will do so." Not with the regent whispering in his ear.

Beast steps forward and wraps his enormous arms around me, as if he could reach back through time and spare me from my past. "Except you," I amend. "You came."

"But not for you," he whispers against my hair.

No. For his sister. "Did you know that was when I fell in love with you? When I learned you had come back for Alyse. Besides," I murmur against his chest, "when it mattered most of all, you *did* come for me." The memory of it — of that impossible escape — causes a lump to rise in my throat. Would that such a daring rescue could save us all now. Afraid I will start leaking all over his be-damned shoulder, I push away and resume trying to piece together a strategy. "You did not see how annoyed the king was to be bothered with such things. How baffled he was that his queen had made such a decision without informing him."

"She made it long before she was queen."

"He did not give her a chance to explain that."

"Perhaps that is what she is explaining to him in private."

"Perhaps."

"I know the queen will argue on my behalf, but I don't know that the king will listen. The regent has done all she can to erode any fragile trust that might grow between them. I am no longer certain he will support her simply to favor his new queen." While the queen is a strong woman, she is not strong enough to grant me this most simple of boons. At least not yet.

"Sybella." Beast does not try to hug me again but instead takes my hand. "If you run, they will chase you. There is nothing you could do that would more incite the king's interest and get his blood up."

He is right. The very fact of having to chase me will guarantee my guilt in his eyes. "I cannot sit here twiddling my thumbs while my sisters' safety and futures hang in the balance. And Pierre's men will come for them if the king decides in our favor. Either way, they are at great risk." I retrieve my hand in order to resume my pacing.

"So what do you always do when faced with a choice of running?"

I stare at him a long moment. "I give Fortune's wheel a spin and use it to launch a counterattack."

Beast folds his arms across his chest and leans back against the wall, waiting.

My mind shuffles all the possibilities and options in front of me the way a trickster might shuffle cards. "We must send the girls away," I finally decide. "I will not run, but the girls can. They're never anywhere near the king, or even the regent. It will take days before anyone realizes they are gone."

"Will the king not call them in to ask their thoughts on the matter?"

I laugh. "He does not care what they think or want. And if he does, we can simply say they have taken ill."

"But where will we send them? Surely such a journey is fraught with its own risk?"

"That is the trick of it," I agree. "Unless . . . unless we did not send them very far. Surely there is a convent somewhere nearby where they could request sanctuary."

"Would Pierre's men honor sanctuary? I also fear it would be the first place they look."

Given my own history of escaping to a convent, there is a good chance he is right. And that is when the pieces of the answer fall into place. "Unless," I tell him, "it is a convent they do not even know exists."

It takes him a moment to grasp my meaning. "You don't mean the convent of Saint Mortain?"

The wheels of my mind churn furiously. "It is perfect. It is far away from court. They will be surrounded by highly skilled assassins, reachable only by boat. Best of all, neither the French crown nor Pierre knows it exists. It is the best place to hide them."

Beast pulls at his chin, nodding slowly. "It is also a ten-day journey. Does that not present a new set of dangers?"

"You can stop in Rennes. Ismae can help you — maybe she will even want to accompany you to the convent."

He takes a deep breath and scrubs both his hands over his face. "I do not like it."

"If you, Aeva, Tola, and the queen's guard accompany them —" Beast opens his mouth to argue, but I rush in. "Think! The only way they can hurt me is through my sisters. The best way — the only way — to protect me is to get them to safety. Besides, we may not have much choice."

I can see he knows the truth of what I am saying, but his eyes also glint with his absolute distate for the plan. "I am not going to leave you here alone to face d'Albret and the regent. And you cannot simply commandeer half the queen's loyal attendants." He is silent a long moment before he finally says, "I think we should consider marrying."

I gape at him. *Marry?*

"As your husband, I can offer you some measure of protection. Not only physically, but legally."

My mind is a swirl of all the reasons I will not — cannot — ever marry, none of them having to do with Beast. Sensing that, he hastily retreats. "I can see by your silence it's a poor idea. And I have little enough to offer you."

"No! It is not you, it is just that —"

"Hush." He steps forward and holds his fingers up to my lips. "You do not need to explain. I should never have suggested it except that there are many things that cannot be done to you or taken from you without your husband's permission."

He is right. It *would* afford me certain protections. I would be his property instead of d'Albret's, and d'Albret could no longer have any claim on me.

But those same protections can also serve as a lifelong trap from which there is no escape. I'm not sure that I can ever let a man — not even Beast — have that sort of power over me again. "We would need the permission of the queen and perhaps even the king," I tell him gently. "And we are already past the point when their protection would do the most good. Besides, while marriage might protect me, it would not help Charlotte or Louise."

His sense of frustration and impotence is so intense it borders on despair.

"But know this. I love you. I will always love you, marriage or not. We are perfectly made for each other, you and I."

He reaches out to cup my face in his hands, his touch so gentle and cherishing, that it nearly makes me weep. "We are that, my fair assassin."

I savor that touch for one long moment before forcing myself to pull away. "I must go," I tell him. "Hopefully the duchess will have news of the king's meeting with the lawyer." And then I hurry from the room before I truly begin to weep.

CHAPTER 83

hen I reach the queen's chambers, she is waiting for me. She is not in bed but sits by the fire. All her other ladies have been dismissed.

"Your Majesty." I curtsy, and she motions me over. She is still fully dressed. "May I help prepare you for bed?"

"Not just yet." There is a chill in her voice that I have not heard before, not with me. She pulls her gaze from the fire, her eyes heavy and solemn. "Lady Sybella, is there something you wish to share with me?"

My mind races over everything I have not told her. The dicing and dagger throwing at her wedding. The assassination attempt. The sneaking and spying on the king. My recent visit with Marguerite. "There are many things I could share, Your Majesty, but I am not certain they are things you truly wish to know."

Her eyes flash in a rare show of temper. "I think it best if you let me decide for myself."

I'm so stunned that it takes me a moment to find my voice. "Where would you like me to start? My past? The methods I have used to keep you informed here at the French court —"

She holds out a hand to halt my words. "Start with Pierre's visit to Rennes before we left for France. You can be certain his lawyer brought it up, and it was a great revelation to me."

I close my eyes. *Merde.* "Your Majesty —"

"Please," she says, her voice softening somewhat. "Sit down."

I give a faint shake of my head and grip the back of the chair instead. "Your Majesty, I told Captain Dunois when it happened, and it was he who suggested I not bother you with it. His reasoning was that he was going to double the guard, and that with the injuries Pierre and his men had sustained they would not be returning anytime soon. He did not see any reason . . ." My words become twisted, tangled. "He was thinking to protect me, Your Majesty. And I let him."

How can I explain to her the sharp, bitter thorns that sprang up around my heart that day? With so many seeing to her safety as my sisters huddled in their rooms, recovering from Pierre's attack? I was blinded by my desire to hoard every crumb and scrap of protection I could for my sisters. I was glad I did not have to tell her and greedily accepted the gift Captain Dunois offered.

"That sounds like the captain." The loss she still feels seeps into her voice. "And is a far more satisfactory explanation than the one Pierre's lawyer offered." She shoots me a tart look. "However, it would have been nice to know about this so I did not appear an idiot in front of my lord husband and the officious lawyer."

"I am sorry, Your Majesty. I should have told you and asked to be released from your service. If I had known Pierre would parade our family's soiled linens before the king and queen of France, I would have." I curtsy and bow my head, hoping she will feel the fullness of my regret. "I am deeply sorry."

"Please rise, Lady Sybella! You have saved me untold miseries on so many fronts. I am not trying to shame you." Her voice carries such firm assurance that it leaves no room for doubt.

"Now, let me tell you what that vile lawyer claimed. And please, do sit down, for it strains my neck, looking up at you."

"But of course," I say as I hurriedly take a seat.

"Pierre's story — relayed by his lawyer — is that he visited Rennes to appeal for custody of his sisters. In answer, I had him attacked and chased from the premises, not even granting him the opportunity for a hearing." She raises one eyebrow. "The king was not amused, was appalled even, that I would act in so high-handed a manner toward one of his vassals. Needless to say, I could only profess my ignorance in the matter."

"Oh, Your Majesty! I am so very sorry."

"You're not the one who lied, so need not apologize for that. However, I would greatly appreciate hearing the full story."

When I have finished telling her of Pierre's attack in the garden, she leans back, her rosary forgotten as she stares into the fire, her brow creased in thought. After a few moments, she turns back to me. "We will simply tell them the truth."

I try to hide my skepticism. "I am not certain how that will help my case."

"Not the whole of it, but that Pierre and his men breached our walls without announcing themselves, killed one of my guards, and threatened those under our protection. I will also explain to the king that Captain Dunois took care of the matter so I would not need to be distracted from my wedding preparations." She blinks, her eyes wide and innocent. "Is that not what a loyal commander is for? To see to such details so that I may contend with affairs of state?"

I smile. "That should work nicely, Your Majesty."

"The king is a stickler for both the rule of law and those precedents that bequeath men their privilege." A faint note of bitterness creeps into her voice. For all that she plays the doting young bride, she sees him clearly for who he is and where his politics lie. "He is much inclined to give your brother custody — not just of your sisters, but of you as well — for he believes, as all men do, that women cannot take care of themselves, nor make decisions over their own future."

"Only because they have made it impossible for us to do so by removing every avenue open to us except marriage, whoring, or the Church," I murmur.

"Furthermore, he feels it is not only Pierre's right, but his duty. To not do his duty would make him a lesser man in the eyes of God."

I cannot help it — I laugh. "As if any d'Albret ever cared how he looked in the eyes of God."

"From what I have seen, I would agree with you on that. One point to our advantage is that all of this is news to the king. If there is one thing he detests, it's being rushed or bullied into a decision he did not come to on his own."

"You have learned much about his nature in the short time you have been together."

She makes a face. "Since it is clear I will have to fight for every scrap of

power I wish to exercise, it seems wise to learn as much as I can about the man who holds the reins to that power. For now, he is inclined to think on it for a few days and weigh the options."

"While I am glad to hear it, I can't help wondering what he is weighing them against. As you say, his own leaning is heavily in favor of Pierre's claim."

She shifts in her chair. "Once the lawyer had been dismissed, I made my case. I explained that you had served me long and well, indeed, had saved my life on more than one occasion. In return for your service, I had vowed to foster your sisters. If he returns them to Pierre, he may salvage Pierre's honor, but he will have stripped the queen of France of her honor. How will that reflect on the crown?"

"Oh, well done, Your Majesty."

She smiles. "I thought so. However"—her face sobers again—"the regent claimed that you had lied to her and that this alone was cause for you to be removed from my circle."

"I cannot say that is unexpected. She has not liked me since I first butted heads with her at Châteaubriant. I am sorry I drew her ire in our direction."

The queen's face grows flushed, her eyes fierce. "Do not apologize for that. If you hadn't crossed swords with her that night, I fear I would have fallen apart with the shame and the humiliation of it. In fighting her, you reminded me that she *could* be fought. By mocking her insistence on such an archaic custom, you reminded me that it wasn't a reflection of me personally."

The queen's words touch something inside me, something deep and raw and yearning.

"I promised your sisters my protection, Lady Sybella, and I intend to give it. I wish I could trust that the king will decide in your favor, or that he would trust my judgment in this, but he may not. I fear if I tell him of my own treatment at the hands of the d'Albret family, it would diminish me in his eyes. But know this. Whatever you need, whomever you need to keep your sisters safe, if it is mine, you may have it."

"Your Majesty . . ."

"I mean it. The Arduinnites, Beast, even the queen's guard, for they are not being allowed to serve their true purpose. Use any resource needed to protect your sisters. Now go. Be with them. I have others who can serve me."

My eyes burn at the enormous generosity of her offer. "Thank you, Your Majesty," I say, around the huge lump of gratitude that has sprung up in my throat.

When I reach my chambers, the room is dark except for the banked fire. The Arduinnites are asleep on pallets on the floor. Aeva raises her head at my entrance, instantly on alert. "Everything is fine," I whisper, then sit down to take off my shoes and remove my heavy skirt and bodice. Dressed only in my shift, I approach the bed and quietly draw back the curtain. Tephanie is asleep in the middle with Charlotte and Louise on either side of her. I slowly lift the covers and lower myself onto the mattress, careful not to jiggle the other sleepers.

As I start to drift off to sleep, I become aware of a moth butting against the window. I frown, for there is no light to attract a moth. Sleepiness forgotten, I raise my head off the pillow. There. Only it is not the feathery wings of a moth, but the beating of a heart.

A heart beats right outside our window. My nerves strung taut, I reach for the knife I have slipped under the pillow, but the beating disappears. I wait one moment, then a second. It is gone, but I know that the Mouse has just successfully completed his first scouting mission.

CHAPTER 84

Genevieve

n the end, when I reach Plessis-lès-Tours, I decide to stick as closely to the truth as possible. Dressed in finery I bought when we passed through Poitiers, I ride Gallopine up to the outer courtyard's entrance. Whether because the guards recognize me or because I present no threat, they allow me to pass. I proceed to the second gate that protects the inner bailey. Old King Louis was so fearful of his person that he built as many layers of defense into the castle as possible.

The guards at the second gate stop me and ask my business. I recognize neither of them. "I am Lady Genevieve, in service to the Countess of Angoulême." They straighten and grow more circumspect. "I would speak with the seneschal, if I may."

This request gains me entrance, and I ride to the main courtyard in front of the palace doors. A groom steps forward to help me dismount as a page appears at my side to escort me up the stairs. When I step inside the main door, the seneschal is already hurrying to greet me. "Demoiselle Genevieve! I must confess I am surprised to see you. We had not received word of your visit."

I ignore the faint reproach in his voice. "I am sorry to hear my messenger did not reach you, but I am not surprised. The road was beset with many hazards. It was too much to hope that he would not fall prey to them."

The seneschal's voice grows heavy with concern. "Hazards, my lady?" The man peers around me. "And what of your escort?"

I blink rapidly and make my voice slightly husky, as if holding back tears. "I fear I am alone. As I said, much ill has befallen my party." He is fair twitching to ask what happened, but is constrained by the formality of his position. "However, I have news that must be delivered to Madame Regent, and turning back offered no safer course than continuing onward."

"My lady, I am sorry to hear of all your misfortune. Alas, Madame Regent has ridden out for the morning. Would you like to rest until she returns?"

I shake my head sadly. "My news and my misfortunes on the road have made me restless. Would it be possible to ease my heart in the gardens? Once I have done that, perhaps I will be able to rest."

Every day that I was at court, after the king's midday meal, he walked in his garden before turning to the social pleasures of the afternoon. I must only position myself and wait.

"But of course. Let me send for one of Madame's attendants to escort you."

I rest my hand on his arm in a fleeting gesture. "Please, monsieur. I am poor company right now, and the attendants would want to know why I am here. It is for Madame to hear first. Truly, I wish only some time alone in the garden to compose myself."

The seneschal's affection for protocol gives way before the weight of my distress. He leads me through the palace to where the doors open out onto the gardens. "Once you have found your peace, send for me and I will have you settled in a room until Madame returns."

I place my hand on my throat in a gesture of profound gratitude. "Thank you, monsieur."

And with that, I am alone in the king's garden.

Nearly an hour later, I hear the sound of voices and footsteps crunching on the gravel. As they draw closer, I am able to pick out a deep rumbling voice I do not recognize. "Send them all back to their brother. They are his to command, no matter what your queen prefers. You do not wish to be seen as weak."

"Surely honoring my lady wife's vows is honorable, not weak," the familiar voice of the king answers. I shift my position in the hedge ever so slightly, trying to get a glimpse of them.

The king is dressed in fine satins and velvet that do not hide the slightness of his figure or the shortness of his height. And no finery in the world can hide the plainness of his face. Nevertheless, it is a face that is nearly always kind, and that is more than most of the people I have known at court.

There are half a dozen men with him, but only one walks beside him, deep in conversation. He is exceptionally tall and towers over the king. He is broad of shoulder and thick with muscle. His features are unrelentingly plain, bordering on ugly. In spite of his looks, he emanates an almost animal virility as deeply compelling as it is unsettling. There is a sense of barely contained civility to him.

Their steps bring them closer toward me and I realize I must interrupt them or have the king pass by altogether and lose my chance to let him know that I am back.

I soften my shoulders, widen my eyes, and step out from the shadows of the hedge. "Sire?"

At the sound of my voice, the king's head snaps up. His companion's hand flies to his sword hilt, but seeing me, he does not draw it.

"Genevieve?"

I take a hesitant step forward, my hands gently twisting together with doubt.

"Genevieve? Is that you?" The king waves his retainers away. The large man hesitates until the king flashes him an annoyed glance.

Alone, the king strides forward to greet me, hands outstretched. He has *not* forgotten, and he is most definitely happy to see me. The two things I don't control have fallen my way.

"Yes, sire. It is I." I sink into a deep curtsy. Immediately his gloved hand is on my elbow, helping me to my feet.

"Genevieve." His voice is low and warm while his gaze sweeps over me, taking in my gown, my shoes, my hair. "I am surprised to see you."

"I am sorry to appear unannounced, but I had news that was best given to Madame Regent in person."

To my immense relief, he does not press me for the news. Either he does not care or has assumed that it is some matter best left to the women of his household. Either explanation suits me, for bringing up the subject of death while attempting to revive an old tendre will not help my cause.

He takes my hands. "That is most thoughtful of you, but you were always that." He smiles warmly, and I realize this fruit still hangs low in the tree. I have merely to pluck it.

I turn my gaze shyly from him to his prized gardens. "And of course, once I was here I had to indulge myself to admire your gardens." I sigh, so soft it could easily be missed — if he weren't hanging on my every word. "I do miss them so."

"As would I if I was not able to visit them whenever I chose." He gives me his arm. "Let us enjoy them together."

There is a loud cough behind us, and the king grimaces. "General Cassel has ridden all the way from Flanders to speak with me. I should not keep him waiting."

At the name, everything inside me stills. It is the general Maraud has been seeking — the man responsible for the murder of his brother. I dare not turn around to look at him. Not with that knowledge in my eyes.

"You will be staying for a while before you return to Cognac." The king does not frame it as a question.

"Of course, Your Majesty."

"Good." He gives my hand a squeeze, then, thinking better of it, lifts it to his lips. "Soon." His eyes are warm upon mine. "I will see you soon. You have my promise."

I curtsy deeply. "You do me great honor, Your Majesty." When I rise, General Cassel is watching me with amused speculation. There is a calculation in his manner that has me believing every word Maraud has said about him. Something in his gaze makes me feel stripped bare, so I lift my skirts and hurry away, careful to keep my head high and my shoulders straight.

CHAPTER 85

eeling well pleased with the day's work, I return to the palace. Before I can so much as search out the seneschal, I stumble upon the regent. She is attended by four of her loyal ladies, and has a distinct air of self-satisfaction about her.

When she sees me, the smile vanishes and she comes to a sudden stop, her attendants having to step lightly to avoid trampling her. "Genevieve?"

"Madame Regent." I sink into a deep curtsy, glancing up from between my lashes to see how she is taking my sudden appearance.

While her face registers mild surprise, the look she gives me is not *unwelcome*. In truth, she looks — almost — glad to see me. Which is odd, as I was never her favorite.

"Come, walk with me." She waves her other ladies back and casts me a speculative glance as she takes my arm in hers. "What brings you here? I had no news of your coming."

"I am sorry for that, Madame. A messenger was sent, but it appears he did not arrive."

Her fine brows draw into a delicate frown. "And where are your attendants?" The faint reproach in her voice is unmistakable, although whether it is for me or my missing attendants, I am unsure.

"That is more bad news, Madame! I fear I bear nothing but distressing tales."

She looks at me sharply. "Come, you must tell me of them." She turns to her ladies. "You are dismissed. I will find you when I have need of you again."

With that, she takes my arm more firmly in hers and leads me down the hall. "We will be more comfortable in my office, where I can hear your tale in its entirety."

"Thank you, Madame." My voice is low, measured, and grateful, but inside I am cursing my luck. While I knew I would have to speak with her, I did not think it would be so very soon.

Her office is finely appointed, opulent even, filled with elegant furniture and decorations. She escorts me to one of the intricately carved Italian chairs facing her desk, then takes her seat behind it. "So, what brings you here, unannounced and unescorted?" She is not as shocked as I feared she would be, which is to my favor. Indeed, she is studying me much as a farmwife studies a freshly snared rabbit.

"It is a long, unpleasant tale, Madame."

"The sooner begun, the sooner it will be over." She settles back in her chair, folds her slim white hands, and gives me her full attention.

I clasp my own hands in my lap. "I come bearing the saddest of news, and met with even more of it along the way. As I told you, the messenger I sent did not make it. Additionally, my own escort and attendants were attacked, near Sainte-Maure."

Her eyes widen at this. "By whom?"

"I don't know. Brigands. Outlaws. I only know that my escorts sacrificed their lives so that I might escape."

She regards me thoughtfully. "You made it all the way from Sainte-Maure to Plessis alone?"

"What choice did I have? To turn back was a longer journey. And since the others paid with their lives, it felt disrespectful of their sacrifice to do anything other than continue."

"You could have sought aid at a church or abbey. They could have provided you with an escort for the rest of your trip."

"I never considered that, Madame. From all that you have taught us, I thought the fewer people who saw me alone, the better."

"That is a reasonable approach," she concedes. "Tell me exactly where you were attacked so that we may send out inquiries. This will not go unpunished."

I describe the small valley where d'Albret's men caught up to us. Even if the wolves or carrion have carried off the remains of the dead, there will be plenty of signs of our struggle.

"I am truly sorry for all that you had to endure," she says. "And you did so because you had news for me?"

I cannot tell if it is my imagination or if her interest is especially piqued. Is she thinking of the prisoner she ordered forgotten? Or is there some other news she is hoping for?

"I do. Tragic news. I am afraid that Margot is dead."

Her pale face grows even paler. "Dead?"

"Yes, Madame." Much to my surprise, my eyes begin to water, and I must blink fiercely to keep them from spilling over. Of all the people with whom I would share my grief, the regent is near the last of my list.

"When?"

"Six days before the royal wedding."

"Why did the count not inform me of this immediately?"

"I am certain he did not wish to darken a joyous occasion with such news."

"That was most thoughtful of him." Her tone is dry. She drums her fingers on the chair arm a moment before asking. "What did she die of?"

I have but a heartbeat or two to decide whether to tell the truth or to protect Count Angoulême. "She died giving birth to Count Angoulême's bastard."

Madame's nostrils flare, and her head rears back slightly before she turns to look out the window. "I am sorry," she says. In those words I hear not only sorrow that Margot has passed, but that Madame herself has placed her in such circumstances. She turns back to me. "How is Louise taking all this?"

I must tread carefully here. "Louise is much concerned with her own pregnancy, and in doing her duty by the count, as you have instructed her. She is sad for Margot's passing, of course, but is not dwelling on it lest the melancholy damage her own babe."

Madame gives a brusque nod of approval. "That is most wise of her." She tilts her head and examines me. "And what of you?" Her voice is as gentle as I've ever heard it. "The two of you have been together nearly your whole life, as I understand it."

I am impressed that she remembers that much about us with as many girls as she fosters. "I miss her terribly. It is why I volunteered to bring the news myself. It is too difficult to be in Cognac surrounded by reminders of Margot."

Because I am so practiced in remaining guarded all the time, it is hard to let the truth of these words show on my face, but she must see something that convinces her. "Poor Genevieve. And you recently lost your father as well, or so Count Angoulême told me in one of his letters."

I school my features so that the surprise I feel will not show. "That is true, although I have not seen him for longer than ten years and can hardly remember him."

She brings her hand up to her chin, one long, slim finger tapping her lips. "And your mother died when you were . . . ?"

"Born, Madame. She died when I was born, and my father's mother lived with him and cared for me until she, too, died."

"So you truly are all alone in this world now."

"Yes." Hidden in the folds of my skirt, my hands clench into fists. *No.*

"Well, I am sorry for the nature of what brings you here, but I cannot be sad to see you."

This is unexpected. I would not have guessed that she would have thought twice about my absence, since it was she who arranged it.

She studies me a moment before rising from her chair and crossing to the window to stare out into the courtyard. "You know that the king is married now, and a new queen sits beside him."

Is this some veiled warning she is giving me? "But of course. I wish them both much joy and good health."

She casts me an unreadable glance. "This is a marriage of political expediency. One for the good of the crown. We all miss our dear dauphine very much."

"I am sorry, Madame." I'm somewhat taken aback by her admission. I don't think we've exchanged words before that did not involve instructions of some kind. Or a reprimand.

"But"—she turns from the window abruptly, her face animated—"your timing is most fortunate, and I believe there is a role for you to play here at court."

It is all I can do not to gape at her. I only wanted for her to believe my story so I could remain in Plessis long enough to seduce the king, but now she is claiming she has need of me? "Of course, Madame. I am happy to serve however I can."

Just as long as it does not come between me and my own plans.

"One of the things I have always admired about you is your pragmatism. That and your wit."

"My wit, my lady?"

"Oh, you try to hide it from everyone, but there is a keen intelligence inside that head of yours. Although you are correct in remaining humble about it," she is quick to add. The regent returns to her desk, carefully adjusts her skirts, then resumes her seat before pinning me with a direct gaze. "You know that the duchess of Brittany and the crown have been on opposite sides of a conflict for a long while now."

I nod.

"The duchess—Ah! But I keep forgetting to call her the queen! The queen is young and beautiful and determined to maintain Brittany's independence at any cost. In short, I do not trust her."

This is precisely the sort of news the convent would have dearly loved to know—if it still existed. "It is not hard to see why, Madame."

"But, as I said, she is young and beautiful, and the king shows signs of being somewhat inclined to indulge her."

I say nothing, but simply nod. In truth, I am speechless at the confidences pouring from her mouth.

"Now that there is an official queen, it makes my own position somewhat more difficult. That is where you come in."

I blink, feeling like I have missed something. I understand that she fears being misplaced by this new queen—it is no doubt one of the reasons she misses the young dauphine, who was like a daughter to her.

She picks up a quill from her desk and runs her fingers along the neatly trimmed feathers. "You have long held the king's affection. For the good of the interests of the crown, I think it would be wise for you to remain at court and reawaken that interest, pursue it to its fullest measure."

It takes me a moment to digest her words. "You mean, you wish me to sleep with him?"

Her fingers stop playing with the feathers and she points the quill in my direction. "I want you to see to his every comfort. He is king, after all."

I must look incredulous. Or mayhap she thinks I have misunderstood her, for she leans across the table. "I wish you to become his new mistress."

"But, Madame!" A distant roar of outrage tries to escape. If she had not sent us to Cognac, then Margot might still be alive. I ruthlessly shove that knowledge aside. "You specifically instructed me to do everything I could to *dissuade* his interest. Including sending me away!"

"Things change. Times change. But France's needs must always come first."

And that's when the fullness of her plan comes to me. "You wish me to sleep with the king so I can share whatever I learn with you."

She smiles as if I am her most prized pupil. "There is that wit that sets you apart."

I am stunned with both the audacity of her plan and the sheer hypocrisy of it. Does she realize she is acting the procurer?

But what leaves me truly breathless is that she has just swept the legs out from under my own plan. Found a way to use it for her own end. She has run out of leverage to bend the king to her wishes, so now wishes to use me as coin.

"Madame . . ."

She puts her hand up to stop my words, her mouth a flat line of displeasure. "Do not say anything you will regret, Genevieve. Do not forget the debt you owe us — me — for taking you in, training you in the ways of being a lady, honoring your family by showing you such favor."

"Madame, as you know, I was convent raised until I came to court. Will you have me go against the very precepts of the Church? I cannot help but think they would frown most severely upon what you suggest. Especially with the king so newly married."

She huffs out a breath. "Kings have always been given great leeway in these matters by the Church, as do the women who serve them."

"What if the queen finds out? Won't she try to have me removed from court?"

A secretive smile tugs at the corners of her mouth. "I will worry about the queen. Your job will be to keep the king happy. Do we have an agreement?"

As she studies me, waiting for my answer, I am filled with disappointment. Not only for the task she has asked of me, but that *she* is the one to ask it. Of all the woman I have known, she is the one who wields the most power. She has commanded armies, conducted treaties, presided over every formal gathering imaginable. She has heads of state and bishops, cardinals and even the pope at her disposal. With all the tools available to her, in the end this is the plan she turns to.

"Madame." My voice is low and heavy with the weight of not only what she has asked me, but my recent grief. "This is much to take in and not something I have ever entertained as a possibility. Not to mention, my heart is still mourning Margot's death. May I have some time to decide if I am worthy of your trust and capable of doing such a thing?"

"Oh, fah!" She waves her hand as if shooing a bug. "I would not have asked it of you if I did not know you were capable of it. I am not such a fool as that."

She will not take no for an answer. If I do not say yes, I will be summarily escorted from court, losing my chance to approach the king with my own intentions.

"Very well. If this is what you ask of me, and what you think is truly best for the crown, of course I will do it."

She favors me with a warm smile, a smile that is tinged with triumph. However, just because I have told her yes does not mean that I intend to do what she has asked. Or, not in the way that she wishes.

But by the time she figures that out, I will have already accomplished what I came here to do.

CHAPTER 86

Sybella

 had not expected Pierre's men to make their move so quickly. Their boldness gives new urgency to my plan, and my conversation with the queen has provided the means — and the permission — to implement it.

There is no point in delaying further.

As I head to the door that will take me to the courtyard, I must pass the regent's office. I slow my steps, debating whether to turn back around if her door is open. She is the last person I wish to see just now.

When I reach the corner before her office, I stop, pulling quickly back.

The seneschal is escorting a girl from the room, a girl I have never seen before. Something catches my eye. It is not the strong, supple grace with which she holds herself, nor the simplicity of her gown. Rather, it is some paradox in her manner — the way her lips and eyes smile politely and say, "Thank you, Madame," even as her entire body seems to quiver with resentment — an internal struggle that echoes every encounter I've ever had with the regent.

The seneschal closes the door behind her, then escorts her in the opposite direction, and I am left free to pass without the regent seeing me.

The stable yard is full of mounted knights and soldiers who have just arrived, reminding me of how Pierre got into Rennes. I tamp down my growing unease and go in search of Beast.

I find him in the armory, surrounded by swords and axes, knives and pikes. Plate armor is stacked against the wall, piled high on tables, or sitting on racks. There is a sharp tang of metal in the air, accompanied by the scent of the oil used to keep the armor clean. He sits in the middle of it all, head bent over a long sword as he tests the edge. "They have you squiring in the armory now?"

At the sound of my voice, his head snaps up and he shrugs. "It was better than pummeling the louts who rode in and nearly foundered their horses. Besides, sharpening weapons helps me think."

"Who are they?"

"One of the king's generals and his retainers, newly returned from Flanders."

"Is it the one rumored to have knowledge of Anton?"

"Possibly. But I will wait until their horses" — meaning his temper — "recover before asking." It would be better to tell him my plan when he wasn't already in an ill humor, but I do not have time to wait.

I run a finger along the flat of the blade he is polishing. "Pierre's man — the Mouse — paid a visit to our bedroom window last night."

Beast's hand grows still, his gaze leaping to mine, his eyes taking on their eerie feral light. "What?"

"He did not get in — did not even try. It was a scouting mission. But it was far sooner than I would have expected."

Beast sets the sword aside and places his hands carefully on his knees. "I will kill them."

"We should. And we will. But not while the lawyer is presenting his case against me. Having four of his men go missing would only cause more attention and closer scrutiny."

"Have you spoken to the queen yet? What did she say?"

"Two things. Pierre's lawyer told the king that Pierre visited Rennes to ask for his sisters back and was summarily attacked and escorted from the premises without receiving an audience, much less an answer."

"An outright lie. Surely the queen told him that."

"She did. But he was not happy with her and she is not certain she can sway him to her favor."

Beast's eyes are bleak, for he knows what is coming. "That is not overly hopeful."

"No. It isn't. And with Pierre's enforcers growing bold, I fear we must get Charlotte and Louise out of harm's way sooner rather than later. They will be safest at the convent."

He looks away to stare at the wall. "The queen has offered her full support," I assure him. "Given me permission to use all the tools and manpower she has at her disposal. That includes you and the queen's guard, as well as Aeva and Tola."

He swears, then rises to his feet. "Do not ask me to leave you to face this alone, Sybella. I cannot do that. I will not leave you unprotected with so many who wish you harm. That has been your fate all your life."

His words fill up the space between us and wrap themselves around my heart, squeezing it painfully. I reach up and place my hand on his rough, scarred cheek. "But my sisters are the most vulnerable parts of me. By getting them someplace where Pierre cannot touch them, you *are* protecting *me*."

The anguish and despair in his eyes feels like it comes from my own soul. "But you are my heart," he whispers. "How can you ask me to leave that behind?"

I lean my forehead against his. "Why do the gods do this to us? Give us choices that wrench the very hearts from our chests?" I whisper. "We always knew this would not be easy. We knew it would take two of us — and all the skills and courage we possess — to stop Pierre."

He does not argue. There is no point.

I do not tell him how hard it is for me to send him away. How little I relish being left alone among my enemies. But I am not seven anymore. I no longer need anyone to save me, but Charlotte and Louise do. "You once pulled me to safety through a nest of vipers. You are doing so again — only this time safety just happens to be in the opposite direction of where I'll be." The smile I send him feels wobbly at the edges.

"And if the king rules in favor of Pierre?" he asks. "What will you do when it is time to produce the girls?"

"I will stall. Claim that they are ill. Then I will run."

"They will be expecting that. Where will you go?"

"I don't know." It sits poorly to go hide in Brittany at the convent. As does leaving the queen, but the truth is my presence — and that of the girls — brings dangers to her door. If I leave, that will disappear. And she has other loyal attendants. "Maybe I will go to Cognac," I tell him, the idea coming to me as I speak. "And see if I can call the other initiates into service. They could return to court and take my place at the queen's side."

That is it, I realize. When I leave, I will head for Cognac and the only two people in France who can help me.

"When must I go?"

"Soon?" I whisper. His fists clench, not in anger, but with sorrow, determination, and a love so overpowering that it fills the very air around me.

His pulse beats rapidly in his neck as he reaches out to stroke my cheek. When he touches me, all that I have been feeling in the last hours, days, weeks, rushes through me in one giant wave that leaves me lightheaded, dizzy, wanting.

Everything I feel in that moment is so big and overwhelming that it cannot be contained in one body. I grip his head and bring his lips toward mine.

He does not resist. Indeed, I have barely touched him, and then his mouth is everywhere, hungry and warm, kissing my lips, my cheek, my throat, his wide hands coming around my waist, sliding upward and drawing me closer. I open my mouth to him, pressing my hands against his chest, feeling the heat of him and the racing of his heart.

He pulls his mouth from mine. "Sybella." It is a wish, a vow, a prayer.

I do not know when I will see him again — *if* I will see him again. I want my body to remember this — the press of his flesh, the cording of his muscles as he holds his strength in check, the desperate hunger of his mouth that is both gentle and demands my very soul.

Wanting the imprint of this moment to stay with me forever, I reach up to unlace the bodice of my gown, slip my arms from my sleeves and press my body along the length of his.

When our skin touches, I am reminded of the Dark Mother and how she causes life to rise up out of our darkest moments. Surely that is true, for the touch of men once brought nothing but shame and despair. But now it brings hope and light, even when I have no reason to believe in either. I wrap my arms more tightly around Beast's neck until I can no longer be certain where my soul ends and his begins.

Chapter 87

Genevieve

hen I descend into the grand hall for dinner, I am dressed in Perrette du Bois's best finery. I try to ignore her as she glares daggers at my back, not only for relieving her of her best gown, but for having come so firmly under the personal attention of Madame Regent.

The hall is aglow with candlelight and flames from the fires roaring in the giant fireplaces. Music plays in the background. The king sits at his high table, and I cannot decide if I am sad or relieved that the queen is not in attendance. I would like to see her for myself, at least once. Through the convent, I have served her all these years. I cannot help but feel that if I could see her face, take her measure, I would better understand why she chose to abandon the convent. If it was her choice.

The fact that she is not present confirms my assumption that she and the king have already grown tired of each other's company — if they ever cared for each other to begin with. It is admittedly less awkward to pursue my designs on the king in her absence.

I am placed with Madame's other attendants at one of the lower tables. None of them speaks to me much — offended as they are on Perrette's behalf and threatened by the favor the regent has shown me. Ignoring them, I pretend to be absorbed in the fine food and the entertainment.

In truth, the food is as tasteless to me as dirt, and the music fair gives me a headache. No, not the music, but the din of the voices and laughter of the courtiers. I have been gone from Cognac for less than ten days, but it feels a lifetime ago, and my taste for the pomp and hypocrisy of court life has run dry.

That I actually prefer the raucous and coarse company of the mummers or even Maraud's mercenary friends should not surprise me. Those are my roots, after all. And these gathered nobles and sycophants cannot see past their own interests or station. The entire spectacle feels as shallow as a poorly dug grave.

The king, alone at his table, is not as subtle in his interest as he should be. Perhaps it is due to boredom — for who wishes to sit alone at the dinner table? While it is intended as a reflection of the king's status, to someone who was raised such as he was — shut away in a castle with naught but his mother and a few men of mediocre wit or intelligence for company — it would feel far more like a punishment. One more way to announce to the world his loneliness.

Our eyes meet, and I look away. I do not even have to pretend to blush, for my cheeks grow red at having been caught thinking of him thus.

Our exchange of glances is quickly noted by the other ladies in waiting and does nothing to further endear me to them. I can already imagine their plots to inform the regent of this development.

I smile into my goblet. If they are looking for her to intervene, they will be sorely disappointed.

When the final dishes have been cleared, four of the lower tables are removed to make room for dancing. As the first chords strike up, the king rises from his table and makes his way to me. Could he not have at least waited until the third or fourth dance? Or until the dance floor was full of others before approaching?

In a rustle of bows and curtsies, the crowd parts before him, and curious whispers follow in his wake. When he stops in front of me, I curtsy deeply. Without a word, he smiles and takes my hand to lead me to the dance floor. As if by some silent arrangement, other courtiers follow suit, remaining a respectful distance away.

We take our positions, standing side by side. "You look beautiful in that gown."

I raise my hand to his, our fingers lightly touching. "Your Majesty is too kind," I demur.

We take three steps forward and rise up on our toes before he speaks again. "I cannot help but hope you are as happy to see me as I am you."

I glance up at him, my eyes wide with surprise. "But of course, Your Majesty! I am honored that you even remember me, let alone wish to spend time in my company."

He throws back his head and laughs. For one brief dizzying moment, a different laugh echoes in my ears, one accompanied by dark stubble and white teeth. "Ah, Genevieve." The king's voice quickly chases away the memory. "You do yourself a disservice by underestimating the hold you have." His eyes capture mine again, commanding my attention, his face growing serious.

I avert my gaze. "Your Majesty. Please. You will have the entire court talking."

The music causes us to step toward each other and bow. He leans in close. "Let them talk. If a king cannot incite his own courtiers to gossip, he is not truly a king."

The truth in his words causes the corners of my lips to turn up in a reluctant smile. "Touché, Your Majesty." And then the moves of the dance force us apart; I go to the gentleman on my right and the king to the lady on his left. I ignore my new partner's open curiosity and focus instead on the movements I must perform.

We change partners twice more until I am once again paired with the king, his hand holding my fingers in a firm grip rather than the light touch dictated by the dance. "Tell me, Genevieve." His voice is a low murmur. He does not look at me but straight ahead. "If I were to send for you, would you come? You broke my heart once. I do not think I could stand for you to do it again."

Before I can reply, the music stops and we must all bow and curtsy. As I kneel before him, my gaze flies to his. "Oh, Your Majesty! Surely I could not have broken your heart! I do not think I could bear such a burden. I thought you were simply being kind and chivalrous in paying me such honor."

The king extends his arm and leads me from the dance floor. "Does that mean you will come?"

I cast my eyes down. "Yes, Your Majesty," I whisper. "If you send for me, I will come."

There is a long beat of silence. When I finally look up, he is smiling. He bows deeply and raises my hand to his lips, careful to turn it so that the palm is exposed before kissing it. Then he folds my hand to enclose the kiss.

"I will send for you." His voice is low and faintly rough with his desire. "You may count on it."

CHAPTER 88

Sybella

Early the next morning, before nearly anyone else is up, I bid Charlotte and Louise goodbye. Louise stands near Tephanie, watching with worried eyes as the girl packs a few belongings into a satchel. Charlotte is sitting near the fire, carefully trimming her fingernails with her small knife. It is such a perfect mirror image of what her father used to do that it's like a fist to my heart. I want to yank the knife from her hand, as if in doing so I can snatch the d'Albret legacy from her slender shoulders.

"But why are we going away? Will Sybella be going too?" Louise asks.

"No, silly," Charlotte says without looking up. "She is too busy attending to the queen to have time to look after us."

Her words are another fist to my bruised heart. I have explained it to her. Does she not believe me, or does she simply delight in worrying Louise?

Just then, Charlotte looks up and sees me in the doorway. I hold my finger to my lips and walk silently to Louise, place my hands lightly over her eyes. "Who is speaking ill of the wonderful and magnificent Sybella?" I ask in a low, gruff voice.

She squeals in glee and whirls around, throwing her arms around my waist. "Only Charlotte, and only because she is showing off with her knife."

I hug her, wishing so much of our lives could be different. That we had oceans of time together. That my duties did not keep me away from her. That my own temperament were better suited to tending children than slaying their foes. But none of that is true, so all I can do is hug her as hard and long as I can when I have the chance.

"It will not be for long, sweeting." As her face falls, I hurry to explain. "Besides, you are going to visit a princess, a most wise and lovely princess who has a fondness for eating small girls."

Louise rolls her eyes at me. "Don't be silly. Princesses don't eat small girls! Ogres do."

I clap my hand to my forehead. "Of course. That is it. I always get princesses and ogres mixed up. Don't you?"

She giggles and shakes her head. After a moment: "Are we really going to visit a princess?"

"Yes," I say, thinking of Annith. "Of a sort. She lives on an island with her darkly handsome consort and her highly skilled handmaidens. Sister Beatriz will want to dress you in fancy clothes and Sister Widona will let you pet and feed the horses. Besides, aren't you getting tired of this stuffy old castle?"

Louise looks around the room, which, while pleasant, is also spare. "No," she says simply. Tephanie looks up from her packing and smiles at me.

"That's too bad, for you will get to wear the new fur cloak you are so fond of. And did I tell you that Beast would be going with you?"

Louise's face lights up. "Will he? Well, then, we will be fine without you."

I put my hands on my hips and pretend to scowl. "Is that how easily you dismiss me?"

"He is stronger than you," she points out. "And will keep us safe."

"Are you worried about your safety, little one? Don't be. There are many who will take care of you. Tephanie, Tola, Aeva, half the queen's guard. And that is just those who will be traveling with you. There are others, including the queen, who are working to keep you both safe and well."

"What about the king?" Charlotte asks. "Does he care?"

I sometimes wish that Charlotte's wit was not so sharp. "It is his job to care for all his subjects and see to their safety." I do not share with her that he and I might have different opinions on how best to achieve that.

"Besides," Louise continues, as if Charlotte had not interrupted, "Beast will let us feed his horse apples."

"Ah, if only I'd known the way to win your heart was to let you feed my horse."

I give them each one last hug, then turn to Tephanie. "You are all right with this?"

"Of course, my lady. It will be hardest on you. Here." She thrusts something into my hands.

It is the embroidery she's been working on. Slowly, I unfold the delicate white linen and find it embroidered with the brilliant red and green of a holly bush. My eyes sting and my vision blurs.

"It's so you have something to wipe your face with, when you need it. I thought the red holly berries would hide the blood."

"Thank you." The words come out in a whisper. I give her a quick, fierce hug and press a fleeting kiss upon her cheek before pulling away.

And then there is nothing left to say or do but escort the small group down the stairs to the side door. Beast, the accompanying queen's guard, and Yannic are waiting with the horses already saddled. Because of the castle's visitors yesterday, only a handful of grooms are about — and their eyes are still filled with sleep. When the girls have been safely mounted with Tola and Aeva, I turn to Beast. I open my mouth but cannot find the words to say goodbye.

He grins. "Do not worry. I will charm any obstacles we encounter with my good looks."

I smile past the lump in my throat and shake my head at his nonsense.

He brings my hand up to press his lips gently against my wrist. "I have ordered Lazare to remain here. I cannot leave you utterly alone." He pauses, growing solemn. "They will be safe, Sybella." His eyes are full of everything he cannot say. "I swear it." At his words, I feel a presence, almost as if Saint Camulos himself has stood in surety of Beast's vow.

<hr/>

When I return to my room, I go to the small trunklet that holds all my most valued possessions. I lift the lid to put Tephanie's handkerchief in with my other treasures, stopping when I see that the holly twig I carried with me from Rennes is still as green as the day I picked it, the berries just as vibrantly red. I reach out and stroke my finger down one of the shiny green leaves and find some small sliver of hope. Perhaps Mortain holds some mysteries in life, as well as death.

CHAPTER 89

am ready when the page arrives, informing me that the king has summoned me to his chambers.

I rise, wondering if a decision has already been made or if I am going to be allowed to present my case. With the girls having safely escaped this trap Pierre has set for them, it is far easier to face whatever comes with a calm heart.

When I arrive, the king is there along with Pierre's lawyer. I do not know where Pierre found him, but surely he is one of the most respectable-looking men to ever have served the d'Albret family. Whether he is new to their service or simply part of the outer circles that I was never privy to, I don't know. Nor do I know how much of me and my history within the family he is aware of, but he is decidedly discomfited at my presence, which is a small victory.

However, my spirits dip when I see that the queen is not in attendance, but the conniving regent is. If Pierre's lawyer's arguments do not sway the king to his cause, the regent will do her best to sway the king from mine.

A sense of grim foreboding settles over me.

I stop before the king and make a deep curtsy. "Your Majesty."

His bejeweled hand waves me to my feet.

"You wished to speak with me?" I have decided to act as if I am unaware of what is going on, instinct telling me it is the least threatening way to present myself to the king.

"As you may have heard, your brother has claimed you and your sisters should be in his care, not serving the queen. I am committed to putting forth the crown's justice, but to do that I must hear all sides before making a decision. Monsieur Fremin, you may go first." He turns to the lawyer expectantly.

"The matter is simple, Your Majesty. The Lady Sybella, Lord d'Albret's sister —"

The king holds up a hand. "I thought she was the Lord of d'Albret's daughter."

The lawyer nods. "I'm afraid her father has taken a mortal wound and has not regained consciousness in nearly a year. The duties and responsibilities of overseeing the family and its holdings have fallen to Pierre, the eldest surviving son."

The word *surviving* cuts deep. Julian. Would the lessons he learned at the end have made him a better overseer of the d'Albret domain than Pierre?

"I am sorry to hear of Lord d'Albret's injuries and will pray to God that he is healed soon."

"Thank you, Your Majesty." The lawyer almost succeeds in keeping the impatience out of his voice. "During the fall of Nantes, the Lady Sybella took her sisters from her father's custody and brought them to Rennes."

"Where she served the duchess," the king interjects.

"That is what we have been told, Your Majesty, but we have no way to confirm that."

"*I* am confirming that." The king's voice is brusque and dismissive.

"But of course, Your Majesty. Nevertheless, the Lady Sybella did not have her father's or brother's permission to leave their custody, nor did she have permission to remove her sisters from their care."

"Why did she do so?" The question comes from the regent.

"We do not know, Madame Regent. Lord d'Albret is most anxious to ask her that same question."

"Could it be," the king offers, "that she thought it a great honor to serve their duchess?"

There is a warning note in the king's voice, but the lawyer is not perceptive enough to hear it.

"Surely that is for their father or brother to decide, not the Lady Sybella."

There is silence as the king eyes the lawyer with displeasure before he turns to me. "Lady Sybella. How do you address these charges?"

"Charges, Your Majesty?" My heart sinks like a dropped stone. I am not here to make my case but to address charges?

"Your brother claims that you took your sisters from his home without his permission. Is that true?"

I fold my hands demurely in front of me. "No, Your Majesty. I did indeed have permission. It was given to me by my brother Julian, who was the eldest surviving son at that time."

The lawyer all but rolls his eyes, as if I am some imbecile they must indulge. "But, Your Majesty, why would this brother give such permission? It makes no sense to send two young girls off on their own with no escort save an elder sister."

The king indicates I may speak. "Your Majesty, it was a time of great political upheaval and confusion. D'Albret had unlawfully taken the city of Nantes from the duchess by force. As you must know, any city under threat of siege is not a safe place for young women."

"That is true," the king concedes.

"But your father was the one in command," the regent points out.

"Yes, Madame, but everyone knows how difficult it is to control men when they are in battle, how unsafe the cities are, especially to the innocent. For our safety, my lord brother instructed me and my sisters to leave. Unfortunately, both my father and Pierre were absent."

The lawyer sighs. "Where did they go, pray tell, with an entire city to put to order?"

I turn to look at him for the first time. "They were in negotiation with the regent on the terms for handing Nantes over to the approaching French army. Which," I point out, "would have made it even more unsafe for my sisters."

There is a long moment of silence at the stark reminder of the d'Albret family's stunning lack of honor, for all that it had turned the tide to the crown. The king's chin rests in one hand while he taps his fingers on the arm of his chair. He turns toward his sister. "Is this true? Did you meet with d'Albret outside the city of Nantes prior to us taking it?"

He did not know! He thought the city simply had bowed before him, pleased to receive him as their king. Which was true enough after d'Albret's brutal reign, but startling nonetheless that he was not in on the plans.

The regent does not so much as squirm in discomfort. Truly, her nerves are forged of iron. "I thought it wise to test the waters and do what we could to assure a peaceful transition. It would do no good to any of us to raze Nantes to the ground as we fought over it."

He says nothing, but considers her coldly, the tapping of his fingers growing more pronounced.

"Your Majesty? If I may?" I use my most humble and self-deprecating manner, which is rewarded by an indication that I may speak. "Count d'Albret was a great soldier and lord, but he had little interest in his daughters. I was only too glad to relieve the men in my family of those duties so they might better concentrate on matters of state. Surely that is what any dutiful daughter should do to ease her liege's burdens?"

The king's face relaxes, almost into a smile. This is the sort of motivation he can accept from a woman. Motivation that does not threaten his own sense of power. One that supports, rather than transplants. "Indeed, Lady Sybella. Would that all sisters chose to see to their brother's needs in so humble a manner."

I silently cringe, not intending my words to be a weapon against the regent — not while she still holds so many threads of power. I was merely trying to assure him that I was a model of feminine humility.

The regent uncoils from her place behind the king, coming out to walk in front of me. "I am not at all convinced you are a suitable model for two young girls. One of the soldiers says he saw you drinking and gambling with the guards the night of the wedding."

My heart sinks again, and I curse my own foolish temper. "I fear your soldier is mistaken, Madame. Indeed, I spent the entire evening with the queen."

The king frowns, and the regent barks out a laugh. "In case you forget, there is a witness to the queen's activities that evening."

"Many witnesses," I agree. "But as I am certain your witness will attest, he was only with the queen a short time. As soon as he left, I arrived in her chambers to attend upon her. You may call her in and ask her. Or ask any of the ladies you assigned to her that night. They can also attest to my arrival.

"Prior to that, I was visiting with the queen's councilors, wanting to enjoy their company before they returned to Brittany. I can only surmise that your soldier has mistaken me for someone else. There were many celebrating the nuptials that night. Besides, I do not play dice or gamble." Except with my life.

The regent purses her lips in annoyance, knowing that if I have named witnesses, I most likely speak the truth. I am not, but I was only absent for an hour — easy enough to blur the timing of that.

"And what of the rumors that you were performing unholy rites with Captain Dunois's body?"

I am careful to keep the shock off of my face. Whatever I was expecting next, it was not that. "Is praying over a fallen commander considered an unholy rite here in France, Madame?"

Her voice hisses into the space between us like a snake. "That is not all you were doing. By all accounts you were touching him, leaning over his body, placing your hands upon him and your face next to his."

My brow clears in understanding. "When he fell from his horse, I rushed to his side to see if I could ease his distress. But I did not know that seeing to someone's ill health was considered an unholy rite." I frown slightly. "You do know I spent a handful of years at the Saint Brigantian convent, do you not? I learned some small healing arts while I was there, and surely those cannot be considered unholy, for even France sends its daughters to be trained by the Brigantians."

Her nostrils flare in irritation. The king shifts in his chair. "Madame, when I said you could question the Lady Sybella, I did not intend that you should scour the country for such sordid gossip. Are there any other questions that are not rooted in rumor?"

The regent's lips flatten into a furious line, and it takes a moment before she can speak. "What sort of respectable noblewoman can wield a knife as you did when your party was ambushed?"

This time it is I who laughs. "Madame, surely you have heard of Joan of Arc, who led France's own armies against the English? Or Jeanne de Montfort, who led the Breton forces in our civil war? Or the Lioness of Brittany, who took to harassing the French fleet after her husband was betrayed and killed? Or any number of Frenchwomen who have had to lead their husband's garrison in order to protect the keep while he was away fighting the king's wars?"

Eyes burning, the regent opens her mouth to speak, but I rush over her words. "Your Majesty, sisters often serve their fathers and brothers in many ways. I have tended my brothers' wounds, entertained my father's vassals, and prayed for all of their souls. But I have also served my family by protecting my sisters from those who might wish them harm."

It occurs to me that on the face of it, this makes me similar to the regent. In as many ways as we are different, we are the same in that. She protects those she is loyal to, and I protect those I hold dear. For all that I dislike her, I also recognize that she does it to protect her brother.

No. In that moment I realize it is not her brother but the crown of France she protects. That is her true loyalty.

"Thank you, my lady Sybella. Now, sister dear, do you have anything further to add?"

She stares at me with an unreadable expression. "I just wonder why, now that the war is over, they should not be returned to their brother. All of them."

"A most excellent point." Pierre's lawyer is pleased to be back on solid ground.

"Well, for one, it pleases my queen to have the Lady Sybella serve as her attendant. It also pleases my lady queen to act as wards to the younger girls, an honor any house of noble blood would be overjoyed to have, would you not agree?" The question is asked in silky tones, but is like a silk rug placed over a hole in the ground. One misstep in the answer could cause a downfall.

Unfortunately, the lawyer sees the danger. "But of course, Your Majesty. Is that your judgment, then?"

"No. Now that I have heard from all parties, I must think and pray on it. I will summon you back when I have decided. You are all dismissed." He waves his hand languidly.

As we depart the room, the lawyer sends me a long, calculating look, and I know that whatever is decided, he thinks he still holds all the cards.

CHAPTER 90

s I leave the king's chambers, I know it is more critical than ever that I maintain appearances. I must keep my shoulders back and head high, as if I've not a care in the world.

It is hard when what I wish to do is gallop after my sisters and disappear off the face of the earth. The painful truth is that Captain Dunois was right about how I would be viewed should my true nature be exposed, and the regent did all that she could to expose it. Fortunately for me, each of the incidents had another, more easily believed explanation.

Except for the dicing and the drinking with the soldiers, but I am not the only woman of noble birth who has done *that*. And it was easy enough to lie about. Even so, I am happy her informant did not see us at daggers.

"How did it go?"

The voice nearly sends my bones leaping from my skin.

"I am sorry," Father Effram says. "I did not mean to startle you."

"Well, if your be-damned heart beat like a normal person's, it would not be a problem."

He smiles in sympathy. "I take it the hearing did not go well."

"It went fine. It is your sneaking that has me on edge."

"But of course."

I sigh. "It was not so much a custody hearing, but more of a chance for the regent to attempt to assassinate my character."

Father Effram frowns in concern, and I find myself relaying my meeting—after all, there is no one else to tell. Besides, he *is* a confessor.

"Truly," I say when I have finished, "my dark nature puts all I have strived for at risk."

He tilts his head as if listening to a particularly elusive melody. "Has it?"

I try not to scowl at his question. "What do you mean?"

"It seems to me that all the actions thrown back in your face by the regent did not come from a dark place, my lady. But one of caring."

I am so startled by his words that I stop walking.

"Of caring for Dunois when he was stricken," he continues. "Of caring who was trying to harm the duchess. Of caring that as few as possible be harmed in the attack against us on the road. You could have simply disappeared into the litter with the rest of the ladies."

"More would have died if I'd done that!"

He smiles. "Precisely my point. Even choosing to draw the regent's ire to lend strength to the duchess was done out of a passionate desire to protect her. And at great cost to yourself. Staying silent would have kept the regent from even noticing you."

I frown. "You know about that?"

He shrugs. "I *am* the queen's confessor."

I blink, wondering what else she may have told him. I start walking again. "You're wrong, Father," I say softly. "It wasn't to protect — or not only to protect — her, but also to stop my own pain at watching her endure that."

The old priest reaches out to pat my hand. "Even better, my lady. It shows how deeply your compassion flows. You act not from some vague notion of chivalry" — my mind goes immediately to the king — "but because you feel others' pain as if it were your own. I can assure you none of the d'Albrets have ever felt that. Indeed, far too few people experience such solicitude." He sighs. "The world would be a far better place if they did."

I start to answer, but he wags a finger at me.

"Nor are you only Mortain's justice, meting out punishment and vengeance. If that were the case, you would simply wait until the vile deeds had been done, then exact justice. You work far too hard to save the innocent from such wrongdoing in the first place." His old blue eyes are vivid in their intensity, as if willing me to feel the truth of his words. "When you act from that place, there is no risk you are dark or evil. You merely understand that to fight evil things — to truly fight them and protect others — you must sometimes use those same methods. Ah, I see that we have reached the chapel."

I glance in surprise at the door to the servants' chapel.

"I shall leave you to your prayers, my dear."

He bows before disappearing down the hall while I am left standing at the door to a chapel I had no intention of visiting. "Father Effram!" I call out.

He pauses at the end of the hall and looks over his shoulder.

"Thank you."

He smiles, knowing full well I do not mean for leaving me to my prayers.

In truth, his words feel as if they have turned me inside out so that I must look at all the parts of myself anew. This is as good a place as any for that.

When I step into the chapel, I realize I am not alone. Someone else sits quietly in the front bench. I nearly turn around and slip back out, then recognize the woman whom I saw leaving the regent's office yesterday. Curious now, I step behind one of the stone columns and observe her more closely. Her head is bent, the curve of her slender neck graceful. She does not wear a fancy headdress like those favored here at court, but a simple coif.

My interest sharpens. But someone else approaches — a page. I pull back behind my column as he glances around the chapel, his gaze finally landing on the other woman. He hurries down the aisle, bearing a message in his hands. "My lady?"

"Yes?" she says.

He hands her the sealed parchment and waits for her to read it. When she does not, he shifts impatiently. "Do you not wish me to carry back a reply, my lady?"

"No. When I have one ready, I shall find someone to deliver it. You are dismissed."

Once the page has left, she rises and approaches the bank of lit candles that sit in front of the chancel. When she reaches them, she holds the message out over the flames.

It takes a moment for the flame to catch, but eventually it does. When her fingers are in danger of being singed, she finally drops the last of it into the burning wick.

She heads to the left side of the chancel, where nine niches are carved into the wall. I am surprised to see that they hold nine burning candles. Has Father Effram placed them there?

She pauses at the first one — Mortain's niche — raises her hand to it, then bows her head briefly. When she has finished her short prayer, she turns on her heel and walks away. Her steps are not hurried or lingering, but carefully measured. The sort that do not call attention. As she passes by my hiding place, I am able to see her more clearly. Her cheekbones are sharp, her lips full, her chin determined. And then she is gone.

I wait a handful of moments before approaching the small alcove.

A single red holly berry rests against the white candle. My heart gives a leap of hope.

I reach for the pouch at my waist and the crow feather I have carried for weeks. I pat futilely for a moment before realizing I did not attach it to my belt this morning as I dressed for my audience with the king.

Even so, she is from the convent. I am certain of it.

When I arrive at the queen's solar, it is obvious at once that the queen is not there. The ladies sit in a circle amongst themselves, heads bent, whispering. At my approach, they stop talking and resume their needlework.

I ignore their clumsy attempts at subtlety. "Where is the queen?"

"She has returned to bed as she did not feel well. Elsibet and Heloise are with her."

"Thank you." I lift my skirts and head for the queen's chambers. When I

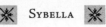

knock, Elsibet opens the door. "Oh, Lady Sybella. We were hoping it was you. The queen is not up for visitors."

"Your Majesty?" I say softly as I approach the bed. Her face is pale, a fine sheen of perspiration on her forehead and upper lip. Her eyes flutter open, and without thinking to ask for permission, I reach out and take her wrist, laying my fingers over her pulse.

It is strong, not weak or fluttery.

She smiles faintly. "Lady Sybella. How did your audience with the king go?"

I kneel beside the bed. "Your Majesty, we can speak of that later. Right now I am more concerned for you. How are you feeling?"

"Tired. And weak." She grimaces. "And no wonder, as I have been unable to eat anything all day."

"Indeed," Heloise pipes in. "Just thinking of food makes her turn green about the gills."

I frown. "What was the last thing you ate?"

"Supper last night. What we all had. Venison, pheasant, eel pie."

"I have warned you about eel pie." I keep my voice light as I examine her eyes. Her pupils are a little large, but not alarmingly so. "Eels are notoriously dubious."

"Believe me, I will remember your warning next time they are offered."

"Very good." The regent would not poison her, would she? No. But Pierre might. I think of the Mouse and how easily he can slip through cracks unnoticed. I rub my fingers along the palm of her hand, then once her eyes flutter closed again, bring them to my nose and sniff.

There is no smell to indicate any of the poisons I am familiar with, but I am not reassured.

"I know of something that might help. Let me tell Heloise to have it prepared for you."

"Thank you," she whispers without opening her eyes.

"What do you think is wrong with her?" I ask Heloise.

"I truly think the eels did not agree with her, my lady. Why?" Her gaze sharpens. "Do you sense something amiss?"

"No, but I am trained to look for the darkest answers to such questions. Do you think a tisane of comfrey and ginger might help? The pois — herbal mistress at the convent used that on occasion."

"I do think it could help. I will go to the kitchen and prepare one immediately."

"Good. Hopefully that will provide her some relief."

When she has left, I turn to Elsibet. "Has there been any news among the regent's attendants of a new lady joining their ranks?"

"Why, yes, Lady Sybella! That is all they have talked about since yesterday. Apparently her name is Genevieve, and she used to be one of the regent's pupils." She leans in close and lowers her voice. "The king developed a tendre for her, and she was sent away to Cognac."

I blink at her in surprise. "They told you all that?"

"Oh no, my lady. But I am small and easily overlooked."

"Only by fools," I mutter.

CHAPTER 91

he next morning, I am ordered to return to the king's chambers to hear his decision. It has come more quickly than I expected.

My plans to seek out Genevieve hastily put aside, I dress carefully, in my most somber and responsible-looking gown. Holding my head high, I look neither to the right nor the left as I follow my escort to the king's chambers. My stomach feels as if it holds a nest of newly hatched serpents, all writhing and struggling to get out.

As my feet carry me closer to the king's decision, I am fiercely glad the girls are far away from here. With them out of harm's way, no matter what else happens in the meeting, I will have won.

A guard opens one of the large double doors, then steps aside for me to enter. The king sits in a large chair at his desk, the regent standing behind his right shoulder. She does not look at me, and I don't know if that is a good sign or a bad one.

Monsieur de Fremin is already there, barely making an effort to contain his impatience. While it is irksome that he arrived before me, his open impatience will not sit well with the king. I cannot decide if he is a stupid man or merely an overconfident one.

The king sets aside the document he is reading to give us his full attention. "I have given this matter much thought and many hours of prayer," he says without preamble. "The law is clearly on the side of Lord d'Albret having custody of his sisters so that he may provide them with good marriages." Fremin visibly puffs up at this encouraging announcement. I keep my face as still as stone.

"However," the king continues, "matters of honor and oaths are involved. My own lady queen has sworn to oversee the d'Albret girls' safety and well-being, and I do not wish to force her to forsake her word. There is no honor in that for anyone."

A tiny leaf of hope unfurls in my breast.

"I have decided that for now, the girls will remain in the queen's care. Surely Lord d'Albret will agree that there is no better custodian for his sisters than the queen of France?"

The lawyer wants — desperately — to argue with this. "But, Your Majesty, the girls must be married —"

The king holds up a hand, stopping his words. "Of course they must. But as his liege, their marriages have to be approved by the crown, do they not?"

While this is true, it is often a mere formality. The lawyer cannot risk pointing this out. "Of course, Your Majesty, which he would duly obtain, but —"

"So for now, the sisters d'Albret will be privileged to serve the queen until such time as marriages can be arranged for them. We ourselves will give these unions some thought, and of course, if Lord d'Albret has marriages in mind, we will be happy to consider those unions as well."

I do not dare to let myself react. I did not expect for him to grant me outright custody — there is no legal precedent for that. This is the very best I could have hoped for.

The lawyer opens his mouth to argue again, then stops it when he sees the king scowl with displeasure. I briefly wonder if Fremin has been threatened with some dire punishment, should he fail in this task. Before he can do anything to sour the king's mood, I curtsy deeply. "Thank you, Your Majesty. I can think of no greater honor for you to bestow upon the house d'Albret than to allow me to serve your queen and grant us your protection and guidance in these matters."

That pleases him, and he settles back in his chair. "You are welcome, Lady Sybella. And you, Lord Fremin. You may take this decision back to your liege."

"If I may, sire . . ."

Astounded that he is questioning his dismissal, we all turn to stare at him.

"Would it be possible for me to see the girls before I take my leave, so that I may assure my lord as to their good health and well-being?"

His words confirm my biggest fear. He is looking for an opportunity to snatch them from me. I turn and give him a horrified blink. "Are you suggesting the queen has in some way threatened their well-being?"

"No! Of course not. But ... my lord has messages of affection he would have me pass along, lest they forget how much he cares for them."

I nearly laugh out loud at that. "Ah, you may tell them to me, and I will share them with my sisters. I am afraid both have taken a fever with the recent winter storm, and it is best that they not have visitors right now."

The look the lawyer shoots me tells me that in his mind, this is far from over. And he is right. I just don't think it will end the way he expects it to.

CHAPTER 92

Genevieve

s I am dressing for supper, the king's summons arrives, delivered by the chamberlain himself.

He waits outside while I finish my preparations. I don't have much to choose from, but even so, I take care with my appearance. Not in an attempt to appear prettier, for that part of the game has already been won. But the more care I take with my appearance, the more he will feel I am honoring him.

When I am finally ready, the chamberlain glances at me with approval, then escorts me in silence to the king's apartments. When we arrive at a pair of thick double doors, one of the guards steps forward to open it for me. I cannot help but wonder what my mother and aunts would think of one of their own sleeping with the king of France himself. I give a regal nod of thanks and smooth my skirts before stepping into the private bedchamber.

The room is huge and made welcoming with rich oak paneling and exquisitely rendered Flemish tapestries hung on the walls. There are two fireplaces, a fire roaring in each one. Along the farthest wall is an enormous canopied bed with deep blue velvet curtains embroidered with gold fleur-de-lis.

The king himself rises from a couch covered in the same blue velvet. He is but a young man, only a handful of years older than I. Even though he is king, I am struck by how vulnerable he looks without his retainers and the trappings of state. "Genevieve! You came."

I curtsy. "But of course, Your Majesty. I said that I would."

When he reaches me, there is an almost palpable uncertainty lurking behind his regalness, and I realize that I am well suited to this task. Desire is my mother's stock in trade, and surely I am my mother's daughter as well as my father's.

He smiles shyly and takes my hand. I squeeze his fingers lightly. "Your Majesty, I am honored to be here."

It is not a lie. It feels as if my entire life has prepared me for this moment. It is the same feeling I had in the abandoned village when Maraud was attacked by outlaws — I knew what to do and that the moment I had practiced and trained for was finally at hand.

He tugs gently at my hand. "Come sit by the fire and let me pour you some wine."

I raise my brows slightly. Kings do not dress themselves or wash themselves or put on their own shoes, so I did not expect him to pour his own wine. But it appears that he has dismissed all his attendants, and for that I am glad. What will pass between us is not something that is meant to be witnessed by others.

"Your rooms are magnificent, Your Majesty. I did not know such finery existed in all the world. And so many books! Have you read them all?"

He smiles with shy pride and turns to his collection, a stark hunger shining in his eyes. He is as consumed by lust for them — for the knowledge they hold — as he is by the lust for a woman's body. "Not yet."

I take a sip of my wine. "The court was all abuzz with your ruling today."

He looks away from his books, surprised. "Were they? I did not think news would have traveled so quickly."

"This *is* the French court, Your Majesty," I tease.

"True." His mouth twists into a grin that holds more pathos than humor.

"They say it was a most generous and noble decision," I tell him gently. "And that your protection of those under your care is in keeping with your chivalrous nature."

The crease between his brows disappears. "They say that, do they?"

"Well, some do." I set my goblet down. "I do."

"Many of my lords are displeased, fearing it calls into question their rights over their own daughters and sisters."

"Do you have any intention of exercising such rights over them?"

He looks taken aback. "No."

I smile. "Then their worries will prove unfounded." I allow myself to grow more serious. "Your Majesty, it was a well-thought decision. You protected innocent lives as well as spared their liege any censure or embarrassment, granting them the honor of serving in your queen's household. And," I add, slipping off the bench so that I am kneeling in front of him, "you gave full support to your queen. If that is not both wise and chivalrous, I do not know what is."

If I were to lean forward, I could press my body against his knees, but I do not wish to appear too brazen. Instead, I reach for his hand. "May I?"

He looks puzzled, before realizing I am asking permission. "Of course."

I take his hand in mine. "Your Majesty, if I can ease the burdens you carry, even just for a handful of hours, and bring you joy — you who have the weight of so many others on your shoulders — I will count myself honored to be of some small value to you."

His face shifts imperceptibly, and I can see that I have touched him.

Good. For I do not lie. He is a kind man and tries to be just and generous.

To my surprise, he gently pulls me back up so that I am half on the couch and half in his lap. "It is you who have honored me with the pleasure of your company. To be simply a man for an hour or two, albeit a very lucky one." Without looking away, he draws closer, pressing his lips to mine.

His mouth is eager and warm and as soft as an overripe pear. His tongue thrusts too rapidly, like a maid with a butter churn. One hand leaves my shoulders to caress my arm, then moves to my rib cage and upward until he is cupping my breast. His fingers begin squeezing and kneading so forcefully that I am reminded of a farmer milking his cow.

He pulls away, his eyes heavy lidded with desire. "There is a more comfortable place to do this," he murmurs. He stands and pulls me up alongside him, then leads me to the huge canopied bed. It is cooler here, away from the fire, and I shiver.

He smiles. "Do I make you shiver, dear Gen?"

He is so very hopeful that I must cast my eyes down. "Yes, Your Majesty."

"Good." With quick and practiced fingers, he unlaces my gown. When he slips it off my shoulders, he presses his lips to my collarbone, kissing a trail down to the swell of my breast. I wonder how he would best like me to act. He is moving so fast, there is not time to anticipate his needs or wants. As he tugs off my sleeves and bodice, exposing my breasts, I realize that I don't need to react so much as simply *be* here. He is taking pleasure from doing things *to* me rather than with me.

He unties the laces at my waist and I step out of my skirts as they pool to the floor. The king steps back to gaze upon my nakedness, as pleased as a child with a new toy. "You are beautiful." His voice is husky and reverent.

I open my mouth to respond, but before I can get a word out, he backs me up to the bed and gently pushes me onto it, my entire body exposed to his gaze.

He puts his hands on my knees and starts to coax them apart. I place a palm on his chest. "Will you not take off your clothes, as well, Your Majesty?"

"See the effect you have on me?" he whispers. "I forget even the most basic of niceties." As he struggles to remove his doublet, I arch my back, but in such a way that he will not be aware that I have done so, making my breasts more prominent. He casts his clothing aside with a grunt of frustration. Then he is upon me, his hands going immediately to my hips to position them. Then he thrusts.

There is no art or finesse to it. He barely even looks at me.

It is a pity, because there are so many things I could do to make this more enjoyable for both of us. Instead, he simply expects me to lie beneath him like a rug while he spends himself. For all that he claims it was me he wanted — I could have been anyone.

Fortunately, it does not take long. There is a final flurry of thrusts, a shout, followed by a grimace. Then he collapses on top of me, his body damp with sweat.

CHAPTER 93

Sybella

am waiting for them when they come.

For a brief moment, I consider enlisting Genevieve's assistance, but I have not come face-to-face with her nor even had a chance to give her the crow feather yet.

Besides, this is not the convent's business, but mine.

As I wait in the dark, I marvel that I have no qualms about killing these men. I do not know if Father Effram's words soothed something inside me or if I simply no longer care as long as it keeps them from pursuing my sisters.

Or it could be the nature of the men themselves. While they would call themselves soldiers, their crimes are not those of soldiers or mere acts of war. The Marquis, when d'Albret occupied Nantes, accepted the city nobles' hospitality as one of their own. When they would not swear allegiance to d'Albret, he gutted them at their own table.

Le Poisson will be the easiest to kill, for his list is the longest and the pleasure he takes in his deeds is unnatural. It is not born of passion, but of a cold, detached curiosity. He was responsible for a large number of the deaths when d'Albret took Nantes as well, but his were conducted more slyly, in darkened city streets or tavern corners, or as he crept among the duchess's loyal retainers who refused to swear allegiance to her enemy.

Maldon has always perplexed me. While he has committed many

atrocious acts, he atones for them every time, lashing his own back so often that it is rumored to be naught but a huge welt of scars. And there are boundaries he will not cross. Like the time the wives of the Nantes burghers took sanctuary in the cathedral and he refused to enter the church and drag them to their deaths. Others did, but he would not. And for whatever reason, d'Albret never punished him for such disobedience. Odd that I've never wondered about that before.

In that way, Father Effram was wrong. I do relish serving justice to those who would escape it otherwise, for that is exactly who these men are. They commit the sorts of crimes that would go unpunished. Whose victims are not remembered or allowed justice. I was too late to protect those innocents, but I will at least see that they receive justice. To not do so only serves the wicked and allows them to grow stronger.

Although in truth their biggest crime will be showing up in this room tonight.

The Mouse is the first one in, coming through the window. I have studied that wall for hours, trying to determine how he was able to climb it.

I could not.

There is a *snick*, followed by the faint creak of iron as his knife pries up the latch. It swings open, and, quiet as a shadow, the Mouse slips in, closing it behind him.

Even though I have a knife aimed straight at his heart, I do not throw it. Not yet.

He leaves the window, glancing briefly at the canopied bed as he crosses the room. I resist the urge to pull farther back against its curtains. They are drawn, but not completely shut, allowing me to see into the room. Moving only risks giving away my position.

The Mouse opens the chamber door, leaving it ajar, then returns to the window. He props himself on the casement and waits, glancing every so often toward the bed.

Does he not plan to take part in this himself, but is only here to grant the others access?

I do not know if that earns him a stay of execution or not. To my knowledge, he has never killed anyone. If so, it was not something he boasted of or even, I think, took pleasure in. It was likely either in self-defense or to prove his loyalty to d'Albret. I also know this is not the life he chose, but instead had it thrust upon him, and having no choices is not unlike being a victim.

I consider him carefully, trying to determine my best shot. His tunic is loose around the shoulders where he has pulled his hood down. As long as he doesn't move ... With a hard flick of my wrist, I throw my knife. It whips through the air, catching the bulge of fabric on his left shoulder before sinking into the wooden frame of the window behind him.

He gapes in shock, but before he can call a warning to the others, I speak, keeping my voice pitched low. "If you remain quiet, you may yet live. I don't know you for a killer or a snatcher of children. As of now, all you are is a thief in the night. A way to gain entrance to places that are locked. If that is truly all you are, you may leave this room with your life. But if you so much as squeak and give me away, you will die with a knife in your throat before the words have passed your lips. Nod if you understand me."

His head bobs up and down as he squints at the bed, trying to locate the source of the voice. "Excellent. Now be quiet and try to look as if everything is normal."

I am not sure why I take such a risk. If my sisters were here, I wouldn't. But I still fear stepping too far off the path that Mortain once set for me, and to kill a mere thief, no matter whom he works for, feels like abandoning that path.

The door creaks faintly, and the Marquis comes into the room. He glances briefly at the Mouse, who jerks his head toward the bed. The Marquis gives a brusque nod in return and pulls a length of cord from his belt. He taps it lightly against his thigh as he approaches.

I return my second knife to its sheath and grab my own rope. A garrote is more infallible — the thin wire cutting hard and deep, making it nearly impossible to fight back. But it is messier as well, and the less evidence I leave under the king's nose, the better.

The Marquis steps through the drawn curtains and stops at the side of the bed, staring down at the bolsters I have placed under the covers to mimic two sleeping girls. His expression is unreadable. Does he feel any remorse? Any reluctance?

He grasps the cord with both hands, pulling it taut. I frown. Surely his orders were to tie them up, not strangle them?

I step from the hidden corner of the bed canopy, a whisper of movement he barely registers until I have slipped my rope around his neck.

His body erupts, dropping his weapon and reaching over his head to grab me. But I have the advantage of surprise and position, and use my body weight to pin him against the bed. He scrabbles at my hands. Thankfully, his leather gloves keep him from doing too much damage. But he is strong, and I have no time to waste.

"Such a nobleman," I whisper in his ear. "Praying upon two young girls for a few gold coins and the favor of a man who has no soul."

Just as I'd hoped, he tries to turn around to see who is speaking, which gives me the leverage I have been looking for. I shift my grip, bring my arms up around his head, and give a sharp twist.

His death is nearly instantaneous, and it feels as if his soul is ripped from his body. It surges upward with a howl of fury that he has been bested. Bested by a woman who has wrung his neck like a farmwife with a chicken. It is a weak, thin gruel of a soul, with anger and resentment the only pleasure it took in life. If I did not know all the vile deeds he had committed, I would almost feel pity for him. But this soul is beyond even that. Besides, another man is coming through the door. I shove the Marquis from my mind and turn to meet Yann le Poisson.

His pale skin is stark in the moonlight. He glances at the Mouse, who shrugs in silence. A faint cold smile plays upon Yann's lips. The knife he carries is long and sharp. But when he sees the Marquis kneeling against the bed, he frowns. I pull a thick stave from my belt and do not move again until he steps through the bed curtains.

My stave is there to greet him — catching him full in the throat. There is a crunching sound as his windpipe shatters.

He drops his knife, hands flying to his neck, grasping and clawing, as if there is something he can do to make his breath whole again. Falling to his knees, he gasps like the fish he is named after, his face already turning blue.

There is little time to enjoy that victory, for Maldon the Pious, no doubt wondering at the delay, pokes his head into the room. He does not see me, but sees the two men sprawled upon the bed. He swears in disgust.

"These are our lord's own sisters." His hoarse whisper is thick with revulsion, and for that, I hate him a little less. As he draws near the bed, he reaches out a hand for each man, intending to pull them back. Ultimately, it is his decency that is his undoing. I have ample time to slip up behind him, loop my rope around his neck, and jam my knee into his back, eliminating his balance. He is not tall, but he is thick with muscle, and I must work to maintain my hold. After a few moments' struggle, he grows still, drops to his knees, and raises his chin. Startled, I loosen my grip enough that he is able to speak.

"Do not make it quick," he gasps hoarsely. His tunic gapes slightly, revealing the faint traces of thick white scars at the base of his neck.

"If you wish a more painful penance, I will not deny you." With my hands still pulling on the rope, I stretch two fingers out to twist the black stone on my ring, uncovering its single sharp point. When I jab him with it, his eyes widen. "Poison?"

"Not just any poison, but heretic's lament. It will spread through your limbs like a holy fire."

His face relaxes into a smile that, while not unexpected, is unsettling nonetheless.

"Down!" From the corner, Lazare's voice cracks across the room like a whip.

I let go of Maldon and drop to the floor, feeling the air above me stir as something passes over my left shoulder. I roll to the side, then rise to a crouching position just in time to hear a dull *thunk*. I wait for a beat, maybe two, but no more weapons appear, so I cautiously rise to my feet.

Lazare stands near the window, staring down at the Mouse, crumpled at his feet.

I step around Maldon, whose body is stretched out in agony, his lips twisted

in a grimace of pain, and kneel next to the Mouse. "I had planned to let him live."

"I would not have interfered with that plan if he hadn't tried to skewer you with your own knife. I don't want to have to answer to Beast for that."

I look down into the Mouse's face. I had wanted to spare him. To give him another chance at life — a life away from the influences of my family.

When his heart finally stops beating, his soul slowly rises from his body, timid and uncertain. That is when I realize he feared retribution if he took the chance I offered him. "You are safe now," I whisper, catching his attention. "You have gone where they can no longer reach you."

His presence . . . *expands* is the only word I can call it, growing lighter, more buoyant, and he floats up to the far corner of the room.

When he is gone, I turn to find Lazare's shrewd eyes filled with something akin to wonderment. I scowl at him. "What?"

He shakes his head slightly. "That's some gift your god has given you."

I snort. "I am not sure it is a gift to be able to see so deeply into men's hearts. Most of them are dark and grim beyond bearing."

"I'll not argue with that," the charbonnerie mutters.

Just then, Maldon finally succumbs to the poison. His soul bursts from his body as if being released from bondage, and the room is filled with a sense of remorse and self-loathing so thick that I am sure I could grasp it in my hand.

"What is that?" Lazare whispers.

"You can feel it?"

He nods, then almost shudders. "It's uncanny."

"It's Maldon," I say quietly. "Even as he was compelled to horrible deeds, he repented of them, but it was not enough, and his soul knows it."

Instead of approaching, as most souls do, Maldon's hovers just above his own corpse, as if milking every last drop of penance that he can. At that moment, death claims Yann as well, and his soul slips silently from his body, regarding me flatly, coldly. The sensations that pulse over me are not of remorse or regret, or even sadness at his own death, but more of a never-ending hunger that it will no longer be able to fill. It is as unsettling as anything I have ever encountered, and I am glad when it decides to ignore me and slowly drift away. I wonder if it will linger long and come to haunt the castle? I will have to take precautions that it does not.

As I stand there, my heart beats quickly, not with effort but with . . . exhilaration. They are gone. They will no longer be able to harm those I love. Justice has been served. Given the choice between protecting the innocent without Mortain's grace or risking eternal damnation, I will protect others every time. My own true nature has nothing gentle or restrained about it. I am darkness made flesh, but it is the darkness of mystery, the endless night sky, and the deep caverns of the earth. It is the darkness that can love a man like Beast. The darkness that will protect those I love with my last breath.

"Are you going to stand there praying all night or are you going to help me with the bodies?" Lazare grunts.

I turn to see that he has already hauled le Poisson to the window. "I wasn't praying," I mutter as I hurry over to help. "I was gloating."

"Ah, that's all right, then. Please feel free to gloat while others do the work."

"Why are you here, again?"

"Because Beast insisted I stay behind to cover your back, so cover your back I will. You can thank me for it later. Now grab his feet. Father Effram can't spend the whole night waiting for us down in that cart."

Once we have removed the bodies, Lazare slips away to help Father Effram dispose of them while I put the room to rights. When everything has been straightened, I build a small fire and toss in a handful of fragrant herbs to cleanse the pall of death from the room. I also sprinkle a faint trail of salt along the base of the walls to cleanse the room of any lingering spirits.

When every last bit of my work is done, I glance about the room one final time. Now that my own family mess has been dealt with, it is time to call Genevieve into service. With Beast and the others gone, I cannot be the queen's only ally. Especially now that the regent has shown she is willing to dance with the devil in order to achieve her ends.

CHAPTER 94

Genevieve

s we lie with our limbs still entwined, my body is utterly unsatisfied. Four times now, I have taken a lover. Each time has been different, but each has satisfied something within me. The first time, with Margot, was curiosity — and that was easily — if not skillfully — satisfied. The second was lust, pure and simple, for a well-shaped, handsome knight who I thought would satisfy not only my curiosity, but my flesh as well.

He did.

The third time was simply because I wanted it, although with Maraud the want felt far more like a need. A need that still plagues me. I brutally shove that memory aside and turn to my current lover — the king. While I did not desire him, nor lust after him, I did give him what he wanted so that he would, in turn, give me what I want.

The king bestirs himself just then, his hand reaching out to stroke my back. He puts his arm around my waist and pulls me closer, putting his mouth up against my ear. "What magic have you wrought, dearest Gen? I am not a handsome man, nor a graceful one. I cannot even claim to be worldly, for all that I have tried to make up for my sheltered upbringing. But lying with you, I felt all of those things."

"Your Majesty, I am honored that anything we did together

brought you so much pleasure." I turn around to face him. "That you should feel thus brings me great joy, Your Majesty."

He reaches out and captures my hand, pressing a kiss upon it. "I wish to give you a gift such as you have given me. I will make you my court favorite and shower you with whatever you desire. Your own chateau. A new wardrobe. Jewels. Silks. A retinue of attendants. Name it, Genevieve, and it is yours."

It is all I can do not to gape at him. I had hoped for some small reward, a gift perhaps, that I could refuse and instead ask for the convent. But he is offering me every gift I could ever imagine — and all at once. "Your Majesty is far too generous."

If I had time, I could simply refuse any of the gifts and continue our arrangement until the moment felt right to ask my own favor. But by sticking her long nose into the matter, the regent has forced my hand. She will want reports, ask questions, summon me. And word of those meetings and summons will inevitably work their way back to the king. I can think of nothing that would enrage him more than believing his sister was behind our affair. "Your Majesty, I have no need of a chateau, or jewels. Nor can I imagine what I would do with a troop of ladies trying to see to my needs. I fear all your gifts are too grand for the likes of me."

He smooths my hair back from my face. "Do not be so modest, my dear."

"I am not being modest, so much as practical."

His laughter feels like an invisible velvet rope looping about my neck.

I push to a sitting position. "Truly, I have no wish for such things. Knowing that I brought you pleasure is reward enough." Risky words to utter, in case he takes them to heart.

"Well, as my mistress you may lead as simple a life as you wish. No one will dare comment upon it."

Tiny wings of desperation begin to beat inside my breast. "Your Majesty," I whisper, "I cannot be your court favorite."

For the first time in hours, he frowns, and a faint note of arrogance colors his voice. "Why not?"

"You are newly married to a young queen. A queen who is soon to be crowned in front of all your subjects. They will be hoping for an heir, and soon. To have a court favorite so early on feels as if it risks their goodwill."

He, too, sits up. "I am the king. I do not need their goodwill."

"Of course not, but the new queen does. And even kings can benefit by the goodwill of their people."

He says nothing, but I see the truth of my words reach him. He takes my hand, holding — trapping — it in his own. "I will have you by my side, official court favorite or no, and I will give you something to show my deep appreciation and regard, whether you choose it or I."

"A gift, a true gift," I tell him, "is to be given freely, with no thought of receiving something in exchange."

"I know, and you are one of the few who has done precisely that — given to me of yourself freely and without expectation." It is all I can do not to squirm at this lie. "And now I wish to do the same for you."

"Very well." I fold my hands, place them on my stomach, and stare at the ceiling.

He watches me a moment, then leans forward. "What are you doing?" he whispers.

"I am praying, Your Majesty. Praying to see what gift I should ask you for." It is not — quite — a lie, for I am praying, but I am praying that I do not overstep again. After a few more minutes pass, I turn on my side and prop my head on my elbow. "The gift I would ask is not for me, but for those whom I care about."

His face softens. "Who are these that you care about, and what can I do to help them?"

I close my eyes and steady my breath. "It is a convent, Your Majesty. The convent where I was raised."

"But of course I will help a convent!"

I grimace faintly. "I have heard this is not a convent that you care for, and I fear in asking for them that you will think less of me."

"My dear, Gen! How can I think less of you when you have shown such nobility of spirit and generosity toward others? Please, name your convent and how I can help them."

"It is the convent of Saint Mortain. I would ask that you not disband them, but allow them to continue their worship."

He manner cools, his body easing away from mine. "The convent of Saint Mortain?"

"Yes, Your Majesty."

"And what is your connection to them?" He is vexed, even though he said he would not be.

"It is the convent where I was raised before my father had me sent to court."

My stomach dips as he abruptly rises from the bed. When he shrugs into a chamber robe of deep blue velvet, I become painfully aware of my own naked-ness. "A convent that serves the patron saint of death seems an odd place to send a young girl to be raised. One can only question your father's judgment."

The ice beneath my feet is thin; one miscalculation, and it will crack. "It was the tradition in his family. They sent their daughters there for generations. He thought only to continue that tradition."

He is quiet as he pours himself some wine. He does not offer me any. "What does one learn at the convent that serves the patron saint of death?"

His words sow further seeds of misgiving. "Your Majesty, surely you know, else you would not have made the decision to disband it."

"Surely I *do* know, but I wish to hear it from one who was raised there. I will confess that I have not spoken directly with one of his novitiates before."

What — or how much — to tell him? Mayhap, hearing directly from one of us will help change his mind. But how much did he know of our practices before he closed the convent door? Giving myself time to choose my words care-fully, I scoot up so that I am sitting against the bolster at the head of the bed and drag the thick coverlet up around my shoulders, more to ward off the chill than to cover my nakedness. Even so, the king's gaze dips down to my breasts. "We learned many things, Your Majesty. We learned of the complex nature of death, how it is not simply something that sneaks into our lives unwelcome, but can serve as justice or mercy or simply a passing." I must be honest enough with him that if he is testing me, I will not fail. "We learned of the ways death can be delivered — through illness and weapons, disease and poison."

At the word *poison*, he gaze drops to the goblet in his hand. I hurry to add. "We also learned of antidotes and means of protection, but mostly that all death comes through Him."

His fingers on the stem of the goblet tighten. "The Church says such things come from God." His voice is expressionless, telling me nothing.

"Of course they do. But once God has decided, it is Mortain to whom the task falls. Just as while it is God who grants us protection or safe crossing, it is Saint Peter or Saint Christopher who carries out our deliverance."

"Ah." He takes another sip of wine. "Now tell me why you think I've disbanded them."

"Your Majesty, I am in no position to question your judgment. I am only asking for an act of mercy for those that I care about."

He smiles again, fleeting but genuine. "No. I mean, tell me why you think the convent has been disbanded. I did not even know of its existence until you told me of it just now."

It feels as if someone has grabbed my stomach and hurled it down six flights of stairs. Cold dread seeps into my limbs. "Then I am sorry to have bothered you with such a trifling problem. Clearly the information I received was wrong." Angoulême lied to me! But why?

I remember how closely I checked the letter, and I would still swear it was not a forgery.

"Clearly, and I would like to know who gave you this information."

"It was Count Angoulême who told me, although he did so after receiving a letter from the abbess."

His eyebrows shoot up into his hairline. "Count Angoulême was in communication with the abbess?"

Rutting goats! This ditch I had no intention of digging is now threatening to swallow me whole. "But of course, Your Majesty. She would occasionally inquire after my welfare. She was fond of all her pupils and would ask after me upon occasion. But again, I fear I must have misunderstood the message the count conveyed on her behalf."

The king studies me with hooded eyes. "I wonder . . ." he says, tapping his finger on the stem of his wineglass. After a moment, he abruptly sets it down, then walks away from the bed. "Tell me," he says, his voice drifting over his shoulder, "do you know why I was raised so far away from the court, stuck in a lesser castle like a prisoner?"

As he turns around, I see that he is carrying my gown. When he reaches the bed, he tosses it to me. "You may get dressed."

Afraid to take my eyes off him, I move out from under the covers, to the side of the bed, and pull my chemise over my head. It feels good to be covered, as if somehow the fine cotton fabric can protect me from whatever is brewing between us.

"Do you know?" he prompts.

"No, Your Majesty." I grab my skirt and step into it, donning my clothes like a knight his armor.

"You have seen how well guarded Plessis-lès-Tours is, yes? The traps, the snares, the cunning passageways one must navigate to reach the castle itself."

"They are most elaborate." I slip my arms into my sleeves, then begin lacing the bodice of my gown.

Slowly, he pushes my hands aside and laces my gown himself. "And deadly."

"And deadly," I agree, my heart racing. When my gown is laced, he takes my shoulder and pulls me around so that I face him.

"It is because, more than anything, my father feared for his safety. He feared for my safety. Some thought him crazed with it, a fearful old man fretting at the dark. But others, Generals Trémoille and Cassel among them, swore his fears were well-founded.

"Do you know what he feared most, dear Genevieve?"

My mouth is so dry that I can scarce get the words out. "No, Your Majesty."

"Assassins." He studies me carefully, but I have long practice at this and am able to keep my face impassive.

"And it's odd, when you were explaining what you did at the convent, once you said the word *poison*, that was all that I could think about — my father's fear of assassins."

His eyes are guarded now, but not so very guarded that in addition to his ire and anger, I can also see that I have hurt him with this admission. He lifts a finger to trace the rapidly beating pulse at my neck. "I have half a mind to fashion a thick silver chain and drape it around your lovely neck and fasten it to my bed."

"But why, Your Majesty?" My heart beats even faster, but I do not so much as blink. "I have told you nothing but the truth." My voice comes out calm and cool.

"I know."

"Indeed, I would not have said anything, had you not pressed me. I was content to leave things as they were."

His hands drop from my shoulder. "You were. That is one point in your favor."

Is there only one?

"Does the queen know of this convent?"

Wishing to somehow contain the damage I have just inflicted, I lie. "I don't know, Your Majesty. In generations past, the dukes of Brittany have used the novitiates of Mortain for protection, much as your father used the snares at Plessis, but whether her father passed that knowledge on to her before his death, I do not know."

A look of understanding, as if he has just figured out some piece of a puzzle, crosses his face, then he shakes his head.

"They told me Bretons clung to old superstitions and beliefs that should have been discarded long ago, but I thought them to be simply folktales. Now you tell me that they are actively worshiping the patron saint of death and that he has novitiates who serve him. Novitiates who have studied all the ways that death can be delivered. Can you see, dear Genevieve, why I must express some dismay, if not outright anger, to learn of such things? And from my mistress, who I now learn is one of them?"

It does not seem a good time to point out that I am not his mistress.

"Have you been sent to kill me, Genevieve?"

His question is so unexpected that I blurt out, "No! Your Majesty, I have not been sent at all. Not since five years ago when I was came here as a child to serve Madame Regent."

"Ah, but now I must question such things, mustn't I?"

That is when I understand what I have truly done. He did not know, never knew. It was my own eagerness to save the convent that led me to expose its existence.

He taps his finger on his chin. "Well, I will not chain you to my bed. But you will be confined to the palace for the time being, and you will make yourself available when I send for you. I will have many, many questions you will need to answer. As will my wife," he adds, under his breath.

"But of course, Your Majesty."

He looks at me one last time. It is a look full of longing and crushed hopes, of disappointment and the inevitability of betrayal. Then he crosses to the chamber door and calls for his chamberlain to escort me back to my room.

CHAPTER 95

s I leave the king's chambers, I move slowly, carefully, afraid that one wrong move and I will shatter into a thousand pieces.

I do not even know what to believe anymore. Did the convent send me a letter to cut me loose from their service? Or did Count Angoulême lie to me? The choices are equally breathtaking.

I remember so clearly being called into the abbess's office prior to being sent to France. She explained precisely what would be required of me. If she thought I would balk, she was mistaken. The daughter of a whore does not have many reservations about the nature or value her body can provide, the doors it can unlock, or the secrets it can shake loose. Even so, I asked her what my other options were, for only fools do not weigh all their options before committing to a course.

She told me that if I did not wish to serve Mortain, she would find me a husband, one suited to my station in life, with whom to spend the rest of my days. She pointed out that while most girls opted for serving the convent, not all did, and some had gone on to have quite normal lives.

As if that were a good thing. Surely it is to escape such normal lives that we end up at the doorstep of the convent to begin with.

And yet, after my swearing to follow Mortain's path, wherever it led, after being isolated with no guidance or so much as a note asking if I was still alive, she has suddenly decided that I should live a normal life after all.

Or has she?

The other possibility is that Angoulême lied, but to what end? He cannot be so determined to bed me that he would betray his relationship with the convent. What other purpose could he have for destroying my ties with them? It makes no sense. Unless he is trying to ingratiate himself with the king or regent, but then, surely he would have been the one to tell them of the convent's existence.

I finally reach my room, no closer to anything resembling understanding. When I let myself in, I sense immediately that someone else has been there. I pause, but hear no sound of movement or breathing. I close the door behind me and take a cautious step into the room. When nothing happens, I hurry to the cupboard where my knives are hidden in my saddlebag. I snag one before turning back around to face the room. "Show yourself!"

The only answer is silence. Keeping my eyes on the darkness in the corners, I light the candles, relieved when the soft yellow glow of their flames chases away the thick shadows. Truly, no one is here. But someone was.

I return to the door and lock it before studying the room more closely. There. Something is on my pillow that was not there when I left. As I approach the bed, I am consumed by an impending sense of dread, as if some deeply hidden part of me recognizes the object before my eyes do.

It is long and black, like a knife blade. My knees weaken, and my heart races as I reach out and lift the crow feather from my pillow.

After five long years, it has finally come.

AUTHOR'S NOTE

As with the original His Fair Assassin trilogy, the broad political brushstrokes and people in *Courting Darkness* are based on historical events and personages. Near the end of the final conflict in the French-Breton War, France held nearly all of Brittany and had besieged the city of Rennes, where the duchess had fallen back behind the city walls. Full-scale war was averted by the Treaty of Rennes, in which King Charles VIII of France and Anne of Brittany agreed to marry. (Though history has no record of Arduinna's arrow!) In order to do so, both Anne's proxy marriage to Maximilian, the Holy Roman emperor, and the king's betrothal to Maximilian's eleven-year-old daughter had to be annulled by the Church. By all accounts, this troubled both participants greatly, although both were assured by their advisors and bishops that it was not only necessary, but morally acceptable.

One of the greatest liberties I have taken is compressing the timeline of the historical events that occurred. In reality, the major events in the His Fair Assassin trilogy and *Courting Darkness* occurred over the course of two and a half years, during which there was a great deal of tedious waiting while messengers were dispatched back and forth. I pulled most of the major events of 1490 and 1491 into 1489, the year in which the story takes place. The wedding that occurs in *Courting Darkness* did not actually happen until the end of 1491.

An unfortunate result of this compressed timeline is that in *Courting Darkness*, Anne is only fourteen when she marries, rather than her actual sixteen years of age. Despite popular misconceptions, marriages at fourteen were not commonplace. When they did occur, it was most often between royal families and noble houses eager to seal alliances and treaties. Commoners, as well as second sons and daughters who were not heiresses, often married much later in life, needing to establish some economic security for themselves first.

Even when these earlier marriages took place, families often allowed for time to pass between the marriage and the consummation. Sadly, however, the records indicate that there were a number of royal marriages consummated when the wife was fourteen. To not do so was to leave an avenue for annulment —and too much was at stake. While fully public consummations had receded in popularity, semipublic consummations such as Anne of Brittany's were still conducted.

It can be hard to fully grasp how a society as obsessed with the Church and getting into heaven as fifteenth-century western Europe was could also have had such a laissez-faire attitude toward sex. They were far earthier than we are, the Puritans not having come along yet. During the late Middle Ages especially, sex and prostitution flourished.

Louise of Savoy did indeed live side by side with her husband's mistress, and they were by all accounts good friends. She raised his illegitimate children alongside her own and even provided for them once she came into power in her own right. Anne of Brittany also grew up in a household that included her father's mistress and her half siblings.

Prostitution was viewed as a necessity, often regulated by cities, states, or town municipalities and having a guild, like many of the medieval trades. Prostitution establishments were by and large run by women, and many sex workers were daughters, widows, or wives of poor craftsmen.

That is not to say their lives were ideal. As with sex workers today, some were forced into the trade while others chose it, and still others drifted in and out of it as financial needs dictated. Medieval prostitutes had no legal standing, so they could not act as witness in their own defense in a court of law and had few legal protections. However, they were widely accepted as a part of society and often participated in city processions and festivals.

I have probably taken the most grievous liberties with the d'Albret family. Count d'Albret was one of Anne's most ardent suitors. Except for the recording of his death, which transpired in 1522, Count d'Albret disappears from the annals of history after 1491, and I have taken great license with this disappearance. He left behind seven children, including Pierre, Louise, and Charlotte. Sybella was not one of his historical daughters; she is my own invention. By all accounts they were a brash, abrasive, politically ambitious family who betrayed the duchess multiple times, including handing over the capital of Brittany to France.

While the nine old gods in *Courting Darkness* did not exist in the exact form they are portrayed in the book, they were constructed from earlier Celtic gods and goddesses worshiped by the Gauls, about whom we know very little. As the Church struggled to convert an entire population over the centuries, as a matter of policy they adopted pagan deities as saints, painting over the original myths with their own Christianized narrative. They also built churches on pagan holy sites and organized their own festivals and celebrations to coincide with earlier pagan celebrations to make them more palatable for the local populace. In later years, the Church became much less accepting of such divergences in religious practices and became more watchful and far less tolerant of irregular worship and heresies.

ACKNOWLEDGMENTS

This book was lucky enough to have two amazing teams help bring it into the world. I am forever grateful to Betsy Groban, Mary Wilcox, Linda Magram, and Karen Walsh for believing in and supporting this book when it was naught but a hopeful gleam in my eye. That support came at a critical time and meant the world to me. This book would not exist if not for them.

Nor would it exist without the continued support and enthusiasm of Lisa DiSarro, Maire Gorman, Catherine Onder, and Veronica Wasserman.

I am truly among the most fortunate of writers for having the opportunity to work with so many incredibly talented people. I wish to thank Billelis for his amazing cover art, which captured the mood and feel of the book in such an extraordinary fashion. Thank you also to Whitney Leader-Picone and Cara Llewellyn for their spectacular design skills and vision.

A most appreciative round of thank-yous are due to Diane Varone, Emily Snyder, Chloe Foster, Lily Kessinger, and Kristin Brodeur for their unflagging patience in keeping the mysterious wheels of the Publishing and Production Process turning smoothly in spite of delays caused by wildfires, floods, and mudslides. And to Mary Magrisso, Ann-Marie Pucillo, Erika West, Emily Andrukaitis, Alison Miller, and Ana Deboo for their expert eyes and attention to the intricacies of punctuation and grammar that often escape me (and who will, no doubt, have to copyedit even my thank-you!). They have the patience of saints.

Thank you also to the incredible marketing and publicity team at Houghton Mifflin Harcourt, specifically John Sellers, Tara Shanahan, Tara Sonin, Amanda Acevedo, and Catherine Albanese.

Fellow writers Leigh Bardugo and Holly Black were kind enough to listen to me babble about my plotting conundrums, and then, being brilliant, made extraordinarily helpful suggestions. Deva Fagan, Tessa Gratton, and Shae McDaniel gave me equally brilliant, essential feedback on the manuscript, making it stronger in the process.

And last, but perhaps most important, the deepest, heartfelt gratitude to Erin Murphy and Kate O'Sullivan, who never wavered, never doubted, and never ceased to believe.